The thirteen former U.S. presidents featured in this chilling collection have one thing in common: an uncanny ability to get into trouble. Imagine Abe Lincoln solving a fifty-year-old case of international espionage left over from the Washington administration ... picture Ulysses S. Grant forced to choose between his two children in a tale of domestic blackmail ... and watch as newlywed Grover Cleveland solves a murder in Deer Park!

As each man uses his own particular powers of observation, detection, and common sense, history is revealed as a fascinating trove of dangerous secrets and timeless mystery.

Also edited by Martin H. Greenberg and Francis M. Nevins, Jr.

HITCHCOCK IN PRIME TIME

MR. PRESIDENT, PRIVATE EYE

Edited by

Martin H. Greenberg and Francis M. Nevins Jr.

BALLANTINE BOOKS • NEW YORK

Library of Congress Catalog Card Number: 88-92136

ISBN 0-345-34493-6

Manufactured in the United States of America

First Edition: January 1989

Acknowledgments

Mr. President . . . Private Eye

An Anthology of Short Fiction Featuring Former United States Presidents

Introduction

Francis M. Nevins, Jr.

Presidents of the United States involved in mysteries? What an absurd notion (you might be thinking). Surely our chief executives have always been much too busy and serious-minded to fool with such trivia. Right? Wrong.

Connections between American presidents and mystery fiction go back to Abraham Lincoln, who was an avid reader of Poe's short stories of crime and detection. Early in the twentieth century Theodore Roosevelt developed a fondness for Arthur B. Reeve's "scientific detective" tales about criminologist Craig Kennedy, and when Reeve heard that he had a fan in high places he sent Roosevelt a specially bound set of his works. In 1918, after a newspaperman noticed Woodrow Wilson reading J.S. Fletcher's *The Middle Temple Murder*, the publicity that followed his article turned the book into an instant bestseller. Perhaps the most enthusiastic mystery fan to occupy the White House was Franklin D. Roosevelt. At an informal supper in May 1935 he tossed out the germ of an idea for a thriller—how could a man make himself and five million dollars vanish without a trace?—and one of his guests, *Liberty Magazine* editor Fulton Oursler, also known as mystery writer Anthony Abbot, assembled a team of authors to develop F.D.R.'s notion into a collaborative book, *The President's Mystery Plot*, which was published in *Liberty* as a serial and later in hardcover. The volume found on Roosevelt's bedside table at his death in 1945 was a paperback reprint of Carter Dickson's *The Punch and Judy Murders*. More recently, a few kind words from John F. Kennedy made superstars out of an obscure espionage novelist named Ian Fleming and his character James Bond.

The use of fictitious or unnamed presidents as characters in novels was rare until the Kennedy assassination in 1963. As the nation passed through that trauma into the era of Vietnam and Watergate, there developed, in the words of mystery scholar Marvin Lachman, "a literary subgenre predicated on a picture of the president as either victim or villain. He will not survive his term—or, if he does, he will not deserve to." Thriller writers of one political persuasion filled their White Houses with corrupt toads and Machiavellian warmongers while their opposite numbers conjured up a legion of presidential patriots beset by traitorous peaceniks in their midst. Lachman's article "The President and the Mystery Story" (*Mystery*, May 1981) surveys both camps with insight and wit.

Hundreds of espionage and political intrigue novels with fictitious presidential characters have been published in the past quarter century, and a few recent whodunits of the old school have been written or at least signed by members of first families and have cast other first family members, like Eleanor Roosevelt, in the role of detective. Over the years, however, neither imaginary nor real presidents have figured often in mystery short stories. The best known of the handful, and clearly the inspiration for one tale in the present book, is Ellery Queen's "The President's Half Disme" (1947), in which Ellery grapples with a riddle left behind by George Washington more than a century and a half earlier. The use of a genuine president as the *main* character in a short mystery has been almost unheard of.

Until now.

Mr. President . . . Private Eye brings together twelve tales never before published anywhere, by eleven writers, about thirteen chief executives, each of them centrally involved in a mystery. The protagonists are Washington, Van Buren, Millard Fillmore (!), Lincoln, Andrew Johnson, Grant, Hayes, Cleveland, Teddy Roosevelt, Coolidge, Hoover, Truman, and Gerald Ford. Our authors include a number of well-known names—Joe L. Hensley, Dorothy B. Hughes, Edward D. Hoch, Stuart M. Kaminsky, Henry Slesar—and others likely to be just as well known in the not too distant future. What the stories have in common is simply that each is a good mystery about a person who is or was or was to become a president of the United States.

Hail to the Chiefs!

Widely considered to be the current master of the modern crime story, EDWARD D. HOCH has published over 650 short stories in a career that has spanned more than thirty years. He is one of the very few writers who make a living writing short fiction. His monthly story in Ellery Queen's Mystery Magazine *is eagerly awaited by his legion of fans. In 1967 Mr. Hoch won an Edgar Award from the Mystery Writers of America for his story "The Oblong Room."*

The first of two stories in this volume by Edward Hoch features both our first president, George Washington (1732–1799), and our most famous, Abraham Lincoln (1809–1865).

THE TRAGEDY OF 1799
★ ★ ★
Edward D. Hoch

It was a stormy December along the Potomac, an area that was more often tropical than wintery. On Thursday the 12th, nearly two weeks before Christmas, the snow began falling at Mount Vernon around ten o'clock. It soon changed to hail and then settled into a cold rain that was to last the day. George Washington had ridden out to inspect his farms shortly before the storm hit. At sixty-seven he still considered himself a vigorous man, one not to be deterred by a little bad weather. He had recently drawn up a four-year plan for the rotation of crops in his fields and he was anxious to see that the proper winter preparations were being made.

He did not return to the big three-story white house until midafternoon. Then he was surprised to find a small middle-aged Frenchman waiting to see him. He'd known Leon Ferreux slightly during his years as president, but he hadn't so much as thought of the man in more than two years.

"President Washington!" Ferreux exclaimed. "I must see you on a matter of importance."

"It is General Washington now, Mr. Ferreux. I will always be a general, but now we have another president."

"You are wet from the rain," the Frenchman observed.

"No, no. My greatcoat kept me dry. Come into my library. What brings you all this distance from Philadelphia?"

"Actually I rode down from Federal City," Ferreux told Washington, following him into the book-lined room. "Construction is all but complete. President Adams and the rest of the government will be moving there in a few months."

Washington nodded. "A new capital for a new century. I chose the site for the District of Columbia myself. It will be a magnificent place."

"And that is what I come to you about, General. My visits to Federal City during its construction have turned up some shocking information. There is a traitor in the government, a man sworn to deliver our capital and our nation back into the hands of the British."

Washington leaned forward in his chair, rainwater still dripping from his hair. "This talk of conspiracy is always with us, Mr. Ferreux. Any information you have should go to President Adams, not to me."

"The man I suspect is an advisor to Adams. I cannot go there. Already I fear for my life. It is known that I have certain information—"

Washington's keen eyes detected a bulge beneath the other's coat. "You have this information with you?"

"Yes."

"All right," Washington said with a sigh. "Let me see it."

Leon Ferreux pulled the bulging documents from his inner pocket. "These concern a young man named Stephen Eton. He is barely thirty but has already made a name for himself in government circles."

"I have heard the name," Washington confirmed.

"He first came into the government by working on some

of the architectural plans for Federal City. Now he is close to President Adams and others. Read this document, if you will, General. It is a copy of a dispatch he recently sent to London. In it he proposes a plan for a British landing near Federal City and a burning of the new White House!''

"These are very serious charges," the former president agreed as his eyes scanned the dispatch. "Where did you obtain it?"

"From a French seaman friendly to the American cause. He assures me it is an authentic copy, with Eton's own signature traced from the original."

Washington was silent as he read through the several pages of thick foolscap. Presently he said, "Let me keep this. It is a serious charge if true, and the matter must be investigated."

"Do what you think is best, General. I brought the information to you because there is no one in whom I have more trust."

"Thank you for that, Mr. Ferreux."

"I believe he would kill me if he knew I had given you this document. My life is in your hands from this moment on."

He rose to leave and Washington walked him to the door. "Our two nations have always been allies, Mr. Ferreux. Together no one can defeat us—not even the British."

The Frenchman gave a wry smile. "When I read the dispatches from Paris these days I do not know what to think. Napoleon Bonaparte has been appointed first consul of France. I believe the man wants to be emperor!"

They shook hands at the door and Washington watched him mount up and ride away. With the coolness of late afternoon, the cold rain was turning back to a wet snow. Washington studied the document in his hand and tried to think where he could hide it.

Leon Ferreux was a few miles north of Mount Vernon, riding hard along the River Road, when he saw the mounted figure up ahead. Though he could not make out the face through the wet snow, somehow he knew it was Stephen Eton.

"Halt there!" the other rider demanded, drawing a flintlock pistol. Ferreux recognized it immediately as a Queen Anne pocket pistol, a weapon much favored by English gentlemen.

"Let me pass, Eton. You've come too late. The copy of your dispatch is in the hands of General Washington."

"Damn your hide!" Stephen Eton raised the pistol and fired once at point-blank range. Ferreux shuddered and toppled from his horse.

Eton quickly dismounted and searched the body of the fallen man. When he was satisfied the document was not in his possession, he rolled the body some twenty feet to the edge of the embankment and watched it sink beneath the roily waters of the Potomac.

There were three inches of snow on the ground at Mount Vernon by Friday morning. Washington awakened with a sore throat but thought nothing of it. He did not ride out again in the storm, however, and only walked a bit outside in the late afternoon when the sky had cleared. During the evening he sat in the parlor with Martha and his secretary Tobias Lear. He was cheerful but his voice became hoarse and he had difficulty reading aloud from the newspapers.

Between two and three on Saturday morning Washington awakened his wife to tell her he was feeling extremely unwell. He could scarcely speak and was breathing with difficulty. A doctor was sent for at daybreak, and by afternoon three physicians were on the scene. Washington was bled several times and his condition worsened. The membranes of his throat were so inflamed that he could hardly breathe.

Finally, toward evening, he asked Lear, "Do you understand me?"

"Yes, sir."

" 'Tis well."

Those were Washington's last words. Shortly before midnight, with Martha and Lear still at his bedside, he died.

Stephen Eton heard about Washington's death the following morning in one of the nearly completed buildings of Federal City. He learned the news with a sense of relief, as if a burden had been lifted from him. Now it would not be necessary for him to assassinate the nation's only former president.

* * *

It was a summer's day in Springfield, Illinois—hot and lazy with only a hint of redeeming breeze. Abraham Lincoln was back in his law office after a single term in Congress. Elected overwhelmingly in 1846, he watched his support melt away with his opposition to the Mexican War. Though his Whig party had captured the White House in the election of '48, Lincoln found himself without friends or influence in President Taylor's administration. Now he was dejected, and further disheartened by his failure to win appointment as commissioner of the General Land Office in Washington. Returning to the practice of law before the Sangamon Circuit Court was the last thing in the world he wanted to do, but he had no choice.

It was his law clerk, a young man named Lew Samuels, who tried to bolster his spirits one day that summer by asking, "Mr. Lincoln, do you know what year this marks the anniversary of?"

"It is the fortieth anniversary of my birth," Lincoln replied grouchily, "and I am feeling every day of it."

"Well, sir, it is the fiftieth anniversary of George Washington's death. Our first president died on December 14th, 1799. It seems to me some tribute should be mounted this December to honor the occasion."

"If I were still in Congress, Mr. Samuels, I would propose it myself." He went back to studying the law briefs on his desk.

"You know, sir, I did my master's thesis on the death of Washington. There were some mysterious elements about it."

"You mean he was poisoned, as some claim of Napoleon?" Lincoln asked with a playful smile, laying down his papers and deciding a few moments' talk with his assistant might be just the relaxation he needed on a hot, frustrating afternoon.

"No, no!" Lew Samuels insisted. "Historians and medical men now believe his death was caused by either diphtheria or a streptococcus infection of the throat. I was referring instead to a mysterious visitor who arrived at Mount Vernon two days before his death, and to rumors of a traitor within the government at that time. The visitor was never identified with any degree of certainty, but the body of a Frenchman named Ferreux was taken from the Potomac a few days later, not far from Mount Vernon. He had been shot and dumped into the river, apparently in the hope that his body would wash out to sea.''

"You believe Ferreux was this traitor of whom you speak?"

Samuels leaned back in his chair. "No, sir. I believe Ferreux brought the former president proof of the traitor's identity, and then was murdered on his way back to Washington."

"It wasn't called Washington then," Lincoln corrected with a slight smile.

"No, it was Federal City while it was being built. Congress later changed the name to honor our first president. But my point is that Washington may have died with this proof in his possession, hidden somewhere at Mount Vernon. Ferreux's widow certainly thought this to be the case. I believe a cursory search of Washington's papers was even made with this in mind, but nothing was found."

"He had a secretary, didn't he?"

Samuels nodded. "A man named Tobias Lear. He saw nothing of the mysterious visitor. It had been a miserable day at Mount Vernon, with morning snow changing to hail and then to rain. Washington had been out riding in it all day. Lear reported that when he returned home around three in the afternoon his neck was wet and there was snow hanging on his hair. But you can read all that in my thesis if you're interested."

"The idea of an unknown traitor and a missing document cannot fail to intrigue me, Mr. Samuels. I would like very much to read through your thesis when I have the time."

The young man seemed gratified. "I will bring you a copy tomorrow."

He was true to his word, and though Lincoln had not planned to plunge into the lengthy thesis so quickly, he found himself picking it up the following evening with uncommon interest. Perhaps it was partly the result of all those months of frustration at the wreckage of his political career. If he was to be exiled from Washington, at least he might find some solace in speculating about past events.

Lincoln began by reading over his young assistant's thesis.

He supplemented this with some books from his own library, especially James K. Paulding's two-volume *Life of Washington* and a twelve-volume *Writings of George Washington*. He pondered Washington's last days, his last hours, his last words. He studied especially the weather on the day of the mysterious visit.

There was something wrong—

"Where can I find some information on this man who was killed—Leon Ferreux?" Lincoln asked his aide the next morning.

"There isn't much available, sir," Samuels told him, pleased to see Lincoln caught up in the endeavor. "I do have some notes about him, information I came across while researching my thesis."

Lincoln went home that night and pondered some more, much to the displeasure of his wife Mary. They'd been married only seven years and the marriage was not an easy one. "Your sons want a father at the end of the day," she told him, "not someone with his nose in a book!"

"Hush, Mary. This is an interesting and important matter." Later he told her, "I may have to go to Washington for a few days."

"What in heaven's name for? I would think you'd have had enough of that city to last a lifetime."

"I want to visit Washington's home at Mount Vernon."

With his first sight of the big white mansion Lincoln tried to imagine what it must have been like in the president's day. Young Lew Samuels had made the journey with him, and they paused first at the plain brick tomb of George and Martha Washington.

After a brief prayer, Lincoln paused to stare up at the mansion on the hill. "It is rapidly falling into decay," he observed to Samuels. "What is its status now?"

"It has passed through the hands of many relatives since Martha's death in 1802. It went first to Washington's nephew Bushrod, since the president had no children. It is now owned by John A. Washington, the son of a nephew of Bushrod's. Two years ago he offered the property to the United States Government for $100,000, but the offer was refused."

Lincoln nodded. "I remember that. Polk should have bought it. I hope one day some group will purchase it and restore it to its full glory."

John Washington was not in residence that summer, and Lincoln quickly convinced the caretaker that they should be allowed to wander about the grounds. The fact that he was a former congressman apparently impressed the man, a circumstance that made Lincoln chuckle. "I should tell him the antics of some former congressmen!"

"What do you hope to find here, sir?" Samuels asked as they prowled about the estate.

"The hiding place of this document Washington received two days before his death, if such a document exists."

"But the place is too large for any sort of search, Mr. Lincoln! There are two hundred acres of land on the main estate, not even counting the surrounding farms."

"It is not too large if one knows where to look. Come with me."

In little more than fifteen minutes Lincoln was holding the missing document in his hand, smiling broadly.

"How did you know—?" Samuels began.

"There will be plenty of time for explanation later. This appears to be a copy of a dispatch, written in October of 1799, advising London of a plan for invading America, seizing the capital, and burning the White House. It was written by one Stephen Eton. Can you research that name for me at once, Mr. Samuels?"

"We will have to ride into Washington, to the Library of Congress."

"Then so be it!"

It took Lew Samuels much of the following day to confirm an incredible fact. He hurried to tell Lincoln the news. "Stephen Eton is still alive, sir! He's eighty years old, in poor health, at a hospital in Virginia."

Lincoln was galvanized into action. "We must hurry! I've come this close. I don't want to lose him now."

The hospital was only an hour's ride from the capital, nestled in a country setting of rolling farmland and tiny villages.

A stern-faced nurse led them down a corridor to a little room where a wrinkled old man sat alone in a chair.

"Are you Mr. Stephen Eton?" Lincoln asked, extending his hand.

The old man answered with the briefest of nods, neither speaking nor taking the proffered hand.

"Let me introduce myself. I am Mr. Abraham Lincoln, late member of Congress from the state of Illinois. This is my legal aide, Mr. Lew Samuels. We come to you on a matter of great urgency concerning an event of fifty years ago: the death of President George Washington."

The old man in the chair gave a start, and now he spoke for the first time. "I don't know you. What do you want?"

"Simply to talk," Lincoln said. "We were lucky to find you still alive."

He took the document from his pocket and held it up for Eton to see. Moving faster than they would have imagined, he made a sudden grab for it. Lincoln was an instant faster, yanking it back out of reach. "I think we understand each other now, Mr. Eton."

The old man tried to rise from his chair but then slumped back. "Where did you find that?"

"In the place George Washington hid it, at Mount Vernon. It is proof of your treason against this nation, Mr. Eton. It might also tend to implicate you in the murder of a Frenchman named Leon Ferreux."

"That dispatch was only fiction," the old man insisted. "It meant nothing."

"You might have a difficult time proving that, Mr. Eton. The invasion plan as you outlined it in 1799 was very close to the one followed by the British in 1814 when Washington was indeed captured and the White House was burned along with other public buildings."

He seemed to sag in his chair. He was too old to fight or even to argue. Lincoln felt he was witnessing the life drain out of the man. "Where did you find the dispatch?" Stephen Eton asked again.

"The events of Washington's last few days were carefully documented by the president himself in his diary and by Tobias Lear, his secretary. Washington described the weather on December 12th as snow in the morning followed by hail and a cold rain, yet when Lear saw him upon his return he wrote that his neck was wet and there was snow hanging on his hair. How was this possible? How could snow from the morning still be clinging to Washington's hair some five hours later if it had rained all day? There is only one explanation. After his return, but before Lear saw him, Washington went out again. The rain had changed back to snow, and it clung to his hair. We couple this with the story of a visitor—possibly Leon Ferreux—who gave him an important document, and the meaning becomes clear. Washington went outside again in the falling snow to hide the document somewhere. Perhaps he feared that Lear or one of the servants would find it if he hid it in the house. It was a matter of great importance to him, and to the nation.''

"I went there," Eton admitted. "I tried to find it myself after his death.''

"Washington told the world the location of the hiding place. He told it with his dying words, knowing the importance attached to the dying words of great men. He asked Lear, 'Do you understand me?' to make certain he was clearly heard, and then he said, ' 'Tis well.' I knew before I ever visited Mount Vernon that I would find the hidden document in the one place that exists on every farm and estate: the well.''

Stephen Eton closed his eyes, as if accepting a cruel jest of the gods. "The well," he repeated.

"There were several wells at Mount Vernon, of course, for the various farms. This was the well nearest the main house. Mr. Samuels here was prepared to climb down it if necessary, but I suspected the sixty-seven-year-old Washington would have had a hiding place he could reach from the top. It was in a metal box about the size of a brick, set into the inner wall of the well. From above it seemed like another brick.''

"A dying message," Eton mumbled.

"One that took fifty years for someone to decipher," Lincoln told him.

The man's head drooped onto his chest. There was nothing more to be said. Presently, Lincoln and young Samuels went away.

"What will you do now, sir?" Samuels asked. "Which are the proper authorities to notify?"

"It is too late for that," Lincoln said as they strode down the path to their waiting carriage. "Too late for the nation and too late for Stephen Eton. His punishment will be that someone else knows his secret, and for the rest of his days—however few they might be—he will never know when that secret will be revealed."

As they rode away, leaving the hospital behind, Samuels asked, "What now, Mr. Lincoln? Back to Springfield?"

"For the present, for a few years perhaps. But the capital has not seen the last of me, Mr. Samuels. I feel today very close to our first president. In a sense I have read his mind, and I have completed his unfinished task. I will reenter politics one day soon, and when I return to Washington, perhaps it will be as president of these United States."

DOROTHY B. HUGHES is best known for her novels that were made into Hollywood films: The Fallen Sparrow, Ride the Pink Horse, *and* In a Lonely Place. *Eleven of her fourteen novels were published in the 1940s, and we are particularly pleased to present you with this story, since she has published less than a dozen works of short fiction. An accomplished literary critic as well as a novelist, Ms. Hughes was awarded an Edgar in 1950 for her criticism—and she was made a Grand Master of the Mystery Writers of America in 1978.*

Martin Van Buren (1782–1862), America's eighth president, won the election of 1836 after serving as governor of New York and as a senator from that state. Perhaps his greatest accomplishment was his installation of an independent treasury system for the U.S. Government.

FROM THE JOURNAL OF . . .

★ ★ ★

Dorothy B. Hughes

KINDERHOOK
MONDAY
MAY 1851

At fifteen past six this morning, there came a discreet knock at my bedroom door. It was, of course, Cush, he being the only man I know who forgoes making loud bangs on a closed door. His sound does not make you jump; it is always muffled. Cush, more than anyone I know, has the understanding to put himself into another's shoes.

12

But what Cush was doing at my bedroom door at that hour was beyond credibility. He never comes upstairs in the early morning; he is below in the kitchen wing assisting his wife Anah in the preparation of my breakfast.

Having just dabbed a bit of Bay Rum into the palms of my hands in order to dress my burnsides, I called out, "Enter, Cush." The Whigs and the Virginians and their pamphleteers are always speaking in their derogatory fashion of my "perfume." I have never used any scent with the exception of ordinary Bay Rum, used after a shave by all men I know. But that is politics.

Cush entered and stated, "You have a visitor, Squire."

I turned from my pier mirror to make sure I heard aright. "At this hour?"

"She arrived close to six, Squire. She is waiting in the kitchen."

Now I was perplexed. "You put a visitor in the kitchen?"

Cush speaks as softly as a Southerner although he was born right here in New York State, not far from where I was born. The only time he has been in the South is when he and Anah went with me to Washington City.

He spoke softly now while explaining, "She is a colored woman, Squire." He added, "But it was Anah who admitted her. I was out in the henhouse gathering your breakfast eggs."

I was too old to take so many odd happenstances in stride. All I could say was, "I'll be down presently."

Cush said, "I will so inform the lady." He closed the door behind him.

Strange and stranger. The colored folk hereabout wouldn't come to my home but to my law office on the main street uptown. Which to be sure would not be open at six of a morning.

I brushed my whiskers, adjusted my cravat, rinsed my hands, and followed Cush downstairs. As always the polished mahogany of the broad banister gave me a distinct pleasure. My father had built well, and the additions I had made to the old house made it even more comfortable. Not a great house as the Virginians fancied, but more beautiful to me in its New England simplicity.

Cush would have used the back stairs down to the kitchen.

I had to round the newel post below and go down the corridor to find out what this was all about. The door into the kitchen was ajar. Anah stood by the table stirring batter which would become my morning biscuits. The visitor was seated at the end of the table with her back to me. All I could see of her was a dark straw poke-bonnet, daisy-trimmed, and narrow shoulders covered by a dark pelisse.

Anah spoke. "Good morning, Squire."

I responded, "Good morning," as the visitor rose and turned to me. Surprise is too mild a word; I was astounded. When I caught my breath, I could only say, "Babbity, is it really you?"

I opened my arms and she came swiftly to their embrace. "Uncle Martin."

After a moment, I held her off by her shoulders to look again upon her face. I wondered how Anah could have known she was colored—there must be some unknown quality which gives man recognition of his own bloodline. Babbity was a mulatto, but of the palest tan in color, no more than the sun gives a face in summertime. Cush had used the word "lady" for her, a term not used for a colored woman. But Cush, always discriminating, had known she was indeed a lady, and all that word conveys. "How long has it been?"

"Almost ten years," she replied. "I'm surprised you recognize me."

"Could I forget my little Babbity?" Unobtrusively Cush had returned to the kitchen and I spoke to him. "Set another place at the table, if you please," and to Anah, "Make plenty of biscuits and ham gravy," a dish I had learned to savor in the South. "Cush, another thick slice of our ham, from my own farm, Babbity, oh, and Anah, some of your best strawberry preserves, the ones you save for company. Didn't you recognize Vice-President Johnson's little girl? This is Babbi, the littlest one, all grown up."

They each gave Babbity a smiling welcome.

"All grown up and prettier than ever." I escorted her through the swinging door into the dining room and seated her, the while questioning, "Where is Sisty now? And your father, how is his health? And your mother, where is she?"

Cush came in to set the place for Babbity. He needed no

directions, as we used the best silver and china daily. Both were made for use, not for saving. Shortly after, he brought the bowls of oatmeal porridge and pitcher of milk to break our fast while Anah was cooking the breakfast. I must say our milk is more cream than any you would find in the city. As we ate our porridge, Babbi brought me up to date on family news. "Sisty is married to a fine man, born free. They live in Ohio. They have two boys, one named Martin."

I crowed at that. One of my sons has a boy named Martin, but that is to be expected in a family. This Martin was a chosen name.

She continued. "My father is none too well. He is aging. My mother will not leave him. We worry for her, particularly with the passage of the new Compromise and the possibility of more stringent applications."

"But your father manumitted her years and years ago," I protested.

"Yes. Sisty and I were both born free. And my mother's manumission is a legal record in Beargrass."

"Now called Louisville," I interjected.

She nodded to that and continued. "My father has manumitted all of his household slaves since then. But after a master's death, a freed Negro can be called a slave and sold at auction. A slave hunter does not have to prove the Negro is a slave, not under the Compromise. He only has to present an affidavit to the United States commissioner in the district. No proof at all. You can well imagine the persuasion of those named commissioners in the slave states.

"And the Negro has no rights, none whatever. No right for a jury, no right to call witnesses, no right to testify in court. We worry about our mother," she repeated. "You know, even in a free state, how little chance there is for a Negro called a fugitive to keep from being taken by a slave hunter. Under the new Compromise, the marshals and deputies can be fined a small fortune—up to one thousand dollars—for refusing to execute a warrant, or for permitting a fugitive to escape, aiding his escape, or concealing him for rescue. Each of these 'crimes' has a thousand dollar fine, and even a possible prison term for not obeying the new laws."

I knew. I had been embroiled in the issue of slavery

throughout my years in Washington City. As all of us in government knew, the Constitution came close to failing to be passed by those delegated to compose it, because of the cleavage between the North, which would have done away with slavery, and the South, the dominant South, which believed slavery to be a way of life, even calling upon the Bible to back them up in their domination over black men. Their recalcitrance was impossible to comprehend when they had just fought and almost lost a war based on freedom of men from tyranny. For the South, freedom was for white men only. For the South, the Declaration of Independence was amended to: "We believe all men to be free and equal—except black men."

I put away my bitter thoughts. Cush had brought the platter of country ham and new-laid eggs, the special strawberry preserves, and the basket of hot raised biscuits. I kept a standing order at the port in Albany for coffee beans shipped there from the West Indies. Cush poured the rich brown brew and set the bowl of clotted cream between us. Babbi had a trencherman's appetite. Either that or she had been on starvation rations for weeks. Or perhaps food didn't affect her slight frame as it did my stocky one.

I took a recess, touching the bell to signal Cush for more coffee. "And where are you living now?" I asked her. "Are you married?"

"No, I'm an old maid." We both laughed at that. She couldn't be older than her midtwenties. She'd been no more than fifteen years when she was with her father in Washington City. "I've been too busy for husband hunting." Quickly she added, "Not that Sisty indulged in that. She was pursued by Jabez from the moment he laid eyes on her. They are so happy. They almost make me look for my Prince Charming." She became serious again. "I'm still living on the farm in Beargrass. As long as my father lives, I am safe there. As is my mother." She lifted her hand to forestall my next query. "I already have the escape route planned for both of us."

I had another question waiting to be asked, the important one. "What brings you here?"

She didn't reply at once. It was as if she were not sure of

what or of how much to tell me. At last she replied, but with a question. "Are you familiar with the name Levi Coffin?"

I was surprised at the question, though in retrospect I should not have been. "Yes, I am," I replied. "A Quaker gentleman. As a matter of fact, I once met him on a brief visit to New York City."

"Then you know of his establishing an Underground Road for fugitive slaves?"

"Now called the Underground Railroad," I affirmed.

"I am one of the workers on the Railroad."

I was momentarily speechless. That this gently bred young lady could be engaged in something so dangerous was beyond my imagination. I managed to ask, "And you are here for this reason?"

"That is correct, Uncle Matt. But I don't want you to be placed in jeopardy because of me. It is better you don't know my mission."

"Nonsense," I returned. "I can handle these Virginians. I have before. I want to know what this is all about and what help I can give you." The hall clock struck eight. "You will tell me all this evening, yes? But now I must be off to Chatham, as I have an appointment there this morning."

"I can't stay here, Uncle Matt," she began, but I cut her off.

"Indeed you can and shall." Instead of summoning Cush, I helped her up from the table and together we reentered the kitchen. Cush and Anah were at the big table finishing their breakfast. I spoke to Anah. "Will you air the sheets and prepare the west guest room for Babbi?"

"I really can't stay," she began again.

"We'll talk about that later," I insisted. "When I return from Chatham."

She sighed a mock sigh, giving me my own way. Then said, "I too must go to Chatham today. May I ride over with you?"

"A pleasure. We shall go together." I then asked Cush, "Will you harness The Princess and bring the buggy around? Finish your breakfast. It will take me fifteen minutes to wash up after that fine repast, for which I thank you, Anah." I then directed Babbi. "Upstairs. You have traveling bags?" Even as I spoke I saw where Anah had placed them, in the hallway. I took one and she the other and we climbed the stairs together. I opened the door of the guest room she would occupy and pointed out the bathroom to her. I then went to my own room at the front of the house. At Lindisfarm my room looks out at meadows and the Berkshire hills. Here in the village I like to look out on the village street. Both landscapes are equally engaging to me.

When I had finished refreshing my hands and face, and had brushed my burnsides into place, I descended to the hall below. Babbi was already there. I escorted her out to where Cush waited at the head of the horse and buggy. He handed Babbi in and helped me into the driver's seat. My old legs, and my girth, made climbing in unaided a bit difficult. As we drove through Kinderhook, I told her, "I'm meeting this morning with my old friend and colleague, Judge Vandervoort. We shall have dinner at the Chatham House, I shall attend a few errands, and return to Kinderhook around four this afternoon. Will that give you enough time for your business?"

"I'm certain it will."

It was a mild spring day, a beautiful day. The fruit trees were still in blossom, and the elms and maples were bright with new green. I saluted friends on the village street as we passed, and then we were on the road to Chatham. Her work with the Underground Railroad was too much on my mind not to talk about it. I asked, "How did you come into this dangerous work?"

"It is impossible not to be in it. If you live in the South and have black ancestry."

"You have much more white than black in your ancestry."

She reminded me, "One drop of black makes you a Negro."

This I knew. And also knew how her white father would rant and rail at this perversion. But it was a general belief among whites—especially in the South. But even in the North it was rule and law. Her mother, who was called Susannah, was a quadroon. From Susannah's color—she was a beautiful "bright" woman, as women of light color were described in the South—it was most likely that the one black grandparent also was a quadroon.

Babbi returned to the main subject. "Beargrass is on the escape route. It is close to the border of both Indiana and Ohio. There is only the Ohio River to cross and you are in the North." She repeated, "How could I not be involved? Runaway slaves are often hidden on our farm until it is safe to make it to the river. We help them reach the next station."

I was familiar with the meaning of *stations*. They were safe places to prepare for the crossing. Where once it had been safe merely to be in the North, with this new Fugitive Slave Act safety could only truly be found in Canada, where the United States has no authority. England had outlawed not just the slave trade but slavery itself.

"You help the fugitives reach Canada?"

"Yes. The shortest route is by way of Lake Erie to Niagara. There is only the bridge to cross and you are in Canada. But that is not as safe as before. There are other routes. And we will develop more."

"There are stations around here?"

"There are stations everywhere. Until this new Compromise, it was relatively safe anywhere in the North. There, the provisions of the Fugitive Slave laws of 1793 were essentially ignored. Now the Underground will go further underground."

Henry Clay's Compromise had put sharp teeth into those old laws. But not sharp enough for Old Calhoun and his followers. He was too feeble to speak his sentiments; his speech to the Congress had to be read by Senator Mason of Virginia. Seward, of course, and Jeff Davis had plenty to say in support of his virulence.

Congress passed the Compromise with little open dissent. They probably would not have if Old Zack had still been president. But he had died in March, cholera morbus, in the middle of the fight. Millard Fillmore, who stepped up from the vice-presidency, the first to achieve top office in that fashion, was and will always be a knucklehead. Sometimes I am ashamed of New York State; I don't know where the Whigs ever found him, but then they didn't exactly. He found them just when they needed a knucklehead who wouldn't bother Zack.

This Compromise would solve nothing, only extend the time before the final solution. Which was coming, even if most of us old-timers wouldn't see the day. I brought my thoughts back to my companion. One thing in particular puzzled me. "If you are working with the Underground Railroad in Kentucky, how does it happen you are here in upstate New York? You'd be closer to Buffalo from Ohio."

It took a bit of time for her answer, with the only sound the clip clop of The Princess's hooves. She was a fine mare, a gift sent me by Dick Johnson when she was a foal. Beargrass was a horse farm.

Finally Babbi had sorted out how much to confide to me. "You might call this a special assignment. Recently, you may have read in your Albany newspaper that the patriarch of the Virginia Featherstone family died. His will stipulated that the slaves of his plantation, all two hundred and thirty-five of them, were to be sold on the auction block in Washington City." Her voice flared. "That will be the last of such auctions, the shame of our nation's capital city, when the Compromise becomes law in January next."

True, there were some good things in Clay's Compromise.

"That auction took place and the Featherstone heirs have their ill-begotten fortune." She swallowed her anger after a moment. "The slaves were sold to a rice plantation in Louisiana. Among those sold were kinfolk of my mother. Of me. Her cousin was a house slave, married to Jared, a skilled carpenter, one who was frequently rented out to other planters because of his fine work. I don't know if they were able to escape being shipped out. But they were able to arrange the escape of their daughter, Amberly, a child no more than ten years of age. The Underground of Washington City got word to me at Beargrass. I was asked to go to Philadelphia where she would be turned over to me. I would then escort her to Canada, where other members of Jared's family would care for her."

"And this you have done?" I must admit a chill went through me in spite of the warmth of the morning, to think of the danger to Babbi. She could have been taken as a slave and transported to the deep South before her credentials as Johnson's daughter reached proper hands. If ever.

"By water as far as New York City. There I learned that she had been missed and that a slave hunter had been dispatched to find her."

"But she is only a child. Why would they care if one child was lost from the lot?" I was becoming what the New Englanders call "het up." "What value has she for them?"

"The value of a brood sow."

I admit that I was shocked speechless. Yes, I had read the many pamphlets that revealed the unconscionable horrors of slavery. In particular I had studied Theodore Weld's "Slavery As It Is." One hundred thousand copies of that were printed and are still circulating. It was Weld who more than anyone was responsible for the antislavery bloc in Congress in the 30s. He was a friend of Quincy's, and Quincy headed the bloc; no one better, as no one is as intransigent as he, whether it is for or against a proposition. I had of course also read Fanny Kimble's Diary and been sickened by its revelations. But never before had I heard firsthand, from someone as close as family to me.

Babbi continued holding her emotion in check. "Have you not read the words of one overseer for a well-known and honored Louisiana planter? He estimated the life of a slave in the rice fields as no more than seven years. By then there would be a new generation raised for replacement."

While I was recovering composure, Babbi began crooning, almost to herself, some of Mr. Greenleaf's powerful words. These had been set to music:

> Gone, gone—sold and gone
> To the rice swamp dank and lone
> From Virginia's hills and waters
> Woe is me, my stolen daughters . . .
>
> Toiling through the weary day
> And at night the spoiler's prey,
> Gone, gone—sold and gone
> Woe is me, my stolen daughters.

I could speak again. "Where is the child now?"

"She was stolen from me when we stopped the night in Hudson. Someone must have informed. There are always informers, they are well paid, you know. Amberly was sleeping in a bedroom with other children, white and black. No one heard anything in the night. No one else was missing. This is why I know she was the one they were hunting."

"And you are here trying to find her."

"Yes." We were approaching Chatham by now. "I heard at the Hudson station that her abductor is still in the neighborhood awaiting a night wagon of runaways by way of Philadelphia. She must be hidden out near here. Undoubtedly it is Theophilos Bunn who seized her, or his most perfidious hired hand, Smoot. Both are well known at the auction blocks in Maryland and Virginia and in Washington City. Bunn is presently stopping at Chatham House.

"Then I may see him. Judge Vandervoort and I will have our dinner there. Would you join us?"

She refused. "I will be busy all day." Quickly she interjected, "You will not speak openly on this matter?"

"Never fear. I shall not speak until I may criminate them. Do you not know that it has been said of me often that I row with muffled oars?"

She could smile at that.

"You will meet me there late afternoon? We will drive back to Kinderhook, have a light repast, and to bed early as is my wont."

"If I cannot be there, Uncle Matt, I shall send a message to you." We were on Main Street, and she pointed out the milliner's shop. "Will you let me off here?"

By the reins, I spoke to The Princess. Babbi needed no help in descending. In spite of her many years living in the city, she was as independent as any girl who had called a farm home. "Thank you." She smiled up at me, quite as if there were no heavy thoughts in her heart. I watched until she was safely within the shop, after which I drove to the livery stable where I could leave horse and buggy for the day, greeted my friend, Waldo, the proprieter, took up my ferruled walking stick, settled my hat, and made my way to the Vandervoort building across from the County Court House.

* * *

KINDERHOOK
MONDAY, LATER

It is always comfortable to have a visit with my old friend
Henrik, now Judge Vandervoort. We had a good many things
to decide regarding the coming elections in the autumn. Both
of us were part of what my political enemies have dubbed the
Albany Regency. Both of us had served as governor, my own
tenure brief, as Andy Jackson wanted me with him. Someone
he could trust, he always said.

He came to Washington City as seventh president of the
United States. What a man he was! Both physically and men-
tally powerful, not often do you find both qualities in one
man. He took plenty of abuse in office, but it didn't budge
him or even cause him to waver about what he stood for. In
my opinion, and that of many of my colleagues, he was the
greatest president we've had. I wager there'll not be one
greater ever again.

Of course, I never knew George Washington. He is considered the greatest by those who did know him, whatever their
political bent. The Adams knew him well, as did Tom Jefferson. Just as they knew old Ben Franklin, the greatest of all
those who had to do with the writing of the Constitution and
the Articles, although he took no credit, not like Jefferson
who claimed it for himself. Or Monroe, who "wrote" Quincy's "Monroe Doctrine." Not that Quincy is a friend of mine.
Quite the contrary, but give credit where credit is due. Andy
met with Washington but briefly. Andy, being a Tennessean,
was not a member of the Massachusetts–New York–Virginia
Revolutionaries, who, after England was chased out, shaped
the rules and regulations to set up a union of the States. If it
wasn't for those Virginians, we wouldn't have slavery now.
It's been the number-one problem since our country was
patched together.

I have been asked often why I say the Virginians and not
the Carolinians or Georgians or those of any other Southern
state. I can speak out why. The Virginians have always been
arrogant. When this New York was Nieuw Amsterdam, it was
the Virginians who helped themselves to our Fort Nassau.
They had to be driven out. Not peaceably. They aren't peace-

able, then or now. Fort Nassau was the beginning of Albany, our capital city in the state of New York.

But I saw George Washington once. I was just a little shaver, not yet seven years, the day of his inauguration as first president of the United States. My father took me with him on the night boat from Albany to New York City. That was our national capital the first year. We arrived at the Battery before he did. He came up from Philadelphia by boat and when he disembarked at the Battery you could have heard the roar all the way to Londontown. The throng followed him to the steps where he took the oath of president. He was so tall that my father, not a tall man but sturdy enough to bear me on his shoulders, could see him. I saw the president clearly. And he was elegant, with his powdered wig and pale breeches, the style of that day. Yet somehow he was humble, shy of his honors. With all that has happened since, I call that the most important day of my life. How I wish I could have known the man.

But I ramble. An aging man remembering.

Henrik and I had a good morning, making our political plans. We will go up to Albany next week to discuss it with our friends there. You must plan early to win an office.

After that I told him, "We have a kidnapper here."

He wasn't surprised. "Yes, I've heard there is a slave hunter in the village. The notorious Theophilos Bunn and his helper. Do you know who they are after?"

"They have already taken her. Kidnapped her from the woman who was caring for her. She is just a child."

"Kidnapping is against the law," he said sternly.

"Yes. But we must have proof. First we must find where she is hidden. For this I want your help. I want a document declaring me to be representing your office in seeking the stolen child and apprehending her malefactors."

"You can do that without a document, Matt. Everone hereabouts knows you and the many government offices you have held."

"But I want something legal—strictly legal—to display to these men when I apprehend them. With Clay's new Compromise and its vicious Fugitive Slave Act passed by the Congress, slave hunting is made legal and we who would prevent it made illegal.''

"Not until January next.''

"Do you think our Southern brethren will wait to put it into action if the occasion arises earlier? We must stop this evil while we can or we will be liable for thousands of dollars if we hinder the villains, or may even be sent to prison. You and I, Henrik, will be treated as common criminals if we help the helpless.'' Having delivered myself of these heartfelt sentiments and taken a cooling breath, I said half in jest, "I rather fancy making a try at being a Dutch Monsieur Dupin, that investigator in Mr. Poe's stories, who thinks out the problem and deduces from that the answer. He is successful, why not I?''

Henrik was laughing out loud by now. "I don't read fiction, Matt. Only Dickens. But I have heard of this Dupin, evidently a popular character. Very well, I shall issue a document declaring you to be my investigator. If not, I fear I shall faint from hunger before you allow me my dinner.'' He took pen from his desk and wrote words on a sheet of paper which would inform all and sundry why I was empowered to act. He flourished a signature and affixed his gold seal of office to the paper. "There you are, my friend. Flash that. Now let's to dinner. It is half past the noon hour.''

As we walked together up the street towards Chatham House, he told me, "You may have an opportunity to view this Theophilos Bunn. At this time of day he is usually to be found in a porch chair observing passersby. Landlord pointed him out to me the day the man arrived, as he does any stranger, but particularly one who seems somewhat shady.''

We lifted our hats to Miss Willa Tichnor, the milliner, as we passed on the street. I had known her since boyhood, a proud spinster, a pillar of our Dutch Reformed church, and the last person in town you would think of as being a leader in the Underground Railroad movement. Seeing her, I warned, "Remember, no whisper of anything I have told you to anyone, no matter how trustworthy you may know him to be. Not even by the blink of the eyelid which might be construed.''

"Never fear, Matt. I am accustomed to court secrecy.''

We had come near the porch steps of Chatham House. I noted the man before the judge said under breath, "That is Theophilos Bunn." He was a pudgy man, red-faced under a planter's straw hat, and wearing a planter's linen coat. I looked for black boots. He was that much a copy of an illustration of an overseer in books about the South. Only the whip in hand was missing. While I was observing him from the corner of my eye, he was quite openly examining me. He would know me again.

The landlord had a welcome for us, and after seating us at the judge's regular table, unasked he brought each of us a dram of schnapps. The dinner that followed was excellent. A rich clam chowder to start, followed by a joint of beef, over brown potatoes and garden vegetables, and for savory, a cheese and an apple tart. The coffee was strong, sweetened with brown sugar. His wife was a splendid cook.

We sent our congratulations to her as we went on our way. Theophilos Bunn was still in his rocking chair on the porch. I walked with the judge toward his office until I caught sight across the street of a man I wished to talk with. "I'll leave you here with my thanks," I told Henrik. "I'll be dropping by in a day or so with a report on my progress as an investigator." I signified the gold-sealed paper was stowed in an inner pocket of my coat. "I want to speak to Honest John."

The judge raised his arm in greeting to the man as I crossed the street. Honest John Flanagan was a builder of houses from Kinderhook to Ghent and all the Chathams between. He was from Ireland but not of the caliber of those loutish Irish troublemakers in New York City. There had been a large number of emigrants from Ireland in recent years, being starved out of their home country by the British—who else? You would think that Americans, having fled the same tyranny, would have welcomed their fellow sufferers, but not so. There was even a movement at present to deny them citizenship.

John had come upstate to Chatham on his arrival in New York about ten years ago. He bought farmland and built a house for himself and his family. His intention was to farm, and farm he still did. But seeing what a fine house and barn he had built for himself, other men in the community hired him to build for them. Wherever you go in these parts, houses are pointed out with pride as "one of Honest John's."

Because he was up on a ladder most of the time where he could observe the comings and goings on the village streets or country roads, he would notice strangers. As I greeted him, he whipped off his cap. "And a good day to you, Squire Martin." He spoke as a man of some education, not in that accent called a brogue which comic actors employ when portraying an Irishman. We exchanged a few civilized inquiries as to families and the vagaries of the weather before I came to the point.

"Whereabouts are you working at present, John?"

He was slow speaking, a quiet man. "I have two houses I'm putting together in Ghent. That town is growing as big as Chatham, it seems."

"Have you noticed any strangers thereabouts lately?"

He gave it a thought. "I can't say I have. Of course that man Bunn has been driving by." In a small town everyone knows names and faces. "With his sneak, now what is his name?"

"Smoot?" John nodded, and I asked, "Sneak? In what way?"

"Prying into other people's business. Asking questions. Looking in windows when the lady of the house is out. Everyone in Ghent is talking of it. Some say he's after a runaway slave."

I pondered this. "Have you heard anything about an Underground Railroad station hereabout?"

"Not exactly. If people know of it, they aren't talking."

"What is this Bunn doing while Smoot is sneaking about?"

"Sometimes he drives on toward Philmont. Mostly he just sits rocking on the porch of Chatham House."

"Keep your eyes and ears open, John. If you hear anything that should be known, pass the word to Judge Vandervoort. Or to me if I'm around. We don't want slave hunters in our village."

"No sir! That we don't."

We bade each other "Good afternoon," and started on our separate ways. But before I had gone two steps, he called after me.

When I turned, he came up to me. He spoke with some hesitation. "I thought perhaps you should know about this. The people in Ghent have seen lights at night in the Old Cemetery. They think it is ghost light. I don't know that I believe in ghosts carrying lanterns."

I was indeed intrigued. "I appreciate your telling me. I would think grave robbers rather than ghosts. And we don't want grave robbers either around here."

Again we went our separate ways. His disclosure gave me thought. I knew I should examine the graveyard myself. Something was going on there at night, that was evident.

By then it was close to three o'clock. A conversation with Bunn might have some value while I waited for Babbi to join me. I returned to Chatham House, seated myself a chair apart, giving him the option of speaking to me if he chose.

He spoke as soon as I had settled myself. "You visiting here?"

"No," I responded. "I'm just here for the day."

"Where you from?"

"Kinderhook. A town not far from here."

"Up by Albany?"

"Not that far."

He leaned across and offered his cigar case. "Have a cheroot. I get them right off the boat from the West Indies."

I declined. "I smoke only a pipe."

"Burns my mouth," he told me.

Now I asked a question. "Are you staying long in Chatham?"

"I don't know perzactly. I'm waiting for a shipment." Now he was chortling inside at me.

If I'd been Andy Jackson, I'd have hung him by his head by now. But I'm not and have never been a physical man. I have neither the physique nor the taste for it. So I returned his earlier inquiry to me. "Where are you from?"

"From Virginny, sir," he boasted. I doubted it, not that all Virginians are fine gentlemen. He did not know my opinion of Virginians. "Do you often visit the Congress in Washington City?"

"No sir! I'm not a politician." He was again inwardly laughing as he said, "I'm an outdoor man."

"Indeed." I looked him up and down. "I would not take you for a farmer."

"Down in Virginny white men don't work the farm. We got slaves for that."

I could take no more from this oaf without dressing him down. I pulled out my watch, consulted it, and said, "I must be on my way. Good day, sir." I did not wait for his response. I was up and stomping down the steps and away. When I reached the millinery shop, I slowed my pace. It occurred to me that I could leave a message for Babbi and wait for her at Waldo Smith's Stable. I would not return to the Chatham House while that man was visible.

Miss Tichnor's shop door has a bell attached that jingles when you enter. She came from an inner room before I'd closed the door behind me. "Sorry to bother you, Willa, but I was wondering if I could leave a message here for Miss Johnson."

"You can give it to her personally, Matt. She's in my work room. I'll summon her." She parted a heavy green tapestry curtain and disappeared. Willa has small feet, and her quick steps were like a pitter patter. She returned with Babbi.

"Not to interrupt your fitting," I told them, going along with what would be their excuse for Babbi being in and out of the shop. "But I'm changing our meeting place. I can no longer stomach that Bunn."

"Him!" Willa Tichnor snorted.

"I'll be at Smith's when you are ready."

"I'm ready now, Uncle Matt," Babbi said. "I'll just get my belongings."

She was no longer than a minute. Willa and I had time only to exchange a few words on the weather before she returned. The two women spoke their goodbyes quietly aside, and Babbi and I were on our way downstreet to the livery stable. Waldo had my horse and buggy ready in no time. As we passed Chatham House, I could see Theophilos Bunn peering at my companion. Then we were in open country on the road to Kinderhook. As The Princess carried us along, I told Babbi what I had accomplished with Judge Vandervoort and inquired as to her day.

"There is still no trace of the child. The Chatham Underground has heard nothing and as yet they have not uncovered the informer, although it is believed he or she lives near Ghent.'' She turned the subject. ''Tomorrow I go to Albany again. I will be away on the first coach and will stay the night with friends there.''

''This same affair?''

Her nod was brief, her words also. ''We are advising another route for those who were to come.'' She sighed. ''It takes interminable time to reach stations that are neither on a steamboat or a railroad line. Messages were sent last week when we discovered Amberly missing. But we don't know if they were received in time to change plans.''

Shortly we were back home. Both of us changed to informal attire before coming to the dining table. In warm weather Anah banks the kitchen stove after the noon dinner. Our suppers are cold. We had hard-boiled eggs, cold baked chicken, and Anah's fresh baked white bread with sweet butter. For dessert she had baked earlier a cobbler with her own blackberry preserves. Both Babbí and I ate heartily.

After dinner we repaired to the library. Although young ladies do not drink wines, I prevailed upon her to accept a small glass of sweet sherry which I had received from Spain by way of the West Indies. It would help her to sleep. For myself I poured a glass of Madeira. I had many questions to ask about her work, but she was too tired tonight for serious conversation. Instead I talked of family. ''Do you ever see Abraham when you are in Washington City?''

A change of subject had been a good idea. Her face lighted. ''Oh yes! I had dinner with him and Angelica when I was there only a few weeks ago.''

My beloved wife, Hannah, had died young and I could not ever have married again. The loss was and is too encompassing. My four boys and I had kept bachelor house when we moved to Washington City, even as we had in Kinderhook and at Lindisfarm.

Dolley Madison was at that time again a lively leader in the social scene of the capital city. She had moved back to Washington from Virginia after the death in '36 of James— her dear Jemmy. It was Dolley who decided we needed a hostess at our house. And that Abraham, my eldest son, named for my father, needed a wife. Dolley sent for a favorite young cousin of hers in South Carolina to come for a visit with her.

Just one meeting between Angelica—and she is an angel—and my son, and I was on my way to acquiring a daughter-in-law. She and Abraham have continued to live in Washington City. He is a lawyer of substance, and, like all my sons, a part-time politician.

Babbi talked of the happiness of his family and I then asked, "And John. Do you see Prince John?" This was a nickname hung on him when he visited London and danced with young Queen Victoria at a ball.

"Indeed yes. Whenever I'm in New York City."

My second son, John, also of the law and politics, lives there. Babbity cocked her head. "Don't you know your son John is for the abolishment of slavery. He does not hide his sentiments. He strongly supports our Underground Railroad."

I couldn't resist a smile. "John has always been a fighter."

"Like his father."

"To the contrary," I countered, "I have always been one to hold to the proverb 'A soft answer turneth away wrath.' "

"And you were a Barnburner? And your son John with you?" she mocked. "Of the radical and reform wing of the party?"

"You quote mine enemies, Babbity. I stood against slavery, then, now, and always."

"I accept your justification, Uncle Matt." And then she added, "Why did you stand for election again last year? There was no chance for the Free Soilers against the Whigs and Democrats."

"Yes, I knew that. And I don't hanker for political power ever again. I'm too old for that. However, the Free Soilers express my own sentiments." I quoted, " 'Free Soil, Free Speech, Free Labor, Free Men.' If I could help them, I would. I've taken villification and I've taken mockery from my opponents, and yes, my enemies, and I'm just what I've always been, a stubborn Dutchman who will stand up and be counted."

"You're a fighter. Just as much as your friend Andrew Jackson was. Only you do it your way."

"And you're a fighter, too. As your father has always been. He knew he'd be part of a fight when he decided to introduce his daughters to Washington society."

She could laugh at it now. "And the fine ladies with their noses in the air walked out of the Assembly Hall."

"Led by Mrs. Calhoun with her nose so elevated she couldn't see the doorway. Just as, for other reasons, she had walked out of President Jackson's soirees."

"John and I often laugh about those days. He was my escort, you remember, that night. Although it still makes him angry. What angers me is that my father was rejected as a presidential candidate because of Sisty and me."

"Not that in particular," I told her. "For the most part, his rejection was because of his association with me, and mine with Andy. The antislavery Democrats were determined to scotch all who were Jacksonians." The clock in the hallway chimed eight bells. "But no more politics tonight. Not if you're to make the early coach to Albany. It comes in from Hudson about seven-thirty. I will put you aboard. The coachman knows me, as I travel with him frequently. He'll take good care of you."

I walked her to the staircase and watched as she climbed the stairs to the upstairs hallway, where a night lamp was glowing. This beautiful girl, beautiful in soul as well as body, to have been ostracized because of one drop of Negro blood!

Slavery would come to an end. But it was taking a long time. How can purportedly civilized men persist in such perfidy?

As yet there are no answers, only questions.

KINDERHOOK
TUESDAY
MAY 1851

This morning I walked Babbity to the tavern where the coach to Albany boards its passengers. It was the tavern my father had inherited from his father, a place where men could gather together around the fire in winter and outside by the doorway in summer for a stein of beer or a glass of schnapps. And incidentally, a place where my father sold his extra farm-produce to those of the village who did not farm. It was there I worked as a tap boy. And there I learned about politics, listening to the men's talk, all in Dutch; few people in our village spoke English then. We had been a Dutch settlement since the 1600s. Whatever the language, politics was the main concern of all Americans in those days when the Constitution was being put together.

I waited with Babbi until the stage arrived and I had bade her goodbye. I then returned home for my breakfast. Today I would go to Lindisfarm. Lysander ran the place for me in the years when I was away in politics. Now that I can no longer do heavy farm chores, he is permanently in charge. He has a Yankee surface dourness, but beneath that, he is a shrewd, easy-natured man. I needed him for my planned snooping tonight, and hoped he'd be willing to join me.

After breakfast Cush brought the buggy around, and I was off to the farm. It doesn't take fifteen minutes to drive there. Lysander was in the side yard mixing paint, from the looks of it for the fence that surrounds the house. His greeting was a laconic, "How'ya, Squire?"

But his wife, Ellie, was at the screen door immediately, calling out, "Well, Squire, it's been quite a spell since you've been around. You been in good health?"

"Indeed yes." I went over to shake her hand. "I've been busy in Albany lately."

"Politicking. Always politicking. It's in your blood. Will you have a cup of coffee?"

"I've had too many cups this morning. Maybe a glass of buttermilk?"

"I'll fetch it soon as I finish cleaning up the breakfast dishes."

I walked down to where Lysander was. "Painting the fence today?"

"Ellie says it needs a new coat."

"Could it be put off till another day?"

"Reckon it could." He relinquished the stick with pleasure and gave me a shrewd gimlet-eye. "What's going on?"

"I have a piece of snooping I'm figuring on doing tonight. I could use a helper."

"As long as it's for you, she won't make a fuss."

"Don't tell her what for." Ellie by nature is garrulous. She'd tell anyone who came by what we were up to.

"Never fear, Squire. I been married thirty years to that woman, and I know what's best be left unsaid."

Ellie was moving across the yard with a mug of fresh buttermilk. Nothing tastes better unless it's her head cheese.

I thanked her and Lysander said, "Squire wants me to go into Kinderhook with him."

I added an explanation. "A little work I'd like him to do for me up there."

"W-e-l-l . . ." She was suspicious. She knew he didn't want to do that painting today. "I reckon the fence can wait. Go change your clothes, Lysander."

"We'll be working, not socializing," I said.

"He can at least put on a clean shirt and a coat jacket."

I gave Lysander the eye and he said, "Won't take me long to get ready, Squire," while she was saying, "You close up that paint bucket before you go wash up, Lysander. I don't want my chickens to get in it. Or the cats. Dogs got more sense."

I finished the buttermilk and listened to the latest farm gossip until Lysander returned. I didn't know how to broach the idea and sort of hemmed and hawed it. "Might be better if Lysander stayed the night, Ellie. We might be late finishing up the work."

To my surprise she agreed with me.

"Now that's a good idea, Squire. I wouldn't want you to have to drive him back after dark. We all are getting too old for driving around at night." She was a good ten years younger than I, but Ellie has that innate sense of phrasing the truth so it is palatable.

When we'd said our goodbyes, The Princess took off at a good clip. On the way I half explained to Lysander. "There's slave hunters waiting around Chatham. And one runaway is missing." I didn't mention that she was a child. He and Ellie had raised children, all married by now with their own broods. The idea of a maltreated child would have taken over his thinking for today. Later I would explain more. "I have a notion where she might be," I interjected before he could question me. "A female. And I have a document from Judge Vandervoort with his gold seal on it giving me leave to investigate."

"You want me to go along with you."

"Yes. Someone who can testify to my actions and to whatever we find out. Also someone who can move faster than I can."

"I should have brought along my blunderbuss."

"I can loan you one of my pistols or a rifle, but I don't think there's need for today."

Being Lysander, he asked no questions as I drove past my house. I volunteered, "We're on our way to Ghent."

"Haven't been there in some time. Not since before Christmas when Ellie and I drove down to Philmont to see her Cousin Bess visiting from Worcester."

"Do you remember Colonel Johnson's girls? Stopped at Lindisfarm one summer about maybe fifteen years ago."

"Yea-ah. School girls, weren't they. Used to a farm."

"Raised on one in Kentucky. The girl they called Babbi—for Baby—is presently stopping with me in Kinderhook. She thinks the slave hunters have the female locked away while they wait for some other runaways who are expected to come this way."

"She an abolitionist?"

"No sir!" I was emphatic. Abolitionists are not popular anywhere. Not up here in the Northern states any more than they are in the South. They are radicals, preaching unlawful dissent, almost as trouble-making as the Secessionists. "But she is actively opposed to slavery. As her father has been for years, although he is a Kentuckian and has slaves. My son John is for abolition; he takes a strong position in favor of New York's Personal Liberty laws."

"States have got rights," Lysander volunteered.

I didn't mention the Underground Railroad. Least said is soonest mended. Instead I jibed him, "You're not a Secesh, are you?"

He just gave me a look.

"You know what Andy Jackson said he'd do to the Secessionists? And Tom Benton told that South Carolina senator, when Andy says he'll hang somebody, you can start looking for the rope."

By now we were in Chatham, and as we trotted by, I ventured a glance in the direction of the Chatham House porch. Bunn was there as usual, talking to whomsoever occupied a near chair. The while, he didn't miss a trick of who was passing by. I doubt that he saw me, as Lysander was lounging in the passenger seat on the far side, and Lysander is head and shoulders taller than I am.

As we continued on towards Ghent, I informed Lysander of why we were going there. "We'll leave the buggy off the road by the Old Cemetery and we'll amble into the grounds and among the tombstones. As if we're looking for family plots to see if they're tended properly. I'll give you the word when to change direction." He may have been puzzled, but he was not inquisitive. We found a good shade tree near the gates where The Princess could graze. There were no people in sight, although there may have been some across the way peering through their lace curtains. Once inside the gates, Lysander and I took separate paths. He stayed slightly aside and behind me where he could keep an eye out for signals. What I was making for, in devious fashion, was an old stone tomb near the rear, the oldest part of the cemetery. When we were some yards distant, I crossed over to Lysander. "That is the old Sedgewick tomb. There behind me. I'm going to circle around it. You join me in a minute or two. I want a closer look at it."

We followed the plan. The tomb was too small to be a proper mausoleum, it was more the size of a storage shed. The carvings and the biblical verses were eroded by time and weather. One angel on the roof had lost a piece of wing, the other most of the face. There were, of course, no windows, and the door, at the rear, was secured by a large and strong padlock. We strolled away, now together, now apart, back to the gates, and moseyed out to the road.

"That's a new padlock," Lysander commented. "New brand. Just came in to the Kinderhook harness shop."

It was something to discuss with the judge tomorrow. I consulted my watch and said, "I have one more stop to make here in Ghent and we'll be on our way.'' We climbed into the buggy and I guided The Princess down the road a bit and on to a turning. You could hear the pounding of hammers over the mare's hooves.

Honest John and a helper were on adjacent ladders at the front of one of the houses he was building. He descended at once. ''Good day to you, Squire.''

I greeted him and introduced Lysander. ''Have you heard any more about the matter?'' I queried.

''Nothing new. But the ghost lights keep happening.''

''No one has investigated?''

He smiled at that, and said, ''Nobody around here is going to investigate 'ghosties and ghoulies and long leggity beasties,' as the Cornishmen say. No more than my people would investigate the cry of a banshee.''

''And you've heard no wailing?''

''Naught.''

''My thanks to you, John.'' I turned The Princess and we were on our return to Chatham. I told Lysander, ''We'll be in Kinderhook in good time for dinner. I asked Anah to postpone it until one o'clock today. After dinner you can take the buggy and go into the village for the afternoon. Do whatever suits you. I have some letters to be answered and may later even take a nap. We'll be going back to Ghent again this evening.''

Dinner was ready when we got back to the house. Sauerkraut and dumplings, simmered Dutch-style, with roasted pork and all the trimmings, and for dessert fresh gingerbread with clotted cream.

After coffee he was on his way and I to my desk. Later I did manage a small nap. Lysander spent the afternoon in Kinderhook dallying with friends, without Ellie there to hurry him along as on their usual trips to town.

When we met at six for early supper, I told him more of my plan for tonight. ''It may be a long watch. It may even be a futile one. But I have reason to believe these slave hunters come by night to the tomb.''

''You figure the prisoner is held there.''

''I do. But tonight we take no action. We observe. We must

find a place where we will be out of sight but can keep an eye on the cemetery.''

Lysander may have catnapped a bit as we sat by the library fire after our supper. No matter how warm the day, it is cool by night in the Berkshires. Having had no time earlier, I read the *Albany Argus*, which is delivered daily to Kinderhook by coach. A neighbor boy distributes the paper to subscribers. The columns are still filled with the reactions to the 1850 Compromise. And there is always news of local government, Albany being the state capital.

By eight o'clock it seemed time to set out. I put Lysander in the driver's place. I see none too well in dark. We were in Ghent by nine. There were no ghost lights visible. We found an excellent watchtower just around the curve of the five mile run.

It was a clear night, dark of the moon, but the stars were bright. The cemetery gates were clearly visible below. It was perhaps ten o'clock before two dark figures appeared. We were near enough to hear the gates creak as they were opened. The men must have been cloaked, because the light of the lanterns appeared only intermittently. We watched as the two went round the tomb to the padlocked door. They would not be visible to the houses across the road. They set the lanterns down and I could clearly see Bunn. I took the other man to be Smoot. Bunn carried a large lunch basket, which he handed to Smoot while he himself used a key to open the lock. They entered with the basket, and there was no more light.

''We can go now. We'll lead The Princess up the road until we're out of earshot. Just in case they can hear within the tomb.'' After a stealthy circling, we got in the buggy and were on our way home. ''This must be the hour when they bring her food and water. They can't let her die.'' I spoke bitterly. ''They wouldn't be paid.''

We drove through Chatham, the House dark by now, and on to Kinderhook. ''Tomorrow night we will return. Could you take another night of this?''

''Yes indeed, Squire.'' And then he surprised me. Unlike the usual laconic Lysander, he said, ''Kind of exciting, ain't it?''

We were home by 11 o'clock. Cush was waiting up as

always to unharness the buggy and stable The Princess. I told him, "Come in and have a nightcap with us when you've finished." I led Lysander to the library. The tray was on the table with decanters of Madeira and of brandy. "What is your choice?" I asked him. He chose the brandy and I poured Madeira for myself. It wasn't long before Cush joined us. He too was a Madeira man. We relaxed over our wines, but none of us lingered.

It isn't only old men who get tired.

KINDERHOOK
WEDNESDAY
MAY 1851

When a man is accustomed to years of waking at a certain hour, he wakes at that hour even if he has been up too late the night before. The time clock inside our brain isn't easily readjusted.

I was awake at quarter to six as usual and wide awake. The bathroom was unoccupied, the door ajar, and I decided to take time for a bath now; there would be no time later.

There is nothing more civilized than to have hot bath water in the house. I had had a boiler in my Kinderhook house years before I caused comment in Washington City by having one installed in my house there. Once cleansed of yesterday's dirt, I took no time in dressing. There were too many things to be accomplished this day.

Lysander was up ahead of me. He was already breakfasting at the kitchen table with Cush, Anah plying them with more hot biscuits and ham gravy.

And in the kitchen rocker was Babbity!

She rose to embrace me, enjoying my surprise.

I told her, "I didn't expect you this early."

"I took the early coach. I was eager to know what had developed here. I've been waiting for you to be up to have breakfast with me."

"A pleasure." But first I had to arrange things with the men. "When you and Lysander finish breakfast, Cush, will you drive him down to the farm? And Lysander, if you'll come back tonight around suppertime with the team and a farm wagon, we'll make our final plans. It will be another late night, so let Ellie know you'll be staying here again. But don't tell her what we're doing.''

"Never fear," he said.

I was certain that he could give her some explanation that would keep her pacified for at least another day. "I won't get my plans all worked out until I've been to Chatham today to talk it over with the judge." With that I escorted Babbi into the dining room. She allowed me only a few spoonsful of my porridge before she began questioning.

I gave her a full report on yesterday's activities. "Tonight we shall rescue the child," I concluded.

"It is to be hoped," she added.

She, too, wished to go into Chatham today. Cush would return with the buggy shortly. "What is the news from Albany?" I asked her, and learned that the message they had sent had been received in time. The runaways expected here were approaching Buffalo by way of the Pennsylvania border. I did not have to warn Babbi against revealing anything of our plans for the night. She was more aware than amateurs like myself about secrecy.

Cush soon returned with the buggy, and Babbi and I were in Chatham by nine in the morning. "I'll be returning early," I told her, "possibly by midday. If that doesn't give you sufficient time, Cush will come back for you later."

She wasn't certain how long she'd be and asked that I stop by Miss Tichnor's before retrieving the rig from the stable. She would let me know then, or if she wasn't there, she would leave a message for me.

The morning went well for me. I conferred with the judge, refusing his dinner suggestion. I preferred not to be visible at Chatham House this day. After, I went over to the jail house and had a talk about my plans with the constable, Fred Fischer, Will Fischer's boy. Will had a farm up around Canaan Four Corners. From there I made the purchases I needed for the night, and by twelve I was at the millinery shop. Babbi was there and also ready to return to Kinderhook.

And so we were home before one o'clock, Anah having agreed to another late meal. Today she had made one of her rich beef-and-gravy stews with potatoes and onions, carrots, turnips and some home-preserved tomato slices. She had also baked a cinnamon-crusted apple pie, a toothsome dish. Cush had brought fresh buttermilk from the farm that was just the right drink with the pie.

After dinner Babbi returned to her room. I hoped it was to rest. She'd had a strenuous regime since arriving in our Columbia County. I managed some paperwork before taking my needed afternoon nap.

At six we met for our light repast. Lysander arrived by seven, driving the team and wagon. When Cush had finished his supper, we gathered in the library. There was considerable discussion before we agreed on the plan for this night. Babbi would ride to Ghent with Lysander in the farm wagon. He would find a place where he could safely leave the wagon, not too far from the cemetery. Close enough to keep an eye on the gates, as we had last night. Cush and I would drive to Chatham in the buggy. He would let me off at the Vanderveer house on Payne Street, where I would wait for Constable Fischer. In this way I could avoid passing the Chatham House. Cush would then proceed to Ghent, where he would find a safe place to tether The Princess and the buggy, probably near the houses Honest John was building on the side road. There would be no one there at night, and it was an advantageous point from which to observe the cemetery.

I would drive to Ghent with Constable Fischer in the police wagon. He would leave me with Cush while he found the place where Lysander waited. Separately, on either side of the road, our two parties would keep a careful watch on our goal.

And we would wait. And wait. It seemed forever, remaining silent, not daring even a whisper that could endanger our plan. Hardly daring to move in place, much less walk about to unkink muscles. But eventually the waiting time came to an end. The cloaked figures and their dimmed lanterns approached the gates. Cush and I moved as silently as possible nearer the main road, where we waited until the lanterns disappeared into the tomb.

We were quick crossing to the gates, but the others were ahead of us. Without words, the five of us made toward the tomb. The door of it was closed so that no chink of light appeared. But the padlock was open, hanging loose from its heavy chain.

I gave the signal, Cush opened the door, and we burst in, Lysander with his *donderbuss*, Cush with one of my shotguns, and I with one of my duelling pistols in hand. I had not told the others I meant to carry it; I was afraid they would try to dissuade me from the idea. It was one of a handsome pair. I had never used them, but in my young days, they were something a gentleman must needs possess. Cush, who recognizes quality, keeps them cleaned and oiled.

Andy once killed a man in a duel, back in '06, a young Tennessee blade who profaned the name of Jackson's wife, Rachel. He never talked of it to me, although more than once he related how he and the then governor of Tennessee had an "altercation" on the streets of Nashville. For the same cause. No one could ever speak ill of Rachel in Andy's hearing. She died shortly after he became president.

Heretofore I could never understand how a man could shoot to kill another man. But tonight I could do it. The evil these hunters had done to a helpless child actually made me hope one of them would get out of line.

Fred Fischer has a good loud voice. On our entrance, he thundered, "Stand aside from that child." Not that the little girl was visible; there was only the wadded covering of a thin blanket. When Bunn and his helper did not obey quickly enough, Fred aimed his police gun. "Move! Over there." He used the gun barrel to point to the corner away from the bed of straw. Without taking his eyes off the men, Fred further spoke, over his shoulder: "Cush, Lysander, see if they bear arms."

Bunn did. A pistol in his coat pocket. He looked at Cush as if, given a chance, he would kill him with his hands. Lysander removed a dangerous hunting knife from each of Smoot's boots. "Keep your gun aimed at them, Lysander," the constable advised. "You too, Cush." He then called to Babbi, who had remained in the dark by the door, "Come get her."

Babbi came quickly into the lantern light. I wouldn't have known her. She was wearing pantaloons like a boy, stout boots, and her hair was stuffed inside a boy's cap. She rushed to the bed and pulled away the dirty rag that covered the child. Babbi had brought a warm wool blanket. She wrapped it around the child and lifted her. The while she was crooning softly to her, "It's all right. You're safe now. I'm here with you."

The child was so emaciated she was no burden. As Babbi started to the door with her, Bunn began screaming, "You can't do this. You can't take her." He was actually screaming, not shouting. I don't know that I'd ever heard a man scream before. The only thing which kept him from lunging forward was Lysander's steady blunderbuss and the shotgun Cush was holding.

As soon as Babbi and the child had passed him, Fred told Cush, "Get them to safety. Better carry your gun along in case there are others." He took Cush's place guarding the hunters.

I walked back with Cush to where Babbi waited. I urged her, "Stay the night. She needs a good sleep. Give her a hot bath, and Anah will prepare whatever food you ask. She usually has some kind of soup in our ice chest. All it needs is warming. I suggested she keep the fire up tonight. I will be remaining here until these villains are under lock and key."

When I returned to the others, Bunn was still screaming imprecations. Smoot hadn't uttered a word, just stood there cringing. Both Lysander and Constable Fred had their guns pointed. Fred told me, "Hold your pistol on them, Squire, while I shackle them." He removed two sets of handcuffs from where they dangled from his belt.

"You can't do this to me," Bunn kept repeating. The constable paid no heed but yanked back the man's arms and clamped the cuffs tight about his wrists. He did the same with Smoot.

"I have a warrant for that runaway slave's arrest," Bunn warned. "Look in my pocket. I have a certificate to return her to her master."

The constable interrupted him. "I bet you don't have no warrant for breaking and entering a tomb. Grave robbing. And kidnapping is a criminal offense up here in New York, whatever you call it down south. You can show the judge all the warrants and certificates you got in your pocket, but you aren't about to get off for what you done. You just may swing for it.''

Smoot whined, ''I didn't do nothing. I just was helping out on feeding the girl.''

''You tell the judge,'' the constable said. ''I bet he'll know what to do about someone who helps kidnap a little girl and breaks open an old tomb and puts a padlock on it. Let's go.''

Lysander used his gun to prod Bunn from behind, while Smoot scurried, trying to keep up with the constable. I held my pistol aimed as I brought up the rear. I almost wished Bunn would try to break away. I may not have duelled, but I've hunted plenty, and I'm a pretty decent shot at a moving target.

Fred had brought the lanterns, so we had some light by the door. ''Get the key,'' he told me. It lay on a ledge. ''I'll lock up for safety of the exhibits inside. Tomorrow I'll come back and write a report on what they've messed up here.''

Bunn began again, ''I got a . . .''

The constable cut him off. ''You told me what you got. The judge'll tell you what you'll get.'' He laughed uproariously at his own joke. Lysander joined in, and I must admit it prompted a smile from me. We returned to the road and clambered up the slope to the police wagon. Fred locked the two prisoners inside and, at his request, I rode beside him, pistol at the ready, into town. We went directly to the jail house, but he waited for Lysander to catch up before he unlocked the cage. He and Lysander each prodded a prisoner into the cells while I stood at the ready, pistol in hand. He put them into separate cells. Chatham has only two cells. It is a law-abiding town.

The three of us returned to the front desk. ''It's too late to call the judge tonight,'' Constable Fred said. ''Tomorrow's soon enough. Maybe the next day. He's pretty busy. Might be next week before he gets around to talking to them.'' He was telling me he would allow sufficient time for Babbi to get safely away with the child before the men would be released. If they were.

I thanked him for his help. ''Say hello to your pa when you see him.''

''I'll do that, Squire. Reckon it was a good night's work.''

"It sure was," Lysander agreed.

Outside Lysander helped me into the wagon. For which I was truly grateful. My old bones were beginning to creak.

KINDERHOOK
THURSDAY
MAY 1851

When I woke this morning, Babbity and the child were gone. Cush, always guarding the house even in sleep, heard them leave before daylight. A closed carriage had come for them. Lysander, too, had gone.

"Lysander had to get back to painting the fence," Cush said. There was a twinkle in his eye. And Anah said, "I bet Ellie won't believe the half of it."

Propped against my water glass at the dining table was a note from Babbi. It said only, "Thank you, Uncle Matt. God bless you always." And it was signed by the name I gave her when she was a little girl: Babbity.

The table seemed lonely without her. Cush noticed it. When he came to pour my coffee, he said, "Seems quiet, don't it?"

Too quiet. I made a decision then and there. I had intended to give back to the judge my document with the gold seal naming me his investigator. I decided now that I wouldn't. It would come in handy if ever I took it in my head to look into some other villainy. Who knows when another might be uncovered. Even in our quiet Kinderhook.

EDWARD WELLEN is one of the most underrated of contemporary crime writers—in part because he has published only one novel, Hijack, *which is science fiction. His several hundred published short stories, mostly mystery and suspense, but including tales of fantasy and science fiction, contain some of the cleverest plotting around. Although he is now a full-time writer, much of Edward Wellen's time is taken up with serving as president of the board of directors of his co-op apartment in New Rochelle, New York.*

Millard Fillmore (1800–1874), America's thirteenth president, became chief executive with the death of Zachary Taylor in 1850. (Fillmore had become vice-president in the election of 1848.) Not known as a decisive man, Fillmore has been the subject of much humor in recent years, and a Society has been established in his "honor."

JAPANDORA'S BOX

★ ★ ★

Edward Wellen

After the hurrahing of the crowd and the banging of the band at the Buffalo railroad station, the stuffy quietude of Millard Fillmore's home came as a balm to my nerves. While his wife took my wife to freshen up, Fillmore sat me down in his study with a neatly measured drink in my hand. We had not much to say on our carriage ride here but pleasant generalities. When you have little in common, you run into a string of abrupt starts and awkward silences once you get past the howdys and the weather. To aggravate this stiffness on both sides, I knew he set no great store by me and he knew I thought him without spunk. He deemed me no great shakes when it came to linking the split land; I felt you might as well try to strike fire from a cake of tallow as get him to show the spark of leadership.

I studied the study. One item seemed out of place, a bit of bright orientalia that appeared not to belong in this dull setting and that stood out all the more interestingly. A japanned box of fine workmanship and great beauty, with colorful designs on the smooth black background, rested in lone splendor on a wall shelf. I made out painted mushrooms and suns and pearls, all greatly luminous.

A side glance showed me that Fillmore had caught me staring at the box. A slight quirk of his mouth bolstered my belief that he had positioned me so that I could not help notice the box.

I played along. "That's some box."

His mild eyes lit up and his chubby face livened as he launched into his tale of how he had come by it.

"As you may recall, sir, I sent Commodore Matthew Perry to Japan with orders to open that benighted land to our seamen and traders. I provided Perry with my letter to the shogun and a letter of credence. These letters were in a rosewood casket, which Perry presented to the shogun. In '54, when I had been out of office a year, an aide of Perry's showed up one day at my door. He handed me that box, saying that the shogun had presented Perry with it, apparently in return for the casket."

"What was in the box?"

"He did not know. No one had been able to open it."

"A puzzle box?"

"It would seem so, for it had no other purpose as far as anyone could see. It felt empty—at least it did not rattle when shaken. After the aide left it with me, I tried many times to open it, always in vain. To tell you the truth, I felt relieved that it would not open."

I could not help work at raising nettle rash on Fillmore's fleshy face. "Sour grapes?"

Fillmore looked at me as though he had just tasted sour grapes. "Not at all."

"Now that puzzles me. Why would you fear to open the box?"

He flushed slightly. "I should call it prudence rather than fear. After all, the shogun had no cause to wish me well and every cause to wish me ill. Our modern fleet had forced him to yield to our demands. True, our demands were just—that the Japanese not mistreat shipwrecked seamen, and that the Japanese provide coaling stations for vessels in need of refueling. True, our demands were made respectfully and presented punctiliously. But that they were demands he had no power to refuse humiliated him. So I looked upon his gift as a—" he slid his eyes at me "—Japandora's box."

"Japandora's box." I slapped my knee; I had presence of mind to do so with my unoccupied hand. "That's a good one." I had not thought Fillmore to have had a whit of wit, and I now regarded him with more respect. "Just what misery and evil do you suppose boil for release?"

"Oh, I do not *suppose*; I *know* what's inside."

"And what might that be?"

"Nothing."

I raised an eyebrow. "Not even hope?"

"Not even hope."

"Then you did find the dodge and open it at last?"

"Not I, but another. But before I tell you about that, let me say what I fantasized might be inside. I thought of Asian plague, of noxious fumes, of poison-tipped needle. Why should I not think so? It has since come to light that, during the audience, samurai crouched under the floor ready to spring out and cut Perry and his staff down at the first hostile gesture."

He got up and took the box off its shelf. It looked one of my hands long and one of his wide. He held it fondly. "From frustration and annoyance, I came to satisfaction and acceptance. I thought of this box as safely housing a measure of Japanese air for a measure of eternity. Once the box opened, that alien atmosphere would be dissipated forever. So I had a superstition against opening it."

I could see his point. Besides, the box was enough just to look at. Why not let it be a thing to behold and admire? Life isn't a puzzle till you try to solve it.

"But you say someone opened it."

He nodded. "Just this past year, an Oriental, though in American garb, presented himself at my door with a strange tale. I gathered, by piecing together his broken English, that he had come to thank me for having enabled him to escape from Japan on one of Beriri's ships."

"Beriri?" Then I raised my hand to keep Fillmore from giving me the answer. "That would be Perry."

Fillmore smiled. "That would." Then he made his eyes big. "I was horrified. I wished to know nothing about the man's case. His escape and our part in it, had the news become known, could have made the entire mission go wrong—and even today, if made public, could raise a diplomatic ruckus to imperil relations.

"Apparently he read my face as expressing wonder and interest, for he went on to convey, largely with gestures, the details. Though a young man of good family, he had long felt boxed in by his closed society; the coming of the black ships opened his eyes to the wide world and awakened his mind to the main chance. The night before the fleet upped anchors and pulled away from Edo, the youth swam out from a headland, climbed an anchor line of the *Powhatan*, and stowed away. He did not come to light till the fleet reached the high seas. Perry had to make a judgment. Keeping the Japanese national aboard seemed more practical than putting back to shore and more humane than setting him adrift. So it was that Perry smuggled him into these United States. By then, my successor was in office. I never did get it clear whether or not Buchanan got wind of the matter—and I have not wished to roil the waters by asking." He shot me a sudden sharp look. "I trust this will go no further?"

"It goes without saying that it will go without saying."

He blinked. "But that is neither here nor there. We are talking about this box. Ikurijo—did I say that was the young man's name as best I understood it?—broke off his jabbering and gesticulating. His glance had lit upon the box. It stood then on my desk, not on the shelf that I have had built for it since.

"After a quick deep bow to me, he moved to pick up the box, and held it reverently. He threw me a questioning look.

I did not quite know what he meant by that, but I took it that he asked if the box was indeed from Japan, so I nodded.

"Before I could open my mouth to tell him to stop, he pressed the box at this point and at this—and the lid popped up as you see it do now."

The box lid sprang open on hinges. I put on my specs. The glossy unlined interior was empty. "And it was this empty then? No pestilences flew out?"

Fillmore smiled. I suddenly liked the man.

"As to that, I cannot swear. An invisible abomination or two may have wafted out along with the merest whiff of staleness." Then his face grew sober. "But I do know I felt a chill."

As he said that, I felt a chill in turn, for I had sensed something floating about on the air, without heft or substance, just like a lock of cat fur where cats had been fighting. I started, but then I quickly saw it for what it was: the shadow of a cloud, passing across the sun, cast upon the wall.

Right about then, the ladies announced themselves freshened up, and I made quick work of my drink. Fillmore shelved the box and whisked the glasses out of sight, and we adjourned to the parlor.

It was back to the small talk now, and I rubbed my new whiskers trying to find something I could compliment Fillmore upon. I stopped short of asking him to vouch for the story that his mother used a maple-sugar sap-trough as a cradle for him. But I did reach back to his early days as a New York State representative.

"As a lawyer, I most admire you for having put two bills through the hopper, reforms that spread to the other states: the act to abolish imprisonment for debt and the act to make religious belief, or the lack thereof, no requirement for testimony as a witness. The latter especially. You showed the inconsistency of the old system that made the oath dependent upon a theoretical belief. Till your reform, someone who knew all about a murder could get out of testifying by professing that he did not believe in God or a future state of rewards and punishments."

Mrs. Fillmore, who had been engaging in some fashion of domestic cross talk with my wife, pricked up her ears and caught the tail end of what I said. She was Fillmore's second wife and I reckon did not have a handle on his early accomplishments. She stared over at him and said, "Mr. Fillmore, was that really your doing?"

He hung his head modestly. "Why, yes, Caroline my dear."

She said, "Well, I never. I hope the Reverend Doctor Hosmer—pastor of the Unitarian Church where you will worship with us during your stop—," she asided to my wife and myself, "has not heard of this." And then she seemed thunderstruck by another thought. "Why, if it had not been for you, my cousin would not have hanged because of a heathen's word."

As in all the noise and commotion a mother hears her child crying, so in the sudden silence I heard a story. Just as I like to tell stories, so I like to hear 'em, and I vowed to get this one out of them despite Fillmore's discomfort and his wife's dismay at seeing herself spill the first bean.

So I beat down their sudden concern for the hour. Fillmore did the honors.

"Steven Brent is, was, a first cousin of Mrs. Fillmore's. The whole horrible train of events goes back two years. Or much further, for Steven Brent had a long-standing quarrel with Kimball Ashworth. The two, surly single men in their forties, were half brothers and near neighbors, living on adjoining farm properties outside of town. On the fatal day, as I reconstruct the murder and its aftermath, matters came to a head. In the heat of the moment, Brent struck Ashworth down without considering the consequences.

"The consequences were twofold. One, Brent could be tried for murder. And two, Ashworth, by dying then, predeceased the aunt who had willed him her estate. Under the terms of the will, which I had a hand in drawing up, if the estate came to Ashworth, and Ashworth died, the estate would pass to Brent.

"No doubt Brent lived through an eternity-long moment of panic. Then he came to his senses. He had to hide the corpse to avoid prosecution for murder, yet keep the corpse handy and fresh. He needed to preserve the corpse in condition such that it would seem Ashworth had outlived the rich aunt.

"Brent could not tell, short of taking on the prerogatives of the grim reaper again, how long that might be. He did not know how long he would have to wait, yet he had to make sure Ashworth would keep. Brent had curing tubs and he had a smokehouse.

"The rule of thumb is four days in the cure per pound of flesh for safe storage in the smokehouse over summer without ice. Ashworth ran to about one hundred and fifty pounds. That comes to six hundred days. Brent put Ashworth in the cure for two years, then removed him to the smokehouse, partitioned off behind the hams to keep him out of sight."

Mrs. Fillmore looked both pale and flushed, and fanned herself hot and cold with a souvenir program of February 16th and 17th, 1861, that she gripped in her gloved hand.

(The program had very little validity. Threats against my life were and are causing me to vary from the scheduled events of my journey to Washington for the inauguration. In my pocket at the moment was a telegram—for which miracle I suddenly realized I had Fillmore to thank, he having got Congress to back Morse's invention. The wire was from Pinkerton and asked me to meet him when I stopped in Philadelphia. He wanted to chaw over an assassination plot his agents rooted out in Baltimore. But that is all by the way. At that moment, the only matter of concern was to give the plainclothesmen detailed to guard me time to mix with the crowd at city hall and get the feel of it.)

My wife, too, found the details of Ashworth's preservation unsettling, though I knew by her glances that she was mostly vexed with me for stirring the brew.

"Meanwhile," Fillmore went on, too busy chasing his own tale to catch anything else, "the world knew only that Ashworth had gone away without telling anyone but Brent that he was going away. Brent put it out that Ashworth locked up and made peace with him and asked him to look after the stock, saying that he meant to try his hand at placer mining in California."

I scratched my chin whiskers. "Brent's own greed for gold shows through in his choice of that for a story."

Fillmore frowned politely. "Possibly, possibly. In any case, the world took Brent's word for the cause of Ashworth's absence, though as the years passed people wondered if Ashworth had come to grief in California, or on the way there or back, for no letters or word of mouth came from Ashworth in all that time.

"Mrs. Sally Ashworth, Kimball Ashworth's rich aunt, his closest relative in all senses of the word, held to the belief that Kimball would return one day. And so she never called me in to change her will, which named Kimball as her primary heir. She gave up hope only when she gave up the ghost. All was still left to the missing Kimball Ashworth. And five years remained before Ashworth could be presumed legally dead: a tricky point you will appreciate. The estate remained in escrow pending determination of Ashworth's status.

"Three months after Mrs. Sally died, Ashworth returned briefly to life. No one but Brent, however, could swear to having seen Ashworth alive. The way of it was this. A glow in the night sky south of town, and a great boiling of smoke, led townsfolk to a fire at the Ashworth homestead. The first volunteers to get there, too late for a bucket brigade to save the house, found Brent, grimy with smoke, gasping for air over the body of Ashworth. Ashworth's body was badly burned but perfectly recognizable.

"When Brent could speak, he said Ashworth had appeared at his door earlier that day, dusty and destitute. Ashworth said he had skirted town so that he would not run into anyone who knew him. Ashworth cheered up mightily when Brent informed him of Aunt Sally's death. Ashworth whooped and said that, while it seemed he had taken the long way and the wrong road to riches, it sure looked as if he had found his fortune after all. He said he was bound for home to dig a bottle of rye whiskey from his cellar to celebrate, and Brent was welcome to share it with him—though, true to his nature, he let Brent understand that was all Brent would ever share of his.

"Brent turned down the offer and watched Ashworth head for home. An hour or two later, Brent said, he saw the first flames and came running. Ashworth had been celebrating the inheritance prematurely and too well. An empty whiskey bottle and an overturned oil lamp told the story. That was all Brent had time to observe, for the flames engulfed him, too, as he strove to pick Ashworth up and carry him out. That was all he remembered, he said, till people arrived and he found himself bent over the body of Ashworth.''

I felt an overwhelming sadness. ''And did the voice of his brother's blood cry unto him from the ground?''

Fillmore looked puzzled. Then his brow cleared. ''You see an analogy to Cain and Abel.''

I saw another analogy, but I did not speak of it. To remind him of it would rub him raw, though he had good reason to sign the Fugitive Slave Law when he did, against his convictions. In '51 the North was not as prepared for war as it is now in '61, and the Union would have been destroyed. The compromise had put off the day of reckoning, but that day is at hand, and the blood will be on my hands.

''Yes,'' I said. ''Cain and Abel.''

Fillmore smiled. ''No, the blood did not cry out.'' Then, with a forthright look at his wife, he said, ''But justice did cry out, if in the voice of the heathen.''

Just a guess, but Orientals of any denomination would be rare in these parts. I leaned forward. ''Ikurijo?''

Mrs. Fillmore's brow creased. ''What kind of Jew would a Hickory Jew be?''

''One that may eat smoked ham,'' I said.

''Our honored guest is pleased to be facetious,'' Fillmore said. ''My dear, do you not remember the name of the eye-witness? Ikurijo?'' He turned again to me. ''Yes, the very same Oriental. He was proceeding on foot, on whatever journey he was making after visiting me, and his way took him past the Ashworth farmstead. When the first volunteers appeared, they found him hurrying away from the fire.

''Suspecting him to be a tramp who had vandalized and fired the abandoned house, they seized him and took him with them to the scene. Though Brent's story seemed to clear the Oriental, they were still suspicious of him. He managed to convey to them that he had been to pay me a visit, and that is how I came into it.

''A constable apologized for knocking us up at midnight,

informed me of the death by fire and of the claim by the suspicious character apprehended in the vicinity that he knew me, and drove me, hastily bundled up, to the scene. The constable had little information, or none that he was authorized to give, so we rode in silence save for the horses' hooves. I even fell into a doze, but came out of it when the horses grew balky and the driver cracked his whip and I smelled the embers. The Ashworth farmhouse, which I had never seen standing, lay in smoldering ruin. A clutch of police officers stood guard over a horseblanketed form I took to be that of Kimball Ashworth, over a burly man I knew to be Steven Brent, and over a shivering Ikurijo. I unbundled myself and climbed out stiffly, not rebuffing the driver's helping hand. Brent acknowledged my coming with a short solemn nod; the slight reserve I put down to his awareness that I had drafted Mrs. Sally's will in accordance with her wish that he succeed to her estate only after Ashworth's death. The officers restrained Ikurijo from leaping to greet me.

"Our brief acquaintanceship hardly qualified me as a character witness; on the other hand, during that short period I had come to view him as a man of courage, honor, and innate nobility. So, after confirming his movements insofar as I was aware of them, I did not hesitate to voice my conviction that he was to be believed.

"The peace officer in charge, a political appointee I had no great respect for, asked me sneeringly, 'Is he, now? Is the heathen to be believed when he says he saw Mr. Brent take Ashworth *into* the burning building, whereas—as we can all see—Mr. Brent took Ashworth *out* of the burning building in a brave attempt to save his life?'

"Steven Brent lowered his head modestly, but I caught the shadow of a smile at one corner of his mouth and a glint from under the hooded eye that slid Ikurijo's way.

"Then I went back to what the peace officer had just said. My first thought was that the man had got Ikurijo's meaning the wrong way because Ikurijo had got the words the wrong way. Only natural; English was not Ikurijo's native tongue. Tongues, the Bible tells us, got twisted on the Tower of Babel. For aught I knew, *out* might mean *in* in Japanese, and *in* might mean *out*.

"I turned to Ikurijo. 'I know you know the difference between in and out, but do you know the difference between the *words* in and out?' He bowed as deeply as the hands holding him allowed. 'I know what is in and I know what is out.' He nodded toward Brent. 'That man pick up'—he nodded toward the blanketed form—'that man and bring him *in*. I see.'

" 'I see,' I echoed, though he had not meant what I meant and though I did not see how his maintaining that Brent brought the body into the fire squared with Brent's having brought the body out of the fire.

"My equivocal, not to say weak, response apparently encouraged Brent. Brent stirred. From looking almost cornered, Brent began to look evilly cunning. He passed his sooty hand across his sooty brow and his face took on the look of dawning remembrance. 'Well, now, come to think of it,' he said, 'when I reached Kimball's house, and it fairly ablaze, I saw this here stranger like he mought have just turned out of the front walk. He give me a look like a skeered rabbit and hightailed it 'tother way with a sack of plunder over his shoulder. I hollered and started arter him, but just then the flames licked up and I saw Kimball Ashworth flat on the floor. So I let the stranger light out while I burned shoe leather to fetch Kimball out of the fire.' "

Fillmore shook his head. "Even I began to wonder if I had not misread the signs. Here a fellow white man told a tale totally counter to that of a foreign yellow man. I looked from Brent to Ikurijo and back. I had qualms, but blood or upbringing pressed me to stand by my own kind, to wash my hands of the stranger. But then reason ruled. Not color of skin but character of truth and truth of character determined my own kind. I looked from Ikurijo to Brent and back, and I knew which of the two I believed.

"I smiled at Ikurijo and I nodded at him to show I stood by him. My smile felt masklike, for I knew how little good my support would do him in the face of reality: without hard evidence, Ikurijo's word meant less than nothing. But my smile and my nod must have meant much to Ikurijo. He bowed.

"Another fire showed itself just then in the east: the beginning of dawn. With the lifting of darkness, the neighboring farm and its buildings grew visible. I made out Brent's farmhouse, barn, and what would be his smokehouse.

" 'Where there is smoke . . . ' It may be that Ikurijo bowing threw me back in thought to the moment when he had bowed and taken the shogun's gift box in his hand. I know it struck me, as I stood frozen on the frozen earth, that a house is a box—on end, if you like—and that houses, like boxes, may have secrets. However it may have come to me, what came to me at that moment was that *both* actions had taken place. Ikurijo *had* seen Brent take the body into the fire; and Ikurijo, knowing nothing good was toward, hurried away. Brent *had* taken the body out of the fire—after allowing the fire time to do its job, long enough for the fire to singe the corpse and burn away any bruises but not long enough for the fire to char the corpse beyond recognition.

"That left us—or I should say them, for I had not yet made the yeomen of the law party to my thinking—with Brent's believable word against Ikurijo's antisensical one. I knew how little weight a jury would give the heathen's. And I knew that, lacking other evidence, any case against Brent would never come to trial. The grand jurors and the prosecutor and the judge would be of the same clay as the men there before me.

"Unless I uncovered corroborating evidence at once, Ikurijo might well take the blame and suffer the punishment for Ashworth's death, while the true murderer would not only go unpunished but be rewarded for his crime. I brought my standing to bear, for awe of office does attend even a former president and I am not yet entirely dead politically, and prevailed upon these representatives of the law to humor me; they did so, ill-humoredly.

"We struck out across the fields toward the smokehouse, the frosty ground and the stubble crackling underfoot. 'Bear with me,' I told the grumbling chief officer, and indeed, as Brent dragged his feet more and more the nearer we got to the smokehouse, the minions of the law saw this and grew less and less unwilling.

"An officer forced the door open and shone his lamp inside. The room was half filled with hanging hams. We crowded inside. I took a lamp and played its light on the empty hooks, looking for a shred of cloth that might match the burnt vestiges of Ashworth's clothing. I found not a scrap—not on the hooks, not upon the floor.

"At our puzzlement, Brent began to straighten and even to swell. I pushed past the swinging hams. I thumped the rear wall and drew a hollow sound. 'Find the door,' I said. Suffice it to say, the smokehouse proved to be a box with a hidden compartment. Behind a partition in back of the hanging hams we found a space with the hook Ashworth's body must have hung from. A shred of cloth, no more than a few threads wide, but enough. Further search of the property uncovered the curing tub Ashworth's body must have soaked in for two years.

"Even then, Brent did not break down and confess. He bluffed and blustered. But the evidence proved enough to bolster Ikurijo's testimony, and a jury of twelve good men and true found Brent guilty." The rest Fillmore left hanging in the air.

At this point, an aide whispered into the parlor. He let us know that it was time and past time for the doings at city hall. The mayor could not hold the crowd, which seemed mostly good-natured but getting out of hand at the delay. The aide said that Major David Hunter of the regular army had dislocated his collarbone trying to keep order.

I shook my head, got to my feet, stretched, and thanked Fillmore and his missus for their hospitality.

"You are not shed of us so easily," Fillmore said as we shook hands. "We are to be on the platform with you, though center stage is certainly yours. And tomorrow you are to attend Sunday services with us, then to dine here."

"My pleasure," I said, and I gave Mrs. Fillmore a Japanese bow.

We all drove to city hall, mounted the platform built out front for the occasion, and waved to the loud and rowdy crowd.

As we sat together upon the rostrum during the mayor's welcoming and Godspeeding speech, Fillmore suddenly clutched my sleeve and leaned toward me.

He spoke low. "Do not get up at once to respond when

the mayor finishes. I do not like the looks of that photographer.''

I followed Fillmore's gaze to a figure in the process of shrouding its head and shoulders under the black cloth of a camera set high upon a tripod at the forefront of the crowd. The photographer worked awkwardly, his right arm appearing to be impaired. Despite jostling, he managed to hold the tripod steady and to keep the speaker's place in clear view.

Fillmore did not give me a chance to question him; he had already turned to speak urgently to the aide who came from the wings at Fillmore's beck. I could not hear what Fillmore said, but I saw the aide whirl and trot down the steps. It was tolerable plain that Fillmore felt something was up.

I heard my name, then a thunder of clapping and a rumble of hurrahing, with a leavening of catcalls. The mayor stood, handing me the floor.

Mindful of Fillmore's warning, confirmed by a slight shake of his head and wobble of his jowls when I glanced at him, I took my time. While my wife coughed her disapproval, I fumbled in my pockets as though feeling for my notes. I retied a perfectly good knot in my shoelace, and generally dawdled till a commotion took place out front.

The aide and two others closed in on the photographer. He sensed their coming or saw them through his peephole, and shoved camera and tripod at them to hold them off while he backed up and snaked away through the crowd.

The whole thing was so local and over so fast it went largely unnoticed. I got up then, shook the mayor's sweaty hand, and stepped to the speaker's stand. I spouted the speech I had been giving at all the stops, thanking all of the people for the big turnout and bidding them farewell.

After I got through it, I took Fillmore aside at the first chance. ''What in tarnation,'' I said, ''was that all about?''

Fillmore used his body to shield his hand from everyone but me as he drew a pistol part way from his pocket. ''This is what it was all about. They found this in the camera, which was not really a camera.'' He shoved the pistol back down out of sight.

I could have used a heavy shawl about my shoulders just

then. If Millard Fillmore had not . . . But how the mischief had he known? "What raised your hackles?"

Fillmore's eyes shone. "The so-called photographer carried no spare plates. It did not seem reasonable to me that a genuine photographer, bent upon recording this occasion for posterity, would go to all the trouble for one risky shot. That turned my thoughts to the camera. A camera is a box. If the box were not to be used as a camera, what then might it hold?" He shrugged.

Now that Fillmore pointed it out it grinned out like a copper dollar.

"I owe you my life."

Fillmore flushed. "It would be tragic if you were to be cut short."

I nodded. "You bet. My feet would not reach the ground."

Fillmore went beet-red to the roots. "I meant—"

I grimaced at myself and quickly rested my hand on his plump shoulder. "I know what you meant. Pray give me your presidential pardon. That was only a bit of nonsense to help me over my scare."

Fillmore smiled.

I glanced over at my wife, who had begun to look moody again. I did not want her to know and to worry. I turned back to Fillmore. "Let us keep this quiet for the present."

"Of course."

And so we parted warmly till we met again the next day for churchgoing and dining.

A maid handed Fillmore a telegram during dinner, but Fillmore waited till after we had eaten and the two of us were alone to tell me the latest news.

"Yesterday, shortly after the ceremony at city hall, someone stole a bay horse from a livery stable. The telegraph line was cut between Buffalo and Rochester. They have just repaired it, and the alarm has gone out. This telegram is the first response. The bay was found grazing on a patch of grass near the train station in Rochester. I'm afraid the would-be assassin has made good his escape. Take great care the rest of your journey to Washington."

"Thank you. I shall."

As we parted for the last time, I tried to say with my eyes and my grip what I could not say with my voice.

Rochester went smoothly enough.

Albany deafened me with a roar of artillery, but nothing else untoward happened. I did not see how anything untoward could happen. Troops lined the streets, and the people held back by the troops seemed excited but friendly.

My wife was in a much better mood, even giggling girlishly with the wife of the Albany mayor as our carriage drove down Green Street. I smiled to hear my wife breathe, "Isn't he the handsomest man?"

The parade route was just then taking us past the Gayety Theatre, and the two women whispered about the actor appearing as Pescara in *The Apostate*.

"What happened to his arm?"

I shot a look at the crowd before the theatre. A darkly handsome man stood staring back at me, his right arm bandaged and tied to his side.

"You know how active he is on stage. The other night he fell upon his dagger and stabbed himself in the armpit. He has had to suspend performances since, but I hear he will resume tonight."

"Tonight! How unlucky for us. We depart Albany this evening."

"Maybe you will see Mr. Booth in Washington another time."

"Maybe." But my wife sounded well on her way to moodiness again.

The man's fixed stare puzzled me. It seemed strange that an actor should show absolutely no emotion. But whether the man with his arm in a sling wished me ill or well, I wished him well in the time-honored way, as I understand it, of those who tread the boards.

"Break a leg," I thought at him.

Joe L. Hensley, when not writing mystery stories, is Judge Hensley of the Fifth Judicial Circuit in Madison, Indiana. His background with courts and the legal system serves him well in his fiction, especially in the adventures of Donald Robak, his series detective—a criminal lawyer. One of Mr. Hensley's strengths is character development, which he shows to great advantage in two non-series novels: The Color of Hate *(1960) and* The Poison Summer *(1974).*

Andrew Johnson (1808–1875), our seventeenth chief executive, served as governor of Tennessee and in the United States Senate before becoming president after the assassination of Lincoln. He successfully fought off impeachment in one of the most famous incidents in American political history.

THE DARKENED ROOM

★ ★ ★

Joe L. Hensley

    Andrew knew she waited each afternoon for his visits. It was a major part of what remained of their lives. He also knew that she'd sensed, for weeks now, that something was badly wrong, that he was worried and afraid. She had asked many questions, but so far no one, servant or family member, had told her. The secret he'd ordered remained a secret.

    He sat in a chair by her bed. He watched Eliza stifle a cough by force of will and smile up at him. The scent from the cut flowers that the servants brought daily for Eliza mingled untidily with the odor of the sickroom and other smells from the open sewer that emptied into the nearby tidal marsh. The result was an indescribable mix of cloying sweetness and final decay.

She'd asked him before and now she asked him again: "Tell me what it is that bothers you so much this spring, Andrew?"

He looked away from her and wondered what it was that always gave him away so instantly to her. It couldn't be his physical appearance. He was, as always, impeccably dressed. "The tailor," they called him. He'd visibly aged a bit in the past difficult months and maybe that was part of it, but he decided it was more probable her reasoning came because she'd known him so well and long. It gave her the ability to read his mind and moods and see through his attempts to put on a jolly face when he came to visit.

He smiled for her. "Only wear and tear on a lame-duck president."

She shook her head. "More than that."

He considered her. She'd stopped reading the papers many months ago because of her disease and because she'd tired of the constant savage stories about him. That had given him the opportunity to spare her. He'd warned both servants and in-house children not to speak of present problems. Her health was frail. Soon he feared she'd get her wish and join their son, Charles, a surgeon thrown from his horse and killed five years back during the war. At times she babbled of meeting Charles in dreams. She was a woman who remembered all and mourned all.

Andrew didn't believe he could bear her death. Even though physical love had ended long ago because of her wasting disease, spiritual love remained.

He arose from beside her and walked to the window. The blinds were kept down, but he pushed them momentarily aside and looked out. On the walk in front of the White House, a quiet crowd watched and waited. The only noise was the shrill sound of the cicadas. Andrew had been told that the crowds near the Senate were as thick as those cicadas and that seats to view his trial were being sold for high prices.

"It's something bad," she said plaintively. "It festers inside you."

He cast about in his mind knowing that if he gave her

nothing she'd worry on until she became more ill. To hide the greater truth, he gave her a minor possible truth.

"There are whispers, and we have reports that there are those who plot to assassinate me."

She watched him for a long moment, perhaps assaying his answer. "I've dreamed on that, Andrew. I've dreamed that those who killed Mr. Lincoln will again come for you. You must prepare for them. There are many soldiers who guard you. Use them. It's said that sometimes you succeed in eluding them to go off on your own. You must stop that and allow them to accompany you at all times. You must not complain about it."

"Yes. I agree, Eliza. But the whispers imply it will be someone close. Poison perhaps, or a knife. Maybe it's to be a servant in this house or someone I think is a friend."

She nodded, accepting his answer. "Plan against it, Andrew. You're intelligent. Stop them." She looked up at him intently, eyes feverish. "I've spoken to you before of my dreams, but not told you all of them. Sometimes I think I faintly see you and Charles together. Once I thought I saw both of you with Mr. Lincoln." She turned her head away and then back. "Plan, plan. You must live for me and this poor and desperate country. I need you and it needs you."

Andrew nodded at her to quiet her. "I believe they probably would try to use a person who serves us here, and so I've asked Robert for a list. We pay so wretchedly that our servants come and go like gypsies. A spy could easily be hired. And this house falls to pieces around us. The bricks are soft and need pointing, the windows should be replaced, and the house smells—always it smells. It's May and the flies are drawn to us by our open sewer." He looked up at the ceiling. "I don't complain to those in the House or Senate because most would enjoy knowing we suffer."

"Remember how it was when we first came to Washington?" Eliza asked. "It was better then." She coughed fitfully into a handkerchief, and he noted that she forced herself not to examine the results.

"I should take you back to Tennessee," he said.

She shook her head in alarm. "No. My place is here at your side. I would pine away and soon die in Greeneville."

She smiled up at him and played the game they sometimes now played. "Who would take care of you?"

He nodded to calm her. "You're right. I need your help and counsel. But for today I don't wish to tire you more. Would you like for me to read to you now?"

"Yes. Please read to me. Perhaps from Shakespeare's sonnets there on the night table." She settled into her bed. It was warm in the room, but he saw that she was cold. She smiled up at him without complaint.

Andrew Johnson read to her as she had taught him to read, long ago now. After a while, seeing that she'd fallen asleep, he softly closed the book. He watched her for a time, remembering their young years. He brushed her forehead with a kiss and tiptoed out.

There was to be the inevitable dinner that night. Despite the disrepair of the White House and the hue and cry surrounding the president, dinners were expected protocol. With Eliza unable to manage, Andrew Johnson's oldest daughter, Martha Patterson, had taken charge. She'd done a fine job, and Andrew reflected that her few failures had not been her fault, but his, for he had no taste in social honors.

Both tonight and at functions tomorrow, there would be guests friendly to the Stanton cause. It might be best to start in the morning. It was more informal.

Johnson walked down a faded but ornate hall to Robert's office. Once Robert had been a bold cavalry colonel—a fighter and killer. When Charles was killed, Eliza had insisted that Robert come to Washington. He'd been restless at first, but now the war was a memory and he was Andrew's good right hand, a swift thinker and a ruthless politician—a doer.

"Ah, Father," Robert said, looking up. "You've been upstairs. How is mother? Did you try the new ploy on her?"

Andrew nodded. "I tried it and now she sleeps. Her room seems very warm. In a month it will be unbearable there."

Robert shook his head. "Heat doesn't much bother her. Cold weather does. Last year I thought she enjoyed the summer."

"She's much worse than last year," Andrew answered darkly. "Sometimes I wish a symptom of her illness was less ability to read me."

"Perhaps the spy stratagem will work," Robert said.

"And there just might be something to it."

"How soon will they vote in the Senate?"

"A day. Perhaps two. Our people are working. It could be close."

"She's still not to know. Be certain no one tells her of the trial. Let only the most loyal of the servants enter her room, and tell them not to dally or gossip as they deliver her meals and clean the room."

Robert inclined his head. "As you will, Father. At times I think she'd be better off knowing, better able to withstand it if—"

"No," Andrew ordered. "I know her better than anyone, better even than you and the other children. When the time arrives, when my fate becomes fact, then I'll hope she can accept it. But she would worry herself to a quick death if she knew now. But she knows me so well that she senses something is wrong. So I gave her this latest rumor, as you and I planned. This hocus-pocus about a supposed plot against me, the current conspiracy."

"It could be truth," Robert said calmly. "Whispers sometimes are based on facts. Those who plot against you have no scruples."

Johnson shrugged. "So you said. But you knew I planned to use it with Eliza when I asked you to make me a list of the newest servants."

"I agree I did. But if you want her to believe you now, you must act seriously. I've finished the list. There are but four arrivals in the last six months. One's a secretary I hired; the other three are house servants."

"Tell me what you know of them. Whether it's worthwhile or not, we'll play out a small charade with them to please your mother."

For a few minutes the president listened. When his son was finished, Andrew said, "Here is what we'll do as we play our game."

As planned, Robert brought the first of the new servants in during breakfast the next morning. Another older servant then took the new one in hand. The new servant was young, black, and dressed in server's clothes.

"This is Michael Anthony Jones," Robert said to Andrew, purposely interrupting the conversation Andrew was holding with two senators and a congressman, all suspect. "When you've finished your breakfast, perhaps you'll take time to talk with us. Mr. Jones wants to discuss matters with us at your convenience."

Andrew noted that the people from the hill were watching carefully. He ignored them and returned to his breakfast. All information overheard in the White House was matter to be carried back to the hill caucuses. Andrew still had a few friends there, but there were many more he counted as enemies. And even friends could turn away from him just now.

"I'll talk with you after a while," Andrew said crossly. "Certainly I can't just now."

At luncheon, over a cool dessert, and with a known Stanton supporter ten feet away, Andrew spoke in low tones to two new kitchen servants. Both were young men, both white, and both embarrassed to be conversing with the president while they were in the midst of serving lunch.

Andrew smiled conspiratorially with the men, talked with them in whispers about their home states and their jobs, and gave each of them a gold piece when the conversation was done.

When the meal was completed, the Stanton supporter was the first to hurry away. *Reporting back*, Andrew decided.

Robert watched the Stanton man's departure with half a smile. He moved close to Andrew. "You are a proper player, father."

Andrew permitted himself a curt nod, aware that other eyes were still on them.

Before dinner, while discussing a map of the West with a senator from Ohio who both fawned on him and hated him, Andrew brought the last of the new employees in. The final man was a secretary. Robert had equipped him with paper, pens, and ink, and dressed him as the other secretaries were instructed to dress while in the White House. The clothing was cheap, but correct.

"My son, who is my chief secretary, has told me your name is Joseph Alsup," Andrew said cordially. "Forgive the guards, but it's known that there are those who plot against me.'' He smiled at senator and servant, excluding them. ''In these crazy times, one must take proper care.''

Alsup inclined his head and waited patiently.

Andrew reached inside his coat and drew out Alsup's letter of employment. ''My son and I thank you for this information you've furnished us. We hope your stay with us is beneficial to both you and us.''

The secretary looked at the paper Andrew studied, recognized it, and said nothing.

The president turned back to the map and the senator. ''Now, back to our discussion.'' He looked up at Joseph Alsup, who was watching him alertly. ''You're dismissed for now, but we'll want to talk with you further at a later time.''

Alsup looked down at the floor and walked quickly away.

The next morning Robert came down to breakfast, something he seldom did. He sat next to Andrew and spoke in a low voice. ''One man took the bait. We appear to be short a secretary. Alsup never returned to his rooming house last night and failed to show up for work this morning. I went to his address personally and sought him. He wasn't there and no one could remember seeing him after yesterday morning.''

''Perhaps he left because the waiting crowd outside informed him what his prospects were of retaining his job,'' Andrew said cynically.

''I only know he appears to have left us.''

''And the other three?''

''Still under our roof,'' Robert said, nodding. ''Tell me why he ran.''

''We don't know that he did, but now I have something to tell your mother. If he has left, he either became afraid or, more likely, someone became afraid of him. When Abraham was killed, vengeance against those who committed the crime was terrible and swift. The country wanted instant justice. If someone sent Alsup to spy or to kill, that someone could take no chances.'' He shrugged, not knowing. ''But it will make a jolly story for your mother.'' He watched Robert. ''Will they vote today?''

''I believe almost certainly. Our poll in the Senate shows you have some chance.''

"Spread the word on the vanished secretary," Andrew said. "It might help."

"I've already set the news afloat. It could be of help to you."

Andrew looked down at his plate, appetite fading. "No," he said with finality. He had come from initial hot anger to being philosophical. He had prepared his speech, the one he planned to give when he was found guilty. "They will have me—fried, boiled, or broiled. Then this poor country will die in anarchy. Our imperial Congress has threatened others, Tyler and Washington among them. Now they will do away with me. Dire events will follow. The crowd waiting outside wants me gone. A new president could mean new appointments, new jobs."

Andrew sat in the darkened room again. Eliza slept restlessly. He turned to his own reading. He read from Addison's *Cato*, trying to commit pertinent passages to memory. He thought that the book would soon be useful to him.

He knew he'd be convicted, knew it with sureness. He felt it was his destiny.

The wasted woman on the bed began to move about. He momentarily put aside his reading and wiped sweat from her face with a damp washcloth.

She came to semiwakefulness. "Are you here with me, Andrew?"

"Always, Eliza," he said soothingly. "And now I'm safe. The person who invaded our house to spy or kill has now vanished."

"You said that to me when you first came here this afternoon," she said querulously. "But you still worry. Why?" She shook her head and turned her body toward him. He sponged her face again. After a time he was rewarded by a faint snore.

Outside the door Robert waited, the results of the vote in hand. He wanted to knock and enter, but was aware of the strict orders his father had given about harboring the truth from his mother. Robert paced and waited. Thirty-seven for and nineteen against conviction. One vote short. Andrew Johnson had won a vote he'd been certain of losing. Robert was exultant.

* * *

Inside the sick room Andrew listened to the mating call of the cicadas in the trees on the White House lawn. Soon they would breed and die, their short lives finished. Soon, he knew intuitively, his own life would end.

He went to the window and looked out. The crowd had diminished, but some curious citizens lingered.

He pushed the shade closed again and returned to his vigil. "I am not guilty," he whispered to the shadow woman in the bed, who lay unhearing. "I am not guilty, but they will find me guilty. Then you will die because of my shame and I will die because you have died."

He lowered his head. He was very tired and so he let himself flee backward into the past, back to the time she'd taught him how to read, taught him the way to be much more than he'd ever thought or hoped to be. He slid into uneasy sleep.

When he came back to wakefulness, it was to a real world, a world where he knew he'd be found guilty, where chaos would reign. He opened his coat and fingered the pistol he carried, but that was not the way. Again he read several pages from Addison.

Outside the door his son waited a few moments longer before descending the steps to greet a visitor in his office. He put the results of the winning vote in his inside pocket. He would reveal the happy news to his father when he emerged from the sick room.

At his desk Robert listened with interest as a policeman explained that the body of one Joseph Alsup had been found an hour before in the White House's open sewer.

Robert nodded and made notes.

The vote lay hotly in his pocket, but there was another thing his father would never know. The night before, Robert had followed Alsup, avoiding the troops at the corner, as had his prey. He had caught up with Alsup in a dark, lonely place. When the fleeing secretary had brandished a revolver, it had been proof enough for Robert. Certifiable proof of guilt.

And in the short scuffle, Joseph Alsup had died.

Robert smiled and waited.

P. M. CARLSON formerly taught psychology at Cornell University and has published several critically acclaimed novels featuring Maggie Ryan, an amateur sleuth and statistician. Maggie stars in Audition for Murder, Murder Is Academic *(nominated for the 1985 Anthony Award as best paperback original),* Murder Is Pathological, Murder Unrenovated, *and* Rehearsal for Murder. *Dr. Carlson is the co-author of the textbook* Behavioral Statistics.

Ulysses S. Grant (1822–1885), America's eighteenth president, was a relentless warrior, a devoted husband and father, a loyal friend—and head of a notoriously corrupt administration. Insider stock trading information, payoffs for Indian trading posts and for surveyorships, and the Whiskey Ring tax frauds were among the methods used by Grant's associates to profit in the boom-and-bust period that followed the Civil War. One bright moment in Grant's scandal-ridden years in office should have been his daughter Nellie's White House wedding on May 21, 1874—but this silver lining, too, had its cloud.

THE FATHER OF THE BRIDE; OR A FATE WORSE THAN DEATH!

★ ★ ★

P. M. Carlson

1

"Hush, Bridget Mooney!" Aunt Mollie hissed at me. "Do you want them to hear us?"

"Oh, bother them all! I'm freezing here," I grumbled. "And my bustle keeps snagging in these damn branches."

"Enough sass! You'll never be rich and famous if you can't be a proper lady!" Aunt Mollie began, then broke off. "Lordy! They're coming!"

I peered over her cloaked shoulder and through the needles of the evergreen shrub where we had been huddling for—how long? An hour? A year? Till the last syllable of recorded time?

Beyond the new fence I finally saw them, cloaked and bundled like us against the chill and leaden sky. A frisky boy in his teens led the way, followed by a stout lively woman on the arm of a dapper man with a trim pointed imperial beard. Then, escorting a lovely girl with eyes as luminous as a fawn's, came the man we had been waiting for—a short muscular man with brown beard and kind thoughtful gaze. President Grant! I'll admit it, yes indeed: I was thrilled! I wanted to wrap myself in bunting and sing the "Battle Hymn of the Republic." He paused to light a cigar, and I noticed more people emerging from the White House behind him: a thickset young man with a dark mustache; a restless middle-aged man with reddish hair and pockmarked skin; a handsome, large, fleshy man. Then the entire party strolled toward our edge of the lawn.

"Papa, tell me!" I heard the fawn-eyed girl ask. "Why is a telegram like a blushing maiden?"

"Why, I don't know, Nellie." The president smiled at her. "Why?"

"Because they are both red quickly!"

They laughed. Aunt Mollie tensed as they approached, surreptitiously gathered up her skirt and cloak, and flung herself out of our hiding place and up against the fence just as the president reached the nearest point to us in the trajectory of his walk. But hurling myself after her, I found my head suddenly snapped backward as though someone had slipped a noose around my throat.

Bridget Mooney foiled again! Always the comic relief. My bonnet had caught on an evergreen branch and I was snared like a rabbit.

Muttering unladylike words, I set myself to untangling my

bonnet as Aunt Mollie called sweetly through the fence, "Mr. President! I have important news for you!"

The president glanced in her direction. Aunt Mollie was an earnest, pleasant-faced woman, her hair no longer red like mine but streaked with gray like last year's peppermint candy. Her face was rosy with cold. He asked kindly, "What is it?"

"People are cheating you," she explained. "Thousands of dollars. I've got a friend, you see, works at Inverness in St. Louis . . ."

The president sighed and made a gesture of dismissal. "Thank you, madam. Consult my staff, please." He turned back to the girl on his arm and moved on.

"But I've got proof, Mr. President!" Aunt Mollie skittered crablike alongside the fence to keep pace.

The men with the president moved toward her in a leisurely way that made me think of big hounds that had spied a luckless turtle. The reddish-haired one said, "Move along, now, madam."

"But I must show him!" Aunt Mollie, waving a green-ribboned packet, was on the verge of tears.

The dapper man took pity and said, "Look, madam, write your name and address here. We'll try to get you an appointment."

"Hang it, this is important!"

The reddish-haired one was lean, excitable, and brusque. "Hundreds of people petition the president every week. Every day! He can't listen to everyone, can he?"

The big fleshy man had a thick beard and a kindly smile. "He needs time with his family, madam. Now, run along. We'll contact you."

They strode away to rescue President Grant from an onslaught of curiosity-seekers at the next turning. Aunt Mollie came storming back but didn't pause for me. I had finally disentangled my bonnet strings from the shrubbery. She swept past and across the clean, satin-smooth breadth of Pennsylvania Avenue.

"Wait! Wait for me!" I exclaimed, darting after her and narrowly escaping the wheels of a speeding carriage.

She was still in a pout. "Look who's here! Precious little

help you were, Bridget Mooney! And it's your prospects we're trying to improve!''

"My bonnet caught," I explained meekly.

"It's always something. Well, come along. Back to the boardinghouse to decide what to do. Maybe I should just hand them over to that newspaper editor. Fishback. But confound him, he won't pay.''

"Back to the boardinghouse?" I squawked. "But you promised we'd go shopping after this! I didn't come all the way from St. Louis to hide in bushes!''

"Oh, Bridget, you are such a cross to bear! If I hadn't promised your dear mama—'' That was only partly true, I knew. I was the bright hope of Aunt Mollie's life, her ticket to a moneyed life far beyond the means of a government copyist. But I'd never earn my way—and hers—to those flowery beds of ease if I couldn't get the training I needed.

I said, "I'm twenty-one, Aunt Mollie. Almost. You needn't treat me like a child. You won't even tell me what you're trying to do!''

She sighed, seeing the justice of my argument. "I reckon I could tell you. Here!''

She pulled the flat little bundle tied in green ribbon from the side placket of her skirt. I opened it: merely papers.

"These are from General McDonald's office! Is that all?'' I was bitterly disappointed. I had expected the crown jewels, at least.

"It's proof, silly goose! He's been cheating the government, and . . .''

Maybe it was the *silly goose* that got my dander up. I was tired of her bossiness, tired of standing around shivering in the cold when the nation's capital cried out for exploration. What a capital it was, new-minted now ten years after the exhausting war. Buildings were rising everywhere; streets were in chaos from the laying of gas lines and new pavement; noble young trees had been planted everywhere. Pennsylvania Avenue, an amazing broad ribbon of silky asphalt instead of St. Louis's broken cobblestones, beckoned me. I was young, pretty—well, pretty if you didn't mind freckles and low-class Irish red hair. I was on holiday, supposed to be having a splendid time. I stuffed her papers into my muff and skedaddled. "Come on, Aunt Mollie," I hollered, "I'm going shopping!"

I know, I know, a proper lady doesn't go galloping through the streets of the national metropolis. But my tomboy years, shooting squirrels with my big brother in the Missouri hills, had taught me some useful skills. Yes indeed. Aunt Mollie chased me stoutly a block or two, then huffed despairingly, "And you wonder why I treat you like a child! Mark my words, Bridget Mooney, you'll come to a bad end!"

I had a splendid time, especially in the dry-goods stores. St. Louis had nothing to compare with the fine imported goods available here. Shopping without much money can be delightful—no need to make decisions about any of the glorious possibilities that present themselves, as they are all equally unattainable. In imagination, I costumed myself lavishly in fine velvets and French lace—as Juliet, as Cleopatra, as Rosalind, even as Lady Macbeth. But by two o'clock I began to feel guilty. A clerk had left a nice bit of Lyons velvet ribbon unattended on a counter. I hooked it as a peace offering for Aunt Mollie and turned back toward our boardinghouse.

I know, I know, Aunt Mollie would scold, too, but she knew value when she saw it. She'd keep it. And shouldn't clerks learn to be more careful?

There were two or three elegant taverns near the turn into my street. As I passed the first, a young man, well-dressed and devilishly handsome, tumbled out the door and against me. He clutched at my cloak to keep himself from falling, then hauled himself upright, blinking and swaying. "Oh, I shay, I'm terribly shorry," he exclaimed. An Englishman. A real swell. Reeking of drink.

I straightened my cloak with dignity. "Sir, you are rather rough. Please let me pass."

"Rough? Shorry. Really." But he didn't move, just swayed a moment as though collecting his woolly thoughts. He had a neat mustache, soft appreciative eyes, and a long, handsome, and somehow familiar, nose. He said carefully, "My lips, two blushing pilgrims, ready stand/To smooth that rough touch with a tender kish—um, kiss."

"O villain!" I retorted, "thy lips are scarce wiped since thou drunkest last!"

His velvety eyes glowed and he fell to his knees before me. "Shakespeare! On this benighted shore! Loveliest of sylphs, I shall be your slave forever! Come live with me! Or," he added more practically, standing and brushing off his elegant knees, "at least share a glash of wine?"

I put on my most ferocious Lady Macbeth glare. He shrugged, bowed, and disappeared into the next tavern while I stalked righteously around the corner into our street before I began giggling.

I waved gaily to the landlady from the stair hall. Mrs. Carter was fat as a walrus and almost as whiskery, and she seldom moved from her capacious rocking chair. She didn't respond, and I didn't know if she'd not seen me or merely needed more time to lift her plump arm. I ran up the stairs. Aunt Mollie and I had one of the two rear rooms on the second floor. The steps led up directly to our door. It was ajar an inch or two, and I was groping for the ribbon I'd found for her as I pushed the door open with my foot. It was jammed against something. I peered around the edge and saw Aunt Mollie sprawled on the floor with a great bloody gash in her throat.

A proper lady would have felt for her pulse, or wept, or shrieked. A proper lady would not have thought first of her own throat and how very much she preferred it ungashed. A proper lady would not have turned away from that partly opened door and marched calmly down the stairs, still waving cheerfully at Mrs. Carter. Or walked straight back to that second tavern with a brazen smile for the young Englishman.

His sweet drunken eyes glowed welcome as he stumbled to meet me. "O joy! I thought you'd left my life forever!"

My hands were trembling in my muff and I couldn't even remember my Shakespeare. Aunt Mollie's image still shuddered at the back of my cowardly mind. I said simply, "Can't a girl change her mind?"

My favorite melodramas would claim that I was asking for a fate worse than death. But frankly, after seeing Aunt Mollie, I reckoned any other fate would do.

2

I woke the next morning in a splendid velvet and brocatelle bedroom amidst silken sheets wildly tumbled from my night-time thrashings and exertions. Not that my handsome Englishman had been in any way involved. Whatever his original intentions, he'd been sound asleep long before his man and I had lifted him into bed, and while I'd flailed about in the throes of hideous dreams, he'd lain there leadlike and stinking all night long. In any case, I didn't fret much about my virtue anymore. I'd been late to fill out and Aunt Mollie, always clever in business, had taken advantage of my long time in the bud to sell my virginity. For a good price. Four times. The takers were St. Louis businessmen, proper gentlemen every one. Yes indeed.

During the sleepless intervals between nightmares last night, I had come to some conclusions. Without Aunt Mollie as guide and adversary, I was effectively alone in the world. Mama had died of a fever shortly after my birth; my older brother, after teaching me to shoot squirrels, had in turn been shot in the Civil War. Papa, though he adored me, had lost a precarious livelihood playing stage Irishmen because his love of the bottle caused him to miss too many cues, and he now spent his hours tippling at Uncle Mike's saloon. Uncle Mike would take me in, I knew, as a barmaid—his word for tart. Aunt Mollie had warned me away from that. To get on, she'd explained, a girl had to please people with money—in other words, men. Without a rich father, my choices were few: to be a servant or a tart, and remain poor; to marry a poor man, and remain poor; or to develop my talent for the stage and improve my chances. So I studied my Shakespeare, while Aunt Mollie put out my virginity money at six percent and schemed to amass the remaining sum necessary to achieve the finer future she envisioned: rich, famous, perhaps even proper. I resolved now to aim for that future.

But first I would find the person who had killed her. Perhaps it was guilt for leaving her at the crucial moment; perhaps fury at the injustice of it. In any case, I'd go right back to that boardinghouse, talk to the walrussy Mrs. Carter and her servants, look for clues like Hawkshaw himself. Oh, I know, I know, a proper lady doesn't go hunting cutthroats. She weeps prettily, and clever servants and heroes appear to fight for her cause. But weeping prettily did not seem to be a very practical strategy. For one thing, I was rather short of clever servants at the moment. And as for heroes . . .

I looked across the room at the only hero who had yet happened by. He was sitting ashen-faced in the armchair furthest from the light of the window, wearing slippers and a satiny maroon dressing gown, his head bowed, seemingly studying the handsome top hat that stood nearby. His man was preparing some Seidlitz powders for him. But when I sat up his great pain-fogged eyes met mine and he attempted a smile.

"How is't with you, my lady?"

"I suspect my head feels better than yours," I observed. I tossed the sheet about me Grecian style and went to the washbasin.

"I hope so. Look here, sylph, who are you?"

"You wish an introduction, at this late juncture?" I wasn't sure I wanted this drunk and foreign stranger to know my horrid situation. What if he talked indiscreetly? There were people in this town who cut other people's throats.

"I know that you are either Mollie O'Rourke or Bridget Mooney from St. Louis," he said, swallowing the Seidlitz powders. "It would seem appropriate to know which."

He must have been reading my papers. I concentrated on my goddesslike attire and looked at him, heavy-lidded, with what I hoped was aplomb. "And you, in turn, are either John Bull, or else not."

He smiled. "Fair enough. My name is Algernon Charles Frederick Sartoris." He pronounced it Sar-triss.

"How grand!" I exclaimed. "With all those names you must be related to a duchess."

"Merely a countess. Oh, and this is my man, Littimer. Immortalized by Mama's late friend Dickens."

I bowed my head to Littimer, a highly respectable stiff-necked fellow with smooth short hair, and then looked back to my elegant host. Perhaps he was telling the truth. "Delighted to meet you, Algy," I said. "I'm Bridget. Do you usually ransack a lady's papers on first acquaintance?"

"I must confess to a certain curiosity about you," Algy admitted. "Generally speaking, tarts do not quote Shakespeare."

"Nor do they stay long to assist gentlemen numbed by drink."

Algy looked uncomfortable. Littimer smirked and said, "There's tarts and there's tarts," with as much innuendo as he could muster.

I whirled on him imperiously, nostrils flaring. "You block! You stone! You worse than senseless thing!"

"Littimer, leave us a moment. The lady is not a tart," said Algy with a weary wave of his hand, and Littimer sidled out, still smirking the smirk of the respectable. Algy turned back to me. "Littimer believes you hope to trap me into marriage."

"Marriage? Of course not!" I was appalled. "Then I'd have to leave the stage!"

"An actress! I should have guessed! What parts do you play?"

"Oh, the Colleen Bawn," I said, trotting out the best.

"Ah, yes, the pretty girl milking her cow," mused Algy, then threw back his head and sang in a surprisingly strong, trained voice, "Brian O'Linn had no breeches to wear, so he bought him a sheepskin to make him a pair."

I couldn't help joining the spirited air: "The skinny side out, and the woolly side in, 'They are cool and convenient,' said Brian O'Linn."

We grinned at each other, then Algy asked shrewdly, "And nothing else but comic-relief parts, right? Your voice is attractive but rather untutored, you know."

"Yes, I know! Aunt Mollie was going to get me voice lessons!" This was something of a sore point. The fourth St. Louis businessman had paid for my virginity by giving me a role in the theatre he managed. The laughter and applause that the audience had lavished upon me confirmed the passion for the stage I had harbored since seeing the greatest actress of the century when I was thirteen. But I had not been retained, because my St. Louis speech habits were suitable for too few roles, and in spite of Aunt Mollie's efforts, we had not yet accumulated enough for first-rate elocution lessons. I reported none of this to Algy, of course; I still felt it unwise to tell him the full extent of my difficulties. I concluded bravely, "In any case, most people think my voice is fine."

"Philistines," he declared. "Though perhaps my judgment is better trained than theirs. My mother sang opera before she married. My aunt was an actress, and my maternal grandparents. Perhaps you've heard of the Kembles?"

I could not have been more astonished if he'd suddenly sprouted a halo and risen on a cloud of cherubim. But on the heels of my shock came recognition. I fell to my knees before him, reached up timidly to touch his face. "The nose!" I breathed. "The Kemble nose!"

Algy drew back impatiently. "Look, colleen, Kembles are no more than ordinary mortals like the rest of us."

"Algy, you're just wrong!" I sat back on my heels in indignation. "Papa took me to hear your aunt Fanny when I was thirteen. Her Midwestern tour. She read *Richard III* and took every role. I was enraptured! She was an army of people! No ordinary mortal can do that. She is the idol of my life!"

"Well," said Algy cruelly, "she does at least have a trained voice."

Clearly, kneeling before him was not advancing my case. I gathered my sheet about me regally and went behind the little screen. Someone, probably Littimer, had neatly arranged the items of clothing, Algy's and mine, on benches and hooks. It took time to don all the camisoles and petticoats and bustles required. When almost done, I picked up my bonnet. Underneath was the ribbon I was going to give Aunt Mollie. The unexpected sight triggered a wild fit of tears.

"Here, here!" Algy was around the screen in a flash. "I say, what's the matter?"

His dressing gown was embroidered satin, and I fear that I snivelled all over one side. He patted my shoulder awkwardly, and said, "There, there," and other equally useful things, and finally inquired, "Look, colleen, what have I done? Ruined your reputation? Insulted your voice? Forgotten to offer you a glass of wine? Tell me my sin, so that I may atone!"

I realized that I'd have to explain my tears. "My aunt's dead," I sobbed. "And I'm angry and miserable."

"Yes, I see. Your aunt. Was this recent?"

"Just after we collided yesterday, I found her dead. That's why I came back to you. I was frightened. And alone."

"Ah." He nodded. "I suspected there was more to it than my noble Kemble nose. My poor Bridget!"

"You've been kind, Algy." I pulled a handkerchief from my muff, noting uneasily that my papers were gone.

"I understand. My older brother died a year ago. One is naturally sad. Tell me, how did she die?"

"She was . . . knifed." The mere thought of it made me quail.

"Knifed! On the street?"

"In our room."

"Well, ah, did you do it?"

"Me?" I stepped back indignantly. "What do you mean?"

"Look, colleen, at the facts. Your aunt is killed, in your room at Mrs. Carter's boardinghouse, correct?"

He had definitely been reading my papers. I nodded.

"And you disappear at the same time. What would any reasonable person conclude?"

Thus challenged, I realized that there had been a logic to my thoroughly improper behavior. "Look, Mr. Sar-triss, sir, we only just arrived yesterday. And the only people we've met are Mrs. Carter and her servants. We went there because friends in St. Louis recommended her establishment. Said it was decent and would accept ladies traveling alone." I plunked my bonnet on my head and tied the strings. "But it can't be all that decent, can it, if the ladies are murdered?"

"You weren't followed from St. Louis? You met no one on the journey?"

"I wanted to, but Aunt Mollie made sure we kept to ourselves."

"And Mrs. Carter is the only person you met here?"

"Unless you count the president of the United States."

Algy's soft gaze became suddenly intense. "The president? You met him?"

"Oh, Algy, for heaven's sake! The president doesn't go about knifing people!" I remembered Shiloh and Petersburg, and added, "Well, except maybe Rebels. And anyway, we didn't really meet him. Aunt Mollie just had this silly idea. Thought she had proof that someone in St. Louis was cheating the government, and—"

I broke off. A new train of thought had suddenly presented itself. I had to go back to that boardinghouse, I realized. Not only to make sure poor Aunt Mollie was properly taken care of, but also to establish that I didn't do it. And to collect my things, and to see if Aunt Mollie had left anything that might tell me who her killer was. I'd been sure he was in Mrs. Carter's employ; now I saw that perhaps he was not. But whoever he was, I resolved, he was going to suffer a fate worse than death.

Algy, waiting for me to finish my sentence, prompted, "And what?"

"Nothing. She wouldn't tell me any details." I picked up my cloak.

"Did she tell the president?"

"No. We only saw him through the fence. He wouldn't listen. He was taking a walk, and just told her to get an appointment and then went on his way."

"Was anyone with him?"

"Several people. Family, I suppose, and four men."

"A girl? Your age, or a bit younger?" he asked eagerly.

"Yes. Dark hair, pretty. His daughter?"

"Nellie," sighed Algy. "Those eyes!"

Philanderer. I was vexed; how could he sigh over Nellie Grant's eyes when he'd just spent the night with me? Well, it hadn't been truly romantic for either of us, I'm bound to admit. And if he was acquainted with Nellie's eyes, he might be able to tell me about those people. I followed him across the room and said, "There was a young man. Thickset, mustache."

"That would be Nellie's brother, Lieutenant Colonel Fred. Fine young scamp. Went to West Point, you know. In discipline, he graduated forty-first in a class of forty-one." Algy seemed to approve.

"Even so," I said, "he seemed more disciplined than the middle-aged, nervous fellow with reddish hair and bad skin."

"Ah, yes, the terrifying General William 'Cump' Sherman."

"Also a well-dressed fellow with an elegant imperial beard. And a large, handsome man. Very genial."

"Grant's personal secretary, General Babcock. The large man had a beard?" I nodded and he said, "General Belknap. Secretary of War."

"Do any of them go about knifing people?"

He looked at me thoughtfully. "Did your aunt mention that she had proof?"

"No more than mention. You didn't answer my question."

He seemed a little distracted, fiddling with his stylish curly-brimmed top hat. "The answer is no. They are all close to the president, of course, and honorable men."

Like Brutus, I wondered? I was sorry now I hadn't pressed Aunt Mollie more about what she knew. It had all seemed just another of her blame-fool ideas to get me on stage. She'd planned to sell her knowledge to the President, then get me voice lessons from a professional in New York, and live off the fabulous earnings that would eventually ensue. I was in favor of all that, of course, but did not believe in it as fervently as Aunt Mollie. All I'd really expected from this plan was a trip to Washington. But Aunt Mollie had always been able to spot a good business deal, and if the papers she had hooked from her most recent employer's office were in fact of value—or danger—to someone . . .

I addressed Algy again. "Do you know of a man named McDonald? Collector of internal revenue for the St. Louis district?"

"No, I don't know of him." Algy left his top hat where it stood and walked over to the great velvet-draped window. There were now some papers in his hand. With a sudden sense of horror, I recognized my boardinghouse card and Aunt Mollie's green-ribboned packet.

"You wretch!" I cried, lunging for the papers.

He laughed and held them high, out of my reach. "Come, colleen, allow me to finish inspecting your most interesting collection."

I hauled up my skirts, kneed him where it would do the most good, snatched the papers from him as he doubled over moaning, and ran out, slamming the door behind me. It was becoming more and more difficult to be a proper lady these days.

Littimer had repaired to a respectable position by the staircase. "Your master is having a bad morning," I told him. "Better go see to him." He bowed without comment and was striding back to Algy's aid as I sailed downstairs and out the tavern door.

Today Mrs. Carter's entry was locked. I rang the bell and set my face in carefree lines. "Oh, Mrs. Carter," I bubbled brightly as she wheezingly opened the door, "I have so much news for Aunt Mollie! Did she tell you I met my father's cousin Emily, and went to stay with her last night? Oh, there are so many . . ."

"Poor child!" Mrs. Carter's small puffy eyes were brimming. "You don't know! Oh, a terrible thing happened to your aunt yesterday. I never knew of such a thing! A robber, it was."

"A robber? What do you mean? Everything was dandy when I ran in yesterday to ask permission to stay with Emily."

"Yes, I thought I saw you. Oh, my poor Miss Mooney, she's dead."

"What? I don't believe you!" That was my cue to run up the stairs. Still, it was an effort to take the dreaded next step. I told myself that Mrs. Carter had the place firmly locked, that she and the servants were near and probably innocent. I reassured myself that if I saw a man with a knife I could scream for help. But it was hard to keep my heaving stomach under control because I wasn't sure I could face Aunt Mollie again. As I pushed the door slowly open, I prayed that they'd taken her away.

They had. But I didn't bother to scream for Mrs. Carter, because the same moment that the cold blade touched my throat, a hand clamped across my nose and mouth.

3

"No noise, now," murmured the voice in my ear as the door closed behind me. "Yer little windpipe slits as easy as the rest. If ye understand, whisper yes."

I understood, yes indeed. Voice lessons couldn't do much for a slit windpipe. As he released my mouth I whispered, "Yes."

"Good. Sit down, now. I have need of a quiet conversation with ye." He pushed the door closed while the knife nudged me into a chair.

"All right," I whispered, and added for good measure, "*sir.*"

"Who are ye? Why are ye here?"

I could see him now. He had a Union soldier's cap pulled low on his brow and a soiled scarf about his bristly chin, but the warty nose and pale eyes and listing posture reminded me of someone. St. Louis, I recollected. At General Mc-Donald's office, where Aunt Mollie did copying. She had pointed at this man once across the courtyard, wondering why he was hanging about. But it didn't seem wise to let him know I recognized him. "Whisht, I am but the housemaid, sir," I said, sounding as low and Irish as I possibly could in a whisper. Papa would have been proud of me.

"Oh, ye are, are ye?" The knife point pressed a little closer. "And why the fine bonnet and muff, then?"

He was right; my meet-the-president costume was woefully inappropriate to this role. I improvised. "Sure and haven't I been visiting my fine cousin Emily? But it's a bit late I am getting back. I thought to start in, sir, before the old lady Carter missed me."

The knife point eased a little. "Aye, she's a bit slow, that one. So ye're the one who does up this room?"

"Yes, sir, that I am. And a fine jumble it is today, sir." It was true; drawers, carpetbags, wardrobes, all were open and the contents strewn about. I tried not to look at the dark stain on the carpet near the door.

The pale eyes glinted with something like craftiness. "Perhaps the two of us can make a little agreement, me girl. I've been sent to find some papers in this room, the rightful belongings of me master. Give me a little help and I'll let ye be.''

"Of course, sir, being as the papers are rightfully his.''

"That they are. Now, me girl, I've searched this room and found nothing. With yer practiced eyes perhaps ye'll have more success. But remember, if ye make any difficulties, the knife will put an end to them quick.''

"Yes, sir.'' He had been talking softly; but I still whispered. It seemed to me that the muff was giving off sparks from the presence of the packet tucked inside. I was fortunate, I reckoned, that this fellow hadn't seen me with Aunt Mollie. While I did not realistically expect to be in this world much longer, his ignorance had granted me a few more terrified moments of life while I searched for an escape from this dilemma. "How many papers, sir?'' I asked.

"He didn't say. They're done up in a packet, he said, with a green ribbon.''

Suddenly, we both became aware of a commotion in the hall.

" 'Shcuse me, madam! Just looking for my cousin!'' There was a crash, and our door sprang open. Algy lurched into the room, clinging to the doorknob for balance. "Cousin!'' He beamed.

"Who's this?'' My pale-eyed companion was again grasping me tightly, knife at my throat.

Algy giggled. "Pirates! What a jolly idea! I shay, let's shail away on the bounding main!'' He snatched the counterpane from Aunt Mollie's bed, waved it in the air, and dropped it neatly over the warty-nosed head. I jerked away at the same moment, so fast that I stumbled back over the chair.

The knife came slashing out through the counterpane, but Algy lifted the oil lamp and thumped it soundly down on my unpleasant companion's head. The counterpane-wrapped rogue collapsed at my feet. I snatched the knife from the limp folds, tucked it into my boot, and sat down on the bundle.

Algy, breathing hard, surveyed the situation and sat on the other end.

For a moment we both were motionless. I waited for my pounding heart to slow before I said shakily, "So now you're my cousin?''

"From across the billowing sea. Or so I told your rotund hostess when she asked if I were the cousin."

"Unfortunately for your clever story, I told her my cousin's name was Emily."

"Easily remedied. Poor Emily married a drunken Englishman."

"Yes, she's so impetuous. Should have held out for a better match."

We grinned at each other, but I was uneasy. We had not exactly parted friends, yet Algy made no reference to his recent discomfort. I fidgeted on my lumpy seat. "Warty-nose here is rather bony," I said. "Why don't we drop him on the back porch roof outside the window?"

We rolled him unceremoniously onto the roof. Then I locked the window and turned back to the chaotic room. "Terrible mess," Algy observed.

"Well, I'll just throw it all into our carpetbags," I said, and began to do so. "Would you mind settling with Mrs. Carter about the lamp and counterpane? She's been through rather a lot, and I'll have to find what she's done with Aunt Mollie."

"You're afraid she won't tell you what she's done if she hasn't been paid for the damage?"

I shrugged. "*I* wouldn't."

"Mm. All right." Algy hesitated a moment, then asked, "Bridget, what is it you want?"

"At the present moment? I want a decent burial for Aunt Mollie, and a place to stay, and breakfast, and a good cry."

He nodded. "Right. But I meant—from life."

"From life?"

"Well, you're a deucedly odd sort of girl. For example, you seem in no hurry to contact your family in St. Louis."

"Aunt Mollie was all the family I had." Papa and Uncle Mike weren't worth mentioning.

"I see. And unlike your mythical cousin Emily, you don't seem bent on marriage. Rather the opposite."

"I love acting. And even your Aunt Fanny, the idol of my life, found that marriage and the stage don't combine easily."

"That's true enough. And the stage is what you really want?"

"Yes. Eventually. But first two other things. I need voice lessons, so people don't laugh at my Shakespeare."

"Good idea. And the second thing?"

I pulled the knife from my boot and tested the edge with my fingertip. "I want to find the man who killed Aunt Mollie."

Algy looked surprised. "Weren't we just sitting on him?"

"Oh, yes, Warty-nose. A hired hand. I want to find who hired him." My rage was very near the surface again, but I dissembled: Patience on a monument, smiling at grief. I said, "I've seen Warty-nose in St. Louis, Algy. Near the place Aunt Mollie worked."

"Connected with this McDonald you mentioned?"

"Perhaps."

His beautiful brow furrowed. "But your aunt was killed here, in Washington."

"Yes, that's part of the problem. Who is Warty-nose's master? And what's his interest in St. Louis?"

"If my ear at the keyhole didn't deceive me, Warty-nose wanted your aunt's papers."

"Yes." I looked straight into his disarming velvety eyes. "And so do you. Right?"

"Well—" He smiled boyishly. A good trick; if I hadn't understood him so well I might have been on my knees instantly, begging him to accept the packet as a small token of my esteem.

Instead, I said coolly, "You didn't follow me here out of love, Algy, not after what I did to you. I do appreciate the heroic rescue, but perhaps we could manage our business more efficiently if you told me what *you* want from life."

He hesitated, and seemed to decide on the truth. He said, "Nellie Grant."

I was startled. "The president's daughter? Truly?"

"I met her on an Atlantic crossing a year ago. We—well, I want to marry her." The man was actually blushing.

I turned away to slide Warty-nose's knife into my muff. "How sweet of you. I fancy that her fortune and connections don't repulse you either. An American princess. I take it there is opposition to this marriage? Your illustrious family, perhaps?"

"Well, they profess to be shocked, thinking all you Americans rather wild and uneducated. Aunt Fanny had a bit of bad luck with an American husband, you recall."

"He was a damn Rebel."

"Well, yes. But my family will consent if I press matters. And Nellie's mother is pleased enough with my connections. No, the real difficulty is the president. He dotes on Nellie, as well he might. And people close to him are advising against the match. So he makes excuses. First he said she should marry a countryman. I offered to become an American citizen. That was before my brother died, of course. Then he said she was too young. His advisors say—well, he finds countless excuses."

"Including, no doubt, that his daughter should not marry a drunken man who takes strange young ladies to his room at night?"

He looked disconcerted. "Bridget, you can't prove that! Littimer is incorruptible!"

I slid my fingers into the muff, next to the knife, and pulled out an extremely distinctive shirt stud.

He said angrily, "You'll ruin your own reputation, too!"

"Algy, Algy, what do you take me for? Of course I don't mean to do anything with this shirt stud. But perhaps we can help each other."

"Ah. Yes."

I extracted the green-ribboned packet from my muff. "No, no, I'll hold it," I warned him, jerking it away from his eager grasp. "You may look, but must agree to tell me what it means. Then we'll discuss the price."

He nodded his consent. I undid the ribbon, rather rumpled from its strenuous adventures, and unfolded the enclosed paper.

It was only a short note. It said, "Tell J. the case against Inverness is now strong enough to ensure cooperation." It was signed "Robert E. Lee."

I watched Algy read it, saw the flash of excitement, quickly veiled. He said guardedly, "Actually, I'm not sure what it means."

"Well, then, " I said regretfully, "I suppose I'd best sell it to a newspaper." I folded the note.

"No, no wait! It's not from Robert E. Lee!"

"I don't need you to tell me that, Algy." My voice dripped scorn: Katherina the shrew.

He blurted, "Inverness is a distiller. In St. Louis."

"I know that, too. But you do tell me one thing of interest. I take it you have an idea what to do with this note."

"An inkling," Algy admitted. "Whereas you have no idea at all."

I reflected a moment. He was right: although I had an idea, it was far too vague. I knew only that the place to ask questions was the White House. Warty-nose had instructions to fetch the green-ribboned packet. Therefore, my quarry was one of the men with the president who had seen the packet. Algy had recognized the writer of the note at a glance, obviously from the handwriting. So I decided to use Algy. A blunder could easily result in death for an unimportant St. Louis visitor. Algy, on the other hand, had the backing of the entire British Empire. If he were murdered, there would be a spectacular investigation.

There was a groan from outside the window. I picked up a piece of Aunt Mollie's scattered stationery and copied the words from the note in a schoolgirl's block printing. Then I tied the copy into the green-ribboned package, opened the window, and tucked it into the moaning man's pocket. He was still too fuddled to notice. I hoped he wouldn't roll off the roof before he woke up. I was depending on him to take the note to his superior, in the hopes he'd leave me alone. I relocked the window, turned back to Algy, and held up the real note.

"The price," I said, "is a situation and a letter."

"A situation?"

"In the White House. Housemaid, perhaps."

Algy frowned. "Not much chance of that. But tell me, how are you at flowers?"

"I can learn anything."

"I believe you, Bridget Mooney. For now, I'll get Sir Edward Thornton to give you a temporary position."

"Who?"

"My host. Her Majesty's impeccable minister to this former colony. With his reference you can move on to the White House as soon as I convince Mrs. Grant to hire you.''

Well, I wasn't likely to get a better offer. Besides, Sir Edward's would offer a safe harbor from which to observe both Algy and Warty-nose before plunging into the deeper eddies of the White House proper. I said, ''All right.''

''And the letter you mentioned?''

''A letter of introduction to your illustrious Aunt Fanny, explaining my desire for voice lessons and touching upon my many virtues, et cetera.''

''Done!'' He in turn grabbed up Aunt Mollie's stationery and, with great alacrity, wrote a laudatory note and presented it to me for my approval. The address was near Philadelphia.

I took the note and handed him the one from the purported Robert E. Lee. ''It's a bargain, then.''

''You give this to me now?'' he asked warily.

I picked up my muff and smiled. ''I trust you, Algy. As long as I have your shirt stud. And a knife.''

He smiled back and gave me a little salute. We understood each other, we two. What a shame that he'd already succumbed to the beauteous Nellie's fawn-like eyes.

4

I arranged for Aunt Mollie to be sent home to St. Louis to be buried, promising her shade that Warty-nose would be punished as soon as he'd led me to his master. I felt guilty for running off to the shops at just the wrong time; I was infuriated at Warty-nose and his phantom superior for cutting short her life just when she was so full of hope and excitement about both our futures. And, despite the demands of the lowly position Algy had obtained for me at Sir Edward Thornton's, I missed her sorely. For a while the world seemed to wear a black border. My every thought had a margin of sorrow. So I spent my last pennies on mourning crepe and plotted revenge.

But Warty-nose had disappeared. Although I spent weeks expecting him to leap out from every dark corner and chop me to flinders, he was nowhere to be seen. Perhaps he was still nursing his broken head.

Algy presented activities of more immediate interest. He in fact spent most of his nights in the beautiful rooms at Sir Edward's, rooms forbidden to kitchen-and-cellar creatures like me. Occasionally he would not come in at all. "Away on business," the respectable Littimer would tell me when they returned. I could guess the kind of business from Algy's bloodshot eyes, yes indeed. But most of the time he was a proper swell, bantering with Sir Edward and ignoring the servants. Including me.

But one day he came out into the yard as I was drawing water from the old-fashioned well by the kitchen garden. My arms were muddied to the elbows and there were smudges on my face and clothes, but I was declaiming "Now is the winter of our discontent" as I remembered the great Mrs. Kemble performing it. Algy said unkindly, "Ah, Bridget! Rehearsing for the wicked red-haired Lady Audley, I see."

I looked at him coldly. "Lady Audley, as I recall, pushed her enemies into the well."

"So she did." He smiled, stepping back out of reach. "I just thought you might like to know that Nellie and I have received the president's consent at last."

"Aunt Mollie's note?" I asked eagerly. "Who did you show it to?"

He held a finger to his elegant lips. "Shh! Telling you that is not part of the bargain."

"Getting me into the White House is."

He nodded. "I don't want to arouse suspicions. But I'll seize the first opportunity."

"Just don't forget who has your shirt stud."

"I shan't, my dear Miss Mooney."

He wandered out the carriage driveway. I debated throwing the pail after him; but he had such a handsome nose.

It was clear that Algy would tell me no more than he had to. The wedding date was chosen; he had what he wanted, or would soon. But the news made me even more eager to get into the White House. I could understand why Nellie would find Algy's dashing ways attractive. But her famous father ought to know better. He'd been the victorious commanding general of a gigantic army of men; he'd maneuvered his way into the presidency. He was a man of the world. Doubtless he understood Algy's character far better than the naive Nellie did. And yet Aunt Mollie's note had persuaded someone who could in turn persuade the most powerful doting father in the United States to allow this unsuitable match. My regard for Aunt Mollie rose.

I fitted another string to my bow by writing a guarded letter to the St. Louis newspaper editor Aunt Mollie had mentioned, Mr. Fishback. If he wanted interesting information about Inverness, I suggested, he should write to me as though from a cousin, Emily, and send the letter to me at Sir Edward Thornton's. Despite my attempt to shelter myself in Queen Victoria's capacious arms, and my furtive posting of this missive, I worried that it might be intercepted. For days afterward I sensed Warty-noses behind every tree; but no attack came, and no answer.

It was depressing. So, on a tender early-spring day of unfolding leaves, I waylaid Algy. "It's time," I said.

"Time?"

"Algy, it's almost May. You'll be off honeymooning within a month. That is, you will be if I get a situation at the White House tomorrow."

"Ah. I see."

"Otherwise," I spelled it out for him, "there is an envelope containing your shirt stud and a letter that explains in vivid detail how it came into my possession. Nellie's name is on the envelope."

He gave me a sidelong glance. "Mm. And where do you keep this letter?"

"Algy! How insulting for you to think I would tell you!"

That boyish grin again. No wonder poor Nellie was besotted. "Deepest apologies, dear Bridget."

"In any case," I informed him, "there's no reason for either of us to become anxious, is there? You want Nellie and her fortune. I want voice lessons and revenge for Aunt Mollie. No reason we shouldn't all attain our goals and be happy as canary birds."

"Ah, Bridget, if only the rest of the world were as reasonable as we!"

The next day he informed me that I was to be interviewed by Mrs. Grant in the White House conservatories. "How should I act?" I asked Algy.

"Just make her believe she is a grand lady."

"Lots of curtseying?"

A smile twitched at his mouth. "Yes, and remember to look her straight in the eyes."

The greenhouses sprawled west of the White House, enclosing a delightful tropical world. I was glad Algy did not attend the interview—he was off murmuring sweetnesses to Nellie, no doubt—because his presence might have sent me into fits of giggles and finished the whole business right there. Mrs. Grant was a short, stocky woman, in mourning because of her father's death last year. Her dark hair was just beginning to be streaked with gray. I found her admirable—a St. Louis girl who had become the most proper lady in the land. Even her chief feature I could have accepted calmly if it hadn't been for Algy's naughty comment: She had a squint that caused one of her eyes to roll wildly off in random directions even while the good one studied me carefully. Look her straight in the eyes, indeed! Algy, you cad! I dropped my own lashes modestly and succeeded in murmuring answers to her questions without inappropriate titters. Apparently my air of confusion did not count against me; she expressed her approval of taking me on as assistant in the conservatories, and even suggested that they might soon need people to assist with Nellie's wedding. She smiled kindly at me, and simultaneously at the glass dome of the greenhouse, and sent me away to my new supervisor.

Algy had chosen my work, I decided, to prevent me from discovering his secret ally. From time to time my tasks took me as far as the basement kitchen of the White House, but for hours on end I was cast away in the alien world of the greenhouses. Gardeners and maids came frequently; Mrs. Grant almost daily; even Nellie once or twice. But the men I most wanted to observe, though tantalizingly near, kept their distance; an occasional glimpse of one or two of them on the South Portico was the best I could do.

But one day in early May, as I was tending the palms, my dream came true: the Grants arrived to inspect the wedding greenery, and a large group of people came with them. I hid my exultation as I noticed Nellie's brother, the supposedly undisciplined Lieutenant Colonel Fred Grant; the large and genial General Belknap with his voluptuous new wife Puss Belknap; the sleek General Babcock with Nellie and a giggling group of young ladies; and the ferocious General Sherman, who glowered at my ferns as though planning a second march to the sea through their midst.

"The devil take you, Sam, you've got a tropical isle here!" he exclaimed. "It wasn't this lush the last time I peeked in! What did you do, annex Santo Domingo after all?"

The president nodded. "Mrs. G. plans to move the entire state of Florida into the East Room."

"Oh, Ulys, don't tease so!" Mrs. Grant laughed, her good eye beaming at her husband. "Of course weddings must have flowers!"

"And bells," agreed the president, "but must they have bells made of flowers?"

"Bells made of flowers, ropes made of flowers, columns made of flowers!" Sherman was striding among the palms and ferns, lean and nervous, his pitted face animated. I bobbed behind a palm, out of his way. "Why did you bother to redecorate the East Room, Sam? Your new carpets will be buried in this greenery! Ah, we saw enough of jungles in Georgia and Carolina, right, Belknap?"

Belknap gave an immense, good-natured chuckle. "Right, we had plenty of jungle there! And swamps!"

"Swamps, right!" Sherman whirled, gesturing exuberantly. "Spanish moss hanging from your new chandeliers! Rice springing up from the carpet—nice for a wedding, eh? Water moccasins twining around the columns!"

"Copperheads slithering down from the North!" suggested General Babcock. Everyone was laughing.

"Hang you, Bab, what do you know?" Sherman asked Babcock. "You and Sam were sitting about, taking your ease, teaching young Fred to smoke cigars, while Belknap and I were doing all the work, whipping the South."

"Yes, and if we'd stopped besieging Lee, where would you have been?" demanded Lieutenant Colonel Fred hotly, but he was stopped by a smile from his father.

"You must let Cump have his way, Fred," said the president. "We must be indulgent of the elderly."

I glanced fearfully at the fierce Sherman, but this appeared to be an old joke between the two men, for Sherman's mirth was undiminished. He said, "Old or not, I plan to leave my frock-coat at home and come to this wedding dressed as an alligator. With bright yellow kid gloves."

"Oh, Papa," exclaimed one of Nellie's giggling friends to General Sherman, "you must stop teasing!"

"Minnie, dearest, the first lady of our splendid republic has a great heart and will forgive her humble servant." Sherman clicked his heels and bowed to Mrs. Grant.

"Indeed I will, General Sherman," said the jolly Mrs. Grant, "but you must promise to stop your slanders and give us advice!"

"My humble opinion in great state matters is worthless, but you are welcome to it," said Sherman. "What is the problem?"

"Why, we are to have a bell, as Ulys told you, formed of snowballs and white roses, or perhaps camellias," said Mrs. Grant. "It's been suggested that we have a wreath, with initials. But what initials?"

"Algy's, by all means," said Lieutenant Colonel Fred, "because he has so many!"

"Oh, Fred, hush!" Nellie exclaimed, "or we won't let you be groomsman!"

"Hurray! Then I won't have to attend this blame-fool affair!"

Nellie gave a little scream and chased Lieutenant Colonel Fred around the ferns so boisterously that I began to fear for the fronds. The lieutenant might have been last in his class at West Point in discipline, but Nellie wasn't much better today. Nor was the president, who picked up a morsel of clay from one of the pots, rolled it into a little ball, and tossed a bull's-eye square on his son's forehead.

"Oh, Papa!" Lieutenant Colonel Fred wiped off his face while Nellie jumped up and down, clapping her hands. A girl of simple mind, yes indeed.

Yet I had to admit that in other respects Algy's taste was impeccable. Nellie Grant was a lovely creature, fresh as springtime, the natural heroine of any scene: eighteen years old, with creamy skin, lush dark hair, and smoky eyes that ranged from dark thoughtfulness to a bright sparkle when she laughed, as now. But could Algy bear to live with that unformed, uneducated mind?

Mrs. Belknap asked, "Julia, why not put all the initials in the wreath? His and hers?"

"Why, that's just what I suggested, Puss," Mrs. Grant told her. "But they say it would become so complex that we wouldn't be able to make out the letters."

"Allow me to suggest two wreaths," said General Babcock. "One on each side of the bell."

"Oh, Mama, that's a good idea!" enthused Nellie.

"Yes, let's ask if they can do that! And now, come see the fuchsia, Puss," suggested Mrs. Grant.

"Oh, Papa, I almost forgot!" cried Nellie, running to her father. "Tell me, when is a door not a door?"

The president's face softened. "How can that be, Nellie? How can a door not be a door?"

"When it is ajar!"

"Ajar! Oh, that's very good! We must tell your mother!"

Into this idyllic scene came Algy, handsome and sleek as a saber. I noticed Mrs. Grant's welcoming coo, Lieutenant Colonel Fred's warm handclasp. Nellie just stood there, rapture shining in those delicious eyes.

"Greetings, one and all!" said Algy; but his gaze spoke only to Nellie. He crossed to the ferns where she stood and caught up her hand to kiss. They were so beautiful, creatures of fantasy: Lancelot and Guinevere, the Duke and Viola, Romeo and Juliet. Algy and I knew it was fantasy, but the others believed—Nellie enchanted with her storybook romance, her family and friends carried along by her joy. I stood behind the palm in coarse servant's black with my red knuckles and freckles, a gross Caliban on the magic isle.

Then I saw Babcock move to the president's side, sympathy in his glance, and I noted what I should have seen before: the president's kind, determined face had darkened just a shade to worry. Babcock murmured something to him and he nodded; but I wanted to cry out, you're right, Mr. President, don't let her do it!

Of course I didn't cry out. For once I was a proper lady—
or at least a proper servant—and tried to remain invisible,
humbly snipping dead leaves from plants and listening avidly
to the conversations. Unfortunately, no one confessed to arranging Aunt Mollie's death, nor even to having connections
in St. Louis, save the president himself, who was telling Sherman and Belknap of the excellent horses he kept on a farm
there.

Babcock interrupted them. "We really must settle the
Richardson resignation, sir," he said quietly to the president.

"Oh, the devil take Richardson!" exclaimed Sherman.

"The treasury is important even to the army," commented
Babcock with a smile.

"Sherman and Belknap prefer to live on the land," said
the president. "Look, Bab, you go draft the papers and I'll
talk to him again. Right now I want to tell these fellows about
my fine old horse, Butcher Boy."

Babcock bowed and left the greenhouse. Watching him, I
suddenly became aware of Algy at my elbow. He still held
Nellie's hand, but his gaze shone on me kindly. As though
from a great distance, he asked, "How are you, Bridget?"

I curtsied. "Quite well, thank you, sir. Though I wonder
that General Babcock does not seem as much a general as
the other generals."

"Very astute, isn't she, Nellie? General Babcock was only
a colonel in the war. But don't underestimate him. He was
chosen to make arrangements for the surrender at Appomat-
tox. He's been a most capable assistant to Nellie's father for
years."

"That's right," Nellie affirmed, smiling at me with winning sweetness. "And he's ever so nice."

How could I argue with that well-reasoned testimonial? I
changed the subject. "Mrs. Belknap's frock is lovely."

"Oh, isn't it?" Nellie enthused. "It cost a thousand dollars!"

Quite a sum for the wife of a glorified soldier with nothing
but his government salary. I murmured, "The triple pillar of
the world transformed into a strumpet's fool."

Nellie looked blank and Algy broke in. "Nellie, here's one

for your papa," he said. "Why is Ireland like your rich friend Commodore Vanderbilt?"

Nellie giggled. "Like Commodore Vanderbilt? I'm sure I don't know, Algy!"

"Because its capital is always Dublin!"

Nellie squealed with delight and ran to her father. I tossed Algy a look of contempt. "She has not so much brain as earwax," I quoted.

He didn't smile but his eyes were laughing. "Good Thersites, come in and rail!"

"Seriously, Algy, it's a pretty wrapping, but can you live with the emptiness inside?"

The elegant Sartoris brows rose. "Ah, Bridget, 'twas cruel fate that your papa was not elected president! But since he was not, I shall have to forage for my Shakespeare in the highways and byways, and make do with the pretty wrapping at home."

"You're a holy martyr, Algy."

"Now, Bridget, be kind, or I shall take your letter home again."

"My what?"

He handed me an envelope. "For you, care of Sir Edward," he said. "From my wife."

"Your wife?" I glanced after Nellie in confusion.

He smiled. "Your cousin Emily in St. Louis. And I was so sure you had invented her, dear Bridget!"

"You'll be a bigamist soon," I said drily.

He laughed and went to join Nellie.

The letter had been opened, and I feared for the future of my quest if Algy had read—as he doubtless had—the letter from my "cousin." But Mr. Fishback was a clever journalist. The letter, a perfect morass of cousinly gossip, spun a credible tale of the supposed Emily's acquaintances and activities in St. Louis. But in the midst of this chaff was a grain of pure wheat: one of the St. Louis characters discussed, a Mr. W. Ring, had recently moved to Washington, "Emily" claimed; and she gave his address on J Street.

I memorized it and burnt the letter that night.

My work increased as the wedding approached, but took one happy turn: in the ever-increasing frenzy, I was occasionally sent into the White House proper. The day before the wedding, as my colleagues polished and swept, I was dispatched with a forgotten bouquet to give to a chambermaid in the upstairs family quarters. I risked a detour on my return trip past the president's office down the hall.

It was empty.

I stole in, looking about at the mantel, the handsome shield-back upholstered chairs around the table, the clever clock with built-in calendar and barometer. The scent of aging cigar smoke clung to the room. There was something familiar about the stack of documents on the table. I tiptoed closer, intent on deciphering the topmost, which seemed to concern funds needed for the army, when a step sounded behind me. I whirled to find the president himself frowning at me.

"Here now, what's this?" he asked.

I made a swift mental calculation and pulled out a silly giggle. "Oh, sir, I was sent with the flowers, and I made a wrong turn, sir." I peeked at him with merry eyes. "And I have something to ask you, sir."

"To ask me?" He was lighting a fresh cigar, but some amusement had crept into his demeanor in response to mine.

"Yes, sir, if I may be so bold, sir." I gave a gawky shrug. "Why is a victory like a kiss?"

He was delighted that I was not asking for money or favors. "Why, tell me then! Why is a victory like a kiss?"

"Because both are easy to Grant," I told him, and giggled.

He guffawed. "Saucy girl! Easy to Grant! Well, you are right!" He leaned over and kissed me. I giggled again to cover my confusion, and he took it as an invitation to kiss me again. Then, chortling, he turned away and went toward the stairs. "I must tell my wife," he called over his shoulder, and was gone.

And I'd best be gone, too, I realized. I was weak with fear. Would he tell Mrs. Grant I had invited his kiss? Worse yet, would he realize why I'd been so interested in the papers on his table?

The papers, you see, had been in the same hand as Aunt Mollie's note.

Puzzling over my next move, I returned to my day's work

helping move tropical plants into the recently redecorated East Room for the great nuptial the next day. We worked late, wrestling palms into place and draping greens about the beautiful new gas chandeliers, and I returned wearily to my tiny lodging that night still perplexed by the new answers and questions the day had presented. I missed Aunt Mollie's guidance more than ever. I closed the door behind me and turned up the lamp on the table.

The glow revealed Warty-nose sitting on my cot.

No knife this time. He'd come up in the world. He was holding a sleek army-issue Colt revolver.

5

He seemed to have a similarly heightened opinion of me. "The place ye're working now is a bit more elegant, me dear."

"Yes, thank you, sir." I tried a curtsey, but my legs most vexatiously threatened to collapse. I clutched the edge of the table for support and groped for hopeful signs. There were only two. First, a revolver was not as silent as a knife, and he might therefore be slightly more reluctant to use it. Secondly, he did not seem angry; indeed, the peculiar expression on his face might even have been a grin. Slightly emboldened, I said, "Sir, I would appreciate learning the purpose of your visit."

"Just clearing up yer story, me dear. I've been in St. Louis."

"I see."

"And I worry a bit about someone who says she is not related to her own dear aunt."

"Sir, I gave you the green-ribboned parcel!" I exclaimed.

"Yes, that's in yer favor, me girl. But I also heard in St. Louis that yer aunt did copy work for the whiskey tax collector."

Relief mingled with anxiety. He still thought I was ignorant, and that I had done what he'd asked; but he knew far too much about Aunt Mollie. Hoping my clumsy tongue would move, I said, "Well, then, you know the story."

"I want to know if she made copies of other papers. And what she did with the originals."

"The original must be at her office, don't you think?"

He smirked. "No. The original turned up right here in Washington a few days later."

"Are you sure?" I feigned astonishment.

"My chief is sure. Now, where did it come from?"

I frowned, making a great show of the ignorant niece in deep thought. I had learned something of great importance: Warty-nose's chief, whoever he was, had seen the note I'd given Algy. Most probably was the very man who had been convinced to speak to the president in Algy's favor. Therefore, he was endangered by the note; and furthermore, he was able to sway the president even on a matter touching the happiness of his beloved daughter. It all fit: Algy's success, Warty-nose's reappearance, and the papers I'd seen on the president's desk. But who? The savage General Sherman? The punctilious General Babcock? The impulsive Lieutenant Colonel Fred? The expensively wedded General Belknap? Any one of them might have reason to accept money in exchange for easing the tax load on distillers. But I couldn't solve that problem now, not with that Colt poised in Warty-nose's hand.

So I sold Algy. I replaced my thoughtful frown with a *eureka!* look and exclaimed, "That young man! In the boardinghouse!"

"Oh?"

"I gave you everything in Aunt Mollie's package, but she had other papers." This was true. "That young man must have taken them!"

"He said he was yer cousin," said Warty-nose, so craftily that I was sure he knew who Algy really was.

I snorted. "He'd seen me on the street. Thought I was pretty and followed me in. Then stole my papers."

Warty-nose nodded. "That fits. There was more than one other paper, ye say? And he took them all?"

"As far as I know."

"And what did ye get in exchange?"

No sense in lying if his chief already knew about Algy and me. I said, "He got me this job, sir."

Warty-nose smiled. "I'm happy to see ye've become an honest woman."

I used my wide-eyed misunderstood-ally look. "I was frightened before, sir."

"And now ye aren't?" He waggled the Colt.

"I must admit, sir, I am. But before, with that blade on my neck . . ." I shuddered at the memory.

He laughed, enjoying the thought of the blade on my neck. And on Aunt Mollie's, too? I clenched my hands to keep from showing the surge of rage that welled up within me. This man, too, would be punished, I swore by Aunt Mollie's ghost, once he'd served my purpose.

He said, "And where are yer aunt's papers now?"

"At Sir Edward Thornton's, I'd say."

"Where that young fellow lives?"

"Yes. Where I worked for a while. Of course, I'm not certain, sir, but the young man keeps a box secretly in the cellar."

A crafty look stole into his eyes. "You know where?"

"Behind the pickles and preserves, sir."

"I want you to get it for me."

"This late?"

"So much the better."

He motioned with the muzzle of the Colt, and I led the way into the night. "Your chief must trust you a great deal," I observed companionably as we and the Colt walked through the dark toward Sir Edward's.

"Aye, that he does. We've been together since Petersburg, you see. A long friendship."

"Yes, you soldiers are very loyal to one another, sir," I observed.

We crept into Sir Edward's carriageway and to the backyard. "There's a door to the cellar from the back porch," I explained. "Do you want to come in, or shall I bring it out?"

"Bring it out."

I nodded. "Yes, sir. Here, you can sit on this little wall, sir." I guided him by the dim glimmer of moonlight to the low ledge.

"Why don't I stand next to the door?" he demanded suspiciously.

"Of course, sir, if you wish," I said dubiously. "But I thought, as a soldier, you'd prefer to have a view of the carriage drive. And if anyone comes, you can run into the kitchen garden behind the well."

Warty-nose grabbed my arm, nudged me with the Colt. "There'll be trouble if you try anything," he growled. "Remember, I can always find you." But as I hurried to the porch door, I noticed that he did stay where I had suggested.

I didn't underestimate him. He'd been a soldier in a long and bloody war, and survived. He'd been hand-picked for this job by a military expert, an associate of the great General Grant's. He would kill in an instant if it suited him. But now that he'd told me who his superior was, it was time to settle about Aunt Mollie.

I slipped inside the porch door, left my foolish bustle dress in a heap next to it, and pried the loose bolt from the cellar door. I scurried through the cellar, past the potatoes, shelves of preserves and marmalades, to the coal bin. I smeared my bloomers and camisole and skin with coal dust, then continued to a front corner of the house and out the low window, like a sooty muskrat emerging from its bank, then circled through the shrubbery that bordered the yard, back to the kitchen garden.

Warty-nose was edgy. His Colt ready, he peered alternately at the carriage drive and the door where I had disappeared.

I glided through the shrubs behind him and slammed his skull with a two-quart jar of Algy's favorite ginger marmalade.

He dropped like a stone. I tucked his Colt into the band of my bloomers and heaved him up onto the low wall. His scant hair was sticky with marmalade and with something warmer, so I covered it with his Union soldier's cap. Then I opened the plank top. "All yours, Aunt Mollie," I murmured, and slid him into the well.

I know, I know, but what do you expect a poor cowardly girl to do? Challenge him to a duel?

Feeling queasily akin to the villainous Lady Audley, I closed the well, retrieved my bustle, and went home to prepare for a wedding.

6

Thursday morning, the White House was a frenzy of activity. The wedding was scheduled for eleven in the morning, followed by a reception and wedding breakfast. We had already begun moving plants into the East Room the day before—not only from our greenhouses, but also fresh imports from Florida. Now we banked flowers everywhere: by the fireplaces, arching over the doors, spiraling around the fluted columns that the Grants had installed. The dais under the east window where Algy was to be married was a masterpiece—a canopy of ferns and vines, with the great floral marriage-bell and the two rings with the couple's initials swinging from ropes of smilax on either side. The beauty of sight and scent was almost overwhelming. I was surprised that every bumble-bee in Washington was not in attendance.

Obeying orders, I ran about fetching pots, trimming fern fronds, arranging bouquets—in and out from the green-houses, up and down ladders. Sometimes I was called upon to help with the flowers on the banquet table, where a twenty-six-course wedding breakfast would be served: crab gâteaus, tongue aspic, little halved snipes broiled on toast, puddings, a splendid white bride's cake.

A time or two I ran upstairs on the pretext of checking the bridesmaids' pink and blue bouquets. Nellie's dress was a glory: white satin with point lace that was twined with white flowers, green leaves, and tiny oranges. The wedding was the celebration of America's dream come true: the lowly tanner's son had become a great general and a beloved president; now he was uniting his family to European noble blood and artistic fame. Every patriotic American should have felt aglow at the rightness of it all. Yes indeed.

By ten o'clock I had been running in and out, upstairs and down, for hours. Bridesmaids and friends were milling about, as well as servants galore. But even though I'd inspected all the rooms from kitchens and greenhouses to bedrooms, I still had not seen my quarry. Perhaps he had not yet arrived; but, just in case, I seized a bouquet of orange blossoms and tuberoses to serve as a pretext and slipped up the office stairs.

The cabinet room was empty; but General Babcock,

astoundingly enough, was hard at work in the office next door. I hid behind the connecting door because he was talking to someone about the appointment of a new secretary of the Treasury. When the man had left, he bent happily to his work again.

I squinted through the crack on the hinge side of the door, pulled Warty-nose's revolver from its hiding-place in my bustle, and levelled it at General Babcock's ear.

Then the hall door opened and the president came in. He looked even more glum than usual. "Bab," he said abruptly, "I don't know if I can go through with it!"

General Babcock went over to him. Not wishing to become an inadvertent John Wilkes Booth, I waited. Babcock patted the president's shoulder and said, "Every father is naturally sorry to see a lovely daughter leave the nest."

"You know it's more than that. Young Sartoris is just not sound!"

"It's mere wild oats," Babcock soothed. "With a wife as sweet as Nellie, he'll settle down."

"Perhaps. But I wish they'd wait."

"They're young and eager." Babcock hesitated, then added, "And as I told you, I don't think young Fred realized that his arrangements could look so shady. In the wrong hands, the evidence young Sartoris showed me could ruin Fred's future. He'll be far safer with Sartoris in the family."

What a liar the man was! I'd seen that evidence, had given it to Algy. It tied only one man to the St. Louis briberies, and it wasn't Fred.

But President Grant seemed to have little faith in the son who, after all, had been last in his class in discipline. He sighed, "Why am I forced to choose between my children?"

"But Nellie loves him! And he's well connected," Babcock reminded him. "And fathers aren't always the best judges. Julia's father thought you would never amount to anything, and look at you now!"

"I hope you're right!" The president shook his head in despair.

"By the way, I have a report on Bristow," said Babcock, as though the rest had been preliminaries. "Do you want to look it over? He's far from ideal, but he has no marks against him, and he'll quiet your critics.''

''You take care of that.'' The president wandered sadly out again.

Babcock returned to his chair and I raised the revolver again. But I had just realized something very important.

President Grant was a man who enjoyed his beloved family, his fine horses, the glory and the popularity that came with being president of the United States. But he didn't much like the work.

General Babcock, on the other hand, loved it.

By funneling information to the president, by taking on the tasks that Grant least enjoyed, he had seized great power. He controlled government appointments, policies, even swindles, like the bribes the St. Louis whiskey distillers were paying to avoid legal taxes. He could decide life or death for those who threatened to expose the corruption to the president.

For Aunt Mollie, he'd chosen death. Algy, better connected, had been paid for silence. On the pretext that young Lieutenant Colonel Fred would otherwise be endangered, Babcock had convinced Grant to sacrifice his daughter.

I found that the muzzle of the revolver had drooped. I was not going to shoot this man, I realized. He did not deserve a quick, clean soldier's death. He must be stripped of his beloved power and publicly shamed. I slid the revolver back into my bustle and picked up my orange-blossom bouquet. Suddenly, I knew what had to be done.

But my thoughts were rudely interrupted by a hard hand gripping my arm. For a wild moment I thought it was Wartynose, escaped from his watery grave to torment me again. It was almost a relief to see Littimer.

''My master wishes to see you, if you please,'' he said.

''I'd think your master would have other things on his mind,'' I grumbled; but despite the respectable *if you please*, refusing to go was not an option. Littimer took me to the room where Algy was waiting for the ceremony to begin. He looked a prince, of course; both illustrious families in his lineage fitted him for great public moments like this. I imagined myself for an instant in Nellie's lace and flowers, sweep-

ing down the grand west staircase and along the marble
corridor, placing my hand in Algy's under the beautiful
marriage-bell in the East Room. The very thought of such a
moment might make one swoon.

But Algy ignored my admiring gaze. "Where was she?"
he asked Littimer.

"Eavesdropping on General Babcock," said Littimer.

"I was fixing the bouquets!" I protested, holding out my
little bunch of blossoms as proof. I had stuck a little silver
banner in the center that said "Love."

Algy took it from me. "I fear I underestimated you, Bridget
Mooney," he said.

"I've lived up to our bargain!"

"Yes, yes; and so have I. Let me explain that I had not
expected you to pursue your aunt's killer quite so doggedly."

"I know. Proper ladies don't do that sort of thing," I admitted glumly.

He smiled. "Your talents do not lie in being proper,
Bridget," he said, and it sounded almost like a compliment.

"Well, what's the problem?" I asked.

"Threefold. First, Sir Edward's servants found the well by
the kitchen garden was clogged this morning."

"Oh."

"I had not expected you to take the villainous Lady Audley
so thoroughly to heart. Littimer arranged things, of course,
but it's rather annoying on one's wedding day. Second, I find
you eavesdropping on Babcock."

"No worse than blackmailing him into supporting your
marriage, is it? And he's the one who had Aunt Mollie
killed."

"How do you know?"

"His handwriting on papers he prepared for the president
matches Aunt Mollie's notes, as you knew at first glance. And
our pal Warty-nose gave him away. He said he'd met his chief
at Petersburg. The other suspects, Sherman and Belknap,
were marching through Georgia at the time. Lieutenant Colonel Fred was only fifteen. So Babcock is the one I'm after."

"And you're welcome to him—but not till I have Nellie
safe. Which brings us to the third item. I can't help but remember that you have my shirt stud."

"I won't trouble you about that, Algy."

"But surely you understand that in the light of the discovery in the well, it becomes more ominous. I have this nightmare vision of an overly theatrical scene in the East Room, in which a wronged St. Louis girl flings herself at the president's feet, pleading for the groom to do right by her and make her an honest woman again."

"What a lovely idea!" I said with relish. "But it might work, you see. And I do not wish to marry you!"

"Perhaps not. But I must be certain. Where is the shirt stud?"

"At my lodgings," I fibbed.

"I think not. Littimer looked there." Algy glanced at the clock ticking on the mantel. "Come, Littimer, let's search her."

They were certainly quick and efficient at stripping the clothes from a girl. Long practice, I imagine. Littimer gagged me and Algy swiftly removed my dress and petticoats. Littimer was going for my bloomers with a not-so-respectable leer when Algy said, "Wait, I think we have something here."

He had found the pocket I'd sewn into my bustle, damn him. I watched helplessly as he pulled forth my most precious possessions, clucking over each of them: the revolver, his own note to Fanny Kemble, a packet of Aunt Mollie's, and the envelope addressed to Nellie Grant.

This last he opened. He sighed with relief when he saw the shirt stud, then flicked open the letter. The beautiful Sartoris brows rose higher as he read, and he raised my little bouquet to his handsome Kemble nose. When he'd finished his eyes rested for a steamy moment on my blushing near-nakedness. "My, my, Bridget," he said, and cleared his throat. "We seem to have had quite a jolly time. It's a pity I was too drunk to notice."

It's not easy to look disdainful in bloomers, with a gag, but I did my best. Algy turned to Aunt Mollie's papers. "And these—my God, Bridget, you little vixen, you would have had dear old Bab in the palm of your hand! Such corrupt dealings—and in his own penmanship! How grateful he'll be to me for these!"

Littimer said, "Ahem," with a meaningful glance at his respectable hunting-watch. It was a few minutes to eleven.

"Oh, right," said Algy. "Littimer, tie her up and hide her dress, just in case. Release her just before you depart."

"That's all?" Littimer sounded disappointed. "She could fall off a horse, like your brother."

"How many times must I tell you? I do not approve of what happened to my brother!"

Littimer's smooth respectability was a little ruffled. "You're the heir now, sir, begging your pardon. And it did save you from having to become an American."

"Do be quiet, Littimer. This occasion is quite different." Algy held up my things. "Note that our sylph here has been defanged. Besides, at some point in the future, I would like to find out if she really would do all those wicked things for the sake of a shirt stud."

Littimer shrugged, took me to one of Mrs. Grant's new-built closets, and tied my hands and ankles. I would have struggled more, but the talk of Algy's brother had rather disheartened me. Then Littimer closed the door and I heard them leave.

I sat in the dark, furious, chewing on the gag. In the great melodrama of life, Algy Sartoris clearly wore a big black mustache. Stupid of me ever to think of him as a hero. But then, that's the kind of mistake you make when you're comic relief.

Far away in the great house I heard the Marine Band strike up the "Wedding March." White House servants, whispering excitedly, ran by in the hall outside. The clock in Algy's temporary dressing room ticked away. Every fifteen minutes, it chimed softly. How many minutes did it take to get married? A proper lady would know. Bridget Mooney could only gnaw at her gag.

It came loose at last. Instantly, I turned my attention to my wrists. I had luckily remembered the stories of a fellow actor in St. Louis who had once assisted a magician with his tricks. By proper tensing of the arms while being tied, what looks like a tight bond might be pulled off with the teeth.

The Marine Band was playing again. Algy and Nellie were married.

But the comic subplot was loose again.

I knew I had only minutes before Littimer or even Algy arrived. But I'd recollected something while in the closet. I knew Algy wouldn't trust Littimer with those papers; nor could he hide the parcel in his sleek wedding clothing. But back at the tavern he'd fumbled with his stylish top hat before producing the packet he'd taken from me. Sure enough, I found all my belongings tucked into it, together with a bonus of several hundred dollars in a clip. I left Algy a note: "If Babcock hears, Nellie hears, (signed) Sylph" and ran for Nellie's bedroom. You see, I figured Mr. Algernon Sartoris owed me a dress. So I'd help myself to one of Mrs. Algernon Sartoris's.

As I'd expected, Nellie had packed all her New York frocks to take to England, but was leaving behind many others that were still at the height of fashion. Unfortunately, I had only just made my selection when I heard footsteps hurrying in the hall outside. I dove under Nellie's bed, pulling my new dress after me, and held my breath, peering through the fringe of the spread.

It was Nellie's maid, and she was only the first of hordes of people who passed through the room—Nellie, of course, and her maids and tittering bridesmaids, and even Mrs. Grant herself, who came in to talk excitedly to Nellie or to the chandelier—it was difficult to tell which. After long ages of giggles, sobs, and pointless remarks, the heroine of the day was bundled into her beautiful brown silk traveling dress and sent out to her fine new husband. The room was empty at last. I heard the bells of the church nearby chiming out "God Save the Queen," and knew everyone was watching Algy bear his prize away. I crawled out and donned the frock.

Another, unexpected, step in the hall. I plunged back under the bed and was astonished to see President Grant enter. He closed the door, wandered over to the bed, buried his face in Nellie's pillow, and burst into uncontrollable sobs.

Now, I ask you, is that proper for a great hero who has seen the fields of slain soldiers at Shiloh? But he was right to grieve for his daughter. In a moment he had me feeling weepy myself. Poor Nellie Grant, the natural heroine, had missed her cue and married a villain.

Still, Mr. President, I argued silently, if you work with weasels like Babcock, bad things do happen.

After a long time, they found him, still sobbing, and took him away solicitously.

And the comic relief? I brushed myself off, tucked my papers into the bodice of Nellie's fine frock, and slipped un-obtrusively down the office stairs and out of the White House—a guest leaving late, to anyone who noticed. Since I had Algy's money, I didn't bother to go past my room. There was only one stop to make in Washington, at an address on J Street. Then I lit out straight for Philadelphia and the tu-telage and protection of the illustrious Mrs. Fanny Kemble.

I'd given up on being proper; but I still meant to give rich-and-famous a try.

7

You know the rest of the story. Fishback found an honest member of Grant's cabinet, and together, starting with the papers I'd left at J Street, they assembled evidence that jailed dozens of members of the Whiskey Ring for defrauding the government of millions in uncollected taxes. Grant saved Babcock from jail, but of course dismissed him from the White House. Babcock became a lighthouse inspector. Far from Washington's seats of power, he spent lonely, disgraced, and powerless years on the fringes of the nation he had cheated. In 1884, while attending to official duties in a place called Mosquito Inlet, Florida, his boat went down in a storm and he—like Warty-nose—drowned. The boat, I know, was not at all seaworthy. I remember it well; I had a few days' holiday from my role as Portia in a Southern tour of *The Merchant of Venice*, and I just happened to be in Mosquito Inlet that day myself.

I know, I know; but don't you think that by then he'd suf-fered enough? The quality of mercy, you know.

Nellie Grant Sartoris raised three fine children in England with the kind assistance of Algy's mother; but in every other way the marriage was the miserable failure her father and I had predicted. Algy was soon foraging in the highways and byways, and Nellie excited great sympathy as well as scandal when at last she divorced him. Algy visited me a time or two, for old times' sake; but I didn't really enjoy the encounters, because he'd become so stout and blowsy, and because I couldn't help but be reminded of those moments in Nellie's bedroom, when the heroic general and president of our United States wept for the daughter he'd been forced to sell.

HENRY SLESAR is an accomplished writer of short stories, having created over one thousand to date in the genres of mystery, suspense, fantasy, and science fiction. After a long career in advertising, Mr. Slesar turned to television and was very successful as the chief writer for several series, including The Edge of Night, *for which he was awarded both an Edgar and an Emmy. In addition, he wrote scores of original stories (and adapted many others) that became episodes on* Alfred Hitchcock Presents, *a program with which he is closely identified. Henry Slesar also won an Edgar Award for his acclaimed first novel,* The Gray Flannel Shroud *(1959).*

In 1876, Rutherford B. Hayes (1822–1893), our nineteenth president, won one of the most controversial elections in American history. If several Southern states had not submitted two different sets of electoral votes, this story might have been devoted to President Samuel J. Tilden.

MURDER IN BLUE AND GRAY

★ ★ ★

Henry Slesar

The bullet smashed through the plate glass of the partially shaded window, and with unspent force traveled through parlor and back parlor to burrow itself in the library wall. Later, Lucy told her husband that his hand, guiding a fork to his mouth at the family dining table, never faltered at the sound, that he had indeed tasted, chewed, and swallowed his lamb before putting down the utensil and quietly asking if everyone was all right. It was apparent that everyone wasn't. Lucy's

114

bright black eyes were opaque with fear. Fanny, their daughter, was trembling, and Scott, her younger brother, had allowed a water tumbler to slip from his fingers, drenching the tablecloth. Only Webb, the oldest of the children present, seemed disposed to action. He sprung from the dining room chair and rushed to close the drapes in an effort to foil the aim of whatever marksman had tried to take the life of the president-elect even before he left Columbus, Ohio, to take his oath of office.

He had, of course, been warned. The rage that had burned in the hearts of the Tilden supporters hadn't been quenched by the decision of the electoral college. The risk of assassination was a real one; there had even been public invitations to murder. Don Piatt, editor of a weekly called *The Capitol*, had written:

> *If a man thus returned to power can ride in safety from the Executive Mansion to the Capitol to be inaugurated, we are fitted for the slavery that will follow . . . We do not believe the people of the United States . . . are prepared, without a blow, to part with their hard-earned, bloodstained possession . . . If there is a law against fraud, there is a reason for violence. And to that we make our last appeal.*

The president-elect hadn't fumed at the fiery editorial; in fact, he had protested the arrest of Piatt, and would later be instrumental in having the sedition charge dismissed. But this night, the violence Piatt sought to inspire seemed to be hovering on the very doorstep of his family home. For that reason, it was a surprise to each of them to hear his opening statement at the family conference that followed.

"There will be nothing more said about this incident tonight," Rud Hayes said. "In all likelihood, it was just an accident—a stray bullet—"

Webb exploded, just as his father thought he would. Ever since the disputed election had ended, Webb had appointed himself as a one-man Secret Service to the future president, carrying a gun and dogging his father's footsteps even when he merely crossed the road to visit a neighbor. But Rud Hayes repeated his order with an extra layer of firmness in his voice.

"Nothing is to be said. If I see a mention in the press, I'll know it came from this room. Is that understood?"

"But surely, the police . . ." Lucy made a helpless gesture.

"There's no need for it," he said. "No need to worry about anything." And he gave them a smile that radiated so much tranquillity and confidence that no more had to be said.

But that night, alone in his study, Rutherford B. Hayes composed a telegram to a Pinkerton detective in New Orleans whose name was Barney Schemmerhorn.

It was less than three months since Rud Hayes had sat opposite Barney Schemmerhorn in a southbound railway car, and enjoyed the anonymity of the year 1876. Yes, there had been newspaper photographs of the candidate, but they had shown only one more bearded face, one more set of nondescript features. Without a coterie, carrying his own luggage, Rud was confident of nonrecognition. Traveling incognito was a predilection he would enjoy throughout his presidency, but on this trip, his pleasure was lessened by thoughts of the people he would see and the attitudes he expected to find in New Orleans, where his political enemies might well outnumber his friends.

He was reading the editorial in the New Orleans *Times* when he became conscious that the man in the opposite chair was staring at him, a stare so intense that it seemed to bore though the pages. Rud lowered the newspaper and appraised him. He was a burly, tweedy man with a well-tended handlebar under a long, thin nose. For a moment, Rud thought he might have been recognized, but the man quickly explained.

"It's the story on the back page," he said apologetically. "I didn't have time to pick up a paper before coming aboard . . ."

Rud offered it to him, but the man waved a broad, pudgy hand and said there was no hurry. He knew all the facts, anyway, he said, with a hint of an eager confidentiality, since he had been engaged in investigating them himself. He produced a card which would explain it all. It was from the Pinkerton agency, and it bore his name in bold letters.

"You're a detective, Mr. Schemmerhorn? That must be interesting work."

"Interesting when the case is interesting," Barney Schemmerhorn said sententiously. "And I ask you, sir, what is *more* interesting than the murder of a beautiful woman?"

It was a question Rud Hayes had never considered before, but he realized that his fellow passenger didn't require an answer. He turned to the back page, and read the headlines:

TERRIBLE SLAYING OF CREOLE BEAUTY
MURDER AT SITE OF HISTORIC MANSION
TAPLEY HEIR HELD ON SUSPICION

Rud would have read the details, but Barney Schemmerhorn was anxious to supply them himself.

"As the story says—a beauty." He produced two cigars and offered one to his companion; Rud refused. "And as we know," he said, with a man-of-the-world wink, "feminine charms need no background. That's why she caught the eye of Bruce Tapley. You know the family, of course."

Rud admitted he did not, being a stranger to the region.

"One of the richest in Louisiana. One of the few to come through the war with their estate fairly intact. They're no longer plantation owners, however, and last year the Tapley mansion was given over to the State Historical Society as a museum. It had been used as a billet by General Butler, and it was the scene of more than one heroic action on both sides . . ." He smiled a tolerant smile, recognizing Rud as a Northerner.

"At any rate, the family now lives in a little place called Winderley; I've just come from there. There are only three in the family: August Tapley, his wife, their youngest son. They lost the elder at Vicksburg."

"And they're threatened with *his* loss now?" Rud found himself suddenly interested.

"If this—" Schemmerhorn tapped the newspaper "—proves to be true. That it was Bruce who killed the beautiful Elly Dyer."

"And is that why you were hired? To prove him innocent?"

Schemmerhorn lowered his voice, even though they were alone in the car. "He wasn't innocent of one thing. There *was* an affair between him and this Creole lady. They used to rendezvous on the grounds of the old mansion, after visiting hours. And the night before last, some time after eight P.M., the custodian, in his bedroom, heard Elly Dyer cry out in terror. By the time he reached her, she was at the base of the dovecote behind the mansion, stabbed to death."

"And did they catch this young man at the scene?"

"No, he was arrested at home. The custodian told the police that he had been there with Elly the night before. Signed the visitor's book, in fact, since the law required it. Bruce admitted that he had been with the girl, even admitted quarreling with her. But he claims to have left shortly before seven, alone."

"But there were no witnesses to his departure?"

"None. And the Tapley family swears that Bruce arrived home shortly after seven, at least an hour before the slaying took place." Rud did not comment on the obvious, but the detective seemed to perceive a cynical thought. "Yes, I know, it was only natural for the family to defend their only son. And what's natural for them," he added with another wink, "is of professional interest to me."

"And how do you intend to prove young Tapley innocent?"

"Why, I haven't the foggiest idea," Schemmerhorn said engagingly, gesturing with his cigar. "But the first thing I intend to do is visit the scene of the crime."

Barney Schemmerhorn got his opportunity sooner than anticipated. Still some twenty miles outside of New Orleans, the train suddenly braked to a halt, and a conductor informed the passengers that a section of track had been damaged in a flash flood. Rud was dismayed at the threat of a lengthy delay, and therefore grateful when the detective came up with a time-saving alternative. Fortuitously, the old Tapley mansion was only a few miles from the site of the breakdown. If he could obtain the use of a carriage, he could drive to the scene of the crime and after completing his inspection deliver his traveling companion to his destination. Rud accepted with alacrity, as much out of curiosity to see the old Southern homestead as out of desire to keep his appointment in New Orleans.

It was another two hours before the train telegrapher was able to arrange for the carriage. By the time they left, the sun began to descend over the oak-wooded lowlands and winding bayous. The swamps became more mysterious in the waning light, and the gigantic trees, draped in Spanish moss like the mourning clothes of desolate widows, gave Rud Hayes the eerie feeling of having landed on an alien planet. He was relieved when they arrived at the avenue of live oaks that led to the Tapley mansion.

Distance had a cosmetic effect on the old building. Its Doric columns were stately and pristine, its color warm and soft, like mother-of-pearl. There was a sign at the gate warning them that less than one hour was left for visitors, but Schemmerhorn had no intention of going inside. His curiosity was directed to the dovecote where Elly Dyer's spilled blood was still fresh.

His companion was more interested in the interior. The old black caretaker who met him at the door grumbled at the late arrival of this final visitor, and commanded him to sign the guest book. He hesitated, thinking of anonymity. Then, underneath a signature that was totally illegible, he scrawled his name in full: *Rutherford Birchard Hayes*. He smiled, wondering what the historians would make of it; wondering if history would care.

The mansion was magnificent. The ceilings rose fifteen feet, and the doors and windows were in the same grand scale. A winding staircase spiraled all the way to the mansion's attic. The furnishings were Empire, the tapestries only slightly faded, and there was a monster piano in the center of the main room, sitting bravely beneath a huge crystal chandelier. The only signs of dissolution were the whited triangles on the walls where mirrors had once hung. Now, between the girandoles and ornamental wall sculpture, there were framed letters, photographs, documents relating to the happy and unhappy past of the old house.

His time went swiftly. When he left the building, he found Barney Schemmerhorn in the carriage, making notes to himself, tugging at his handlebar mustache.

"Well?" Rud asked. "Have you found any important clues?" He tried not to sound jocular, but there was something almost comic about the Pinkerton man's concentration.

"There isn't much," he admitted gloomily. "But I'm sure of one thing. Elly Dyer was running from her murderer. But the poor girl simply couldn't run fast enough."

He didn't say much more on the twelve-mile ride into New Orleans. Halfway there, Rud volunteered to take the reins, and Barney Schemmerhorn folded his arms, tucked his long nose into his coat collar, and slept contentedly. Rud wondered if he dreamed of murder.

It was almost midnight when Rud Hayes registered at the Grand Picayune Hotel in New Orleans. He spent an uncomfortable night in the unfamiliar bed, his dreams troubled. But they were forgotten when the hot, sticky morning arrived, along with a delegation that included an emissary of the Louisiana Democrats, a colonel who was also an associate editor of the New Orleans *Times*. Rud spent the rest of the morning answering his questions about what he would do, if elected president, about the conflicting state governments then ruling Louisiana. The rest of the day was spent in other political conferences, and he was glad when the sun went down.

He left the room only once, to eat a solitary dinner in the hotel dining room. He picked up an evening edition of the *Times* when he retired and scanned the front page, wary of bad news. He was startled to read bad news of a nonpolitical nature.

HISTORIC MANSION BURNS

An historic Southern mansion, which figured prominently in both the War Between the States and a recent murder case, was destroyed by fire last night. The building, the former home of the Tapley family, was once occupied by both Confederate and Federal troops. It has been a public monument since 1871, under the management of the Louisiana Historical Society.

The mansion is located twelve miles west of New

Orleans and three miles from the small community of Winderely, where the Tapley family now resides. They were among the first to arrive at the scene of the blaze.

The Tapley mansion became the scene of a garish crime only forty-eight hours ago, when Eleanor Dyer, 22, was found stabbed to death on the grounds. On the day following the murder, police held under suspicion Bruce Powell Tapley, 24, the only surviving son of the Tapley family, who lost another son during the War. Mr. Tapley had been acquainted with Miss Dyer for the past two years, and had admitted meeting her at the Tapley mansion on the evening of the crime. Yesterday, police released Mr. Tapley without preferring any charge. He was home at the time of the fire, and arrived at the burning mansion before the local fire department. The Tapleys attempted to salvage some of the precious documents and furnishings from the mansion, but were repulsed by the flames.

Fire Chief Walter Semple admitted the possibility of arson, due to the sudden "flash" nature of the blaze. Experts are sifting the ashes for clues.

Inspector Samuel Hawes of the New Orleans Police Department was reluctant to make any connection between the fire and the recent homicide. "There is always that possibility," he stated. "The building and grounds were inspected by our investigators, but owing to the historical nature of the premises, a truly thorough search was not possible. If any evidence existed that related to the crime, it might well have been obliterated in the fire. However, we are not yet prepared to agree that the two events are connected."

The mansion's caretaker, Sam Lemcure, suffered a stroke during the attempt to salvage items from the burning building, and is not expected to recover. It was his responsibility to make sure that all visitors signed a guest book before entering, a requirement of the Historical Society. This register has not yet been located, and it is presumed to have been destroyed in the fire. The investigation is continuing.

For a moment, all Rud could think about was the white magnificence of the mansion engulfed in crimson flames. All that beauty turned to ashes, all that history lost to the generations . . .

Then the reality struck him. Suddenly Rud realized that the anonymity that had been essential to his visit was about to be compromised, and in a manner calculated to do the most damage. It would soon be public knowledge that Rutherford B. Hayes, the Republican soon to be president, had made a secret trip south, that he had been the last person to sign the visitors' book at the ravaged Tapley mansion, and—who knows—might even be implicated in the crime of arson!

It was an unthinkable conclusion, of course, but Rud was wise enough in the ways of politics to know that even the unlikeliest rumor could be used to advantage by his enemies. The mansion was a symbol of the South's antebellum greatness, and he was a Northerner after all. He had once been Colonel Hayes of the Union Army, a fighting commander who had been brevetted a general on the battlefield. Before that, he was famed as an anti-slavery lawyer, defending the rights of runaway slaves. . . . It wasn't hard to imagine the innuendos that would appear in the press, the whispers in the taverns, the speeches on the street-corners, implying some act of contempt or carelessness, a lit cigar left behind, a conscious or unconscious desire to burn down the last trace of Southern gentility . . . The effect on his campaign, already predicted to be a losing effort, could be disastrous.

Rud reread the newspaper article, taking special note of the paragraph which stated that the guest book was presumed to be destroyed. That meant he could keep his secret. The old caretaker hadn't known his name. The Pinkerton agent, Schemmerhorn, knew him only as "Mr. Birchard." He hadn't mentioned his visit to the Tapley mansion to anyone. Rud sighed in relief. He could still escape the consequences of his actions. They had been innocent actions, after all; why get involved?

Yet as quickly as that satisfying conclusion arrived, another followed. No, he couldn't leave things as they were. He couldn't simply skulk away from the scene and pretend it never happened. There had to be a way.

He settled upon a compromise. Rather than march into the

nearest police station and declare himself, he would seek out another kind of law officer. Barney Schemmerhorn.

The next morning, forgetting breakfast, Rud went in search of the Pinkerton office on Bourbon Street. There, a burly man who could have been Schemmerhorn's twin advised him that his associate was not available for consultation that morning, but if the gentleman cared to delineate his difficulty—a straying wife, perhaps?—he would be glad to be of assistance. Rud assured him that his business was only with Mr. Schemmerhorn, and he was informed that the detective was at the home of a client outside New Orleans. Without being told, Rud knew he could find his man at the Tapley home in Winderely. Even if Schemmerhorn wasn't there, he might be able to satisfy his obligation to the truth by meeting the Tapley family themselves.

He had no trouble finding the estate. He drove his hired carriage to the mansion road, following the sign that pointed past the oak-lined avenue towards Winderley. But Rud couldn't resist jerking the reins in the direction of the mansion, knowing that the sight of the destroyed building would only sadden him, but unable to resist.

He thought he knew what to expect, but he was shocked nevertheless. The iron gates of the mansion still stood guard, but there was no longer anything to protect. The fire had left only rubble, jagged remnants of the plaster columns, a truncated section of a standing wall, a fallen beam blackened by soot, stumps of furniture, and scorched piles of brick. He was glad to turn away from the sight.

The new Tapley house, just three miles away, was humble in comparison to their former residence, but its fine architecture attested to the family's continuing affluence. It had started to rain, and Rud was gratified when a stable boy came splashing through the muddy courtyard to take his horse to shelter. Obviously, his approach down the long driveway had been noted, and the front door was already opening for him.

The man who greeted him at the brightly lit doorway radiated some inner illumination of his own. He seemed to be perpetually smiling, but it might have been merely the effect of his white, upturned mustaches.

"You've come a long way, Mr. Birchard," he said, seizing his hand. "I'm glad the weather held up until your arrival."

"You seem to have been expecting me, Mr. Tapley."

August Tapley chuckled, and brought him inside. The explanation for his lack of curiosity was immediately evident. Turning from the window with its view of the driveway was Pinkerton agent Barney Schemmerhorn.

"I believe you know Mr. Schemmerhorn," August said. "And this is my friend Jasper Douglas." He indicated the man posing near the fireplace. His head was half again too large for his small, compact body, and he had compounded the imbalance with a military-brush beard and by letting his silver hair grow long.

"We were just discussing you, Mr. Birchard," Douglas said. "From what Barney has told us, you've become part of the history of the old mansion."

"Beware of Jasper," August said lightly. "He's an historian. He's been writing the definitive history of the War for the last ten years."

Schemmerhorn said: "I told Mr. Tapley about our encounter the other night, Mr. Birchard. I tried to reach you at your hotel, but they told me you had rented a carriage and left."

"The rest was deduction." August smiled. "The detective's stock in trade. At any rate, we're pleased Mr. Schemmerhorn was correct, and that you chose to visit us. I assume you have something to tell us about . . . the fire."

"I'm sure you already know what I know," Rud said, uncomfortable under their steady gaze. "The main fact is, I seem to be the last person to have signed the mansion's guest book."

"The book is gone," Jasper Douglas said cheerfully. "So it's no longer a fact—only a memory."

"And memory," August said, his smile thinning, "is what we're most concerned about."

"I don't think I understand."

Schemmerhorn cleared his throat loudly. "You see, Mr. Birchard, the police are convinced that the fire was caused by an arsonist, using a slow-burning fuse that was probably lit even while you paid your call on the mansion."

"Good Lord," Rud said.

"They're equally sure the arsonist signed the guest book in order to gain entrance. And since you were the last visitor—"

August said, "Even though we realize you had nothing to do with the blaze, the police would still be very interested in whatever you might have seen."

"Such as," Schemmerhorn said gravely, "a *name* in that book. The name of the visitor who preceded you. Since that individual is the most likely suspect in the case. Now do you understand, Mr. Birchard?"

Rud sighed with relief. At least there was no suspicion of his own involvement, no need to offer his true identity as evidence of his probity.

"I'm afraid I won't be much help to you," he said. "Or to the police, for that matter. I did see a signature on the line above, but it was nothing more than an illegible scrawl."

"You're quite sure?" August said, his voice quavering a bit. "You wouldn't change that opinion if asked officially?"

It seemed like an odd question, but Rud didn't try to interpret it. "No," he said. "I couldn't change it, Mr. Tapley, since it's the truth. I couldn't make out a single letter of the name, so I can provide no answer to the mystery. I'm very sorry."

"It's quite all right," Jasper Douglas said reassuringly. "Even if we did know the identity of the rascal, it wouldn't bring the mansion back, would it? . . . Gus, why haven't you offered your guest anything to drink?"

Rud wanted to refuse, preferring to be on his way now that he had fulfilled his obligation and been assured that no further involvement was necessary. But two servants had magically appeared, bearing trays of glasses, liquors, tea service, and hearty sandwiches. Rud no longer had a choice.

When they were seated, Rud offered his sympathies at the destruction of the old family home.

"It was a terrible shock," August Tapley said sadly. "My poor wife is still prostrate with grief over it. Although," he added with a hint of slyness, "I think Jasper here suffered the most when he heard the news."

"Because of my book," Douglas said gloomily. "You see, I wasn't writing a straightforward account of the War; there

will be far too many of those. My conceit was to tell the
story from the focal point of one place, one family, one
Southern plantation. I was going to call it *The Mansion*, and
the house was going to be represent the entire antebellum
South . . ."

"I see," Rud Hayes said.

"I've put in years of work," Douglas said. "But there was
so much more to be written. You can imagine my feelings
when we first learned of the blaze—saw it, as a matter of
fact."

"You could see the flames from here?"

"Just the terrible, unnatural glow in the sky. The three of
us drove as quickly as we could to see what we could
save. . . . Poor Bruce burned his hands rather badly trying
to rescue some of the paintings."

"That's why my son hasn't joined us," August said quickly.

"Yes," Rud said, sipping the tea he had chosen over
brandy, aware of a belligerent note in August Tapley's voice.

"I know you're aware of my son's . . . difficulty," August
continued. "But I trust you're also aware that he has been
completely exonerated in that unfortunate matter."

"I know very little about it, Mr. Tapley," Rud said.

"I only mention it, Mr. Birchard, in case you received the
impression that our concern about the visitor's book had anything to do with Bruce."

"It hadn't occurred to me," Rud said, but was aware that
it wasn't quite the truth. As soon as August had spoken the
word *officially*, the police had come to his mind, as well as
the question: could Bruce Tapley have been trying to destroy
evidence in the slaying of Elly Dyer?

There was another shock in store for Rud when the time
came to leave. August Tapley seemed relieved at his departure, but Jasper Douglas wasn't ready to lose a willing lis-
tener. He asked Rud if he would care to visit the guest cottage
where all the memorabilia necessary to his historical opus
was stored. Rud politely agreed to a brief visit.

It was a short walk through a wooded trail, and Douglas
strode ahead briskly with the stride of a much taller man.
When they reached the cottage, he opened the door ceremo-
niously and ushered in his guest with the words:

"Please come in, Mr. Hayes."

His reaction must have been comical, judging from the grin that split Jasper Douglas's face.

"I'm sorry," he said. "I *am* an historian, Mr. Hayes, and my field of interest is the national affairs of the United States. From the moment I heard the name Birchard and your description, I began to wonder about your identity. Seeing you in person confirmed it. . . . You *are* Rutherford Hayes, aren't you?"

"Yes," Rud said ruefully. "Forgive the deception, Mr. Douglas. I did have my reasons for the incognito, and I assure you they had nothing to do with the subject we discussed."

"Oh, I realize that," Douglas chuckled. "But I also know that you've given me a golden opportunity, sir. Your own role in the history I'm writing . . ."

"I'm afraid I really don't have the time to be of much help, Mr. Douglas."

"No . . . of course not. But come in for just a moment."

Clutter was the word that entered Rud's mind, but then he saw that the cottage was merely overstocked. Every inch of wall space was occupied by shelves, and every shelf contained books, files, artifacts, pamphlets, miniatures, and bric-a-brac. When Rud went to scan the handwritten labels on the spines of the speckled file boxes, he was impressed by the careful organization.

"The history of the mansion is in this room," Douglas said. "From the day of its foundation to its unhappy end . . ."

Rud had removed a file box marked "Butler," and Douglas grinned again. "Yes, I thought you'd be interested in that one. As you know, General Butler spent several days in the mansion. The file even contains a copy of his infamous 'Woman Order.' "

Rud removed a folded sheet of faded brown paper and read:

Headquarters, Dept. of the Gulf
New Orleans, May 15, 1862

General Order No. 28:
   As the officers and soldiers of the United States have

*been subject to repeated insults from the women (call-
ing themselves ladies) of New Orleans, in return for the
most scrupulous noninterference and courtesy on our
part, it is ordered that hereafter when any female shall,
by word, gesture, or movement, insult or show contempt for any officer or soldier of the United States, she
shall be regarded and held liable to be treated as a
woman of the town plying her vocation.*

    By Command of   Major General Butler

George C. Strong, A.A.GI, Chief of Staff

Rud smiled reminiscently, recalling the reaction to Order
No. 28, which drew anger from South and North both—but
most of all, anger from the genuine "ladies of the town,"
who pasted the General's portrait to the bottom of their cham-
berpots . . . It was almost an absentminded gesture that
brought the file box marked TAPLEY into his hand. He removed a yellow sheet of vellum, and saw that it was addressed to the man he had just met.

                       23 September 1859

My Dear August,
    *Your steamer sojourn must have you in good health
and spirits. Your old companions at McGrath & Company must be envying you, but I have assured them that
you are diligently keeping in practice at Poker, Faro,
and the other exercises of which you are so fond. Mr.
Lauraine, of the house of Lauraine & Cassidy, has
written me regarding your indebtedness of eight hundred dollars ($800) and I have assured him of payment.
However, this strain upon the family finances makes it
impossible to provide the additional travel funds you
requested. If you find your journey too arduous to continue, you are naturally welcome to return to*

                       Yours,
                       Father

"Well," Rud said. "I gather that your friend Mr. Tapley was a gambling man in his younger years."

Douglas grunted. "His older brother Damon was even worse, and unfortunately, August admired and emulated him. Of course, gambling has always been an obsession in New Orleans, a major industry, you might say. Look at these . . ." He dug into the file box and came out with small slips of paper. "IOUs," Douglas said. "All acquired by Damon and August, from gambling houses like McGrath's and Lauraine & Cassidy . . . His father, Barnaby Tapley, had to buy them back to save the family honor. In fact, the debts became so great that he had to sell half their slaves."

"Apparently, the family recouped its losses," Rud said. Idly, he picked out another letter, and asked: "Is this from Mr. Barnaby Tapley, too?"

Douglas fumbled for a pair of bifocals. "Yes, I think it is. Written some eight months later to a man named Goley. You can see that Barnaby was in desperate straits by then."

The letter was short. It read:

11 May 1860

My Dear Goley:
Our business of this month concluded, would greatly appreciate payment of the one thousand dollars ($1000) agreed upon. My apologies for pressing this issue, as my need is urgent. Am I to understand that the packages will not be delivered to the station as promised? Please advise as I am anxious to see matters settled. Your kind inquiries about my health are appreciated; I am as well as advancing age and declining income permit.

Your Servant,
B. Tapley

"What business was Goley in?" Rud asked.

"I don't have any record of the man, so I don't really know." Douglas replaced the letter carefully into the file box. "At any rate, I'm much more interested in hearing something of your own experiences, Mr. Hayes. I'm especially inter-

ested in a story I've heard about you and General Reno, about
the time you stood up to him when he accused your men of
pilfering . . . Is it true that he drew his pistol on you?''

"The story is much exaggerated,'' Rud Hayes said.

"I heard you might have been court-martialed, if it wasn't
for the battle of South Mountain—''

Rud consulted his pocket watch. "I really must be returning, Mr. Douglas,'' he said. "I've stayed far longer than I
planned . . . I hope you understand.''

"Yes, of course,'' Jasper Douglas said. "But I can't help
but be disappointed.'' He smiled wryly. "As August said,
this book of mine is an obsession. Indeed, it's become my
whole life . . .''

On the way out, Rud's eye caught one last object. It was
the same evening edition of the *Times* that had brought him
to Winderley. Douglas picked it up, and looked at the head-
line. "The last document of my file,'' he said mournfully.

"It's a pity,'' Rud said. "I mean that the final document
couldn't have been the mansion's guest book . . . so at least
the culprit could be apprehended.''

"Yes,'' Jason Douglas said, but it was apparent that his
attention was already back among his files.

Rud Hayes returned down the wooded path alone, heading
for his waiting carriage. The rain had stopped, and the late
afternoon sun was rimming the clouds in crimson. The stable
boy was there, holding the reins, and his horse seemed im-
patient to begin the journey. He was just settling into the seat,
about to cluck the animal into action, when the staggering
truth struck him. Every instinct urged him to shake it out of
his head, to tug sharply on the reins and wheel the carriage
out of the driveway, back to more familiar problems, back to
the family he loved, the challenges he faced. But Necessity
weighed on his shoulders like a yoke, and he could not move.

The boy seemed surprised to see him climb down again,
and approach the Tapley front door. He was no more surprised than August Tapley, now alone in his parlor with his
wife, a pale, frightened-looking woman whose eyes registered even more alarm when Rutherford Hayes, forcing out
each word, told August Tapley that he knew the name of the

arsonist who had destroyed the Tapley mansion, that the illegible scrawl he had seen in the visitors' register was the
same as the scrawl on some long-cancelled IOUs.

August sat in a rocking chair with his hands in his lap,
looking years older. His wife's frightened look had vanished;
she seemed to have gathered strength in the face of her husband's need. Rud marveled at the character of women.

"You can do as you please," he said to Rud. "The motives
I offer may not get your sympathy. But I want you to know
them."

"I would very much appreciate that, Mr. Tapley," Rud
said.

"I suppose it started with that girl, with Elly Dyer . . .
No, that isn't true. It started with *me*, and my profligate
brother Damon . . . But I'll tell you about Elly Dyer first. It
may be easier that way."

He lit a cigar, placed it on an ashtray, and forgot it.

"We did everything we could to discourage Bruce's romance, but Bruce has a stubborn streak in him. Of course,
he never had any intention of marrying the girl; for all his
impulsiveness, he's a practical young man. However, Elly
Dyer was practical, too. She played the usual cat-and-mouse
game. But unfortunately, the mouse developed unexpected
strength."

August paused, moving his lips, searching his mind for the
next sentence.

"They say that every family has its skeleton. The Tapleys
are no exception. There was something that happened to us
almost twenty years ago, something that can only be described as a shameful secret. I've shared that secret with only
one person in my lifetime. My wife Claire." He glanced at
her. She reached out and took his hand. "I did her no favor.
I simply wanted to reduce the weight of the burden by sharing
it."

"We kept the secret between us," the woman said. "But
then, inadvertently, our children learned it . . . That would
have been all right, too, except—" She stopped.

"Except that Bruce got drunk," August said bluntly. "And

one night, after a family quarrel whose nature I can't even remember, he went to see Elly, and he told her.''

"And so,'' Rud said, "the mouse became a tiger?''

"She knew the secret, and she intended to make the most of it, to bring as much shame down on the family name as she possibly could. She put a price on her silence, and it wasn't money.''

"It was marriage?''

"Exactly,'' August said. "It was an impossible dilemma, but it had an unexpected resolution. Because less than a week after Bruce made his fatal indiscretion, someone murdered Elly Dyer on the grounds of the old mansion.''

"I would call that . . . fortuitous,'' Rud said carefully.

"It sounds *damning*! Don't you think we know that, Mr. Birchard? Our problem solved by some maniac with a knife?''

"You're really certain it wasn't . . .'' Rud stopped, not wanting to say the obvious.

"It wasn't my son!'' Claire Tapley said fiercely. "I swear he is innocent, that he was home long before the woman was slain!''

"It's true,'' August said. "We don't know who killed Elly Dyer. All we know is that Bruce is innocent. And when this terrible event took place, I knew that we could no longer live with this secret. And so . . . I fired the mansion.''

Claire covered her eyes, but she wasn't weeping.

"It was my own property, after all,'' August said. "That afternoon, around four, I arrived with a Gladstone bag stuffed with gasoline rags. I went upstairs and spread the cloths throughout the upper floors, and strung a long, slow-burning fuse. . . . I was probably still upstairs when you made your call.''

"Then if I had gone upstairs . . .''

"We would have met sooner,'' August Tapley said wryly. "You see, I never thought there would be a visitor after me. And I was confident that the guest book would be destroyed . . .''

"But then, Detective Schemmerhorn told you about *me*.''

"Yes. And now, I think I must tell you . . . the family secret. So you can decide what to do.''

* * *

"As I said, it was profligacy that started it. My gambling debts were bad enough, but my elder brother Damon's had almost obliterated the family fortune. By the beginning of 1860, there were only a handful of servants on the plantation. The land was sold, finally, having become an insupportable tax burden, and all that my father possessed was the mansion itself and two sons who seemed bent on total ruin.

"Of course, there were greater events occurring in 1860, as you well know. The Underground Railroad was operating at full throttle in the North, its lines constantly traveled, its stations filled with slaves, its conductors helping more and more packages reach freedom.

"At that time, there was a Quaker named William Jemson, a Pennsylvanian who, like many Quakers, was deeply interested in the Underground Railroad. Under the name of Walter Goley, Jemson came to Louisiana and arranged for almost a thousand slaves to board the freedom train. He found a surprising lot of cooperation among the Southerners. Some helped out of conscience; others because Mr. Goley was willing to do business on a cash basis.

"My father was one of those. For the price of about fifty dollars a head, he was willing to cooperate. The mansion borders the Mississippi, and it was Goley's idea to use the house as a depot, and then pick up the runaways by steamboat and run them up North. This meant a lot of slaves would have to be hidden in the mansion waiting for transport.

"Things went smoothly for about three months. According to my father's diary, he assisted the escape of some four hundred slaves, all hidden in the mansion basement, an underground shelter that ran the length of the house. It could easily accommodate a hundred at a time, if not in absolute comfort and sanitation, although his diary states that the greatest number ever assembled there was forty."

August took a deep breath and closed his eyes.

"There were forty slaves in the cellar in the month of September 1860. They had been accumulating there for almost five weeks, and yet the steamboat hadn't appeared. My father kept writing Goley, but received no reply.

"Then the worst happened. My brother Damon came home. After a year on the riverboats, he decided to demand his filial rights. He knew nothing about our father's secret activities, but he quickly learned of them. And when he learned that money was involved, he voiced his enthusiastic approval.

"Then Damon had an idea. Why only fifty dollars a head for such dangerous and difficult work? Why not a hundred per slave, a hundred fifty? If this Goley wanted them so bad, why not make him pay the highest price?

"Father was enraged at Damon's plan, and ordered him out of the house. It was a terrible quarrel, and it ended in my father's apopleptic stroke. He was put to bed, unable to tend to his simplest needs. A loyal servant saw to him, and it was from him that my father learned what Damon had done. Damon had demanded five thousand dollars for the slaves in the cellar of our mansion. When Goley never replied—not because he scorned the offer, but because he had died a month before—Damon construed his silence as refusal. And his revenge was terrible."

It was a long moment before August concluded his story.

"Damon sealed up the cellar. Sealed it up so solidly that it's hard to know it exists. The forty slaves were still below, singing hymns and praying for the deliverance that never came."

August looked up.

"You talk of families with skeletons in their closet, Mr. Birchard? There are forty in ours."

Barney Schemmerhorn sat perilously close to the edge of the library chair, and the look on his face was something Rutherford Hayes would never forget, an amalgam of bafflement, humility, and a dash of belligerence.

"Look, Mr. Birchard—Mr. Hayes, sir—I mean Mr. President—"

Rud gave him a reassuring smile. "Relax, Barney . . . I mean, Mr. Schemmerhorn. I'm not actually Mr. President yet, and I won't be until the fifth of March."

"Oh, you can call me Barney, sir, that's all right. It's just that I'm curious about why you wanted to see me."

"For one thing," Rud said, "I wanted to apologize for

deceiving you when we met in New Orleans, and to thank you for your discretion in the matter.''

"That's all right, Mr. Hayes. Mr. Tapley explained the whole thing.''

"Then he told you about our conservation?''

"Yes, sir, he took me into his complete confidence. I'm perfectly satisfied that he did nothing that warrants legal action. I hope you are, too.''

"I feel nothing but pity for Mr. Tapley. And I didn't ask you to Columbus for the purpose of taking action against him. This is a more personal matter . . .''

His gaze went to the hole in the library wall, and Barney followed his eyes. His professional interest was excited at once. He slid off the leather seat and went to examine it.

"Good Lord, Mr. President! This is a bullet hole! Has there been an assassination attempt?''

"Some people think so. Some think it was merely a stray bullet. But there is a third possibility, and that's what caused me to summon you.''

"What do you mean?''

"There is something you don't know about my New Orleans visit, Barney. You see, after I left Mr. Tapley that afternoon, after he had bared his soul to me, I realized that the story he had told me was still . . . incomplete.''

"In what way?''

"He cleared up the mystery of the fire at the mansion, and he explained the tragic deaths of forty poor souls. The trouble is, there were forty-*one* murders needing explanation. That was why I didn't return directly to New Orleans when I left Mr. Tapley. Instead, I retraced my steps to the guest cottage, to see his friend Jasper Douglas.''

He had blinked owlishly behind his bifocals when he saw Rud Hayes back on his doorstep, and his immediate assumption was that he had forgotten something. The truth was exactly the opposite; it was something Rud had remembered.

"I don't quite understand,'' Douglas had said. His face brightened momentarily. "Unless you've changed your mind about contributing to my book . . .''

"It does have to do with your book,'' Rud said as he entered. "I wanted to tell you how impressed I was by your dedication to authenticity, and by the remarkable research you've done. There was just something that troubled me, about the last letter you showed me. The one concerning Mr. Goley."

Douglas offered him a chair, but Rud preferred to stand. He moved to the speckled file boxes and trailed his fingers over them with a casual air that belied his inner turmoil.

"I was surprised," he said, "that you didn't seem to know who Goley was—that it was the pseudonym of the Quaker, William Jemson."

Douglas gave only the faintest hint of reaction.

"Of course I knew that. I simply didn't want to bore you with a lengthy exposition." He smiled. "I do have a tendency to rattle on too much about these matters."

"I see."

Douglas removed his glasses and began to polish them vigorously. "I've heard of Jemson, of course. He was quite a romantic character. He was killed by a plantation owner on one of his Southern raids. But then, there were quite a few of these heroic types at the time. Thomas Garrett, another Quaker—remarkable man. And of course the amazing Harriet Tubman—"

"But even if you didn't know that Jemson was Goley, Mr. Douglas . . . it seems to me you should have understood the letter better than you did."

"In what way?"

"Barnaby Tapley spoke of packages that were to be delivered to the station. I had no difficulty understanding what he meant, or what business he was conducting. And yet, you acted as if the whole thing was baffling . . ."

"I don't think I understand your point, Mr. Hayes."

"Surely you could have surmised that Barnaby Tapley was referring to slaves when he spoke of packages. You must have known that the station was the mansion itself. How could you possibly have been so ignorant? Or were you just . . . feigning ignorance, for my sake?"

"Why on earth would I do that?"

"Because you didn't wish to reveal that you knew the truth about the mansion. That it was a depot of the Underground

Railroad. You didn't want me to draw any inference, but I'm afraid I did. I brought my suspicions to the attention of Mr. Tapley, and he admitted the truth. That there was more than one blackmailer in his life. Elly Dyer, and yourself.''

Douglas replaced his glasses carefully, allowing his expression to mellow, his eyes to return to their original warmth.

''You're an intelligent man, Mr. Hayes. I have little interest in current politics, but I feel sure I would give you my vote in the forthcoming election. I believe you're a man who is willing to listen to a . . . rational explanation.''

''Yes. I'm willing to listen.''

He folded his hands under his bearded chin.

''You've heard what August Tapley called me, Mr. Hayes. An historian. But only a year ago, I was nothing more than an impoverished, overage scholar, nibbling like a rat on the fringes of the tapestry of history . . . Then something happened. In the pursuit of my obsession, I ran across a small, handwritten volume, part of the pilfered loot of a dead Union soldier . . .''

''The diary,'' Rud said. ''The journal of Barnaby Tapley.''

''Yes. It took me some time to penetrate his almost illegible hand, but when I did, I also penetrated the shameful secret of the Tapley mansion.

''I had several choices. I could be generous, and turn the document over to the historical authorities. I could publish my own account, and attain a mild celebrity. Or I could be truly generous, and return it to the people who were most concerned: the present generation of the Tapley family. In a way, that's exactly what I did.''

''For a price,'' Rud said.

''For a return favor,'' Jasper Douglas said. ''For their help and support for my dedication to history. They gave me a home; they gave me assistance. They gave me friendship—''

''Is that what you call it?'' Rud asked.

''You may call it blackmail if you wish, Mr. Hayes. But I think of August Tapley as a philanthropist, operating an endowment fund for the preservation of the past.''

''But there was a problem, wasn't there? Your endowment fund was threatened, wasn't it, when someone *else* learned the dark secret of the Tapley mansion?''

"I don't know what you mean." Jasper Douglas blinked.

"I'm speaking of Elly Dyer," Rutherford Hayes said.

Barney Schemmerhorn leaned back so far in his chair that it almost toppled backward.

"Good Lord, Mr. Hayes," he said. "Do you suppose that explains it?"

"Explains what?"

"Why, what happened to Mr. Douglas! After he returned from his trip last night . . ."

"His trip to where?"

"I don't know. He was gone for several days."

"Could he have possibly come north—to Ohio, perhaps?"

"I honestly can't say, Mr. Hayes. All I know is, he returned to the Tapleys' guest cottage late last evening. And about ten o'clock, the Tapleys heard the sound of a gunshot . . . They rushed to the cottage, and found Mr. Douglas at his desk. He'd shot himself through the head with that old Colt .45 of his. It belonged to a Union officer; Mr. Tapley said he was surprised that it still worked. . . ."

Rutherford Hayes slumped in his chair.

"In a way," he said sadly, "I suppose you could call it the last shot fired in the War . . ."

On March 5, 1877, Rutherford B. Hayes was inaugurated as the nineteenth president of the United States. Six Secret Service men walked beside his carriage, their duty was, it was said, "to keep a sharp lookout for assassins intending to prepare the way for the accession of Mr. Tilden to the presidency."

Rud Hayes was calm.

GARY ALAN RUSE is the author of two of the most exciting technological thrillers of the 1970s: Houndstooth *and* A Game of Titans. *He is also an accomplished writer of science fiction and fantasy. Additionally, he has a background in art and graphic design. Mr. Ruse is a member of the Mystery Writers of America and lives in Miami.*

Grover Cleveland (1837–1908) was both our twenty-second and our twenty-fourth president. He was a governor of New York before his first election to the presidency in 1884. He is considered one of the most honest and most anticorruption presidents in the history of the Republic, and he has the distinction of being the only president to marry while in office.

MURDER IN DEER PARK

★ ★ ★

Gary Alan Ruse

1
THE PURSUIT

Washington, D.C., June 2, 1886—

It was a summer night in the nation's capital. The American Civil War was two decades past, and the First World War was nearly three decades in the future. America was still firmly entrenched in the Victorian era, barely on the threshold of enormous change, with such conveniences as the telephone and motorcar mere toys as yet unproven. It was a simpler age in many ways, and some Americans would likely be spending their evening sitting in their front porch swings, cool glasses of lemonade in hand. But on this particular night, and in this particular place, a group of dedicated hunters stood poised in the darkness, ever watchful for their quarry. . . .

"What time is it, anyway?"

"Almost eight-forty," said the man next to him. Then he smiled wryly. "What's the matter, Murphy? You getting tired? Go on home if you want. We'll tell you all about it later."

"Hah! There's no chance of that happening, my lad. I . . . look! I think I see something moving!"

"Where?"

"There! Someone passed before that window. See? They're coming out now."

The main entrance door in the South Portico of the White House was indeed opening. Two silhouetted figures stepped out briskly, carrying luggage. As they approached the curving drive that ran before the presidential mansion, a carriage and team of horses appeared out of the darkness and halted before them. The bags were loaded quickly as two more figures emerged from the White House.

"Is it them?" asked the first man among the group clustered at the vantage point on the edge of Lafayette Park.

"And you call yourself a reporter," the one known as Murphy replied contemptuously. "That stout figure of a man can surely be none other than the president, and the slender young thing beside him his bride. The first two are likely servants. But say, where's his aide, Colonel Lamont? I'm surprised he's not traveling with them."

"I certainly would not ask him along on *my* honeymoon!"

"But you're not the president of the United States, and aren't likely to be, either, my lad. Come along quickly now. They're moving out, off to their secret retreat."

" 'Twill not be a secret if we have anything to say about it!"

Across the way, the president helped his bride up into the carriage—gently, as if he feared she might break. He then stepped up and sat beside her. His valet and her maid took their places on the facing seat, latching the carriage door behind them.

With a sharp crack of his whip, the coachman sent his team

forward along the drive. The gateman waved them through with a flourish and a smile that glistened in the darkness. Clattering through the night with surprisingly unstatesman-like urgency, their hooves striking sparks against the paving stones, the horses took a direct route to K Street, where it intersected with the rail fork known as the "Y."

There, at a spot several blocks outside of the train depot, an engine stood waiting, linked with only two carriages, the second a private car. A plume of black smoke, alight with cinders, billowed skyward from its stack.

The president's carriage pulled to a halt alongside the private car and the servants quickly dismounted. Several railroad officials assisted with the luggage as the president and his bride stepped down, and in barely more than a minute the transfer was made. With an urgent command from one of the railroad officials, the engineer was ordered to pull out with all haste. The powerful engine gave a great chuffing *chug*, followed by another, and another, rapidly increasing in tempo, ever faster, as the train receded down the tracks.

Arriving mere seconds too late, the small group of reporters pulled up in their own hackneys. The members of the press were unable to do more than stare down the tracks at the departing train and swear softly.

"We've been had," cracked Murphy, jamming his notepad and pencil into his pocket. "We fared no better than our friends who planted themselves at the depot with the rest of the crowds."

"What do we do now?" asked the younger reporter.

"Simple enough, lad. It's back to the depot for us. Where one train goes, another may surely follow. If we hurry, we may yet catch up with our man before he and his new missus are buttering their breakfast toast!"

Thundering through the night with a speed that seemed dangerous in the intense darkness, the special train continued on its northwestern journey. The luxurious palace car coupled behind the racing engine seemed more a narrow mansion than a mere conveyance. Rich velvet draperies with drawn shades were at the windows, held in place with matching cord sashes. A plush sofa and several armchairs flanked both sides of the private car's parlor, with end tables and a small writing desk well placed between them. The fabrics were all luxurious red, the paneling and furniture walnut, the fittings and fixtures of gold and polished brass. No expense had been spared in creating this marvelous car, and no effort had been spared in freshening and preparing it for this special trip. The splendor was not lost upon at least one of the distinguished passengers.

"It's quite breathtaking, isn't it?" said she, the former Miss Frances Folsom, now the wife of the highest public official in the land. "So much nicer than the common trains."

"Indeed it is," replied her husband, Grover Cleveland, twenty-second president of the United States. He stroked his full mustache, his blue eyes twinkling as they took in the details of the private car. "However, I must say that I find such luxury a bit ostentatious. Makes me feel like a damned Republican!"

"Grover!"

Cleveland's stern look dissolved in a hearty chuckle, even as his young bride's look of reproach gave way to merry laughter. He put his arm around her slender shoulders as they sat on the sofa, swaying slightly with the rhythm of the speeding train.

"Nevertheless," Mrs. Cleveland told him, "we must make sure to thank Mr. Garrett for his kindness. Allowing us to use his private car for our trip was very thoughtful. And," she added, cocking her head slightly, "I think it's quite romantic."

The president took her hand and kissed it gallantly. "As do I, my lovely Frances. And since Mr. Garrett is not only president of the Baltimore and Ohio Railroad but also owns much of the property at our destination, I could scarcely decline his invitation. We are just lucky that the Knights of Labor are at peace with Mr. Garrett. A railroad strike here would have left us stranded. At any rate, they've done a splendid job so far in getting us out of Washington."

His young bride gave a small laugh. "Yes, indeed. As did our coachman. The ride from the White House was exhilarating to say the least!"

"I promised him a bonus if he left in his dust any reporters following us." Cleveland shifted his stout form upon the sofa and examined the plain gold band freshly decorating his left ring finger. With mock wistfulness he said, "Ah, no more the carefree bachelor, I."

His bride leaned closer to him, her hand gently touching the lapel of his formal coat, her dark and soulful eyes exploring his own. "No regrets, Mr. Cleveland?"

The president smiled warmly and squeezed her hand. "None at all, *Mrs*. Cleveland. But what about you? Any second thoughts? You've seen the field day the press has had with us: *President, 49, takes wife, 21*. There were any number of younger men willing to wed a beauty such as you."

"Perhaps. But none brave enough to contest your claim. Frankly, I was beginning to think you would never ask me!"

"I almost did sooner, in the East Room that night, back when you were visiting my sister. But I knew your studies at Wells College were important to you, and I did not wish to propose until after you had graduated."

"Dear Grover. Always so considerate. How could I possibly love anyone else?" She sighed. "My! What a whirlwind this day has been! My mother and cousin and I arrived in Washington only this morning. There were all the preparations, and then the wedding itself this evening. And now here we are on another train, being whisked away to a honeymoon cottage in the mountains. I shall treasure this day all my life."

Cleveland smiled. "The wedding suited you, then?"

"Suited me? What girl could ask for more? A ceremony in the Blue Room of the White House, the place bursting with roses and pansies. The Marine Band playing the wedding march, with Sousa himself conducting. Then a twenty-one-gun salute from the navy yard, and church bells ringing all over Washington. It couldn't have been more splendid!"

"I quite agree. Now, if you have no objections, I shall ring for the porter and have him bring us champagne, for I intend to make a toast to my lovely bride."

She blushed slightly. "You know my view of spirits. But I suppose a sip or two for a toast would not hurt. Just do not tell your sister Rose."

"Fair enough. And after that, I suppose, we really should

think about turning in. There's a long night's journey still ahead of us.''

''Indeed,'' she said coyly.

On through the night rocketed the special train carrying President and Mrs. Cleveland. The landscape beyond the shaded windows was nearly invisible in the extreme darkness of that night. For mile after mile, hour after hour, the train continued. At eleven thirty-seven the town of Martinsburg was reached. The wait at the station was brief, for they paused only long enough to couple on a new engine. After that, the train stopped at Sir John's Run to take on water. The railroad men went about their business promptly and efficiently, and there were no intrusions on the couple's privacy. . . .

2

THE LOVE NEST

Thursday, June 3—

The sun was rising over Deer Park, a small resort town in the western portion of Maryland. Dawn's glow peeped through a sky gray with clouds. A drizzling rain put a sheen upon the valley and the great mountains and forests surrounding it.

Creeping into this woodland setting, its stack creating its own gray clouds, was the engine pulling the president's train. A shrill whistle cut through the crisp mountain air like a knife, echoing and reechoing through the dismal, shadowy hills. Before the sound had fully faded, the train pulled to a halt before the small, picturesque depot, excess steam venting from the cylinders and adding more mist to the air.

The train seemed a noisy intruder in this scenic calm, for though it sat in the midst of everything—the great hotel owned by the Baltimore and Ohio Railroad, the twenty quaint cottages, the murmuring fountain, and the pretty depot itself—nothing else stirred. Not a soul moved about the small community, nor stood upon the station platform.

''Splendid!'' Grover Cleveland beamed as he stepped down

from the train's private car and took in the scene around him. "Peace and quiet, at last!"

As the handful of railroad men who had traveled on the special train bustled about, President Cleveland turned and extended a hand to his young bride as she stepped down to the platform. He held an umbrella over her against the steady drizzle.

Within moments a single coach appeared and drove up to the car. Cleveland and his bride entered and, as soon as the valet and maid were ready and the bags attended to, they were driven across rain-soaked lawns to the cottage the president himself had rented.

Perched on the hillside, two hundred yards above the hotel, the structure was two and a half stories, meaning that it had attic rooms above the first two floors. The sheltering walls were painted dove gray, the roofs and steep gables red. Hooded windows offered a view of Deer Park and the Blue Ridge Mountains, and red window blinds with movable slats insured privacy for those within.

The plainness of the outer walls was broken by several porches and a small piazza, offering quiet, picturesque nooks in which to while away the hours. Near the cottage were six others in various stages of completion, their raw wood dampened by the rain. All were surrounded by a bower of trees that sheltered the buildings and gave them rustic charm.

"This is lovely," said Mrs. Cleveland as they started up the walk to the cottage. "It is even prettier than I imagined."

"The setting is, I agree," replied the president, with a gloomy look toward the sky. "I regret to say, though, that of the many facets of presidential power available to me, controlling the weather is sadly not one of them."

His bride shrugged. "Oh, I'm sure the rain will clear up. Besides, it will only make our sweet haven that much more cozy."

The valet opened the door for them and stood back while they entered. They could see now that the cottage was indeed a cozy retreat. The parlor was simply furnished, with no great deal of ornament, but a toasty fire was already burning for them in the fireplace, and an expensive Weber piano stood at one side of the room.

The president and Mrs. Cleveland took a brief stroll around the first floor while their servants put away the luggage. Besides the parlor, this floor also contained a dining room, kitchen, and pantry. There were all the essential conveniences: hot and cold water, and gas for lights and cooking.

"The bedrooms are upstairs, I suppose?" inquired Mrs. Cleveland.

"Yes—four of them, according to what I've been told. The servants' apartments are in the attic." Back in the parlor now, the president paused by a window and peered out through the blinds. "Ah, good! I see they are on the job already."

His bride joined him at the window. She saw a cordon of men surrounding the cottage, a short distance out. Dark-suited men, many with bowler hats and all with unusually large silver badges pinned on their coats. Their collars turned up against the light drizzle, they strode purposefully back and forth.

"Guards?" she said.

"Sworn constables of the state of Maryland," Cleveland replied. "I requested privacy and protection from intrusion, and the railroad people were kind enough to make the arrangements."

"I'm glad of that. You truly need the rest." She touched his face gently, soothingly. "Dear Grover, you have developed such a careworn look from the constant parade of politicians, office-seekers, and reporters that pester you so in Washington. If I can take any credit for rescuing you, however briefly, from all that, I shall be greatly satisfied."

He took her hand and kissed it, then steered her to the seats facing the fire.

As they sat there before the fireplace, taking the morning's chill off, Cleveland stared into the flames and sighed. "If the people only knew how many nights I've labored until dawn, reading through hundreds of pension bills that Congress has carelessly voted upon and sent for my signature! It's absurd. The Pensions Bureau was established for the purpose of fairly hearing and deciding upon the claims of Civil War veterans, but every shirker and ninety-day soldier, and a good many professed invalids who are strong as oxen, are petitioning their congressmen. And the fools—they vote them pensions, regardless of the validity of their claims. Back in April, the Senate passed four hundred bills in one day! They might as well turn over the keys to the treasury."

"Are they all fraudulent?"

"Not all. But certainly most are doubtful. One widow claimed her husband fell off a ladder because of a minor leg wound acquired twenty years earlier. Would you call that a valid claim to collect a full and retroactive war pension? I think not. And yet I cannot merely veto all the bills. That would trouble my conscience as surely as blindly signing them all."

"Well, that is something you must not think about now. Not here. I want you to relax and forget your cares, and I fully intend to see that you do!"

"I already feel more at peace than I have in a very long time. I thank you for that, my dear Frank."

Sitting next to him, Frances Folsom Cleveland settled her head upon her husband's broad shoulder and took his hand in hers. She watched the cheery flames beyond the hearth and felt true contentment.

By ten o'clock that morning, the quiet community of Deer Park was well awake. The resort season did not begin until June 15, so there were relatively few residents of the cottages and hotel present. But quite a number of country folk from the surrounding towns had heard of the illustrious visitors and had been drawn by curiosity to come and have a look. Another group of visitors were present, larger and more citified, and they had gathered around a pavilion on the property of one of the home owners as if staking out a gold mine.

The pavilion was only a few hundred yards from the very cottage where the president and his bride were settled in, and the journalists, who had arrived about eight o'clock by express train, were making themselves comfortable. They had about them the air of parade watchers or a circus audience, some standing, some perched upon railings, some sitting upon the broad, sloping lawn of the property on which they trespassed. All were facing the tiny cottage in hopes of catching a glimpse of someone through one of the hooded windows. Most of the men had binoculars through which they peered unabashedly. Some had cameras. All had press cards stuck jauntily in the bands of their hats. And they had not come alone. Back at the hotel, a dozen expert telegraph operators were busily setting up their portable telegraph keys and stringing connecting lines, and taking up two rooms for their improvised message center.

At the house to which the pavilion belonged, a shade flew up at the window facing the flock of newspapermen and a man's face appeared framed within. The fellow, an older gentleman with a neat beard, stared out at the group of squatters, his eyes widening, his jaw dropping. That face promptly disappeared from the window and reappeared at the front door, and the fellow rushed out in a manner most irate.

"You there!" he called to them. "You rapscallions! What do you think you are doing? That is private property upon which you are trampling. How dare you! I insist you leave at once!"

Several of the reporters chortled. Others simply ignored the man.

The reporter known as Murphy chose to answer him. "We are gentlemen of the press, my dear fellow," he cried, "and we are here on public business. The Constitution assures a free press, and it is our duty to inform the people of this fair land of the news regarding their president."

"Balderdash!" proclaimed the landowner. "You've got nothing more in mind than selling newspapers, and the Constitution does not grant you the right to trample my lawn in the process. Now be off with you. Leave the poor Clevelands alone, and me in the bargain!"

"We will leave." Murphy gave a tip of his hat. "Just as soon as the president and his missus go back to Washington."

The bearded man fumed, drew himself up, and stalked back to his house, muttering, "We shall see about that!"

The group of reporters exploded into laughter. "Fine talking, Murphy!" said one. "I guess you told him," proclaimed another. "Maybe you should run for president, Murphy!"

Their jocularity soon ended, however, as one of the men thrust a finger toward the cottage and announced, "Look! They're coming out!"

All laughter ceased. All eyes were riveted upon the piazza

fronting the two-story cottage of gray and red. The recognizable figure of the president emerged, followed by his bride. Grover Cleveland held a chair for his wife, then seated himself as well. The act itself was utterly mundane, but it was greeted with enormous interest by the men in the pavilion.

"Ah," remarked Murphy. "The lovebirds have left the nest."

"What's that he's wearing?" said one reporter who had no binoculars.

"It's a black frock coat," another man, lenses to his eyes, informed the others. "And Mrs. Cleveland is wearing a blue tulle dress."

Hasty scribbling followed. Watches were consulted. A voice from somewhere in the group cried out, "How do you spell *tulle*?"

While the journalists continued their watch, scrambling for more crumbs of detail and searching their memories for colorful adjectives and clever turns of phrases, there were others in Deer Park who were also observing the unfolding events. A handful of men stood at the window of a similar cottage across the way, far past the police cordon and the small bridge that was their headquarters, far past the narrow stream which meandered through the valley.

"Bad luck," said one of the men in the shade-darkened room.

The second man, white-haired, and wearing a gold signet ring, extracted a small pair of field glasses from its case and brought them to his eyes. Peering through a gap in the blinds, he said, "This is indeed unfortunate timing. Perhaps we should change our plans."

"Let's not be hasty, gentlemen," the third man told them in a voice that was crisp and smooth and hard. "All the attention seems to be focused over there. Not here."

The man with the field glasses frowned as he continued to watch. "I still do not like it. We shall have to be more careful about our movements."

"We need to be, anyway," came the third man's reply. "At any rate, the others will be here this afternoon. We must wait until then, at least. Then we may make our final decision, though I foresee no difficulties in continuing as planned.''

The other man lowered his field glasses and nodded soberly, his tone uncertain. "Very well. . . .''

The reporters were still at their post hours later, duly noting upon their jotting pads that breakfast was served at eleven, carried from the hotel by waiters who were not allowed to enter the cottage beyond the kitchen door. It quickly became clear that no one else save the president's valet and Mrs. Cleveland's confidential maid would have access to the honeymoon couple. A few of the gentlemen of the press were so brash as to attempt to sneak a look at the food trays, so as to better inform their readers just what delicacies were to tempt the presidential palate. And there was a minor contest on, among those equipped with binoculars, to count the number of letters being delivered to the cottage by the postman.

One young reporter, not caught up in such antics, alternately stared across the way toward the cottage and at his notes in his lap. He shook his head ruefully. "There that carriage sits, parked before the cottage for at least an hour and a half, and nothing happens. How can I write about that?''

"Patience, my lad,'' said Murphy. "In fact, look—if I do not miss my guess, the turtledoves are ready to leave at this very moment.''

The young reporter watched as the president and Mrs. Cleveland emerged from their cottage. Within moments, they were in the fine carriage, heading away.

"Dashing down the avenue toward the charming village of Oakland,'' phrased Murphy, writing as he spoke.

Scrambling to his feet, the younger journalist consulted his watch, jotted the time down hastily, then tucked away his notepad. He started away, then glanced back at Murphy querulously.

"Well,'' said he, "aren't you coming? We can hire a carriage and follow them.''

Murphy gave a shrugging wave of his hand. "You go ahead, lad. They'll be back, and I have my own ways of finding out where they've gone. Right now I want to look around this place—find some local color, that sort of thing. I'll see you later. . . . "

It was late afternoon when the fancy carriage bearing the president and his bride returned. The couple disappeared within the cottage for a while, then Cleveland appeared on the piazza for a time, sitting in one of the large, comfortable wicker chairs, reading a newspaper.

Murphy was polishing his prose, splicing bits and pieces of material together, when he noticed his young reporter friend pacing back and forth. The younger man was glaring at his notepad, trying to stare words into existence.

"My word, lad," muttered Murphy. "Are you still struggling?"

"Yes. *No*. I don't know. It just isn't coming, for some reason."

"Well, maybe you're trying *too* hard this time. Look, don't fight it. Just take what you see, and then make it pretty. Now, what did you see?"

The young reporter stopped in his tracks, gazing off, his mouth twisted in thought. "Well, the president and his wife came back. Just in time, too, since it will be getting dark soon. And the breeze must have been cool on them, for Mrs. Cleveland's cheeks were quite pink. And the president was smiling. Not a big smile, but a pleasant one."

"Very good," said Murphy. "Exactly what I saw. So here is how I chose to describe it: *The shades of evening were falling when the lovers reached their cottage. Her cheeks had already caught fresh beauty from the mountain air, new light sparkled in her eye, and the president himself seemed at peace with all the world*. Neatly done, eh?"

"You don't think that's too . . . well, flowery?"

"Bosh!" said Murphy. "You young fellows have a lot to learn about the fine art of reporting." He glanced over toward the piazza. "Say, you've got binoculars. Can you make out which newspaper the president is reading?"

The young man brought the lenses to his eyes and strained to make out the lettering atop the front page. "No, it's too far away, and the light isn't good enough."

"Well, as far as I'm concerned, Mr. Cleveland is reading

a copy of the *New York Herald*, no doubt the one containing my account of his wedding, and that is precisely what I intend to tell my readers. Now, go craft your own prose, my young friend. I have work to do."

Part of that work consisted of interviewing the carriage driver and learning the couple had been driven to Mountain Lake, returning along the banks of the silvery Youghiogheny River. The rest, later, involved describing a twilight walk for the president and his bride, taking note of the fact that Mrs. Cleveland had changed and was now tastefully attired in a light snuff-colored dress which was very becoming to her graceful figure. And that the two sat on the piazza until a late hour, side by side like true and dear lovers. And somehow, studying them, Murphy found that even his florid prose seemed no exaggeration.

At last, as the day drew to a close and the honeymoon couple retreated once more inside their shelter, Murphy and the others rushed to the bank of telegraphers waiting to transmit their columns home. For it would soon be time to put the newspapers to bed as well. . . .

3
THE BODY

Friday, June 4th—

The morning brought better weather to Deer Park. Dappled sunlight illuminated the little cottage, and there was a dewy freshness to the well-tended lawns and gardens of the picturesque mountain resort.

At a minute after nine, the door to the cottage opened and President Cleveland appeared on the piazza, escorting his wife. His smile broadened as he took a deep breath and sighed with satisfaction.

"Ah, Frank," said he, "you won't find air like this in Washington. It's invigorating!"

"It truly is," Mrs. Cleveland replied, fussing with his collar and polka-dot bow tie. "I'm glad this place agrees with you so."

"My dear, it is not just this place, marvelous though it is, that agrees with me," the president told her. He gave her a kiss, then glanced around self-consciously. "Are our friends from the press still out there?"

"Yes," she said, blushing. "I fear so."

He glared toward the pavilion. "It was bad enough that they followed us here. But I think it is unseemly for them to lurk in the bushes, staring at us through their spyglasses."

She flashed him a playful look. "Shall we give them something really wicked to write about?"

Cleveland gave a hearty chuckle. "I am pleased to see their obnoxious presence has not diminished your sense of humor. Now, what shall it be this morning? I was just contemplating taking a few turns about the property. Do you care to join me?"

"You go on ahead," replied Mrs. Cleveland. "I think I shall just sit here and enjoy this lovely breeze and the beautiful view."

"Very well. I shall be back shortly."

Grover Cleveland took leave of his wife and descended the steps to the gravel walk, enjoying the pleasant crunch of the tiny stones beneath his feet. Heading out along the front of the yard, he strolled leisurely.

He could not help but notice that the scene before him had changed from the previous day. While Deer Park had been quiet and nearly deserted yesterday, today there was a bustle of activity everywhere. Workmen, upholsterers, and decorators were busy making repairs and sprucing up the buildings, apparently in preparation for the imminent arrival of the wealthy and fashionable folk.

Drifting over from the big hotel, some five hundred feet north of his rented cottage, came the staccato rapping of tack hammers, and a wagon load of new carpeting was being carried, roll by roll, into the building. Cleveland knew full well that the summer season was still two weeks away, so the only thing that could account for this sudden flurry of activity was his own visit. He shook his head and gave an amused chuckle, thinking that *he* would not go out of his way to come and gawk at a U.S. president, least of all himself. Ah well, he thought, people are entitled to their diversions.

Cleveland nodded in greeting to the cordon of policemen that circled the area. As he walked toward the side of the property that faced a number of new cottages under construction, he noticed that several of the constables were gathered at the nearest structure, a ways beyond the cordon. Something about the way they stood there, looking down at a tarpaulin on the ground, caught his attention and roused his curiosity. And though he was not sure why, the sight also sent a tiny shiver down his spine.

The president continued walking in that direction now, crossing the perimeter with a courteous "Good morning!" to the guards nearest him. As he approached the half-completed cottage, one of the men standing there looked up and came toward him. It was Lieutenant Brockmyer, the officer in charge of the special constabulary force. He was a burly man under his neat suit, mustached and wearing his bowler hat at a rakish tilt.

"Good morning, Mr. President," Brockmyer said, his manner all grim politeness.

"And good morning to you, Lieutenant Brockmyer," replied Cleveland. His eyes focused past the officer and upon the tarpaulin directly before the cottage wall. "Is there some sort of problem here?"

"Nothing you need concern yourself with, sir. I wouldn't wish to spoil your visit."

Cleveland gave him a comradely pat on the shoulder and gestured him toward the spot. "I appreciate your concern, my good fellow. But I can assure you I am quite used to dealing with worrisome matters. So let us take a look."

As they walked to the cottage wall, Brockmyer cautioned, "It's not a pretty sight, sir."

"I may be president now, Lieutenant, but by turns I have also been governor of New York, a lawyer for many years, and the elected sheriff of Erie County. I am not squeamish."

The office nodded respectfully and reached down for the edge of the tarp. He lifted it cautiously and folded the canvas back to reveal what was beneath.

The body of a man lay twisted in awkward angles. His eyes were frozen in an unnerving stare, and a thin trickle of blood, now dried, ran from the corner of his mouth down his chin and partway along his neck. Inches from his right hand, clawlike in death, lay a pair of binoculars with leather grips.

"Found him this morning, soon as I came on shift and took a look around the grounds," said Brockmyer. "His papers indicate he's a reporter, like those other fellows down the hill. Name of John Finley, *New York Evening Post*."

The president continued to stare at the body, absorbing the details that seemed to grab at his attention. "His neck is surely broken."

"Indeed it is, sir. Looks like his arm is, too." The officer pointed up at the second floor and the open framework of a window not yet finished. "Near as we can tell, it must have happened late last night. The damn fool fell from up there."

Cleveland tore his gaze away and looked up at the window. "Up there?"

Brockmyer had an uneasy frown. "Distasteful though it sounds, the hooligan must have been after a better look at your cottage, sir. He'd have had a clear view of your second floor from here. Then he got too nosy and slipped right out. Probably good riddance, I say."

Cleveland looked from the window above over to the second-floor windows of his own cottage, where the bedrooms were located. The view was clear indeed. And with binoculars! . . .

The president's face colored as some of his usual annoyance with the press briefly flared into anger. But something tugged at his thoughts and his temper cooled.

He looked back to Brockmyer, then once more at the body sprawled so piteously before him. "Something troubles me about this. As you point out, the evidence all seems to be here before us, and yet . . . I wonder. I have, in fact, read some of Finley's pieces, and he does not seem the type of reporter to indulge in Jenkinsism. The *New York Evening Post* is itself a highly respected newspaper. I cannot imagine them sending a man here for such a purpose."

Brockmyer gave a shrugging gesture. "Yes, sir. But here he is."

"Tell me, did none of your men hear anything last night? An outcry? The fall itself?"

"They heard nothing, Mr. President. Just the chimes in

the hotel tower. I questioned them myself, right after I found the body.''

Cleveland gave a frowning pout. "Does that not strike you as odd?"

Brockmyer pulled at his chin and sighed. "Maybe so, sir. I reprimanded the men for being inattentive, but I s'pose there could have been some other sounds that would have kept them from hearing this.''

"Possibly." The president stooped and looked more closely at the body. The laces of the man's shoes were caked with mud, still damp. "It appears he must have crossed the stream to get here.''

"I agree, sir.''

Grover Cleveland cast his sharp gaze back in the direction of the pavilion commandeered by the press. Leaning first one way and then the other, he found that he could not see it, for the foliage of several low trees blocked the view. That meant that if there had been any reporters present in the pavilion at the time, they would have been unable to see this cottage and witness their fellow journalist's tragic end.

Looking to Brockmyer, he asked, "Is there some place the man's body may be kept, until the next of kin are notified?"

The officer chewed his lip as his eyes quickly surveyed the village of Deer Park. "There *is* the icehouse, just back of the hotel. Wrapped in this tarp, I think we can get him there without too much fuss. I'm sure we may count on the full cooperation of the railroad company.''

"Cooperation?"

"Well, sir," said Brockmyer, lowering his voice, "I mean as far as the press is concerned. This ain't the sort of thing you would want in the papers. Could look bad, what with them criticizing us already for keeping them away from your cottage.''

Cleveland inquired, "You are afraid the press might think one of your constables took his duties too seriously and killed the man?"

"It could look that way.''

The president eyed him unblinkingly. "*Did* one of your men do it?"

Brockmyer seemed genuinely taken aback. "No, sir, Mr.

President. I will vouch for all of my men. None of them would have done this."

Cleveland put a steadying hand on the officer's arm. "I believe you, Lieutenant. But I think you are dead wrong in wanting to keep this matter from the press. Rest assured, you will not be able to hide the facts for long, and if you attempt to, you will only aid the reporters in jumping to the wrong conclusion and laying the blame upon your men."

"I see your point. We wouldn't want that."

"If I may advise you, be straightforward with them. Bring some of the journalists up here. Ask if they know anything about the man. If what you suspect about him is true—if he did fall to his death while attempting to spy on my wife and me—then I doubt that is a story the reporters will want to put before their readers."

"All right, sir. I shall. But . . . you are not convinced the fellow's death was an accident?"

Cleveland sighed and shook his head. "I wish I could say I was, but frankly there is something about it which nags at me. Could you do me a personal favor, Lieutenant? Something just between you and me?"

Brockmyer's chest swelled visibly. "Of course, Mr. President. 'Twould be my pleasure."

"Then indulge the whim of an old lawyer and ex-sheriff, and let me have a hand in investigating this matter."

"Well, sir," said the officer with a small chuckle, "I could hardly refuse the president of these United States, even if I had a mind to. What would you like me to do?"

Cleveland once more studied the corpse intently, committing to memory all that he saw. "First, just do as we discussed, insofar as informing the other reporters and seeing that the body is properly tended to at the icehouse. Second, I should very much like to have a doctor examine the man."

"There is one near here in Oakland. I can send a man to fetch him here."

"Excellent! Third, I'd like to examine the man's personal effects. Unless, of course, you object or feel your sworn duties compromised. . . ?"

Brockmyer absently twisted the end of his mustache. "No, I see no problem. Would this afternoon be satisfactory?"

"Yes, I am quite sure it would be." Cleveland shook the officer's hand and started to turn to go. He hesitated. "You know, Lieutenant, if foul play is involved here, it might be prudent to have the railroad ticket agent or a constable keep watch on who tries to leave the area by train. There are other means of leaving Deer Park, to be sure, but that would be one important escape path covered."

"Yes, sir. I'll see to it right away."

"And now, if you will excuse me, I must resume my husbandly duties."

"I understand, Mr. President. Oh—wait, sir. There is something I forgot. Yesterday afternoon while you were out, several gentlemen from the Methodist Sunday School Convention came by to deliver this letter." He fished through his inside coat pockets and finally produced the message, handing it over.

Cleveland took it. "Do you know what it concerns?"

"One of them said something about wanting to call on you and the missus, to congratulate the president and kiss the bride, as I recall."

"Humph," replied Grover Cleveland with a bit of a smile. "I suspect the gentlemen are less interested in the former than in the latter. But you have done your duty and delivered the message. I shall see you later, Lieutenant. Good day."

"Good day to you, sir."

4

THE DETECTIVES

President Cleveland consulted his gold pocket watch. The hands showed a few minutes past ten. As he snapped it closed and put it away, his valet entered the dining room from the kitchen carrying a silver tray with a domed cover.

Seated at the table across from his wife, Cleveland said, "Ah, breakfast."

"Yes, sir," his valet replied. "I am sorry for the delay. The waiters from the hotel brought it just this moment."

The man placed the tray on a stand near the table and

proceeded to uncover it. He transferred dishes of melon slices to each place at the table, then placed glasses of ice water before the presidential couple. He took the empty tray to the kitchen and returned with another, much larger, this one revealing serving dishes, a platter piled with scrambled eggs and sausages, a basket of hot biscuits, and crystal dishes filled with butter and jam. Retreating toward the kitchen once more, the valet said, "I'll have your coffee in a moment, sir."

"Thank you."

Mrs. Cleveland toyed with a piece of melon on her plate for a long moment, then said, "Are you sure there is not some danger to you as a result of what you've told me?"

"Oh, I very much doubt there is," said the president, spearing a large chunk of melon with his fork. "There is probably nothing more to it than Lieutenant Brockmyer surmises."

"And you intend to investigate on your own?"

"Yes, in a puttering sort of way. But do not fear, my dear girl. I will not allow it to ruin our honeymoon."

"I should hope not," she told him with a wry look. "At any rate, if you are determined to play detective, then I fully intend to help you in any way that I can."

Cleveland swallowed his bite of melon quickly. "Oh, I do not think that will be necessary. Besides, this is not a fitting matter for a lovely young bride on her honeymoon."

"Well," she said with a playfully adamant glare, "it is no *more* fitting for a handsome groom on *his* honeymoon. Besides, I strongly believe that a wife should share her husband's burdens, whatever they may be."

He could not help but smile at her spunk. "Very well, then. I shall be grateful for your help and opinions. But first, let us finish breakfast. This fresh air has made me ravenous!"

At the pavilion some two hundred yards away from the cottage, Murphy consulted his watch. It was a quarter past eleven, and the sun was rising toward its highest point in the sky. He glanced up from his watch sharply as the young reporter next to him spoke suddenly.

"Breakfast must be over," said he. "See? They're out on the piazza again."

Murphy squinted across the gap, doffed his hat momentarily, and scratched at his balding head. "Right you are, lad. Ready to begin a new day of idle pleasure. Let us hope for something exciting and colorful."

The young reporter looked toward him soberly. "Seems to me we've already had our quota of excitement for today, if you know what I mean—that Finley fellow?"

"Indeed," replied Murphy, still staring across at the presidential cottage. "Sad . . . truly sad. And shameful, too. You won't catch me trying a stunt like that. I look for my stories in better ways."

The young reporter brought his binoculars up to his eyes and focused on the walk leading up to the cottage. "Now who do you suppose that might be calling on them. . . ?"

On the piazza of the gray cottage, much the same question was being put forth by the new first lady of the land.

Grover Cleveland looked more closely at the approaching figure and smiled. "Ah, that is none other than the gentleman who convinced me Deer Park would be the perfect site for our honeymoon. You have met Senator Davis before."

The senator was passed through the police cordon without difficulty and made his way up the gravel walk. He was soon on the piazza itself, and the president and Mrs. Cleveland rose to greet him.

"Senator, how good to see you again."

"Mr. President, Mrs. Cleveland." Davis shook Cleveland's outstretched hand and kissed that of his wife. "I hope you are enjoying your stay here with us?"

"Yes, indeed!" replied Cleveland. "More than I thought possible. Deer Park is a delightful place."

Mrs. Cleveland added, "Thank you for suggesting it. I could not be more pleased."

"Good, I am glad to hear it," said Senator Davis. "Well, besides paying my respects to the most famous honeymoon couple in the land, I also came to invite you both to have luncheon with my wife and me. At our cottage at one o'clock, if that would be convenient."

Cleveland gestured toward a chair. "We would be delighted to accept your invitation. Won't you sit with us a-while?"

"Thank you, no. Much as I would like to, I really should return. My wife, you see, has only just arrived, and she quite has her hands full caring for a sick grandchild. My son-in-law, Stephen Elkins, is in Arkansas, at the hot springs. His wife is suffering poor health. We expect him back this evening, but my good wife came here at once when she learned the child was ill."

Mrs. Cleveland's face clouded with concern. "I am sorry to hear that. If you would allow it, I should like to go back with you and see if we can be of assistance to your wife." A glance to the president. "Dear . . . ?"

Cleveland nodded. "An excellent idea, if the Senator has no objections."

"Not at all. It is kind of you to offer. Very well, then. I shall escort you there."

"You needn't have bothered to bring along your diary, my dear," Grover Cleveland said gruffly, his eyes quickly scanning the copy of the *New York Herald* in his hands. "Should you wish to refresh your memory concerning anything we did yesterday, you may find it set down in the most minute detail in any one of a half-dozen newspapers fresh off the presses this morning." He tossed it down upon the parlor table where other papers lay. "My word! Can't a man find privacy anywhere these days?"

His wife came forward and gave him a sympathetic hug. "You must remember, dear, that you are not just any man. What the president of the United States does is news, even if it is nothing extraordinary."

"Perhaps. I still think it an unmanly business."

Mrs. Cleveland glanced at the clock on the mantel. "It is half-past two now. Senator Davis will be here by half-past three. We should get ready."

Cleveland gave a shrugging nod. "Yes, I suppose you are right. Are you sure you wish to go?"

"Yes," she replied brightly. "I think it will do us both good. And I think it will do Mrs. Davis good as well, now that her granddaughter is feeling better."

"Very well."

As they started for the stairs, the valet appeared at the doorway. "You have a visitor, sir."

"It's just me, Mr. President," came the constable's voice from the open front door. "I've brought those things you requested."

Moments later, Lieutenant Brockmyer was standing with them in the parlor. He took a folded manila envelope from his coat pocket and emptied its contents on the table. "Here they are, sir. There ain't much, I'm afraid. Just the usual sort of things a man carries in his pockets."

Mrs. Cleveland stood close at her husband's side as the president examined the items. There was a wallet containing his press identification and a few dollars, some loose change, a box of matches, a small notebook and pencil, an envelope marked EXPENSES, and a pair of glasses in a pocket case.

"Oh, and here are his binoculars, too," said the constable, placing them on the table as well.

Cleveland looked them all over thoughtfully. "Did you have any luck finding a doctor?"

"Yes, sir, I did," Brockmyer told him. "One of my men brought him back here just a while ago. He's taking a look at the corpse—forgive me, ma'am—the deceased, right now, over at the icehouse."

"Excellent. My wife and I shall be leaving shortly for a drive with Senator Davis, but I look forward to hearing your report as soon as we return. In the meantime, could you send a telegram to the managing editor of the *New York Evening Post*, just to inquire what they know of their man's business here?"

"Certainly, sir. Frankly, I'm curious about it myself."

"Good fellow!" Cleveland escorted him to the door. "We shall see you later, then. Good day."

"Good day, sir."

The president closed the door after Brockmyer, then returned to the parlor. His brows knit in concern as he saw that his young wife stared down at the reporter's belongings, her eyes welling up with tears.

"What is it, my dear?"

"It . . . it's just made me think of that day, so long ago, when Father's things were brought to my mother after his accident. There is something inherently melancholy about a man's belongings after he's gone."

Cleveland stepped quickly to her side and put an arm around her. "Yes, I know. I'm sorry this matter has made such sad memories resurface."

She blotted her eyes with a handkerchief, then began examining the items on the table. "I still intend to make good my promise to help you. You know, it seems strange there is so little money in his wallet. How did he plan to pay his bills?"

"Indeed," said Grover Cleveland. "Perhaps equally strange is that a reporter's notebook has no notes in it. There are a handful of pages torn out from the front, but nothing new written down."

Mrs. Cleveland picked up the envelope marked EXPENSES and leafed through the contents. "There is nothing here but receipts for meals and lodging. And here is his ticket for the train that brought him here . . . but how odd!"

"What is that?"

"Why, the date," she replied. "The ticket was for the first of June, three days ago. How could he come here before it was known where we would be going?"

"It is unlikely he could have known," said the president, examining the ticket with its punched holes. "I think it more likely the man came here on some other business. It is only the other reporters' presence here that makes it easy to assume he was with them."

"Well, yes," said Frances Cleveland. "That, and the fact that he died in a spot where he seemed to have been watching us."

Cleveland absently stroked at his mustache. "I would not wager any money on that assumption either."

She looked at him strangely. "Why do you say that?"

He placed the ticket back in the envelope and put it on the table, then steered his wife toward the stairs. "I shall tell you, but we had best get ready while we talk, or we shall surely keep the good senator waiting."

"For one thing," said the president in their second-floor bedroom, "the man had dried blood running down his face and his neck. The blood did not run toward the ground, as good sense and the laws of physical science dictate. It ran sideways, lateral to the ground. And that simply is not possible if the man was lying there with a broken neck.''

Mrs. Cleveland was changing into a dress more suitable for an afternoon carriage ride. "I see what you mean. He must have been upright when the bleeding occurred, and it would have been quite impossible for him to get up or move with an injury like that.''

"Exactly. But what if he was carried, say by two men who moved him from some other spot? That would also make sense of something else that has troubled me.''

"Can you help me with these buttons?''

"Certainly, my dear.'' He stepped behind her and proceeded to fasten the pearl buttons running up the back of her dress.

"I did not mean to interrupt,'' she said. "What was the other thing?''

"Oh, just the matter of his shoes. There was mud on them, which suggested he had crossed that little stream out there to get to the cottage. But there was virtually no mud around the bottoms of his shoes. The mud, and quite a lot of it, was caked upon his laces and deep behind them. Now, the mud could not be that deep in a stream that size, so it set me to wondering how he could have acquired it in such a strange fashion.''

Mrs. Cleveland turned abruptly to face him. "Yes, of course! I see what you mean now. Your theory of two men carrying him would fit perfectly. If he were dragged through the stream, his feet would be at an angle . . . thusly!''

She raised the hem of her skirt and tilted her pretty foot so that the toe of her shoe pointed back, her ankle bent sharply. This exposed the top of the shoe and the laces to whatever surface it might be dragged against.

The president nodded in agreement and could not help smiling, both at her enthusiasm for mystery solving and at her winsome appearance in such a pose. "A most dainty demonstration, my dear. And you have grasped my point exactly. I should have spotted the clue right away, an old river fisherman such as I am.''

"The poor man must have met his tragic fate elsewhere,

and merely been brought to that cottage to deceive us all. But if that is so, then his death was surely deliberate. Who are his killers, and what was their reason for such a crime?"

"Ah . . ." sighed Grover Cleveland. "That is a perplexing set of questions for which I presently have no answers. Perhaps a brisk ride in the mountain air will help clear our minds and give us a fresh perspective."

5
THE DOCTOR'S REPORT

The sun was descending toward the mountainous horizon by the time the carriage belonging to Senator Davis returned. Lieutenant Brockmyer was waiting for them on the gravel walk leading to the honeymoon cottage.

"Good evening, sir . . . ma'am," said he. "Did you enjoy your ride?"

"Yes, indeed," replied Grover Cleveland, looking refreshed and at peace with the world. "There is splendid scenery to be found here." He lowered his voice a bit. "You are here, I trust, to tell us what you have learned?"

"That I am, Mr. President."

Moments later the three of them were cozily ensconsced in the parlor.

"Now then, Lieutenant," said the president, "what did you learn from the editor of the *New York Evening Post*?"

"I have his answer to my wire right here," replied Brockmyer, drawing a folded telegram from his pocket and extending it to the president. "Unfortunately, it ain't much help. The editor didn't know what story this Finley fellow was working on up here. Finley hadn't wanted to say much until he had more facts, or some such reason."

Cleveland read through the telegram himself. "Tell me, did your wire to the editor explain the full circumstances of Finley's death?"

"Not how he was found, exactly. Just that it appeared accidental, but that we were takin' a look into the matter in case there might be foul play."

"I see," said Cleveland. "Well, then, how about the doctor? Did he find anything of interest?"

Brockmyer again fished through his pockets. "I have his report here. I had him sign and date it, and I witnessed it myself."

"Good fellow."

"You may have some trouble reading it. It's handwritten, and you know how doctors are. Anyway, he confirmed what we guessed about the man's broken neck and arm, and he also found blood on the side of Finley's head, the side that was on the ground. He said he must have died late last night, maybe near midnight, although he couldn't be positive."

"So I see." Cleveland pointed to a paragraph near the end of the statement. "And what does this refer to?"

Brockmyer leaned over to read it. "Oh yes, the bruises and splinters. The doc found some fresh bruises on the inside surfaces of Finley's shins and knees, which is a little hard to figure. And there were some splinters under his fingernails, too."

"What sort of splinters?"

"Old wood, with paint on it. Maybe he tried to grab at something, like the window frame, when he was falling."

The president stroked his chin thoughtfully. "Yes, that would make sense. But as I recall, the cottage where the man was found is not yet painted. The wood is bare."

Brockmyer frowned, his eyes unconsciously shifting toward the unfinished building that was beyond his view. "Yes, sir. You're right. There is no paint there. So them splinters must have come from someplace else."

"That fits in with something my wife and I were discussing earlier," the president told him, then proceeded to explain his theories about the dried blood and the muddy shoelaces. "I'm convinced the man died elsewhere and was brought to where we found him. But I must confess, the matter of the bruises puzzles me, too."

"A tree," Frances Cleveland interjected suddenly. She had been pondering everything silently until now, but her lovely young face lit up with revelation. "Yes, a tree! When I was a child, going to school, a couple of the boys were real tree climbers. They were always getting bruises on their legs from shinnying up tree trunks. Perhaps Mr. Finley had to climb a tree for some reason.''

"An excellent thought," replied Cleveland. "That may be just what he did."

Brockmyer nodded. "Yes, but I don't think he'd have needed to climb any trees at that cottage. There are no doors hung yet, and the stairs to the second floor are finished. It would've been easy for him to get up there. So . . . the place he got the splinters may be where he climbed something."

Cleveland said, "Tell me, Lieutenant, do you know if Mr. Finley had a room at the hotel?"

"Yes, sir, he did."

"I should very much like to take a look at it. Might that be possible?"

Brockmyer gave the president a wink. "For you, sir? I'd be very much surprised if it wasn't! And if *I* can't arrange it, I am sure a word from Mr. Garrett will smooth the waters. When would you like to go?"

Cleveland glanced at the mantel clock. "About thirty minutes from now, if you can set it up. My wife and I can stroll over there for a little tour of the hotel before dinner. And I hope we can manage to avoid having the good gentlemen of the press tagging along to Finley's door. As much as I want to play square with them, I do not wish to alert the killers to our suspicions."

"Just leave it to me, sir."

"Excellent! We shall see you at half-past six, then."

After the valet showed Brockmyer out, Grover Cleveland turned to his young wife and arched an eyebrow in amusement.

"So, Frank, you know about shin bruises from the wee lads in school?"

Frances Cleveland gave her husband a rueful pout and a retaliatory tweak in the ribs. "All right, perhaps I did climb a tree or two in my childhood. I just did not wish to admit it to Lieutenant Brockmyer. A young lady may keep some secrets, may she not?"

"Indeed she may. And should," replied her husband.

6
THE MISSING KEY

"Heads up, lads," warned Murphy. "They're on the move again."

The gang of reporters gathered at the pavilion came swiftly alert. All eyes were riveted to the front of the honeymoon cottage as the president and Mrs. Cleveland emerged and descended the steps to the gravel walk. The celebrated two-some walked casually, nodded their greetings to the constables on duty, and headed along the roadway in the direction of the big hotel owned by the Baltimore and Ohio Railroad.

"Out for an evening stroll," remarked the young reporter near Murphy. "The president has certainly been more visible today."

"Yes, lad, he's become a citizen of the world again. Since he seems to be talking more freely with people, perhaps he will favor us with a word or two. Come on."

The Clevelands and their entourage reached the hotel in a matter of minutes. It was a sprawling Victorian resort, entirely of wood, with cupolas and gingerbread trim. Bellhops and hotel staff came alert as the distinguished guests entered the lobby, trailing a crowd of newsmen who were growing ever more eager and aggressive. Cleveland and his bride took in the view, admiring the crystal chandeliers, the brocaded silk covering the wall panels, and the fine Oriental carpets.

At that moment, the general manager of the hotel rushed forward, exuding charm, efficiency, and solicitousness.

"Greetings to you, sir, and lady. Welcome to our hostelry. Please allow me to show you both around? . . ."

Grover Cleveland shook his hand warmly. "We would be delighted."

The hotel manager escorted them through the lobby, then led them back to the corridor off which the two rooms of telegraph operators were sending their click-clacking messages. At a pace that was straightforward without seeming hurried, the manager next led them to the great dining room, creating quite a stir among those diners present.

Still following as the president and his wife crossed the

dining room were the reporters, but as they neared the swinging doors of the kitchen itself, the hotel manager dropped back to confront them with polite but firm words.

"I am indeed sorry, gentlemen," said he, "but while we must certainly make an exception in the president's case, the hotel does not allow *anyone* else to enter the kitchen other than our staff. You do understand, I am sure."

As if to underscore his words, several burly waiters took up positions by the doors, closing off that path to the reporters.

Inside the impressive kitchen, Grover Cleveland paused, inhaled deeply of the delectable aromas, and closed his eyes in reverence. But he quickly opened them again and with a shake of his head exclaimed, "Ah well. To work!"

Close at the heels of the hotel manager, the Clevelands strode at march tempo straight through the center of the kitchen, passing the cooks in their white uniforms and aprons, leaving them at attention and gaping after the swiftly disappearing couple. The president smiled and nodded to the kitchen staff, but his attention was clearly centered upon the exit door.

Lieutenant Brockmyer waited at that door, holding it open for them and smiling broadly. As they reached him, he said, "Neatly done, sir . . . ma'am."

"A splendid plan," Cleveland told him, adding a firm pat on the back. "Lead on!"

Brockmyer now took them quickly through a back corridor to the service elevator, which stood open and waiting. A creaking ascent in the spartan conveyance brought them to the third floor, and the lieutenant held the metal-work gate open as the president escorted his wife out into the hall.

"It's just down here a ways, sir," directed Brockmyer, walking with them at a brisk pace. Indicating a temporary workman's barrier separating their portion of the corridor from the public access, he added, "We shouldn't be disturbed for a while."

"You have done well, sir," Cleveland told him with an appreciative chuckle.

Reaching the door to the room with conspiratorial stealth,

the three gathered close around it. Brockmyer produced a hotel key.

"Got this from the manager," he said softly.

He worked the lock and swung it open, peering inside to be sure the room was deserted as it should be. There was enough fading daylight coming through the window to provide illumination.

Brockmyer stepped in quickly and motioned the president and Mrs. Cleveland inside, then closed the door. He turned the gaslights up to full brightness.

"There, that's better," he remarked.

The room was small, but attractive. It contained a bed, a small writing table with chair, a bureau, and a wooden wardrobe.

Grover Cleveland looked around the room, his blue eyes alert. His brow was knitted in a frown and he chewed his lower lip.

"What exactly are you looking for, sir?" asked Brockmyer.

"I wish I knew." Cleveland strode to the wardrobe and opened the doors. The cabinet was empty save for the bare hangers. The president next studied a small suitcase on the floor near the bed. He picked it up, placed it upon the bed, and opened it. Inside were a few items of clothing, a razor, and some toiletry articles.

"It looks to me," said the president, "as if Mr. Finley was either ready to leave, or that he had no idea when he might have to leave and was living out of his suitcase."

"Yes," replied his wife, standing beside him. "I have done that on some trips myself." She peered into the suitcase, gingerly moving items of clothing aside with her fingers. "Mr. Finley does not appear to have been a very neat packer. His possessions look as if they have been thrown in haphazardly."

"So they do," Cleveland said. "Perhaps he was in a hurry. Or . . . tell me, Lieutenant, is it possible someone else has been here before us and searched his things?"

"The manager knew nothing about that. No one else asked for the key."

"But locks may be picked by someone industrious enough,

and even the unskilled may gain entry to a hotel room by bribing a maid or porter.''

"True enough, sir,'' Brockmyer admitted grudgingly. "Shall I question the staff?''

"Yes, later, if you would, please. And tell me, do you recall if there was a key for the room on the man's person? I do not recall seeing one among his personal effects.''

The lieutenant frowned in thought. "No, sir. Now that you mention it, I don't think there was one.''

"Here—'' called out Frances Cleveland "—could this be it?''

She held aloft a key with a brass tag attached to it. It was identical to the one used by Brockmyer to unlock the door moments earlier.

Brockmyer said, "Where did you find that?''

"In the bottom of the suitcase, beneath the clothing.''

"Strange,'' replied the president. "I can imagine his forgetting to take his key with him, but I cannot believe he would have put it in his suitcase. I think you can forget about questioning the staff, Lieutenant. It is likely Mr. Finley had this key on his person when he died, and the killer, or killers, took it to gain entry to his room. I suspect that after their search, in their haste to straighten up, they gathered up the key with the clothes and threw all into the suitcase.''

Brockmyer nodded. "But we don't know if these rascals found what they were looking for. We don't even know *what* they were looking for.''

Cleveland sighed deeply. "That is all too sadly true. That knowledge would likely give us the men's identities and the motive for their murderous act.''

The president began to pace about the small room, his lower lip set in a pout as his eyes studied everything again and again. "I cannot for the life of me imagine what it is, but I feel certain there is something missing here.''

"Money?'' asked his wife.

"No, I don't think so. Though you are right, dear. Mr. Finley did seem to be suffering from a lack of funds. Lieutenant, could you find out if he kept anything in the hotel safe, or perhaps in a deposit box?''

"Yes, sir. Certainly."

"Excellent. Now I think we should return to our staged tour before the gentlemen of the press become suspicious."

"A wise idea, Mr. President," Brockmyer agreed, going to the gaslights to turn them down. He then opened the door cautiously and peered down the hall. "The coast is clear, sir."

The three of them quickly retraced their steps to the service elevator and through the kitchen. Their abrupt reappearance caught some of the reporters off guard.

"You have a fine kitchen, sir," Cleveland announced to the hotel manager, and to all those within earshot.

"Thank you, Mr. President."

"President Cleveland!" called one of the reporters. "May we have a statement, sir? Your opinion of Deer Park would be of interest to our readers."

Cleveland nodded agreeably. "I am more than pleased with my visit. The scenery is charming; the air is invigorating; my health has never been better, and I find the people extremely courteous."

"And you, Mrs. Cleveland," queried the reporter, "is your view the same?"

Frances Cleveland glanced at her husband with a smile that was at once breathless and ironic. "Why, yes. I did not dream I would have so good a time."

Murphy of the *New York Herald* now voiced a question. "Mr. President, it has been reported that you were opposed to the presence of newspapermen at Deer Park. May I ask if you ordered the cordon of police and sworn constables to be placed about your house for that reason?"

Grover Cleveland's eyes narrowed slightly, but his expression remained pleasant and patient. "No, I did not order the guards. I did request strict privacy. I suppose that the railroad company, in their desire to serve me, has placed the constables on duty and given them orders to allow no person to venture within the lines. So far, the reporters here have been gentlemen, and I thank them for the kind words their journals have printed about me. And now, if you will excuse us, my wife and I shall return to our cottage."

* * *

Back in the hotel dining room, at a table not far from the path taken by the honeymoon couple and their tagalongs, sat two well-dressed men at their dinner. They were sheltered by a bank of potted palms, and they strove by their manner and their low voices to attract as little attention as possible.

"That was close," said the man on the left, the white-haired gentleman with the gold signet ring. "Far too close. That workman on the third floor nearly saw us leaving Finley's room. I do not care for the way things have progressed. I think they suspect foul play."

"Suspecting and knowing are two different things," replied the man on the right. "And even if they do know, they still cannot prove anything, or even begin to know what our true plans are. So relax, my friend."

"Relax? How can I relax? I tell you, I am certain they are watching the train station."

The other man leaned closer, a firmness and a hint of menace in his tone. "And I tell *you*, it does not matter. We cannot leave for the moment, anyway. Not until we have assured ourselves and the others that Finley's notes are not left lying about. Are you certain there was nothing hidden in his bag?"

"Yes, quite certain." The fellow blotted his forehead with his handkerchief. "What about the dresser drawers? You checked those?"

"There was nothing there, either."

The first man sipped his coffee. "I wonder if he may not have simply kept it all in his head. There may be nothing else written down."

"Perhaps, but we must make sure. There is too much at stake now. Much too much at stake . . ."

The romantic strains of a piano concerto by Schumann filled the parlor that evening. Alive with music, bathed in the gaslights' mellow glow, the room was indeed a cozy place amid the night-drenched forest setting. In the room just beyond, the dinner dishes had been cleared away. The servants had retired for the night.

Frances Cleveland sat before the piano, her touch upon the ivory keys accomplished and sensitive as she played. She looked up from the keyboard and smiled as her eyes met those of her husband.

Grover Cleveland sat upon the sofa in a pose of utter comfort and contentment. Surrounding him were the various belongings of John Finley that Lieutenant Brockmyer had brought over earlier. Listening to the soothing music, the president let his mind wander as he reexamined the evidence. He turned the notepad over in his hands several times, then picked up the eyeglass case. He pulled the glasses out and held them up before his eyes to peer through the lenses, then put them away again. Next he picked up the binoculars, examining their workmanship and the quality of the leather grips.

His wife kept up her playing, but asked, "Have you found something?"

"I'm not sure," Cleveland replied. "This is an expensive pair of field glasses, though. That much is certain. They are well made, and they . . ." The president hesitated, frowning as his eyes left the binoculars and rose to stare at his wife. "Frank, I think I know what was missing from Finley's hotel room. There was no case for these. None at all, nor was there one found with the late Mr. Finley. Yet they have hardly a scratch. He could not have carried them around without a case and kept them in such fine condition."

"Do you think the killers took the case from his room?"

"Perhaps," Cleveland muttered, looking through the lenses with sudden curiosity and adjusting the focus upon the flowers at the far end of the dining room. After a moment, he set them down again, snatched up the pocket case, and withdrew the spectacles to examine them more closely. "Humph! There is something odd here. I rather doubt the field glasses belong to Finley at all. Both lenses are set the same, for a man with normal vision. But a glance through his glasses convinces me that Finley was nearsighted in his right eye."

Mrs. Cleveland softened her playing but did not lose track of the melody. "But was he not found with the glasses tucked away in his pocket?"

"Indeed he was."

"Well, then, I would think he could not have been looking

through those binoculars, even though they were found so conveniently near his hand.''

"They were probably placed there as part of the deception. Which means they belong to one of the men responsible for Finley's death. That may tell us something useful.''

His wife finished her song and rose from the piano. ''Well, *I* think it would be useful for you to get your mind off such things and think about something else for a while. There are comfortable chairs just waiting out there on the piazza, and a sky full of stars. Could we not spend an hour there before bedtime?''

Cleveland rose from the sofa and reached out his arms to encompass her. ''Your wish is my command, dear girl.''

7
THE NEW PUZZLE

Saturday, June 5—

At half-past seven in the morning, an early caller began rapping on the door of the shaded cottage across the way from the one rented by the president and first lady. It was the very same cottage where a tight-lipped group of men had been observing the comings and goings of reporters and police guards around the Clevelands' cottage.

The rapping continued imperatively, but with a speed that suggested nervousness on the part of the person knocking. A space in the window blinds snapped open and eyes peered out, sizing up the man who waited outside. After a moment's delay, the door swung open.

Framed in the shadowy doorway stood a large man in a tweed business suit. He glared out impatiently at the early caller, and also glanced past him, as if fearful there might be others with him.

''Yes?''

''Sorry to disturb you, sir,'' said the caller, a youngish man wearing a belted coat and slacks. A soft cap covered a wealth of dark, wavy hair. His well-waxed mustache curled up toward ruddy cheeks and alert dark eyes. "It's just that I was instructed to deliver this message to you."

The man in the doorway eyed the proffered envelope suspiciously. "Instructed? By whom?"

"I don't know, sir. The gentleman merely gave me the message and paid me to deliver it."

The cottage-dweller hesitated a moment longer, then took the envelope brusquely. "Paid you, did he? Well, then, sir, you won't be expecting a tip, will you?"

The caller was already beginning to back away. "Well, no sir . . . it . . . it isn't necessary. Good day to you."

He touched the short brim of his cap and quickly turned to leave. His long, easy stride carried him away from the cottage and he soon disappeared from view among the trees and other foliage.

The man in the cottage stepped back inside and closed the door quickly. Returning to the parlor, he was met by two other men, one dressed, the other clad in expensive silk pajamas and a burgundy brocade robe.

"What is it?" inquired the older man in the robe, rubbing at his sleep-filled eyes. His white hair was mussed.

"Trouble, I'd be willing to bet," replied the first man grimly. He tore open the envelope and wrenched out the folded letter within. His narrowing eyes quickly scanned the message scrawled upon the sheet of paper, then slowed to read it again. Finally, he crushed the sheet in a fist that trembled with barely controlled anger.

"My word, man!" said the other suited fellow. "What has happened? Tell us!"

"The last thing we needed, gentlemen. This entire thing is fast slipping out of our control. And I can tell you this, if we do not keep our wits about us and take the steps needed, it could end in the destruction of us all."

At two minutes past eight that same morning, Grover and Frances Cleveland emerged from their cottage to greet a new day. The president was dressed in a comfortable coat and slacks, his ever-present tie jauntily fastened at his throat. His wife wore a light morning dress of thin, soft muslin. Pinned at her waist was a small bunch of wild flowers that her confidential maid had picked for her.

Their morning stroll carried them through the woods behind their rented cottage, and once they had reached a point where they were no longer visible to the band of reporters staking out the pavilion, they angled toward the unfinished cottage whose property was not far from theirs.

"So this is where the unfortunate Mr. Finley was found?" Frances Cleveland said as they neared the structure.

"The very spot," replied her husband, gesturing at the ground where the body had lain.

"What a pity he cannot tell us what truly happened."

"With words he cannot, but in a way he has already set us looking in the right direction."

There was an abrupt scraping sound, soft but alarming in the early morning stillness. It was immediately followed by a dull clank that seemed to come from somewhere around the corner of the uncompleted cottage. Mrs. Cleveland gave a small gasp, looking for the source of the sound, and drawing near to her husband. The president put a sheltering arm around her.

In the next moment, Lieutenant Brockmyer appeared around the corner of the building. His coat was off; his sleeves were rolled up. In one hand he carried a sturdy shovel; in the other he held a parcel. He hesitated a bit in his long, even stride as he caught sight of the Clevelands, then he continued on toward them with the same steady pace.

"Morning, Mr. President. Morning, ma'am," Brockmyer said courteously as he reached them and set down his burdens. "Hope I didn't give you a start."

Grover Cleveland relaxed, but his friendly smile did not hide a certain caution and curiosity. "Perhaps you did. A little. I didn't expect to see you here."

Brockmyer dusted his hands and rolled down his shirt sleeves. "I came on over to take another look. I've had the feeling that something ain't right with this whole thing. And as it turns out, I've found something my sergeant and I both missed yesterday."

"Indeed?" replied the president. "These things here?"

Mrs. Cleveland leaned forward to look. "You think they are connected with the murder?"

"Well, ma'am, I don't see how they could help but be connected."

Brockmyer bent to turn the parcel on the ground. They could see now that it was a loosely wrapped bundle made of oilcloth, resembling a small tarpaulin. It appeared to have been hastily tied with a length of wire, rusty in spots, and something bulky reposed unseen within.

"It was unwrapped when I found it," Brockmyer told them. "I just wrapped it back up quick to bring it over to show you."

The lieutenant untied the wire and laid back the folds of oilcloth. There in the center of the bundle was an ornamented wooden case which looked to be about nine by twelve inches, and four inches deep. The outer surfaces were lacquered and bore inlaid border designs. In the center of the lid was a small Christian cross inlaid in ivory. Brockmyer picked up the box and held it out for the president to inspect.

Grover Cleveland turned it over in his hands. He worked the tiny latch and raised the lid. Velvet of a rich blue hue lined the interior of the box, which was compartmentalized. Marks upon the velvet showed where objects had lain, but the case was completely empty.

"It is surely a jewelry case," remarked Mrs. Cleveland. "And handsomely made."

"Yes," agreed her husband. "There is only some mold about the edges to diminish its fine appearance."

"That's from being buried," Brockmyer replied. "It was probably wrapped well, but not well enough to keep moisture out."

President Cleveland frowned. "Buried? But did you not just now dig it up with that shovel?"

"No, sir. Somebody else did that. And I'm afraid they used the shovel for more than just diggin'. There's some blood on the back of the blade, and I'd be willin' to wager it's Finley's."

"Where did you find these things, Lieutenant?"

Brockmyer gestured behind him. "Over alongside the building, sir. The box and wrapping were lying under some pieces of lumber, and the shovel was nearby. There was a small hole dug near the foundation. I suspect that's where the box was until the other night.''

Grover Cleveland shook his head glumly. "Something like this turning up here, so close to where the body was found, cannot be mere coincidence. And yet it seems to throw my theory of the murder taking place elsewhere into a cocked hat! If Finley *was* killed at another location and brought here to make it seem an accident, then it would make no sense for the killer to bring the murder weapon along and abandon it. No sense at all.''

"I'm afraid not, Mr. President," Brockmyer agreed, almost apologetically. "And there's something else, too." The lieutenant stepped to where the body was found the morning before and pointed at a large dark spot on the ground. "There's a lot of blood there, where Finley's head rested. The dirt was loose, so it didn't spread a lot. You wouldn't have seen it yesterday. I didn't until we moved him. At the time I didn't think anything about it, but when I saw it this morning I remembered what you said about the blood on his chin lookin' like it dried with him upright. But if he was already dead when the killers brought him here, then . . .''

"Then," concluded the president, bending to examine the ground, "there shouldn't be fresh blood here. I can see that it has crystallized around the dirt, and soaked in deeply.''

Frances Cleveland averted her eyes from the darkened blotch on the ground. "But what can this jewelry case have to do with bringing a reporter here on a story so mysterious he cannot tell his editor? Why should he be killed over such a thing?''

"Indeed," said Grover Cleveland. "This grows more puzzling, more frustrating, the deeper into it we go. It's like waiting for the election returns to be telegraphed in, state by state. One moment you seem to be winning, then the next thing you know, your opponent slips ahead." He straightened from his examination of the ground and cast an eye upon Brockmyer once more. "Tell me, Lieutenant, are you familiar with the history of this area?''

"No, sir. Me and some of the other men, we were brought

in last week at the railroad's request. What did you want to know?''

Cleveland handed the jewelry case back to Brockmyer. ''I was just wondering how this ties in with Deer Park, since it seems to have been buried here for some little time. Perhaps if we knew to whom the box belonged, it would provide a clue.''

''I see your point, sir. Perhaps the mayor or some of his people may know. I'll be happy to inquire.''

''If you would, please. The more we find out, the better.''

Brockmyer examined the lid of the jewelry case, his expression becoming sheepish. ''I . . . I hate to suggest such a thing, but with this cross on the case, you don't suppose it could have anything to do with any of those Methodist gentlemen attending that convention, do you?''

''I rather doubt it,'' replied the president. With a trace of a smile he added, ''Granted, they may be sore at me for not arranging to meet with them, but I cannot believe they were enraged to the point of slaying innocent newspapermen.''

The lieutenant gave a short chuckle, then fought to regain his sober look. ''Yes, sir. I'm sure you're right. I'll show this to the mayor as soon as his office opens. Is there anything else you'd like me to do this morning?''

''No, Lieutenant. Just have your man maintain his watch at the train station. In truth, I don't know who to suggest he look for, but if there is anyone suspicious, I would like to know.''

''Yes, sir. Oh, and I checked with the hotel manager last night. Finley didn't have any cash or anything else locked up with them.''

With that, the president bade the lieutenant good day and escorted his bride back to their cottage. The time was roughly half-past eight.

At the pavilion some two hundred yards away, the reporters were well settled in for the new day, though some were still yawning and others were munching on breakfast rolls carried from the hotel dining room.

Murphy was sporting a fresh shirt and a jacket and hat that were carefully dusted. He had a pocket full of pencils and a new pad tucked under one arm as he used his pocket knife to clean his fingernails one by one. He whistled merrily to himself.

The young reporter who had made it a practice to take up a post next to Murphy's spot glanced over at his fellow journalist and said, "What are you so happy about?"

"Ah, what's not to be happy about, lad? The weather is pleasant, the scenery delightful, and I had a good night's sleep and a hearty breakfast. Besides, I'm in a good mood because I shall have a personal interview with the president and his missus today."

"Really? How did you arrange that?"

"In point of fact, I haven't yet. But Cleveland offered last night to see any of us that asked for an interview and made known the paper for which we work, and I intend to take him up on it."

The young man gave a skeptical grunt. "It may not be that easy!"

Murphy flashed a sly wink. "Just you wait and see, lad. Now, what have you seen happening over there so far?"

"Well," replied the young man with a marked lack of enthusiasm, "you already know about their morning walk, and that breakfast came at nine o'clock, judging by the appearance of the hotel waiters. The president came out on the piazza about nine-thirty. He's been smoking a cigar and reading a newspaper—" he cast a wry look at Murphy "—not necessarily the *New York Herald*."

Murphy laughed out loud. "Well, he's a man of good taste, so it's very *likely* the *Herald*." He squinted in the direction of the small piazza at the front of the cottage. "What's that he's doing now?"

The young reporter raised his binoculars to his eyes and directed his aim at the stout figure seated on the piazza. A glassy glint of light sparkled back at him, and he was startled to see, seemingly at close range, that the president was looking back at him through binoculars of his own.

"My word, he's watching *us*!"

" 'Tis only fair," said Murphy.

"At least, he was," continued the young reporter. "Now

he seems to be looking across the valley. I wonder why he's doing that.''

Across the way, Grover Cleveland turned slightly in his seat as he heard his wife step out onto the piazza. He started to rise, but she motioned for him to remain seated and moved to take a chair next to his. Her eyes glanced quizzically at the binoculars in his hand.

''Are those the ones belonging to Mr. Finley?'' she said, adding a small, qualifying gesture of her delicate hand. ''Or whomever?''

''Yes, Frank. I've just been using them to look at the other cottages in the area. I know my first theory seems to have gone awry, but I can't put it out of my mind. I read the doctor's report again and noticed that he specified the actual color of the paint on the wood splinters found under the man's nails. It was yellow. I've discovered there are exactly three cottages with trim painted that color.''

''That narrows it down a little,'' said she.

''Ah, but,'' replied her husband, ''if we take into account your splendid theory of Mr. Finley's tree climbing, then it narrows it down quite a lot, for there is only one cottage of the proper color which has a tree growing close enough to it to provide access to an upper floor.''

Mrs. Cleveland gave him a smile and an enthusiastic pat on the arm. ''That is sound reasoning. You have a real talent for this.''

The president sighed. ''Alas, it is all nothing more than supposition, which as every lawyer knows is next to worthless. Especially given the evidence Lieutenant Brockmyer discovered this morning. Finley must have been killed where he was found. And that invalidates everything else.''

''I'm afraid that's not all.'' Frances Cleveland was holding something in her hand, and she now presented it to her husband. ''I was looking at that notepad, the one with the missing pages, and I remembered a silly little trick someone showed me once.''

Grover Cleveland took the pad with a curious frown. ''There are words here.''

''Yes, I shaded across the top sheet of paper with the flat

of my pencil lead, and the indentations from the previous page's writing show what was there.''

The president angled it to get a better view. Gray streaks ran laterally across the page, while the words themselves were the white of blank paper.

''It's faint,'' said Cleveland. ''But it looks like . . . *inside man, Kol, has key to box, Pruett at Midwestern will back up story of transfer, barons ante up, they joke about ruination of TP*. . . .''

Frances leaned forward in her chair, her intent gaze on the notepad. ''That's what I thought it said, too. Do you suppose the *key to box* refers to the jewelry case Lieutenant Brockmyer found?''

''That is hard to say. It is certainly a box, with a lock, and it is clearly connected with the case. But if that is the explanation, then who are these men the notes refer to?''

''Or women,'' Mrs. Cleveland added wryly.

The president gave a grudging nod of assent. ''At any rate, this is beginning to look like some large criminal conspiracy, and not at all the simple case it once seemed.''

''So . . .'' she looked at him demurely ''. . . are you ready to give it up and leave the matter to other hands?''

Cleveland gazed deeply into his wife's eyes. ''I am certainly tempted to, if only to spend more of our time together here on pleasanter things.'' His lower lip acquired a resolute set to it. ''But I want you to know one thing, Frank. You have not married a quitter.''

''Good,'' said she, squeezing his hand and planting a prim kiss upon his cheek. ''Neither have you.''

The president chuckled warmly, then consulted his pocket watch. ''It is nearly ten o'clock. Let us see if the lieutenant has found out anything yet.''

8
THE FISHING TRIP

Brockmyer was standing by the rustic bridge below the cottage. The spot had become the informal headquarters for those of the Maryland constabulary on guard duty there, and both Brockmyer and another detective speaking with him came to attention as they saw the president and his bride approach.

"Hello again, Lieutenant," said Grover Cleveland as they came to a stop before the bridge. "I was just wondering, have you had a chance to investigate that matter of which we spoke earlier?"

"Indeed I have, sir," Brockmyer replied, pulling a small notepad from his pocket. "I came from Mayor Latrobe's office not more than fifteen minutes ago. He and the village sheriff feel certain they know the significance of the fancy box we found."

"*You* found," Cleveland corrected with a smile. "I do not wish to take credit for another man's diligence."

Brockmyer shrugged. "Well, sir, if not for you, I'd have most likely given up looking for evidence yesterday. At any rate, Mayor Latrobe feels the jewel box must belong to Emmaline Worthington. She's a wealthy matron who stays here frequently in Deer Park, and she reported a similar box missing after a robbery."

"When was this robbery?"

"Late September, last year." The lieutenant glanced at his notes. "It was the end of the season, and the new cottage foundation had been started then, so the timing seems right. The lady claimed there was about four or five thousand dollars' worth of jewelry in the box when it turned up missing."

"Now only the jewelry is missing," said Mrs. Cleveland. "It appears the thief dug it up and discarded the case."

"Yes, ma'am," Brockmyer replied. "It does look that way."

The president frowned. "Was there a suspect?"

"At the time, the lady felt certain the hotel maid was involved, but there'd never been any trouble with the girl before. The only other visitor to Mrs. Worthington's room the day before she noticed the jewelry missing was some professor of divinity whose acquaintance she had made here, but he allowed his room and luggage to be searched when they questioned him. With that, and his background and all, there seemed to be no reason to suspect him or prevent him from leaving. Or so they thought.''

"I take it you are not convinced, then?''

"No sir,'' said the lieutenant. "The reason I ain't is because I spent some time in Baltimore last October, and the city police there told me about a fellow they had in the hoosegow name of Jack Straker. He's a thief and a confidence man. A real sharper, preys on the rich folk; a brain type that hasn't ever been caught with the goods. But the Baltimore johnnies, they had him on some minor charge and meant to keep him locked up for awhile.''

"So,'' Cleveland asked, "you think the so-called professor of divinity may have been this Straker fellow?''

"It wouldn't surprise me. He was said to be quite an actor. They called him Angel Jack, 'cause he looked as innocent as a lamb, no matter how big the lie. Men like that come to no good end.''

"Indeed,'' agreed Cleveland. "Though some of them get elected to Congress. Well, if what you believe is true, then we may assume that either Straker or a confederate of his is responsible for digging up the buried jewelry box.''

Frances raised a pretty eyebrow. "And the murder of Mr. Finley?''

"Perhaps,'' replied her husband. "Perhaps. Yet . . . Lieutenant Brockmyer, what is your experience in such matters? From what I've seen, confidence men are seldom killers.''

The Maryland officer folded his arms and chewed his lip a bit. "True enough, sir. They don't often resort to physical violence. But if Finley surprised him in the act of digging up his ill-gotten loot, then maybe he did.''

Grover Cleveland sighed heavily. "Unfortunately, that still leaves us with the dilemma of explaining why Finley was there at all. Tracking a Baltimore confidence man does not seem his style. His articles before have dealt with larger issues. Anyway, you have done a fine job, Lieutenant. Do you think you could find out if Straker was released, or if he had any partners?''

"Yes, sir. I'll wire the Baltimore police right away.''

"Good fellow. I appreciate your help. Oh, one other thing. Do you happen to know if someone owns, or is renting, that

cottage over there? The one with the yellow trim, two buildings over from the Davis cottage.''

Brockmyer turned to look back in that direction, shielding
his eyes from the morning sun. "I believe I heard that one
belongs to Russell Sage, the big financier from New York
City. Can't say as I've seen him in town, though.''

"All right. Thank you, Lieutenant.'' Cleveland fell silent
a moment as he saw a few of the local townsfolk coming
toward them, and a small regiment of reporters approaching
also. "Well, it seems we are drawing a crowd, Mrs. Cleveland. Shall we face them, or would you prefer to return to
our cottage?''

"Oh, let's sit out here a while and chat with them. I think
that would be pleasant.''

The president sat beside his wife on one of the rustic
benches there. He lit a fresh cigar and struck up a conversation with one of the locals, an old hunter by the name of
Browning, who was only too happy to fill them in on the
history of Deer Park. Browning spun out his narrative in sufficient detail to impress anyone interested enough to follow
it, and at sufficient length to occupy the better part of an hour.

The French chimes in the hotel tower were ringing the
noon hour in as the Clevelands accepted a new set of visitors
into their parlor. It was their second group of callers this
morning, with a purpose altogether different from the first.

Upon being ushered into the parlor by the valet, Murphy
and two other reporters found the honeymoon couple seated
upon the sofa. The table near them was covered with piles of
congratulatory telegrams, but the personal effects and other
evidence relating to John Finley's death had been put away
out of sight.

"You're a sly one, Murphy,'' whispered the young reporter, "letting me think you had an exclusive interview,
when the truth is that the president is seeing us all anyway,
in small groups!''

Murphy quietly shushed him, then said with buttery politeness, "Good day, Mr. President; you, too, Mrs. Cleveland. It is most hospitable of you to receive us.''

Grover Cleveland rose and shook hands with each of the

three newspapermen, gesturing them toward seats. The constable who had admitted them had explained they would have no more than ten or fifteen minutes of the couple's time, but Cleveland was not the sort of man to make them stand even for that short a span.

With greetings aside, the third journalist initiated the first inquiry. "It is reported, Mr. President, that you have signed certain bills passed by Congress and forwarded to you from Washington for signature. Is that true?"

"It is a mistake," replied Cleveland. "I have signed no bills, nor have I signed any legislative documents whatever. I came here to rest. I never slept better, and the air and temperature are simply delicious."

"Yes," Mrs. Cleveland agreed. "I think it a most charming place."

Murphy spoke next. "If I may ask, sir, who were the two visitors who called upon you at eleven o'clock?"

"They were the Reverend John S. Foulke and Mr. Patrick Hammel of the town of Oakland, near here. They invited Mrs. Cleveland and me to attend church services in Oakland tomorrow, and we were pleased to accept."

"Isn't Mr. Hammel the postmaster you appointed in Oakland?"

"Indeed he is."

It was the young reporter's turn now. "I suppose you will remain here for several days if you continue to like the place?"

"Oh, yes," said the president with a widening smile. "I expect to go on a fishing jaunt or two. In fact, Senator Davis plans to take us on just such a trip this afternoon."

Frances Cleveland nodded and, with an elegant twist of her wrist, said, "I intend to show him how to fish in the vogue of France, where I visited before returning for the wedding." Her light and musical laughter followed.

"But," added the president, "if I am going to keep my reputation as a fisherman, I must go where there are plenty of trout!"

"How many congratulatory telegrams have you received?"

"Hundreds, so far," Cleveland told them. "Including one from Queen Victoria. Most are, of course, from friends, public officials, a few press associations, and others in America.''

"Have you received one from James G. Blaine, your opponent in the last election?'' asked Murphy.

"No, we have not yet. I understand Mr. Elkins, who managed his campaign, has said something to him about the matter, and seeing as how I obliged Mr. Blaine with the Augusta postmastership despite the wishes of the Democrats, I cannot see why he would wish to slight us.''

Said the young reporter, "Do you think he will run against you in the next election?''

"Perhaps you had better direct that question to Mr. Blaine himself.''

Murphy leaned forward in his seat and flashed a conspiratorial smile. "He's in for a surprise if he does, sir. I have it on good authority from a prominent western Republican visiting here that the Knights of Labor are solidly against him, and mean to defeat him if he should run again. It's said they have an autographed letter in Blaine's own handwriting, stating his views on labor, that is so unjust, so narrow, so dictatorial, that publication of it would surely ruin his chances.''

Grover Cleveland tried not to look too pleased. "I hope they have it under lock and key!''

"Stashed in a safe-deposit vault, from what I hear,'' replied Murphy, joining in the laughter himself. "On another matter, sir, many of the newspapermen thought they had a good deal of difficulty in getting information about your departure from Washington on the day of the wedding.''

The president gave them a smile. "I made no secret of coming down here. I must have spoken to a dozen persons about it, and supposed it was pretty well known that I was to visit Deer Park. If any one had gone to the White House on the day of the wedding and asked, I have no doubt that the desired information would cheerfully have been given.''

"How about reading us some of your telegrams?'' queried the young reporter.

"All right. They may be of interest to the public, but I leave you to judge their value.''

* * *

By half-past one, the Clevelands had taken a brief stroll through the woods behind their cottage, had eaten their luncheon, and were now preparing for their afternoon outing with Senator Davis. The valet and maid had laid out comfortable clothing that was a shade less formal than their normal garb, and better suited to the outdoors.

"Are you sure you do not mind going, my dear?" the president was asking as he buttoned his shirt.

"On the contrary, I am truly looking forward to it," Frances Cleveland replied. "And if the fishing spot is half as pretty as the senator describes, I would hate missing it."

There was a rap on the bedroom door at that moment. Cleveland called out, "Yes?"

The valet's voice came from the other side of the closed door. "Sorry to disturb you, sir, but the lieutenant is downstairs and wishes to speak with you."

"Please admit him to the parlor and tell him we will be down in a moment or two."

"Yes, sir."

The president finished dressing and loaded his coat pocket with fresh cigars. Out of routine, he checked the box of matches in his other pocket.

"Only one match left," he muttered to himself. "That will not do."

Of all the things he had seen to, or had someone arrange for, before their trip, laying in a supply of matches had not been one of them. Puttering about in the drawers of the bureau and side table in the vain hope of finding some that had been left behind, his eyes fell upon the small pasteboard carton containing John Finley's personal effects. The valet had brought it upstairs when preparing the parlor for visitors, and here it remained. Lying in the bottom of the carton with the wallet and notebook and other items was the box of matches he had seen earlier and promptly forgotten about.

Cleveland picked up the box of matches and turned it over in his hands a few times. He wondered briefly if there was anything wrong with borrowing a few matches from a dead man, then realized with a sigh that borrowing was the wrong term, since replacing them would be a useless gesture. Finley would not be needing them. What harm could it do?

He pushed the box's drawer open with his thumb and saw that it was nearly full of matches. He took out a half dozen or so and put them in his own matchbox, which he returned to the side pocket of his coat. Satisfied, he closed Finley's matchbox and proceeded to lower it into the pasteboard carton once more. But he hesitated as he felt a faint but distinct thump once the box was turned on its side. He had not noticed it before, and he did not think the weight of the matches was enough to account for it.

"That's odd," he mused aloud.

"What's that?" asked Frances.

"I think there's something else in here." He carried the matchbox over to where his wife stood putting the finishing touches to her wardrobe. As she looked with interest at the box, he slid the drawer open fully and dumped its contents into his palm. A small metal object glistened dully atop the pile of wooden sticks.

"It's a key!" his wife said. As her eyes flashed up to his, she added, "Do you suppose it's the key mentioned in his notes?"

"No, I think that unlikely. Still, it must be important, or why would he have hidden it beneath his matches?" Cleveland held it up and examined it. "It looks to me to be the key to a post-office box. You know, a man who traveled as much as Finley did might very well have kept a post-office box to receive his mail."

Frances's dark eyes showed a flash of enthusiasm. "Do you think there might be an important clue there?"

"There is only one way to be sure."

Moments later, Grover Cleveland and his bride were downstairs, showing their discovery to Brockmyer and explaining the significance they hoped it might have.

The lieutenant nodded as he studied the numbered key. "You may be right. Do you want me to contact the police in New York and have them check it out?"

"Let's be more direct," said Cleveland. "Especially since we are dealing with the United States mail. Please send a wire to the postmaster of New York, explaining that you are speaking on behalf of the president and urgently requesting his help. I would like the post-office box rented under John

Finley's name and this number opened, and a thorough description of the contents wired to me as soon as possible. I met a gentleman here earlier today who is the superintendent of the Baltimore and Ohio Telegraph Company. His name is Charles Selden."

"Yes, sir. He's in charge of the whole telegraph operation here during your visit."

"Take him into your confidence. Explain our investigation and see that a trustworthy operator is used to send our message and receive any reply. I do not wish to tip our hand too soon."

"Right, sir. And while we're on the subject of wires, I thought you might like to know what I found out from the police in Baltimore."

"Indeed I would!"

Brockmyer unfolded a telegram and glanced at it, but he seemed to have already committed its details to memory. "Well, sir, that fellow I told you about, Jack Straker—he's supposed to be in jail there, but he ain't. Seems the man who was sharing his cell was supposed to be released last week. And they thought he was, at first. But it turns out the other guy died of natural causes the night before, and Straker apparently changed his appearance enough to pass for him and get released in his place. So they thought they was buryin' Straker. By the time they realized their mistake, he was long gone."

"A most resourceful and opportunistic man, this Angel Jack," said the president. "Did they send a description?"

"Yes, sir, for all it helps," said Brockmyer with a sheepish grin. "They say he's a man of average height, average build and complexion, and stronger than he looks. And he's bald except for a touch of hair on the sides."

"That could be a lot of men," Frances Cleveland said with an exasperated sigh. "But we must presume he is here in Deer Park. Or was."

"Yes, indeed." Grover Cleveland shook Brockmyer's hand fervently. "Lieutenant, I truly appreciate all your assistance in this matter. My wife and I have to leave again for a few hours, but we shall return. I hope you don't mind these little errands I have set you to on our behalf?"

"No, Mr. President. To tell the truth, it beats just walkin' around out there."

"Excellent. I look forward to seeing you, then, after our return. . . ."

The carriage, drawn behind its team of handsome bays, rumbled down a road well sheltered from the sun. Arching over it along a considerable length were the branches of an ancient oak forest, their breeze-stirred leaves scattering pale green light upon the road below.

"This is so beautiful," Frances Cleveland said with child-like awe, gripping her husband's hand tightly. "Almost like the nave of a great cathedral."

In the seat before them, Senator Davis drove beside his wife. "The mountain people call it the Shade Drive. It has been widened and leveled by the railroad company, you see, and is quite pleasant now."

The carriage continued its passage along this path only a few minutes more, then the senator turned his team north-ward, passing by a mountainside and crossing a glade. A forest of pines soon surrounded them, their fragrant young buds scenting the breeze and filling it with soft whisperings. The colors and perfumes of pink laurel, mountain honey-suckle, and azaleas competed for attention, creating an ideal setting.

They quickly reached a glade rich with coarse grass and cut through by the meandering path of Deep Creek, a slug-gish stream with many pools deep and darkling.

"Now, those are trout waters if ever I have seen them!" said Grover Cleveland as he disembarked from the carriage and assisted his wife down to the ground.

"Of that you may be sure," said Senator Davis, adding with a chuckle, "besides, I have let it be known to the fish hereabouts that the president of these United States would be visiting, so that a large crowd would gather for a look!"

Grover Cleveland gave a hearty laugh and said, "Splendid! That is one crowd I shall not object to."

The senator assisted his wife from the carriage, then un-packed the tackle he brought for himself and his guests. They all set about the business of fishing, having chosen a spot on the bank near several promising pools.

"Do you need any help, my dear?" asked the president solicitously.

Frances Cleveland held a hook in one hand and a wriggling worm in the other, and answered with more determination than enthusiasm. "No, I am quite sure I can manage." She gave a light laugh at her own seeming timidity.

The party cast their lines into the water. They had good luck, pulling in several medium-sized trout in the first hour.

The president stowed his catch and, with a feeling of exhilaration, made another cast. Quite without planning, he saw his weighted hook ricochet off a large stone rising above the stream's surface and arc toward the area in which Senator Davis's line plumbed. It landed in virtually the same spot and sank out of sight.

In the next instant, before he could react and retrieve his line, there was a sudden thrashing in the water of that pool. Both lines extending out went taut, jerking with the sudden strength of an unseen opponent. As both men began to reel in their lines a large speckled trout splashed into view, flipping and writhing as they drew it to the bank.

"It seems we have caught the same fish upon our hooks," said Cleveland with an embarrassed smile.

Senator Davis let loose a good-natured laugh. "Now see here, Mr. President. You are carrying bipartisanship too far!"

The men brought the trout up between them, suspended by both lines. They disengaged the hooks and added the trout to their basket.

"It seems," said Cleveland, "that the rascal favored the prospect of two worms over one."

Davis marveled at the size of the catch and at the odd manner of it as well. "I wonder if he struck one hook or the other first, or both at once?"

The president gave a shrugging gesture. "It little matters, for the end result is the same. I tell you, Senator, we shall share the honors, and have a good story to tell in the bargain."

Frances Cleveland hurried over to see the trout and give her husband a congratulatory pat on the back. Her eyes danced with amusement as she stared at the fish, then as her gaze rose to meet her husband's, her pretty mouth froze in an odd expression.

Cleveland himself matched that look as something in his innocent words triggered a thought. His eyes widened a bit as he saw excitement flare in Frances's own gaze.

"My word, Frank!" he exclaimed. "Brockmyer and I have both been right all along! We are not dealing with a simple case of murder at all. We are dealing with two separate events—two separate, overlapping crimes."

"Murder?" breathed the senator quizzically. "But it's only a fish."

"Forgive me, sir, for interrupting a perfectly enjoyable afternoon. I shall explain everything to you on the drive back, for I suspect I shall be needing not only your kind assistance, but your advice as well before this day is through."

9
THE VILLAINS GATHER

"I do hope you and Mrs. Cleveland will take dinner with us," Senator Davis was saying in the parlor of his cottage. "Kate has her heart set on it, you see, and there's no shortage of fresh trout."

Grover Cleveland was peering through the window blinds, bent forward a bit as he stared at a cottage roughly four hundred feet away. There was an intervening building, but it was set back farther than the other and allowed a clear view. It was late afternoon now, and the sunlight was becoming golden. The president turned to look over his shoulder at his host, smiling warmly.

"It would be our great pleasure, Senator. And if you don't mind, this also affords us an opportunity to do a bit of spying."

Senator Davis gave Mrs. Cleveland a crystal goblet of ice water, and shook his head sadly. "It is hard to believe that Russell Sage is involved in murder."

"I do not know for a fact that he is," replied Cleveland,

"or if he is, to what extent. But if my theory is correct, then that cottage he owns is almost certainly the scene of some bit of dusty business. Tell me, Senator, have you seen much of Mr. Sage these past few days?"

"Nothing more than a passing greeting. He mentioned something about coming here to entertain some business friends. I have seen some other men coming and going at his cottage."

"Anyone you know?"

Davis shook his head. "I have not seen their faces well."

Frances Cleveland took a sip of water, then joined her husband at the window. She, too, peered out. "Can you see anything unusual?"

"No. Everything is quiet. Perhaps too quiet. We may have to go calling on them if we are to learn anything. But I should like to have more evidence before confronting them."

A concerned frown clouded his wife's pretty features. "I am not sure you should confront them at all. If there are dangerous men present—"

A rap on the door brought everyone's attention sharply around. Senator Davis glanced at the others in the room, then strode purposely to the door and looked through the small window set into the wooden panel. He turned to the president as his hand went for the latch.

"It's just that constable fellow. He looks agitated."

Davis opened the door and Lieutenant Brockmyer stepped through. The Maryland constable gave a perfunctory tip of his hat to the senator, but his eyes sought out the president. "Afternoon, gents . . . ladies. One of my men told me you were over here."

Grover Cleveland came toward him, leaving Frances at the window. "Lieutenant, have you received a reply?"

"I have indeed, sir. Mr. Selden himself received the message a few minutes ago. Turns out there were only a couple of letters and a bill or two in that box, but I think the one you're interested in is the one Finley mailed to himself the day he came here. The postmaster wired the contents here, word for word."

Cleveland reached out and eagerly took the folded telegram offered him by Brockmyer. He quickly scanned the lines, his eyes glistening with sudden and intense interest in a face grown terribly sober.

"This is really a page or two of his notes and not a letter," said the president. "But it sheds a great deal of light on everything, especially with another bit of information I have learned today."

"What does it say?" Senator Davis asked.

At the window, Frances Cleveland was torn between wanting to rush to her husband's side to read the message and wanting to keep watch. Her gaze was fixed for the moment upon the three men gathered about the telegram, where it had remained since Brockmyer's entrance, but now her sense of duty drew her eyes reluctantly back to the cottage beyond, where the answers to the mystery seemed to lie. As she looked once more in that direction, she was startled to observe that four men were coming out of the cottage and walking to the drive, even as a fifth man brought a carriage and team around the corner from the side of the cottage she could not see.

"Oh my!" she called out to the others. "There is something happening. I think they are leaving!"

Her husband was the first to reach her side. Brockmyer was next, and soon the senator joined them in peering through the blinds. The view that greeted them was not encouraging, for the men at the other cottage were most prompt in boarding the carriage. Their team of dark thoroughbreds whisked them off to the road and beyond view.

"Senator," Grover Cleveland said with urgency, "is your own team still hitched?"

"Why, yes."

"Splendid! Let us use your carriage and follow them!" Turning to his wife, he asked, "Frank, do you wish to stay here?"

She bristled with barely contained energy. "I do not!"

"Very well, then. Let us be off!"

The group of four hastened outside to the shady spot of the property where the senator's carriage and his son-in-law's proud team stood waiting. It took them less than a minute to board and turn the horses down the drive to the main road. The other carriage with its burden of mystery men had a good head start, and none of its passengers seemed aware that they were being followed.

"They ain't headin' for Oakland or Altamont, not goin' that way," Brockmyer declared. "Maybe the train station. There's one due to leave shortly."

"Let us keep them in sight," urged Cleveland. "But not too closely, lest we spook them."

They drove on, heading further into town. But it quickly became clear that the other carriage was not heading for the train station after all. A fact borne out in the next moment.

"They're pulling over toward the hotel," Senator Davis observed. "That seems innocent enough."

"Perhaps," said Cleveland. "Let us follow suit and see what they do."

The driver of the first carriage pulled his team to a halt at the edge of the roadway. He dismounted and tied the reins to a tether post, then joined the other men as they headed up the steps to the Baltimore and Ohio's large hotel. Several of the men were wearing hats with the brims pulled low above their eyes, and they all moved with a certain stiff formality, as if self-conscious about being seen. The driver wore a tall hat, the hair beneath it white. He looked near seventy. There was a glint of a gold signet ring upon his right hand.

"That is Russell Sage there," Senator Davis said softly as he pulled his own carriage to a halt a short distance behind the first. "I still cannot see the others well enough to swear to their identity."

Brockmyer climbed quickly out and hid his large constable badge beneath his coat. He helped Mrs. Cleveland down from the carriage and gave a steadying hand to the president.

The four of them walked at a casual pace toward the hotel, trying to appear nonchalant. Once within the luxuriously appointed lobby, they saw that the five men were entering the hotel dining room, checking their hats and asking the mâitre d' for a table.

"I am going to feel exceedingly foolish," confessed Grover Cleveland, "if they have nothing more on their minds than dinner."

"Shall we go inside, too, sir?" asked Lieutenant Brockmyer.

"I think not," said the president, glancing about cautiously. "We have been lucky thus far to have caught the press napping. That cannot last long, I am sure, and we are already drawing some attention from the hotel guests. I do not relish dragging a crowd of onlookers in there and making things more difficult for us. For now we may as well just stand near enough the door to keep an eye on those men, and pretend we are merely conversing."

They casually moved closer to the dining-room entrance and faced each other. Their faces smiled, their talk was pleasant and innocuous. But the president and Lieutenant Brockmyer were able to glance in often enough to keep the five men under surveillance.

At a large table at the far side of the room were seated Russell Sage and the other gentlemen. They all held menus before them. But their eyes seemed more intent on surveying the other faces in the room. Sage relaxed his hold on the menu and used one hand to drag out a handkerchief to blot his perspiring forehead.

"I do not understand," he said to the others in a nervous whisper. "Why should he demand that we all come here? Surely one or even two of us would be sufficient."

The man seated nearest him, two decades younger than he, gave him a hard-eyed look. Speaking softly, he replied, "It should be obvious. The fellow wants us all where he can see us."

"And so can everyone else," whined Sage. "I do not like this, J. G. Besides, once he has been paid, why should we believe he will not continue to bleed us dry?"

The other man continued to glance cautiously about. "Because once he has given us the notes and we have left Deer Park, his hold on us will diminish. It will not matter what he knows after that, and once we know who he is, we can gauge how to deal with him."

Sage and the other man fell silent now as they became aware of a waiter who was watching them. The man in the trim uniform was staring in their direction with a puzzled look, then he turned and spoke to a large man seated by himself at a table twenty feet away. The solitary diner glanced over his shoulder at the five men behind him and nodded slightly to the waiter.

"This must be it," said the gentleman next to Sage.

As they watched, the waiter left the other table and walked briskly toward theirs. Surveying the men quizzically, he bowed as he reached them.

"Good evening, gentlemen," he said hesitantly. "I . . . that is, this is not my table, but the gentleman over there has requested that I take him something you have brought. I presume you understand what this is all about?"

Sage and the others looked over to where the large man sat by himself. The fellow returned their glance, smiled, and nodded. He even raised his wineglass in a silent toast.

"The nerve of the fellow," muttered Sage.

The man next to him shushed him, reaching into a deep pocket within his coat. He extracted a thick manila envelope, seeming to weigh it for a moment, then presented it to the waiter.

"Just give him this," he directed the waiter. "We are expecting a document in return. Please ask the gentleman to deliver it in person. Here—" he added, giving the waiter a folded twenty dollar bill "—this is for your trouble."

"Thank you, sir. I shall give the gentleman your message at once."

They watched in silence as the waiter returned to the other table and, with his back to them, spoke quietly to the solitary diner. The large man nodded. As the waiter turned to head for the kitchen, he smiled and gave a gracious bow to the man who had given him the large tip.

Several minutes passed. Then several more. All the while, the solitary diner ate his meal and gave not a thought to the men who so eagerly awaited him. At last, when they could no longer bear the tension, the man next to Sage and one of the other gentlemen got up from their seats and strode brusquely toward the fellow.

The man known as J. G. confronted him, his voice low but seething with anger. "All right, sir. You have our money. Now complete the deal. We do not intend to let you leave here without giving us the promised package."

The solitary diner looked up at them blankly, swallowing hard. Gravy at the corners of his mouth quivered a bit.

"What? What's that you say?"

"Enough of your games, sir. Do you deny we've played square with you? Did not the waiter tell you to bring us what we want?"

"Why, no," replied the diner with a blank stare. "He only told me that you fine gentlemen were the owners of this hotel, and that as a gesture of kindness, you were giving me a complimentary meal, for which I nodded my gratitude. But . . . but, I shall be only too happy to pay, if there is some problem."

The two standing men exchanged looks that reflected in close succession abject bewilderment, gasping revelation, then electrifying anger. Their voices spoke as one.

"The waiter!"

Turning, they looked everywhere across the hotel dining room, but the bald-headed waiter was nowhere to be seen. The men rushed to the door leading into the kitchen. Several startled guests gasped, and a dozen cooks and assistants looked up in puzzlement at the men staring into their pristine domain.

"He's gone," said the man known as J. G. "Come on, let's get out of here."

They turned and made as orderly a retreat as they could manage, rejoining the other three men as they left the table. They clustered together nervously for a moment, exchanging accusations and low curses, then J. G. began to stare through the tall front windows of the dining room. He searched in vain for a glimpse of the waiter, then his gaze fell quite by chance upon another familiar face. His arm shot out, pointing at a tall man with black curly hair and mustache, garbed in a business suit and carrying a suitcase.

"There!" he cried. "The bearer of the original message. He may know more than he said. After him!"

There was a side exit leading out of the room, yielding direct access to the outside, and it was through this the five men now plunged. Their headlong flight could scarcely not be noticed by the foursome conversing near the proper entrance and exit.

"They are on the fly, by gad!" declared Senator Davis.

"Quickly!" said Grover Cleveland. "We must catch the lot of them, or justice may be forever foiled!"

10
THE GRAND FINALE

The five gentlemen burst out onto the open porch which ran the length of the sprawling hotel. Fifteen feet or more ahead of them was the object of their intense interest. The tall man with the black curly hair and mustache was just descending the steps leading down to the roadway before the hotel, walking briskly and carrying his small traveling bag with his arm slightly bent.

"You, sir!" J. G. shouted. "Hold up!"

The man jerked his head around in the direction of the voice, and, spying the five running men rapidly approaching, decided to do anything but wait for them. Leaping the last few steps to the ground, he clutched at his hat with one hand and began sprinting down the drive toward the train station. He could see that a locomotive and a string of passenger cars were waiting, smoke billowing from the engine's stack as the fireman stoked the fire to build up a good head of steam. He knew it would be ready to pull out momentarily. He glanced briefly at his vest pocket where the end of a ticket protruded, then set his gaze upon the platform and ran for all he was worth.

The five men set out after him in hot pursuit, clearly less suited to running than he, but making a surprisingly good show of it considering their ages. At this moment, the president and his retinue burst out from the hotel's main entrance.

"There they go!" exclaimed the president. He headed down the steps, taking them cautiously, then hurried off in the direction of the running men.

Beside him, his wife moved as quickly as she could, given the length of her skirt. Senator Davis lagged behind, already panting for breath. Only Lieutenant Brockmyer had no difficulty in keeping up with the chase.

As Brockmyer trotted away from the hotel, he paused just long enough to look in the direction of the police cordon surrounding the president's cottage. Bringing his thumb and finger to his lips, he blew a shrill note that lifted the hair on the napes of nearby necks, and caught the attention of his men. With a swift jerk of his arm, he motioned for them to join the pursuit, then he started off on a dead run after the felons.

"You go on ahead, Lieutenant," Grover Cleveland called after him. "We are not built for this sort of chase. We will catch up with you when we can."

The participants in this peculiar race stretched down the length of the tree-lined street that, like the crossbar of an H, connected the hotel boulevard with the road paralleling the tracks. Each turned the corner as they reached it, angling for the station platform.

With a great shriek of the whistle and chuffing of the pistons, the engine started forward. It moved ever so slowly at first, then gradually built up speed.

The curly-haired man reached the train first and, racing along the platform with its progress, swung up onto the step of the second from the last passenger car. He clung to the handrail for a moment, glancing back, then went up into the car.

Reaching the train five or six seconds behind him, the five men just managed to catch up with the last car. Sage halted, weary and gasping for breath, but the others grabbed the handrail and propelled themselves up into the car one after the other.

Brockmyer came running up next, closely followed by a number of his men who had taken a short cut across the field. He gestured at Sage and yelled to one of the constables, "Hold on to him!"

The lieutenant ran after the last car and managed to board it, with two of his men following suit as the train continued to roll, gaining speed. Entering the car, they caught a glimpse of the four men they pursued just disappearing through the vestibule at the front of the car.

Passengers were starting to react with surprise and concern

as these men raced through the aisle, occasionally colliding with people attempting to change seats.

Entering the next car, Brockmyer saw the men still moving forward and thought he glimpsed the fellow with the curly hair disappearing into the next car. As he raced forward along the aisle, he reached out and grasped the emergency cord, giving it a strong yank.

Wheels squalled against the rails. Several women screamed. Everyone standing gained sudden extra momentum as the brakes took hold and the train abruptly slowed. Brockmyer shot forward into the next car close on the heels of the four men he chased, and discovered that the first two of them had collapsed in a pile upon the man they themselves had pursued. They were wrestling with the fellow and grabbing for the bag he carried. In the tussle the man's hat came off, and along with it his hair. Save for the mustache, he bore a striking resemblance to the waiter who had disappeared. The resemblance was complete when one of the men tore off the false mustache.

Now the train halted completely. Brockmyer hurried forward, flipping his badge into view and drawing his revolver. Leveling it at them, and backed up by his men, he yelled to get their attention.

"Hey! That will be quite enough of that, gentlemen. Don't anybody move until we get this mess sorted out!"

It was only a matter of minutes before the president and his wife appeared within the vestibule of the car, with more constables behind them. Cleveland was huffing a bit from exertion, his face ruddy, but his sharp eyes quickly surveyed the scene before him.

"You have done an excellent job, Lieutenant," he told Brockmyer.

"Thank you, sir. Now what shall we do with all these fine gentlemen?"

"Well, since we seem to have everyone accounted for, I suggest we allow the rest of these good people to be on their way." Cleveland gestured toward the men on the floor. "Let us retire with these fellows to Mr. Sage's cottage. There we may get to the bottom of this mystery once and for all!"

* * *

Grover Cleveland paced back and forth in the parlor of Russell Sage's cottage. Sage and the other four men were seated rather uncomfortably before him, wedged into a sofa and a nearby chair and bracketed by constables standing at both ends of the group. The sixth man, the waiter/messenger, sat in another chair. He was seemingly calm and self-possessed, but Cleveland noticed the man's forehead glistened with a nervous sweat.

"You have no right to hold us!" protested the man identified as J. G. "We are not common criminals."

"Not common ones, that is true," said the president. With a glance toward Senator Davis, he said, "I believe I can guess the names of these men, Senator, but if you would be so good as to point out any whom you can identify?. . ."

Davis cleared his throat and appeared uneasy. "Why certainly, Mr. President. There is Russell Sage, of course, the financier who owns this cottage. Next to him is Jay Gould, noted capitalist. Then we have Collis P. Huntington, Leland Stanford, and Sidney Dillon. These gentlemen are the principal owners and officers of the Union Pacific, Central Pacific, Texas and Pacific, and Missouri Pacific railroads, if my memory serves correct. The other fellow who they were chasing I do not know."

"That is quite all right, Senator," said Cleveland. "I believe we may be certain he is Jack Straker, also known as Angel Jack, a thief and con artist, at the very least. Do you concur, Lieutenant?"

"I do indeed, sir," replied Brockmyer. "Maybe we should just take a look in this bag the fellow was so anxious to leave with."

The lieutenant laid the small suitcase flat upon the floor and quickly worked the latches. Inside was a variety of clothing, packed neatly. There was also a clerical collar, along with three wigs of various colors. Lying on top of a stack of shirts was a thick envelope large enough to contain a book, and beneath the underwear was a cloth pouch heavy with some bulky object or objects. Brockmyer handed the envelope to the president.

"Here, sir. This looks like the parcel we saw delivered in the hotel dining room." The lieutenant opened the pouch and reached in. He drew his hand out draped with dazzling jewelry of gold and precious stones. "I'd be real surprised if these ain't the baubles stolen from Mrs. Worthington last year!"

Breaking the seal on the envelope, Cleveland began to pull out bundles of large-denomination bills, fresh from the bank with their wrappers intact. As he stacked them upon the table nearby, he gave a low whistle of appreciation. "My word, there must be at least two hundred thousand dollars here!"

"Two hundred and fifty thousand," corrected Russell Sage, who then fell silent under Jay Gould's withering glare.

"I stand corrected," agreed Cleveland, thumbing the bundles again. "A quarter of a million, exactly. Practically a king's ransom. Perhaps you gentlemen would care to tell us just why you made such a generous gift to Mr. Straker?"

The five men glanced nervously at each other but remained silent. Jay Gould's features were especially stony.

"Nothing to say?" challenged Brockmyer. He looked next to Jack Straker. "And how about you, sir? Care to tell us how you come by this money?"

Straker gave a low snort and looked the other way.

"So," said Grover Cleveland, "no one has anything to say? Very well. I shall endeavor to compensate for this lack of conversation by putting forth what I know. First of all, I feel certain that you gentlemen and this Mr. Straker had never crossed paths until the night before last, here in Deer Park, and would not have yet were it not for a quirk of fate. Mr. John Finley of the *New York Evening Post*, on the other hand, came here specifically to follow Russell Sage and to spy on his meeting with Jay Gould and the others."

"That is idle speculation," snapped Jay Gould.

"On the contrary," spoke up Mrs. Cleveland, moving close to her husband's side, "we have been given that information by Mr. Finley himself."

The president extracted a telegram from his coat pocket, the one Brockmyer had delivered less than an hour before, and which Cleveland had shown to his wife while on their way to the Sage cottage. He unfolded it and glanced at its contents.

"We have here, sent to us by telegraph, a page of notes

written by Mr. Finley and mailed by him to his own letter box in New York." Cleveland paused, noticing worried glances among the men on the sofa. "These notes tell of a secret business meeting planned by you gentlemen while you, Mr. Sage, were in New York, and the rest of you were visiting Washington to meet with your agents and lawyers. There were apparently matters to be discussed among you in the utmost privacy, and Mr. Sage's cottage here in Deer Park was agreed upon as the rendezvous point.

"I have no doubt," the president continued, "that if you had known of my intended visit here, with its attendant publicity, you would have chosen another location, but such was not the case. At any rate, Mr. Finley's notes explain at least one important purpose of this hush-hush meeting of yours. I, at first, thought the word *kol* impressed into his notebook following a missing page referred to a man. But I now know it to be the initials of an organization Mr. Gould and the rest of you have had a great deal of trouble with this year—the Knights of Labor."

"Yes," said Senator Davis in understanding. "Those strikes that just ended May 4th. Nearly crippled two of the lines."

"The Knights leader," Cleveland went on, "Terence V. Powderly, is becoming very powerful, commanding perhaps eight hundred thousand votes, in addition to his ability to call nationwide strikes. Now, I do not have to be a genius to recognize what a threat such a man must pose to you gentlemen. And according to Finley's notes, he suspected you were plotting to take action to undermine Mr. Powderly and weaken his union.

"So Finley followed you here and set out to eavesdrop upon your meeting. I looked upstairs a few minutes ago and discovered that Mr. Sage has made one of the bedrooms into an office. No doubt the meeting took place there. There is evidence to suggest that John Finley climbed that tree which grows close to the cottage and stepped over to the balcony outside the upper windows, there to listen in on your plans. I do not know how much he heard, but the last page of his notes mentioned an inside man with the Knights of Labor, someone with access to the key to a box. Might that be the safety-deposit box, Mr. Gould, in which the Knights are holding James G. Blaine's incriminating letter? They are counting upon that as a tool in the next election.''

Jay Gould merely averted his eyes and said nothing.

"And this Pruett at Midwestern," Cleveland continued. "Might he be a bank teller at Midwestern National Bank? Have you made arrangements with him to transfer union funds to another account under Powderly's own name? And perhaps to sweeten it with some of your own money, just to make it seem he is robbing his own union?''

The president was guessing on this point, but the facial reaction he got from Russell Sage confirmed that he had guessed right. "Such a plan would take a lot of operating capital. Finley's notes describe it as 'the barons ante up.' I believe you gentlemen have often been portrayed in the press as railroad robber barons? So you pooled your funds and finalized your plans.''

"And joked," Frances Cleveland added, recalling the notebook entry, "about the ruination of TP, Terence Powderly.''

"My word," exclaimed Senator Davis. "I have heard rumors of the monies these men have spent in Washington to buy influence and favorable rulings, but such a plan as this is nothing short of scandalous!''

Grover Cleveland drew back his coat with his thumb, putting his hand upon his hip in the manner of a lawyer presenting his case. "John Finley was going to expose that plan in the columns of his newspaper, but it was his very diligence that resulted in his murder.''

"Murder? No!" Russell Sage blurted out. "It was not murder!''

"Shut up, you fool!" snapped Jay Gould.

"I shall not! Whatever indiscretions or mistakes I may have committed, I shall not stand accused of murder! I tell you all here and now, Finley's death was an accident.''

Brockmyer gave him a skeptical smirk. "An accident? Now really!''

"But it's true!" Sage was mopping at his forehead, where veins stood out against skin nearly as pale as the white of his hair. "It happened just as you said, Mr. President. Finley was indeed out on the balcony that night, listening in. But he made a noise of some sort and we discovered him there. We threw open the window and grabbed for him, but he stumbled back out of our grasp. He grabbed for the railing, but could not hold on, and . . . and he fell to the ground below. We rushed downstairs, but he was dead. There was nothing we could do.''

Cleveland gave them a stern and withering look. "And so rather than face the authorities, you carried his body over to that cottage near mine, and sought to make it look as if he had fallen out the window while spying upon my wife and me? You even placed your own binoculars there to further the deception.''

"Yes, yes,'' replied Sage. "We thought it the best thing. Under the circumstances.''

Brockmyer's gaze swung around to Jack Straker. "Now let me guess. While you fine gentlemen were disposin' of the body and discussin' your predicament, Angel Jack was waitin' to dig up his buried treasure, and heard enough to realize he could blackmail you all for more money than he'd ever dreamt of.''

"Yes,'' said Sage, with a hateful look at Straker. "It took all the money we had brought for our, ah, business meeting, and a little more besides. He threatened to tell the world we had killed the newspaperman. He knew we could not risk an investigation.''

"Indeed,'' replied the president. "But he played you for even bigger fools than you realize. For not only did he not have the other notes he claimed to possess, he also knew one important fact unknown to you: when you carried Finley over to the cottage, he was not dead! He was severely injured, and unconscious, but he was still alive.''

"Alive—?'' exclaimed Jay Gould, for the first time interested instead of merely defensive.

"Yes. I suggest he must have come to sometime after you left, and after Straker dug up the jewelry box he had buried there last September. Imagine Straker's consternation to discover that the key element to his blackmail scheme was not going to cooperate. All that money, slipping through his fingers. There he stood, shovel in hand, fresh from digging, and nothing standing in the way between him and a fortune except a body that was not dead—yet.''

"You must have swung that shovel pretty hard," Brockmyer said coldly, "to break his neck that way. The Baltimore police warned us you were strong."

"No!" cried Jack Straker, his hands gripping the arms of his chair. "He was dead already. I swear! It is they who killed him."

"Impossible," Cleveland told him. "The bleeding from Finley's head wound was too great, and it occurred after his other injuries. The blood on the shovel clinches it. You killed him, all right, Angel Jack, and you more than likely stole the money from his pockets, leaving only a few dollars and some coins to make it seem less like robbery."

The confidence man turned killer sagged in his chair, his actor's mask giving way to the look of a fearful and beaten man. "Should have stuck to fleecing old ladies and frails," he muttered to himself.

Brockmyer directed one of his men to place manacles upon Straker. Then he approached the president with a whispered question.

"May I speak with you outside, sir?"

The president nodded, and he and his wife followed the lieutenant out of the parlor and onto the front walk. Facing the Maryland constable, he said, "Yes?"

"Well, sir," began Brockmyer, "I think you've done a first-rate job, and there ain't no doubt we've got enough on Straker to see him hang for his crime. But what I'm wondering is, what we should do with those other gents. Are they guilty of anything?"

"I am sure they are guilty of quite a lot," replied Cleveland. "But not of murder, in this case. I suggest you present the facts and evidence as you have it to the Maryland state attorney and let him decide what to do. Given the lack of solid proof regarding their plans against the Knights of Labor, and the fact they had not yet acted upon those plans, I would be willing to bet their high-priced attorneys will get them off with nothing more than a fine for some negligible offense. But there is little we can do about that."

"What about the money?"

"I should think that is part of the evidence," said the president. "Now if that is tied up a good long while, then perhaps it will slow down their various schemes. I would also urge you to send wires to the following people: to the editor of the *Evening Post*, apprising him of the truth behind his newsman's demise; to Terence Powderly, of the Knights of Labor, alerting him to the need to protect his union's funds and the document in question; and to the president of the Midwestern National Bank, informing him of the suspected activities of an employee named Pruett."

Brockmyer smiled broadly. "With pleasure, sir."

"As for me," added Cleveland, "I suppose I should express my thanks to that reporter from the *New York Herald*. His information about the Blaine letter got me thinking."

Senator Davis now came down the steps to join them. He was still shaking his head from the revelations within the cottage. "Deer Park will never be the same, I fear." He sighed.

"Ah, Senator!" proclaimed Grover Cleveland. "You are just the man I am looking for. Tell me, does your offer of a fresh trout dinner still hold?"

"Why, yes, Mr. President. Of course it does."

"Splendid! All that running about has given me an appetite."

As they started down the walk, Lieutenant Brockmyer called after them. "I'll have my men back in place around your cottage before you return, sir. If I can help with anything else, please let me know. But then, I guess things won't be as exciting around here now."

"Thank you, Lieutenant," Cleveland told him. With a sly look at his wife, and taking her arm in his, he added, "I suppose if we grow too bored, we can always return to the clamor of Washington."

Frances gave him a look of wry reproach, but said demurely, "I think we shall be here a few more days at least."

Grover Cleveland was in a jovial mood now. "Excellent idea, my dear! It will give me time for another fishing trip or two!"

Our twenty-sixth chief executive, Theodore Roosevelt (1858–1919), won the Nobel Prize for Peace because of his efforts in ending the Russo-Japanese War of 1905. At age forty-two he was the youngest man up to that time to become president— when he was elevated to the position with the death, in 1901, of William McKinley.

THE RIVER OF DOUBT

★ ★ ★

Edward D. Hoch

The Brazilians called it *Rio da Duvida*, River of Doubt, because it was only vaguely indicated on maps and some doubted that it really existed. That was all Teddy Roosevelt needed to hear from the Brazilian government before agreeing to join a well-known local explorer on an expedition to determine the true course of the river. He was in South America with his son Kermit, lecturing in various cities and securing specimens for my employer, the American Museum of Natural History. When the museum learned that the new expedition would take precedence over a planned zoological and botanical quest up the Paraguay River, they sent me to Rio de Janeiro by the fastest available ship to find out what was really happening.

All this was in October of 1913. Teddy had been out of office since 1909, when he became America's youngest former president at the age of fifty. His attempt to recapture the presidency on the ticket of the Bull Moose Party in 1912 failed by more than two million votes, succeeding only in splitting the Republican vote and putting Wilson in the White House.

211

Though we'd met briefly in New York, my first real conversation with Roosevelt came on that October day when my ship docked in Rio. Young Kermit met me and brought me to his father's hotel suite overlooking Copacabana beach. Teddy rose to greet me, flashing his famous grin beneath the bushy mustache. "David Hall, isn't it? We met back in New York. You were lecturing on Mexican birds, I believe, and showing lantern slides of the Montezuma quail."

"I'm pleased that you remember it, Mr. President."

"Call me Teddy. Everyone else seems to."

"I've come about this expedition down the River of Doubt."

Roosevelt dismissed my unspoken objections with a wave of his hand. "I'm here to help collect specimens for your museum, and I daresay we can find just as many unusual ones on the River of Doubt as we can on the Paraguay. In fact, why not come with us?"

"I'm not an explorer—"

"Nonsense! This is the twentieth century! It's as safe as a journey down the Mississippi! What about it, Kermit? Can we sign him on?"

"We have almost a score of men already. One more won't matter. And you'll certainly be able to give the museum a firsthand account of our efforts."

"When are you planning to start?"

"We're still organizing it. The Brazilian explorer, Colonel Candido Rondon, is going with us. He's arranging for the boats and supplies, and it'll take a few months at the very least."

"February," Teddy Roosevelt decided. "I want to start no later than February."

Once I'd agreed to join the expedition, I entered into it with vigor. We worked on our plans through the rainy season, with Kermit and Colonel Rondon doing much of the actual organizing. By late February the twenty-man expedition was ready to set forth into the unknown. We departed on February 27th, one day short of Teddy's deadline, traveling overland across the Mato Grosso plateau.

Colonel Rondon seemed to know where he was leading us, and after a week's travel we reached a jungle stream that looked much like the others we'd crossed on our journey. "Here is the River of Doubt," he announced. "Now we go by boat. I estimate we must travel between 900 and 1500 miles before reaching the Manaus River and then the Amazon."

Our half-dozen longboats were piled high with supplies as Parcha and Amapa, our two Brazilian guides, eased them into the water. Already the Dutch map makers, Sten and Berg, were at work, charting our exact location from the position of the sun. I was helped into the second boat with Teddy Roosevelt and a German botanist named Hans Klepper. Kermit would ride in the lead boat with Colonel Rondon.

"Do not be deceived by all these supplies," Rondon warned as we set off down the river. "If we travel too slowly we could easily starve to death before we reach the settlement at Manaus. And if we travel too fast, the rapids downriver could smash the boats to kindling."

"You've traveled this route before?" I asked him.

"Not for its entire distance, but the natives speak of rough water ahead."

So we set off through the muggy, misty jungle. Although the rainy season had ended, the whole of the Amazon basin and its tributaries could be considered a tropical rain forest, and progress in the early stages was slow. We paused frequently to rest at some clearing along the banks, or to observe the brightly colored plumage of an unfamiliar bird.

"I'm at my best out here," Teddy Roosevelt told me on one of these rest stops during the first week of our journey. The map makers were busy recording yet another offshoot of the river, and Colonel Rondon had gone with the guides on a scouting party into the bush. "Washington was always a bit stuffy for me. Not enough air to breathe."

"But it's a great deal more dangerous in the jungle than back in civilization," I pointed out. "There are wild animals here, and unfriendly natives—"

"Nonsense!" Roosevelt bellowed, and in that moment with his head thrown back, with his bulging stomach and pince-nez glasses and drooping mustache, he reminded me somewhat of the British author G. K. Chesterton, whom I'd recently seen on a lecture tour. "I find your so-called civilization far more dangerous than these jungles. The closest I ever came to death was not at San Juan Hill or in Africa. It was a year ago October in Milwaukee, when John Schrank shot me in the chest from six feet away. If I didn't have my fifty-page speech in my pocket to slow down the bullet, I'd probably be a dead man today.''

''Schrank was a madman. They locked him away.''

''One doesn't find madmen in the jungle,'' Teddy responded, as if I'd somehow proved his point.

I was to remember those words in the weeks that followed.

We'd been on the river some two weeks when the former president was laid low by an attack of malaria and dysentery. He was running a fever and remained in the boat much of the time, even during the rest stops. I began to worry about his condition, but there was little we could do. To stop and camp until he was well again would have cut drastically into our limited food supply. I could see that Kermit and Colonel Rondon were troubled, but they pushed on.

The rainy season had led to a greater than normal runoff of water, and the River of Doubt was deeper than the native guides had ever seen it before. This caused trouble during our third week, when one of the boats was caught up in the rushing water and propelled through the rapids so swiftly that it smashed up on the rocks. Some supplies and food were lost, but no one was injured. Roosevelt was feeling a bit better during this period, but that came to an abrupt end one day when he badly gashed his leg while stepping out of a boat.

Duncan Treymore, a British zoologist who'd studied medicine, was the closest thing we had to a doctor on the expedition. He examined the former president's leg and treated it as best he could. 'It should be all right if it doesn't become infected,'' he told Kermit. ''We'll just have to watch it carefully.''

Treymore had become friendly with me during the expedition, and we often sat together after supper discussing the day's events. ''I don't like it,'' he told me that night after he'd treated Teddy's injury. ''Nothing seems to have gone right on this trip yet. I have a chilly feeling we're all headed for disaster.''

''Roosevelt's come through worse than this.''

"I heard Rondon and his guide, Parcha, talking. We're getting into dangerous territory now. The natives are unfriendly, and they're been known to hunt with poisoned arrows. Some even say there are man-eating fish in the waters."

"You're a trained zoologist, Duncan. Do you mean to tell me you believe in such claptrap?"

"Guides have told me stories of the piranha or cannibal fish. It's little known outside South America, but the stories seem to have some truth behind them. I've met men who claim to have lost a finger while trailing it in the water from their boat. The fish is said to be nearly a foot long, with extremely sharp teeth, and they hunt in immense schools."

"Well, I'll believe it when I see them, and I hope I never do."

The following morning Teddy's bandaged leg was extremely sore, but the malaria seemed better and his fever was down. He had his hunting rifle with him in the boat, and once when a small jaguar appeared on a tree limb over the river he brought it down with a single shot.

"Not much sport there," he conceded, "but he might have decided to drop on our heads."

When we stopped to rest around noon, I noticed that the native guide Parcha remained in the lead boat, dozing in the midday heat. It was some time later, with the sun peeking through the tangled vines above our heads, when I heard Klepper, the German botanist, give a shout of alarm. "The boat is loose!" he cried out.

The boat had drifted into the main current of the river with Parcha still dozing in it. I knew there were more rapids just ahead because we'd stopped to rest before going through them. Now the boat shot forward, and the native guide seemed to loll over without awakening. Kermit and some of the others ran along the shore, trying to stop it somehow, but they were too late. It hit a submerged rock and split apart, hurling Parcha and several bales of food supplies into the water.

Kermit started in after the guide, but suddenly Colonel Rondon yanked him back to shore. "Cannibal fish!" he shouted, pointing at a violent turbulence in the water near Parcha. We watched helplessly, horrified at a momentary glimpse of arm-bone. Then, as quickly as it came, the turbulence subsided. The River of Doubt continued its uninterrupted flow over the rocks.

"A terrible sight," Duncan Treymore said, shaking his head. "I think that answers our questions about the piranha."

"But not about the boat and Parcha's death," I told him as we walked back to the campsite. "How could it have happened?"

Teddy Roosevelt must have been wondering the same thing. He was down on one knee at the water's edge, studying the rope that had been used to tie the boat to a tree. "This rope was cut with a sharp knife," he decided. "Look at how clean the break is! It never split like that accidentally."

"There's something else," I pointed out. "It could be blood."

Colonel Rondon looked distressed. "Who was near that boat and the rope? One of you must have seen something!"

But of the nineteen of us who remained in the party, it seemed that no one had seen a thing. Hans Klepper had been the first to notice something amiss when the boat drifted away from shore with the current. Roosevelt was deeply troubled by the event, and we decided to spend the night where we were before venturing into the river again. The tents were put up, and in late afternoon Roosevelt, Kermit, Colonel Rondon, and I held an impromptu meeting away from the others. Teddy's eyes were a bit wild, and I feared his fever was returning even as he spoke to me.

"David, you noticed a drop of blood on that cleanly cut rope. Does that suggest anything to you?"

I pondered for only an instant. "There was blood on the knife when the rope was cut. Fresh blood. Someone stabbed the dozing Parcha just before cutting the rope."

"That's what I think, too," Teddy said. "From what I've heard of these cannibal fish, they attack at the smell of blood. Parcha must have had a wound on his body to bring them around so quickly in such numbers."

"You're talking about murder," Kermit said. "Why would anyone want to kill our guide?"

Colonel Rondon looked grim. "Possibly to keep us from ever getting back to civilization."

"What about the other guide, Amapa?"

"He's younger than Parcha, but he knows the area well enough. He can get us through."

"And the killer?"

"If there is a killer, we must keep our eyes open."

Teddy started to rise and then slumped back in pain. "I'd better stay off this leg. It's starting to bother me."

"I'll have Duncan take another look at it," I suggested.

But once Duncan Treymore was summoned and had removed the bandage and inspected the leg, his news was bad. "It's infected," he told us. "He really needs proper medical treatment, more than I can give him."

Colonel Rondon was silent, and Kermit asked him, "Is there any chance of our turning back?"

The Brazilian explorer shook his head. "From here it's as far back as it is forward, and we'd be rowing against the current. All we can do is press on as quickly as possible."

In the morning there was even worse news. During the night someone had cut loose another of our boats.

The three remaining boats were large enough to accommodate nineteen people with only a minimum of crowding, but some of the expedition's equipment had to be discarded. We couldn't part with the food, already growing low, so extra tents and cots had to be left behind, along with some clothing, rope, and lanterns. I had a feeling we were never far from the watching eyes of the natives, and I wondered what they would make of these abandoned treasures.

The thought of the natives must have been in everyone's mind. Rudolph Sten, one of the map makers, approached me as we were getting ready to shove off with our cargo of men and supplies redistributed in the three boats. "I think I saw a savage watching us from the forest," he said, speaking with his thick Dutch accent. "One of them might have cut the boat free under cover of darkness."

"It's possible," I admitted. "But yesterday's incident can't be blamed on a native. Surely we'd have noticed a naked Indian approaching the boat where Parcha dozed."

"Even if he came under water?" Sten asked. "He had only to lift his head and arm from the river to stab our guide and cut the boat free."

"The natives must know there are piranhas in this area. I doubt if they'd risk going swimming with them." Still, I had to admit the underwater approach of a native was a possibility we hadn't considered. Perhaps they had a special way of avoiding the bite of the cannibal fish.

We set off downriver once more, making good time as the current increased and the rapids smoothed for a lengthy stretch. I still rode in the boat with the former president, trying to make him as comfortable as possible. "David," he said at one point.

"What is it, Teddy?"

"Keep the rifle ready. There is death all around us."

"You have nothing to fear."

When we stopped for our traditional noonday rest, his son, Kermit, asked me how he was doing. "Not good," I had to admit. "His fever is very high."

Duncan's thermometer bore me out, showing a temperature of 105. The malaria was back, teaming with the infected wound to ravage the fifty-five-year-old body. "He's dying, isn't he?" Kermit asked the zoologist. "Tell me the truth."

"I can't say, Kermit. I've seen men pull through worse."

"In hospitals, not in the middle of the Amazon jungle!"

So we pushed on, down the swollen river.

The next two days were relatively placid, and Teddy Roosevelt's fever actually dropped a bit. The worst seemed to be over, though at times Kermit feared he was out of his mind, especially in the night when his feverish ramblings were often at their worst. Then one morning, as we were striking the tents to continue our journey, the guide Amapa rushed into the clearing.

"Dead man!" he shouted. "Over here!"

I was on my feet at once, leaving Teddy's side. "Who is it?"

"Mr. Sten. He has been stabbed in the chest."

Rudolph Sten, the map maker, lay on his stomach in the tall grass at the edge of our clearing. I turned him over and saw the bloody wound that must have gone directly to his heart. Treymore arrived a moment later and knelt at my side.

"He's dead," he confirmed, if any confirmation was needed. "Probably killed sometime during the night. His fingers are beginning to stiffen with rigor mortis already, despite the heat.''

"There's no weapon. Could it have been an Indian arrow?"

"The wound is wide for an arrow. More likely a knife. Besides, an arrow would probably have been left in the wound. And Indians rarely attack at night.''

"So we're back to the killer among us."

We buried Sten there with a simple funeral service. I think everyone in the party was terrified by this time, with the possible exception of Teddy Roosevelt, whose poor fevered brain could only partly comprehend what was happening. He did see us at prayer around the grave, however, and asked what had happened. "Another murder?"

"Yes. The map maker, Rudolph Sten." I told him about finding the body.

"You must question everyone, find out where they were."

"It will do no good," I said. "Anyone could have killed him in the darkness."

But I did call Amapa over and question him further about finding the body. "What made you go out there? Were you looking for him?"

"No, no. I had gone into the bushes to relieve myself when I saw the body. I was afraid to touch him, so I ran for help."

"Did you see anyone else near the spot earlier?"

"I didn't notice. The men were walking all around. Anyone might have gone back there for the same reason I did."

Rudolph Sten's map making partner, another Dutchman named Berg who spoke little English, was the most devastated by the tragedy. But all of us were in a state approaching panic. We had lost three boats and two men had been killed, apparently by a murderer in our midst. Theodore Roosevelt was still feverish and in real danger of dying from his infected leg. And our food supply was dwindling.

Nevertheless, we got ourselves together and set off once more down the River of Doubt, because there was no alternative open to us. Teddy's waking hours alternated between feverish ramblings and attempts to analyze the facts of the two deaths. "No one is above suspicion," he said, "even you, David."

"Me?"

"You cannot account for your movements during the night—"

"I was sleeping!" I protested.

"—and we have only your word that you did not cut the boats loose."

"You can't be serious, Teddy! What motive would I have?"

"A madman determined to destroy the expedition would need no other motive."

"Do you think I am mad?"

His face relaxed for a moment, though his eyes still had a feverish look to them. "David, you are probably the sanest of us all. I think we were out of our minds to attempt this journey in the first place. Call Kermit in here."

"We're on the river, Teddy," I said as kindly as I could. "Kermit is in the boat ahead. You can see him when we stop."

"Of course! Pay no mind to my ramblings."

That evening as we made camp the best we could with our dwindling equipment, Teddy asked his son to take over the chore of making notes about their journey. Roosevelt was planning to write a book about the trip, but his illness made it impossible for him to concentrate.

"I'm already doing it," Kermit assured him.

Colonel Rondon assigned several of us to two-man shifts of guard duty throughout the night, in an attempt to prevent more killings. "Remember," he told us, "the killer may be someone right here in camp, or it could be an Indian lurking in the jungle. We cannot afford any more deaths, or the loss of another boat."

I was teamed with Hans Klepper for my patrol, and we circled the camp together between midnight and two A.M., never straying out of each other's sight. The German botanist was in a talkative mood, discussing the worsening situation in his homeland. "There will be war before the end of summer, I am convinced of it. The kaiser wants new conquests, and with the help of Austria-Hungary he probably has the strength to accomplish them. Any spark could set it off."

"Let's hope it doesn't come."

"This is something like a war in miniature," he suggested. "We battle the river and an unseen killer."

"Doubt. We battle doubt."

"Yes." Suddenly his body stiffened. "Do you see something near that tent?"

"I'm not sure."

Klepper lifted his hunting rifle and took a step forward. "Who's there?" he called out.

"Don't shoot," a voice answered. "It's only me. I couldn't sleep."

As we drew nearer I recognized Duncan Treymore. "That's a good way to get yourself shot, prowling around at night."

"I thought I heard a noise."

"You'd better get back in your tent," Klepper advised him.

We checked the boats to make certain none of the ropes had been tampered with. Finally, at two o'clock, we turned over the guard duty to the next shift, Berg and Kermit Roosevelt, and retired to our tents.

When it came time to get under way in the morning, Teddy seemed no better. The fever was high and he spoke in confused ramblings. Treymore said the wound in his leg looked better, but another bout of malaria seemed to be keeping his temperature high. "There is nothing to do but push on," Colonel Rondon said again. "We are still several hundred miles from our destination. If we stop now, our food will run out and we'll only provide a feast for the Indians." Rumors of cannibalism were prevalent, though most of us doubted their truth. Amapa kept assuring us that the tribes he knew were always friendly unless provoked or threatened.

I was loading the last of my gear into the second boat when it happened. As I bent down, the boat gave a sudden lurch away from shore. The loosened rope came free of its moorings and I was drifting into the main current of the river. I looked around for help, and several people saw my plight at once. It was impossible to tell if one of them had given the boat a shove with his boot.

I hauled in the trailing rope from the water and tried to hurl it to shore, but I was already too far out. The river was growing wider with each day's journey—wider and more deadly. Though we were some distance from the next rapids, I knew I had to bring the craft under control quickly. I shoved one of the oars into the water and tried to steer with it. Though the boat's speed continued to increase, I was able to edge it a bit closer to the shore.

Kermit had run along the bank, keeping pace with me. Now I hurled the rope again and he was able to catch the end on the second try. He brought it around the trunk of a tree and started pulling. The boat gradually edged into shore and I hopped out. "Thanks," I told him. "You probably saved my life."

"Amapa and Treymore were working near the boat," he told me as we secured the boat and hurried back to the others. "I think Treymore might have loosened the rope and given the boat a kick."

Hans Klepper had the same idea. He'd grabbed Duncan by the front of his shirt and forced him against a tree. "You were prowling about last night, and you freed that boat with your foot."

"You're crazy, you bloody German!" Duncan yelled into his face.

I think Klepper would have punched him if Teddy hadn't spoken suddenly. He was upright for the first time in days, leaning on a tent pole. "Let him go," he commanded in his most authoritative tones. "He didn't kill anyone."

"Then who did?" the German asked.

The former president pointed an unsteady finger. "There stands your murderer!" He was pointing at Amapa, the guide.

Amapa looked trapped and frightened; at the same time he tried to edge away from the others. "What he says is a lie! I am innocent!"

But Teddy Roosevelt was still speaking. "He said he was afraid to touch Rudolph Sten's body when he found it, yet he came back to camp and told you Sten had been stabbed in the chest. How could he know that, since the body was lying on its stomach?"

All eyes were on Amapa now, but the guide moved faster than we could. He grabbed up a machete, waving it wildly about his head. "Keep back, keep back! You come to my land to spoil it, to drive my people away! I killed Parcha for bringing you here and Sten for drawing his maps. I will kill the rest of you, too!"

Treymore made a grab for him, but Amapa shoved him

aside and ran screaming into the jungle. "The man is mad," Colonel Rondon said. "We'd better go after him."

After his moment of triumph, Teddy Roosevelt had collapsed in a faint. Treymore hurried to his side with Kermit, while Klepper, Berg, and I picked up rifles and went off after Amapa.

We followed his obvious trail through the underbrush for nearly an hour before we finally found him, slumped against a tree trunk with a native arrow through his heart.

"They must have been watching us all the time," Klepper said. "They didn't want him back."

I shook my head. "No, I think they just saw a crazy man with a machete running toward them. I think it was as simple as that."

When Teddy Roosevelt regained consciousness, his fever was broken. Oddly enough, he remembered nothing about Amapa and that final scene of accusation. He refused to believe that his fevered brain had arrived at the solution to the killings. We traveled on through the jungle without further mishap, finally reaching the settlement at Manaus on April 30th, more than two months after the expedition began. The Brazilian government was so pleased it renamed the River of Doubt in his honor, Rio Roosevelt. Teddy lost fifty-seven pounds on the journey, and though he recovered from the ordeal, his health was never quite the same. He died less than five years later of a coronary embolism.

I have set down these facts for the public because the account of the expedition and the murders contained in Roosevelt's own book, *Through the Brazilian Wilderness*, is quite different on several counts. Oddly enough, the most lasting effect of the expedition was neither the mapping of a river nor the discovery of a murderer. It was Roosevelt's revelation of the deadly piranha that seized the public's imagination. His description of the cannibal fish was picked up by other writers and repeated almost verbatim. He made a fish famous.

ED GORMAN is a former political speech writer who is one of the most important crime-fiction writers to emerge in the last decade. In that time he has published some dozen novels in the mystery and horror fields, as well as over fifty short stories. His novel The Autumn Dead *was published to much critical acclaim in 1987. Additionally, Mr. Gorman is an editor of* Mystery Scene, *the most important trade journal in the genre.*

Calvin Coolidge (1872–1933), America's thirtieth president, who took office after the death of Warren Harding in 1923, was reelected in 1924. He had become politically prominent when, as governor of Massachusetts, he called out the State National Guard to quell a famous Boston police strike. Coolidge refused to run in the election of 1928.

MY COUSIN CAL

★　★　★

Ed Gorman

1

By morning I had everything I needed to expose the killer. Now it was just a matter of convincing Cal to let me go through with my plan.

The train bearing President Harding's body was in the depot at the San Francisco station. Harding, who had fallen ill with ptomaine a week earlier and who had died suddenly of what appeared to be apoplexy, had been pronounced dead three days earlier.

My cousin Calvin Coolidge, formerly the vice-president, had been spending the summer on the Vermont farm where we'd been raised. He'd been given the oath of presidential office right in his own living room by his own father, who was not only a champion woodcutter but also a justice of the peace.

Cal—or Mr. President as I was now going to be calling him—had then taken the Twentieth Century Limited out here so he could ride with the mourners back to Washington.

Hundreds of citizens—rich and poor, white and black and yellow—crowded the depot. I kept my White House Security badge in my hand, flashing it as a means of getting through the throng. Every twenty feet you saw army men in green khaki uniforms patrolling with the type of Enfield rifles that had been used a few years ago in WW I (Cal always saying that WW stood not for World War but for Woodrow Wilson's War). There had been strong hints in the press that President Harding had not died of natural causes at all but had in fact been murdered by a piece of poisoned crab meat he'd eaten in Alaska (which explained the emphasis on security). Some claimed that it was his wife, a strange woman given to deep belief in astrology, who'd done it. Others claimed it was Harry S. Sinclair himself, owner of the giant Mammoth Oil Company, who'd been his killer.

On board with me I took two things, the silver-plated Colt 1911 that Cal had given me when he'd brought me to work for him as a vice-presidential assistant, and a plain brown leather valise containing all the evidence I'd been gathering.

Finally, I boarded the train, had the black porter called George (all porters were called George for some reason) find me a Pullman, and then proceeded, at least for a time, to relax and hone my plan.

2

By now you've no doubt read about it. The spectacular response of Americans to the death of their beloved President Harding. We'd only been on the rails a day when a reporter for the *New York Times* said, "It is believed to be the most remarkable demonstration in American history of affection, respect, and reverence for the dead.''

And he wasn't exaggerating.

Thousands of people packed the route. It seemed you could not look out your window even in stretches of desolate country without seeing mourners standing by the rails, waving small American flags or clutching their hats to their chests.

On the slopes of western hills we saw cowboys saluting us; in villages we saw freckle-faced children with silver tears the color of mercury sliding down their cheeks waving to us; and in cities the crowds became so overwhelming that the engineer had to slow the train to a crawl lest he kill them.

The mood on board was just as vexed. As twenty-ninth president of the United States, Warren G. Harding had been among the most beloved leaders of our time. Americans liked him particularly because he was not an imperious snob on the order of Woodrow Wilson nor a careless adventurer, however colorful, on the order of Theodore Roosevelt. The press liked to call him ''This country's favorite uncle,'' and I guess that pretty much said it.

Of course, lately his air of industry and fairness had been tarnished by some of the men around him. Various charges of graft and bribery had driven several cabinet members from office.

But at the moment none of the administration's shortcomings were on the country's mind. We meant, by God, to mourn the passing of a decent man, and so we did.

3

I had a copy of *The American Mercury* spread out in front of me and was tracing over a photograph of Lillian Gish, who was that issue's major feature. That's always been one of my frustrations, wanting to be an illustrator but not having the talent. That's how I spent many winter nights in the Coolidge farm home back in Vermont (they'd taken me in after my parents died of influenza), tracing over every magazine illustration I could find.

A knock interrupted me this morning.

"Come in," I said.

"Morning," Cal said, sticking his head through the door. Then he smiled to see how I was spending my time in my compartment. "Tracing. You're never going to outgrow that are you, Bobby?"

"Afraid not, Cal." I laughed.

He closed the door and came into my compartment—a pretty fancy suite, actually, complete with a shiny nickel-plated washbowl and a small dining table on which sat the remnants of my breakfast: hot corn muffins, bacon, and jam.

Cal came in and sat down, a slender man with the sort of robust looks that come from spending as much time as possible with one's family and with God's work in the outdoors. As always, he wore a three-piece dark suit, with a white shirt, gold tie bar, and dark blue tie. He helped himself to his only cup of coffee a day ("caffeine breaks your concentration," he usually told people) and said, "Sorry we haven't had more time to talk the last day and a half." His smile faded. "I thought the ceremonial duties were bad when I was vice-president—"

I said, "Somebody murdered President Harding."

He set down his coffee. "You know what I think about newspaper stories." Though cousin Cal respected the press at their best, he thought that too many of them trafficked in gossip and innuendo. The reaction was typical of Cal. Here I'd just told him that a murder had taken place and he'd responded by mildly telling me that the press was not always to be believed.

"Do you remember how I spent my first years after college?" I asked.

"Of course. Woodrow Wilson's War."

"Right after that."

"The Pinkertons," he said.

"Exactly."

"Afraid I'm not following you, cousin." This he said with something of a New England accent, which was part of his color and charm when he was giving stump speeches. He sounded as down to earth as a New England farm telling you about hickory or syrup. People loved it.

"I'm a trained investigator."

"No disputing that," he said. "And a good one."

"And I've been doing some investigating."

"I see." For the first time, apprehension sounded in his voice. Beyond him, out the window, rushed vast stretches of plains turned brown by summer sun stretched to the horizon. He chewed a bit on his lower lip. I'd only seen him do this on the most pressing of occasions, at the death of his beloved mother (whose photograph he kept in his pocket) and when his wife almost miscarried their first child.

"I need to tell you something," he said.

"All right."

He sat up a little straighter and folded his hands in his lap and looked hard at me with blue eyes lit with their own quiet wisdom. "I'm not sure this country can get through a murder plot—even if it eventually proves to be inaccurate."

I said, "We need to know the truth."

He continued to stare at me. Finally, sighing, he said, "You're right, Bobby. We need to know the truth. What are you proposing?"

"There's a drawing-room car second from the end of this train. A perfect place for a meeting. In one hour I'd like you to bring both Phoebe Harding and Harry Sinclair there."

"They're not on speaking terms." Phoebe and Harry had always had to vie for the president's attention and as a result disliked each other.

"You're the president, Cal. You can order them to be there."

He scratched his head. "I guess I could." Then he raised his eyes to me again and said, "You've got some proof, I take it?"

"Oh, yes."

"That one of them is implicated in his death?"

I nodded to the brown valise on the bed. "Cal, when I open that valise and present the material that's in it, you *and* Phoebe Harding *and* Harry S. Sinclair are going to be shocked."

"I've always trusted you, cousin. I certainly hope my trust won't be misplaced this time." And, happily, he was right. I'd worked for him for two years, handling some extremely delicate matters, and I'd completed each successfully.

He stood up, took his pocket watch from his vest, looked at it and said, again with the Yankee twang, "One hour then, Bobby."

"One hour, Cal," I said.

4

The drawing-room car was fancy beyond necessity, everything red-flecked wallpaper and gilt, with leather furnishings and even padded sills along the windows. Porters in starchy white jackets set out several kinds of refreshment as Cal and I waited for the guests to arrive.

Phoebe Harding came first, a once sumptuous woman given to brocaded dresses and pendants of splendiferous size and ornate design. The pendants each contained some astrological sign. Today she wore a great deal of makeup to cover the dark circles beneath her eyes and the way her cheeks had begun to sag.

She daintily put out a hand for cousin Cal to take but it was too beefy a hand to effect the feminine delicacy she wished. He took it anyway. To me she only nodded.

We had just passed through a town where the throngs had pressed right up to the Pullman windows. "He would have been so appreciative," Phoebe Harding said, pouring herself a healthy dose of bourbon.

Harry S. Sinclair came a few minutes later. As always, he looked angry about something and, as always, he looked like a cartoon tycoon: too much belly, too much ire, too much self-importance. He wore a dark suit and a stiff collar twenty years out of vogue. His face showed whiskey and his eyes showed malice.

He was solicitous as he could be—which was not very often—to cousin Cal. To Phoebe Harding and me, he scarcely offered any sort of recognition at all.

A young man in a khaki uniform came in and said, "Now, sir?"

"Now."

"Just what the blazes is this all about?" said Harry S.

Sinclair, owner of Mammoth Oil and richest man in the country second only to John D. himself.

"A little discussion," I said mildly.

The soldier went down to one end of the car and secured the lock and then went to the other end of the car and said, "Will you lock this behind me, sir?"

"Yes," I said. "You've got armed guards posted at each door?"

"Yessir."

"Thank you."

A few minutes later, fixing myself a straight seltzer water, I said to the three people who sat in front of me, "Each of us here knows something that the press is only speculating about."

"What would that be?" Phoebe Harding said, sounding as innocent as possible.

"That President Harding was murdered."

I let them react, her in her shocked way, Sinclair in his blustery one.

Then I produced the brown valise, setting it like a magician's prop on the table with the refreshments.

The first thing I produced were two sheets of lined paper. In fountain pen innumerable foodstuffs were listed. I handed the paper to Phoebe Harding and said, "Please look at this and pass it around."

Which she did.

Cousin Cal was the last to see it. He handed it back. "It looks like a very long list of groceries."

I took the paper and set it back in the valise. "As you three know, I went to Alaska with President Harding's party. As soon as he was struck by ptomaine, my Pinkerton training took over and I decided to do a little checking with the steward. President Harding ate crab meat—but this list of supplies that I had the steward draw up for me listed no crab meat."

"What are you saying?" demanded Harry S. Sinclair.

"That somebody served the president a very special meal. Very special. One that contained poison."

"But why would anybody want to kill him?" said Phoebe Harding. Again her voice was sweet and pure as a jay's on a spring morning. Only the eyes were old and hard.

I reached into my bag and produced a second document. This one was a letter written on presidential stationery.

I cleared my throat. " 'I am setting this down now in case my sudden passing should be confused by anybody as accidental, which it will most definitely not be.

" 'I write this on a Tuesday evening when the apple blossoms in the White House garden waft on the soft breeze. I am of sound mind even if I am given to despondence.

" 'But who would not be despondent in my position? My wife is having a relationship with my physician Doctor Sawyer, and my secretary of the interior has disgraced both himself and this administration by nefarious and illegal dealings with Harry S. Sinclair, public knowledge of which would bring me down.

" 'So what would these people profit by my death? If I were done away with now, my wife could spend the rest of her years trading on the name of a martyred president, while enjoying the company of Doctor Sawyer. And Harry S. Sinclair would be spared the collapse of his entire financial empire once I've taken this to the press.

" 'Again, I am of sound mind as I write this and I entrust it to Robert "Bobby" Williams, the ex-Pinkerton man who now serves my vice-president, Mr. Coolidge. I have asked Bobby to accompany me to Alaska so as to keep me from peril.

" 'Sincerely, President Warren G. Harding.' "

I gave them the letter to scrutinize carefully, which of course they did. Then I asked for it back.

"Preposterous!" said Harry S. Sinclair.

"A libel!" cried Phoebe Harding.

I put the letter down and faced them both. "The fault here is mine, I suppose. I thought of several ways one of you might have tried to kill him—accidentally falling overboard being the most likely—but I didn't think of poisoning. I failed in my duty."

"And just what do you propose to do with your accusations?" said Harry S. Sinclair.

I said, "Nothing."

"What?" said my cousin Cal.

"Nothing."

I took the two documents—the steward's list and the letter from President Harding—and put them back in the valise.

My cousin Cal stood up and said, "But if you truly believe that one of these people killed the president—"

I held up my hand. "Please, Mr. President, let me finish, if you will." It seemed an appropriate time to start calling him Mr. President.

He sighed then sat back down.

"There are major scandals brewing in this administration," I said. "You, Phoebe, and you, Harry, will only hinder my cousin the president from setting things right. Therefore, I am going to make you a proposal. I will not take this evidence to the press—and let the press decide which of you is guilty of murder—if you agree to withdraw all your interests from my cousin's administration and to leave him entirely alone so he can get rid of all the scoundrels and put the country back on a proper course."

They started to balk.

"Do you want the press to know about you and Doctor Sawyer?" I said to Phoebe. "And live the rest of your life in the public eye as an adultress?"

"And do you, Harry, want me to feed the press the kind of information about how you bribe public officials—information they've been looking for for so long?"

Their ardor for battle simmered.

Phoebe muttered something that former first ladies are not supposed to mutter and Harry stabbed out his cigar in my glass of seltzer.

I said, "I want you and all your cronies and friends—both of you—to be gone from Washington within three weeks. If that has not happened, then these documents will be turned over to the press. Is that understood?"

"You bastard," said Harry S. Sinclair.

"You *dirty* bastard," said Phoebe Harding.

I looked at my cousin Cal and smiled.

5

Three hours later I was sitting in my room, enjoying the clack of train wheels and the sight of piney hills in the distance, when somebody knocked. I was doing some more tracing. "Come in," I said.

"Thought I'd bring these back," my cousin Cal said, coming into the room.

He'd borrowed the steward's list and the letter for examination.

I pointed to a chair and he sat down.

"Beautiful part of the country," I said.

"I read the letter several times, Bobby, and then it finally dawned on me what had happened. All these years of tracing. You've become a forger. The letter's a fake."

I put down the book I was reading, one of the Zane Grey westerns I'm partial to, and said, "But the steward's list isn't."

"Then you admit forging the letter?"

"Of course."

"You're so blasé about it."

"I want you to have a successful administration, Cal. I look out for your interests. There are so many scandals about to hit the newspaper that the entire Harding administration would have been brought down. This is a chance for you to clean house and become a national hero."

The blue eyes stared at me. "A few nights before he left for Alaska, the president called me to his office. You know what he said?"

"What?"

"He told me that he wanted to die."

The blue eyes continued to stare at me. "He told you the same thing, didn't he?"

I thought about telling him what President Harding had asked me to do. To shoot him in such a way that it would look like suicide. The friends he'd trusted who'd betrayed him—including not only his wife and Harry S. Sinclair but his secretary of interior Albert B. Fall and many others—had driven him to the brink of suicide.

"Yes," I said.

"But you couldn't shoot him, could you?"

"No, cousin, I couldn't."

"So you found a gentler way."

"Yes."

"Poison."

"Correct."

"My Lord," he said. "My Lord."

"It was the best way to do it. This way you get rid of Phoebe and Harry and all the others—sending most of them to prison, I'm afraid—and history will officially record President Harding's death as accidental. He won't be thought of as a suicide. I liked him enough that saving his reputation was important to me."

"Then neither Phoebe or Harry killed him?"

"No. But now they both think the other did it and now they'll just want to get as far away from Washington as possible. Neither one of them can stand having the press look into their background and they know it."

"My Lord," he said again. "My Lord."

He followed my gaze out the window to the green hills and the blue sky and the rolling beauty of the prairie.

Then he turned back to me.

"In your own strange way, Bobby," he said, "you're a patriot."

"Oh, I hope so, cousin," I said. "I certainly hope so."

SHARYN McCRUMB is the creator of the clever mystery novels featuring Elizabeth MacPherson, an amateur sleuth with expertise in forensic anthropology. The series began with Sick Of Shadows *and continued with* Lovely in Her Bones *(chosen by the Appalachian Writers Association as 1985's outstanding work of fiction),* Highland Laddie Gone, *and* Paying the Piper. *A non-series comic mystery,* Bimbos of the Death Sun, *was published to acclaim in 1987, then went on to win an Edgar Award. Ms. McCrumb, whose short stories have appeared in* Ellery Queen's Mystery Magazine, *teaches journalism and Appalachian studies at Virginia Tech University.*

Herbert Hoover (1874–1964) served as secretary of commerce before winning the election of 1928 to become our thirty-first president. He will always be associated in the popular mind with the Great Depression that followed the stock market crash of 1929, the major cause of his defeat by Franklin D. Roosevelt in 1932.

SILVER LINING

★ ★ ★

Sharyn McCrumb

"I'm afraid it isn't much of a silver mine, Mr. President," said Milton Zachary, glancing apprehensively at the Humpty Dumpty face in the rearview mirror.

Neither the president nor the first lady had said much of anything since they'd climbed into the car in Pineville, except for the president's remark that the buildings on Main Street reminded him of his hometown in Iowa. He hadn't seemed too pleased about it, either, just as he hadn't been pleased when the town officials had tried to drum up a reception when they'd discovered that the president's train was stopping in town for a few hours. Word was sent to the mayor that the chief executive didn't want a tea party; he wanted to visit a mine. Several frenzied phone calls later, Milton Zachary had been summoned from the Blue Coyote, saddled with the job of entertaining the distinguished tourists for the afternoon. They didn't want a few local Republicans to join the party either. They were vacationing. Zachary could think of better ways to spend one.

When no reply to his remark was forthcoming, Zachary tried again. "No, sir, it's not much of a mine, but I reckon that when the town officials heard you'd be visiting right here in Nevada, they did the best they could on short notice. Of course, you being a mining engineer and all. . ."

"That's right. I would prefer to spend the stopover in useful pursuits, rather than be forced to participate in an impromptu *boirée*, sipping lemonade with the local ladies' club."

"I guess you do a lot of that, sir."

"Of necessity, yes, but I don't feel compelled to in this instance, as I am not visiting here in my presidential capacity. Mrs. Hoover and I are merely on our way to see our son Allan at Stanford. However, I am, as you noted, a mining engineer, and I maintain an interest in the field, so I thought that I should prefer to spend our rest stop refreshing my professional inclinations."

Even his voice is metallic, Zachary thought. And he uses enough two-dollar words to bail out every stockbroker in the country. The coldness must be more than just his manner, or else he'd be stifling in that brown suit out here in the heat. Not the most comforting person to look up to when the bottom's dropping out of the country's bank account. "Of course, we're honored that you'd want to come out and see the mine, Mr. President, but I'm afraid we won't offer much hope of coming prosperity," said Zachary apologetically. "The Blue Coyote had a pretty good surface vein, but it played out quick. I figure in less than a year, we'll be deader than Wall Street."

After a few moments of arctic silence, Mrs. Hoover's silvery voice piped up over the wind noises. "Do you own the mine, Mr. Zachary?"

He flashed her a grateful smile in the mirror. "No, ma'am. Don't know as I'd want to. Why, I'd sooner be a bank pres— I mean—no, the Coyote's owned by a local family, the Fremonts. Last I heard, anyhow. But Frank Blundy, who owns the Little Argentina near Virginia City, has made them an offer for the mine, and we reckon they'll take it. It's not much of an offer, but as Mr. Blundy says, all that's worth saving is the equipment, which he can use in his operation, and whatever he can squeeze out of processing the scrap pile. Then some cattleman will probably take the land off his hands for ten bucks an acre."

Zachary stole a glance at his audience. Judging from the deepening frown in the presidential forehead, his tale of the Coyote's misfortunes was sounding all too familiar to one who had heard little else since October 29.

"Interesting country, Mr. Zachary," said Lou Hoover, nodding toward the window. Her short silver hair was still perfectly in place, and she seemed quite comfortable in her lilac print dress. The president was sweating.

"Well, it's all right," Zachary allowed, accepting the change of subject. "I reckon there's a certain peacefulness in all this flat expanse of scrub grass and no-account bushes. And if you like the color brown, why, you could just about call this paradise. You know what the Spanish said about this place? Six months of *invierno* and six months of *infierno*. That means six months of winter and six months of h—"

"We know what *infierno* means," barked the president. "What did you say you did at the mine?"

"Manager, sir. General manager. As of this week. Last week I was the assistant, but Mr. Hamilton got himself killed last week, and I got promoted. Not meaning it to sound like I'm glad of it, you understand. He was as good a man as you could find, for an Englishman. Knew all about mining and geology, and I don't know what-all."

Mrs. Hoover looked concerned. "Surely they haven't sent us to tour a mine that had a cave-in last week!"

Zachary shook his head. "No, ma'am, nothing as serious as that. Mr. Hamilton was murdered, that's all."

"I am distressed to hear it," said the president, but he didn't sound it. He sounded like someone counting the words in a telegram.

"Well, so was I, sir. Not that I can't use the extra ten dollars a week from the promotion, but I did like Mr. Hamilton, odd as he was. That fellow was forever dragging in plants from out in the hills, and he had a standing offer to pay the miners for any rocks they found with fossils in 'em. It was right pitiful when they found him laying there in that field of yellow flowers, with his head bashed in. I reckon even the pro-union boys minded."

Mr. Hoover straightened up in his seat. "Union?"

"Yes, sir. One of the union fellows had been trying to organize the mine, and Mr. Hamilton was against it, so we figure that they had an argument that got out of hand. That organizer is in jail now in Pineville, and I hope they hang him."

After a few moments' silence, Mrs. Hoover said, "John L. Lewis is a friend of ours. He belongs to our club back in Washington. I can't believe that his representative would commit murder."

Zachary flashed a smile at the rearview mirror. "Ain't that just like the ladies, Mr. President? Always ready to believe the best of a man."

He maneuvered the car around a bend in the road, and slowed down before a vista of red two-story buildings with white-framed windows, nestled in the pines between two steep hills. Stacks of timber sat between the ore chute and the railroad track, and a barren hillside near the depot testified as to the timber's origin. Zachary swung the car into a space near the main building, pumping the horn.

"All the above-ground people wanted to get a look at you," he said apologetically. "Will you be wanting to go below?"

"Yes!" said both the Hoovers at once.

Milton Zachary sighed and shook his head. "Now, Miz Hoover, you wouldn't want to do that. Why, the only way into that mine is in a little open cage that goes down 1200 feet a minute, in the dark, with the water dripping on you all the time." Instead of a gasp and a withdrawal of the request,

Zachary's discouraging words were met with stony silence
from the back seat of the automobile. He tried again. "And
what with the fumes, and the falling rocks now and again,
and—ma'am, I'll tell you what's the truth: ninety percent of
our work force is immigrants from the old country, especially
Eyetalian, and the fact is that they won't allow a woman in
the mine. It's supposed to be bad luck. Why, some of the
time, if they so much as cross paths with a woman on the
way to work, they'll turn right around and go back home."

"His statement has veracity, dear," growled the president.
"I think it best for you to wait here, perhaps in the offices."

Mrs. Hoover smiled. "You promise me that you'll be careful, and you can go alone, Bert. I think I'll take a walk in
these lovely hills."

The president, now attired in borrowed coveralls and a
miner's cap, followed Zachary to the entrance of the mine,
barking technical questions as he went.

"Yessir," said Zachary, who was always one question behind. "It's open stoping, with levels leading off the main
shaft here. Gravity brings the loose ore down a frame chute
into the tunnel, where it—"

"—Falls into cars to be transported to the central shaft,
and subsequently out of the mine." Hoover nodded impatiently. "I know that. Do you use Wiggle-Tails?"

"Hand-rotated pneumatic drills?" Zachary grinned.
"Naw, sir. We called them widow-makers, the way they used
to loosen ceiling rock when we were drilling. No, we switched
to an Ingersoll Water Leyner a couple of years ago."

"Better than in my early days," Hoover remarked. "We
used single-jacking. Ever do that?"

"No, sir. It was double-jacking here. They figured it was
easier on the men to work in pairs, one to swing the eight-
pound hammer, and the other to twist and clean the drill.
They counted on fifty hits per minute thataway."

Hoover scowled. "Bit dangerous, wasn't it?"

Zachary held up a crooked finger. "See that? Our light
flickered, and my partner missed the steel. I'm right glad to
be working above ground these days. Well, here's the chip-

pie,'' he said, pointing to a steam-hoist cage, the mine's 'elevator.' "Do you want to go first, or shall I?''

"Despite other advances in mine technology, I find that the sensations during descent are quite unchanged,'' said the president when he joined Zachary deep in the mine. The musty dampness and the litany of dulled sounds, punctuated by flashes of light as the cage rushed past a mining level—it was the same unsettling ride as ever. Hoover brushed stray water drops from his face and shoulders, and looked about him. In the dark tunnel, bare light bulbs shone on chiseled dirt walls and foot-square timber pillars that supported the roof. "This looks about the same, as well. At one time I thought we would develop a substitute for wooden pillars, to reduce the danger of mine fires.''

"Not yet, sir,'' said Zachary, patting the wood. "Iron rusts, and concrete won't take the pressure. We haven't had any cave-ins, though. About all we've had to worry about here is the fact that the mine is played out—that, and the union.''

"I suppose the owners can't afford to pay what the union wants the workers to receive?''

"Not when they want to pay the muckers same as the miners! They claim it's just as dangerous to shovel and haul ore as it is to mine it. I reckon that's true, but it don't require any skill.''

"And you had an organizer from the union here?''

"Yep. He wanted to call a strike, and Mr. Hamilton put him off the place, and talked about bringing in strikebreakers from Michigan. It ended up being a fistfight, and about six of us heard the union man say he'd be back.''

Hoover squinted into the darkness. "A mine would be an ideal place to arrange an accident for someone.''

Zachary shook his head. "Too many witnesses. Remember, there's only one way out of a mine. I guess the killer just waited for Mr. Hamilton to leave the camp and ambushed him. Mr. Blundy was here that day looking over the operation, and Mr. Hamilton was showing him around. About five o'clock, he told us that he was going out walking in the hills. This was his first summer here, and he was real interested in nature. He saw a wolf up here one winter morning, and he didn't even want to shoot it. I wish one of us had told him not to go, but we never thought twice about it. Mr. Blundy was leaving then, too, and he told him to look sharp for rattlesnakes, but none of us knew to warn him about bushwhackers.''

"Shot then, was he?"

"No, sir. Somebody busted his head open with a rock. When they found him, he was clutching one of those weeds with the yellow flowers, like he knew it was his funeral he was headed for.''

Herbert Hoover looked at his watch. ''A sad business,'' he announced. ''I hope we don't have mine wars here, as we did in West Virginia, but I doubt if I shall be the one who has to worry about it.''

"No, sir," said Zachary. "Would you like to see the concentrator now? It's just down the hill from the portal.''

"Time permits a brief tour, and then I shall have to see about returning to my train. What is the per-ton value of your concentrate?''

Nearly an hour later the president had finished his inspection of the mine and its processing mill. Having shaken hands with a number of miners and machinists, smilingly assuring them that prosperity was just around the corner, he went back to the main building to exchange the dusty coveralls for his brown suit and his habitual frown.

Lou Henry Hoover was waiting for them in the foreman's office, sipping tea from a cracked china mug and chatting amiably with a heavyset man with solemn eyes and a drooping mustache.

"I trust I haven't kept you waiting, Lou," said her husband stiffly.

"Of course you have, Bert, but I quite enjoyed my afternoon. This gentleman has been most kind to keep me company when I returned from my walk, and he would like to shake hands with you, dear, but he really came out to see Mr. Zachary.''

The big man stood up, set his Stetson on Zachary's desk,

and stretched out his hand. "It's an honor to meet you, Mr. President. My name is Clayton Guthrie."

"Mr. Guthrie is the high sheriff of this county," Mrs. Hoover announced. "Such an interesting job, I always think!"

"Have they set a trial date yet?" Zachary asked the sheriff.

Clayton Guthrie shook his head. "I'm afraid we're back to square one on that. Our suspect has an alibi."

"And he didn't say so before?"

"His alibi is married. She didn't come forward until she had to."

"Maybe you ought to hang him anyhow," said the president in his deadpan voice.

Mrs. Hoover's laugh indicated that he had been joking. "I was so glad to hear that Mr. Lewis was not even indirectly involved in your foreman's death," she said to Milton Zachary. "Actually, though, I had decided that even before I met the sheriff. Look at this, Bert."

She reached into her handbag and took out a wilted yellow wildflower. "This was growing in the field where the body was found. There were hundreds of them."

"Monkey flower," said Hoover. "We had them in California, didn't we?"

"Yes, we did. Tell me, Mr. Zachary, is that field part of the land that belongs to this mine?"

Zachary looked bewildered. "Yes, ma'am. We timber for a couple hundred acres in these hills. The Fremonts own all of it. You're welcome to a bouquet of the flowers if you want it."

Herbert Hoover smiled at his wife. "The man who wants to buy the land was here on the day of the murder, Lou."

She smiled back. "I thought he must have been."

The sheriff and the mine foreman exchanged puzzled glances. "Is there something about the flowers?" asked the sheriff.

"Its scientific name is *Mimulus guttatus*," Mrs. Hoover explained. "In school we called it a copper flower because it is found growing on copper deposits. It even springs up in the tailings of a copper mine, where nothing else will grow."

"Copper?" echoed Zachary.

"Yes. Probably quite a good deposit. You sometimes find

copper in veins close to silver deposits. And if that is the case, then the land isn't worthless at all, is it?''

Hoover narrowed his eyes. ''It would seem that Mr. Blundy is not a sharp businessman, merely a dishonest one. He must have known about the copper deposit when he made the low bid for the 'worthless' land. And when your amateur naturalist discovered the copper flowers, he was killed before the owners could be told of their good fortune.''

The sheriff looked at Milton Zachary. ''Can you run tests on that land?''

Zachary nodded absently, still staring at Mrs. Hoover. ''Ma'am, how did you know about copper? Just from being married to a mining engineer?''

''Certainly not,'' she replied. ''We were classmates at Stanford. My grades were higher than his.''

The sheriff examined the crumpled yellow flower. ''Lucky for us you happened to visit.''

Herbert Hoover almost smiled. ''It was on our train route.''

''And Mr. John L. Lewis asked us to have a look at things here, if we could,'' added the first lady. ''He belongs to our club, you know.''

STUART M. KAMINSKY *is a professor of Radio, Television, and Film at Northwestern University and has published critical studies of John Huston, Clint Eastwood, and Don Siegel, as well as textbooks. He uses his knowledge of film history to great effect in his Toby Peters mysteries, all of which are set near the movie world of 1930s and 1940s Hollywood. In addition, he is the author of an excellent series of police procedurals featuring Porfiry Petrovich Rostnikov of the Moscow police.*

Harry S. Truman (1884–1972) was America's thirty-third president, winning the election of 1948 in a great upset over Thomas Dewey. (This, after having assumed the presidency upon the death of Franklin Delano Roosevelt.) Perhaps Truman's most important act in the Oval Office was to authorize the dropping of the first atomic bomb on Japan.

THE BUCK STOPS HERE

★ ★ ★

Stuart M. Kaminsky

"Can you guess what this is?"

We were standing in the storage room of the Truman Library in Independence, Missouri, early in July of 1957 and the question had come from Mr. Truman himself, who was pointing at a broken wooden beam about a dozen feet long leaning against the wall.

I couldn't guess what the beam was. I was tired when I had to be alert. Hungry when I should have been undistracted and attentive. I hadn't slept since my unit officer had pulled

244

me out of a basketball game at a YMCA in Washington, D.C., the day before.

I stood blearily looking at the beam and then over at the ex-president, who smiled at me waiting for my answer. Truman was seventy-three years old, and although everyone from Franklin Roosevelt and President Eisenhower had referred to him as "little," the ex-president stood eye-to-eye with me, and I was slightly over 5′9″. Truman wore a light suit and tie and looked dapper and alert with a white handkerchief in his breast pocket.

"Lieutenant?" Truman asked again.

"I don't know, sir," I said as he rested a hand on the beam.

"This," said Truman in his clipped Missouri twang, "is the beam from the White House that gave way under my daughter Margaret's piano. If it weren't for that piano and this beam, the major reconstruction of the White House might never have taken place. It took the fear of a piano falling on my head to get a few dollars to shore up the most important symbolic building in the United States."

"And that's why you want it in the Library," I said, looking around the room on what I hoped was the last part of the tour. I had a potential assassin to look for and some sleep to catch up on. My interest in history was not at its peak.

How had it happened? When my CO had me called out of the basketball game, I hurried down to the locker, took a fast shower, and got dressed in my sports coat, slacks, and solid blue knit tie. I was standing in front of Colonel Saint's desk within fifteen minutes of the moment he had summoned me.

Saint was drinking a cup of coffee. A matching cup stood steaming in the corner of his desk. He nodded at the steaming second cup and I smiled and took it, even though I don't drink coffee. Saint never remembered this, but that didn't bother me. What bothered me was that he had made the friendly gesture. I was being prepared for something I might not want to hear.

"Have a seat, Pevsner," Saint said, reaching a stubby finger into his cup to fish out something tiny and even darker than the amber liquid.

Saint was fully uniformed, complete with medals on his

chunky chest and with his graying hair Wildrooted back and shiny.

"Thank you, sir," I said, and sat in the chrome-and-black leather chair across from him. Saint struck a pose, two hands clasped around his coffee cup. Behind him and over his head on the wall, President Eisenhower, in his five-star uniform, looked down at both of us benevolently.

"Carl Gades," Saint said, returning his finger to his coffee cup and fishing out a bit more of whatever it was that troubled him.

I didn't shake, shimmer, or show a sign when Saint looked up suddenly for my reaction. I just sipped at the bitter, hot liquid. I could see my face in the coffee. It was a bland, innocent twenty-eight-year-old face showing just what it had been trained to show: nothing.

"You know Carl Gades," Colonel Saint said, putting down the cup. "Damn coffee stinks. How can you drink it?"

I shrugged and kept drinking.

"I know Carl Gades," I said.

"You're the only member of this staff who has met him face-to-face who could identify him," the colonel said, folding his hands on his desk and looking down sourly at the coffee cup. "Kravitz wouldn't remember his mother if she wasn't wearing a name tag. Secret Service has no one who has ever seen him. They pulled your name out of the files. They can get things out of the files, off that damned microfilm, in a few hours now."

I had met Carl Gades only once and I didn't want to meet him again, but I was getting the idea that I might not have a choice. I hadn't made too many choices in my career for more than three years or, at least, that was the way it felt. I'd been drafted right out of UCLA and missed Korea by being pulled out after basic training and sent to Texas for Officers' Candidate School. After OCS I was sent to Washington for intelligence training, and a week after completing my training I was on a mission to Rome with a dyspeptic captain named Resnick. Resnick barely talked to me and barely briefed me. "Keep your eyes open," he had said, and then closed his and slept on the plane all the way to Rome.

My rapid rise in the military had been the result not of my

great promise and intellect but good breeding. My father was a retired Los Angeles Police Department captain, and my uncle was an aging but still active private investigator who had handled some delicate private jobs for people in high places. Oh, yes, there was one other thing that led to my success. I was a *hawk*. I hadn't known I was a hawk. There weren't many of us, and the intelligence services probably bragged to each other about the number of hawks they had.

A hawk is an individual who takes in everything in a scene, isn't distracted by the things that draw the attention of normal people. If I'm walking down the street and hear someone scream behind me, I turn around and see not only a woman shouting at a man running down the street, but I see each crack in the street, the color of the man's socks, the woman's straggling hairs, every window on every building, and the fern sprouting yellow fronds in a fourth-floor window across the street. I see and I retain.

It's a literal photographic memory. I don't remember words or conversations, just images, images fixed that can be re-called. Unfortunately, the images sometimes come back unbidden and they don't always bear any great significance. So, for whatever it was worth, I had this gift or curse, and I was of particular value in sensitive situations where photography would be valuable but for various reasons, usually location and security, photography wouldn't be feasible.

Gades had met with Resnick and me in the Piazza Popolo. Gades had worn a wide-brimmed white hat and a white suit. He had a dark mustache and beard and was careful to keep the top of his face and eyes in the shadow of his Marcello Mastroianni hat. Gades had insisted that we meet at the statue in the center of the Piazza so that no one would be near us but the people driving madly around the Piazza.

Gades was there to trade information. We gave him a name. He gave us a name. I didn't know what either name meant. I was there to record and remember Gades, who, in broad daylight, insisted on patting us both down to be sure we weren't armed with cameras or weapons. He also informed us that he had people checking out the nearby buildings to be sure no one was lurking with a high-power telescopic-lensed camera.

Gades spoke no more than a minute in a raspy, disguised voice, and he gave his information first, confident that we wouldn't dare cross him, suggesting, in fact, that he rather enjoyed having people try to cross him so he could make examples of them and increase his value and public image.

Now, many murders—from Bombay to Kiev—later, Gades, who had become even more cautious, was back in my lap.

"No photographs of Gades," Saint said. "Son of a bitch's too careful. You're the only one who might be able to identify him. Could you?"

I pulled out the fixed picture of that day three years earlier and went over it, the split second Gades had tilted his head up and shown his deep blue eyes, the other second when he had shown a profile, the freckles on his wrist, the turn of his left ear.

"I could," I said.

"Hot damn." Saint grinned. He turned and looked up at Ike for approval, and Ike seemed to give it. "We've got them by the short ones, Lieutenant."

"Glad to hear it, sir," I'd said, finishing the coffee. "Who have we got by? . . ."

Saint leaned forward, straightened his tie, and grinned as he said, "Secret Service, FBI, all of them."

"I see," I said, "but I. . ."

"FBI got a phone conversation on a wired line," Saint said, pulling a manila folder out of his desk drawer and opening it. "Word is that Gades plans to assassinate Harry Truman. How do you like that?"

I didn't like it very much, but I was sure he didn't need me to tell him that.

"Why?" I asked.

"Revenge," whispered Colonel Saint, dramatically leaning toward me over the desk. "Gades's brother, Arthur, died in prison last month. Son of a bitch should have been executed. Tried to blow up a plane for who the hell knows why. Spent ten years in jail. Truman wouldn't let him out, turned down two appeals. At least that's the way Gades feels about it, according to the FBI. It was his only brother. Things like that make would-be assassins careless. You know what I mean?"

"Yes, sir," I said, thinking of my own brother Nate, who was in college back in California.

"People are watching Truman, but they don't know Gades," Saint went on. "Fear now is that Gades probably knows we know. FBI screwed up the whole wiretap operation. Who knows? FBI, CIA, MI, everyone and his aunt thinks Gades'll move fast. You've got a military flight to Kansas City in one hour and a half. Sergeant Ganz'll drive you. I'd like you in uniform, highly visible. Stop off at home, change, and get your ass in gear. You meet Mr. Truman in his office in Kansas City first thing in the morning. 0800 hours. Questions?"

"And I'm . . . ?" I began.

"Hawk," he said. "Spot Gades. Turn him over to the Secret Service. There'll be a couple of agents with Truman. You know Gades's reputation, and he's not likely to deviate this time. He does it himself. He does it in person. No bombs. Doesn't even like guns, though he carries one. Kills up close. Wants to scare the community. Does it, too. Kicks up his price. Let's get the bastard. Ganz has cash for you. Keep decent records this time, Pevsner."

That was it. His mouth moved from a broad smile to a thin enigma. I rose, saluted, took his return salute, and watched as Colonel Saint turned in his swivel chair, looked up at Ike and then, hands behind his head, looked out the window at the U.S. Post Office building across the street. Less than two hours later I was on an Air Force plane headed for Kansas City and drinking a Dr. Pepper handed to me by a frecklefaced airman.

We landed at the Kansas City airport on a side strip reserved for military landings. I had picked up my uniform, but I didn't have time to change into my uniform until I got on the plane. Before we landed I brushed my teeth and shaved.

Colonel Saint had given me enough money to last about a week if I was careful. If it took more, I'd have to ask. It might be a lot more. It might be forever if the FBI information was wrong or if Gades had changed his mind. I had the distinct fear that Colonel Saint wanted Gades so badly he might leave me to turn to fungus in Kansas City.

A khaki-colored Buick was waiting at the airport, and the driver, a Spec Four named Kithcart, took me to the Federal

Reserve Building in downtown Kansas City, where he parked the car illegally and led me into the building where a pair of Secret Service men who identified themselves as Koster and Franklin took me to the elevator and up the stairs to Truman's office. Koster and Franklin were clean-shaven, gray-suited, about six feet tall, brown-eyed, closemouthed, and nearly bookends. I guessed they were both in their forties, but they could have been younger or older.

Truman came to the door to greet me. He shook my hand, a strong grip for an old man, and looked me straight in the eye.

"You're younger than I thought, Lieutenant," Truman said. "But so is everyone but Dean Acheson."

"Yes sir," I said.

"You know I was a captain in World War One?" he asked waking to the corner of the room, putting a white hat on his head, and picking out a black walking stick from an upright black leather container near the window.

"Yes sir," I said.

"Let's go," he said. "I'm not changing my schedule for any two-bit gangster. I'm going to the Truman Museum back home in Independence. There's a construction strike all through this area, and some of the important work has stopped on the Library. Damn shame. Everything is ready for final plastering and floorings. Stacks, shelves, and exhibit cases may not be put in for the dedication. Some carpenters and painters are on the job, but we are not on schedule. You ever been in the White House?"

Truman walked briskly past me and looked back at my face over his shoulder.

"Once, sir. I briefed President Eisenhower on a . . . a delicate mission with General Clark."

"I don't give a damn about the subject," said Truman, amiably gesturing for me to follow him through the door. "I just want to know if you're as good as they say you are. I assume you were in the president's office?"

"Yes sir," I said following him out the door. He walked quickly to the elevator flanked by the two Secret Service men.

We went down the elevator and out the building, heading over to a parking lot, where we got into a big, black Lincoln.

I took in the street, the passing people, and saw nothing and no one I recognized. One of the Secret Service men sat with the driver. The other sat silently with Truman and me in the back seat.

"Microfilm," Truman said as I tried to shake off airplane weariness. "At some point, thanks to microfilm, the Truman Library will have the best collection of presidential papers anywhere. You know that, until Hoover, people simply threw away presidential papers?"

"No sir," I said, which was true.

"One exception," Truman corrected, looking over his shoulder at me. "Rutherford B. Hayes, and who the hell cares about Hayes's papers?"

"I think you do," I said.

"You are right, Lieutenant," he said. "I care about Hayes and Millard Filmore and Tyler. It's the office, Lieutenant. You put a man in the office, and it is his responsibility to fill that space with dignity. No man in his right mind would want to be president if he knew what it entails. Aside from the impossible administrative burden, he has to take all sorts of abuse from liars and demagogues. All the president is, is a glorified public relations man who spends his time flattering, kissing, and kicking people to get them to do what they are supposed to do anyway."

"I'll have to take your word on that, sir," I said, looking at the Secret Service man who scanned the road on the way to Independence and appeared to hear none of the conversation.

The trip seemed long, though Independence is only nine miles from Kansas City. When we hit Independence, we drove down Pleasant Street to the Truman Library, which clung to a knoll in the middle of thirteen landscaped acres.

"How do you like it?" Truman said as we got out of the car and the Secret Service men scanned the parking lot.

"Impressive," I said.

"Gift of the people of Independence," he said.

The Library stood on the highest point of the property, an arc-shaped building of contemporary design with an imposing portico in the middle. There weren't many windows.

We started toward the building. Truman's cane tapped on

the stone path as we moved briskly, flanked by Secret Service men.

"Impressive," I repeated, hurrying to keep up with the ex-president.

"Too damned modern," he sighed. "It's got too much of that fellow in it to suit me."

"That. . ." I started.

"Frank Lloyd Wright," Truman said, picking up the pace.

I couldn't see much Frank Lloyd Wright in the building, and I was sure Wright hadn't designed the Library, but I said nothing, just scanned the building, landscape, and the workmen who unloaded a truck in the parking lot.

"Should have been Georgian," Truman said. "Neld got modern on me, and it was too far along to stop him when I realized it. I wanted it to look like Independence Hall in Philadelphia."

We strode through the doors under the portico and Truman led us past painters and repairmen who looked up at us. None of them was Gades. The ex-president opened a door and pointed through it with his cane.

"Step in," he said, "and tell me what you see."

I stepped in and found myself in the Oval Office, the same office in which I had briefed President Eisenhower two years earlier, or, at least, a near-perfect replica.

"The Oval Office," I said.

"Right," he said, motioning the Secret Service men to stay back as he joined me and closed the door. "But you're a falcon. . . ."

"Hawk," I corrected, scanning the room.

"What's wrong with the room?" he said.

"It's not what's wrong that surprises me, Mr. President," I said. "It's what's right. The mantel isn't a replica. It's the same one I saw in the White House."

Truman's laugh was a silent, pleased cackle.

"Perfect," he said, moving across the room, removing his hat, and placing his cane on the corner of his desk. On that desk near the window was a sign I knew about. It read: The Buck Stops Here. "It is original. When the White House was renovated and we moved into Blair House, I asked them to keep pieces they would normally throw out. That mantel was one of the pieces. I'll show you another.''

He led me through the office and past more workmen, who he greeted by name, and led me to the storeroom where he showed me the famous beam that I failed to identify.

"Stage props of history," Truman sighed. "So, young man, what do we do now?''

I held back a yawn and stopped myself from shrugging.

"Whatever you normally do," I said. "But with me nearby and a little more caution than usual.''

"I've been threatened before in my life," he said, stepping over the beam and placing his hand on a table, a nicely polished table. "That is the table on which the United Nations Charter was signed in San Francisco.''

I looked at the table, but it conjured up no images. I needed sleep or rest. He showed me other items: a wax figure of himself, a rug from the Shah of Iran, a bronze figure of Andrew Jackson.

"You think he has a chance of getting me?" Truman asked soberly but without apparent fear.

"Well. . ." I began.

"Forget it," he said. "I'm not going to get a straight answer out of you on that one. I'd rather not shock Bess when I go, and I'd like to see this place finished. Never did consider myself martyr material, either. We'll just have to see what God decides to do with this one. I like to quote an epitaph on a tombstone in a cemetery in Tombstone, Arizona. 'Here lies Jack Williams. He done his damnedest.' ''

"I'll do my damnedest, sir," I said.

"Almost nine," he said, looking at his watch. "Let's get back to the Oval Office.''

He led the way through the storage room and back to the exhibit space, where the workmen stopped talking as we moved through and into the Oval Office.

Truman went to the desk, opened it, and pulled out a bottle.

"Situation calls for a late-morning finger or two of good bourbon, wouldn't you say, Lieutenant Pevsner?''

"Yes sir," I said with a smile, though I disliked bourbon

even more than I disliked coffee, but you don't let a former president drink alone if you're invited to join him.

I took the small crystal glass he pushed toward me.

"To your powers of observation," he toasted.

I raised my glass and took a healthy sip. Truman downed his in a single shot and pursed his lips.

"That will be my only drink of the day till nightfall," he sighed.

I finished my drink and tried not to make a face.

"And now," he said. "If you want to sit, walk the grounds, browse around, I've got work to do. You are welcome to join me for lunch at noon at the house."

I thanked him and went out the door, closing it behind me as he sat behind the desk.

The Secret Service man named Koster was standing outside the office, arms folded.

I nodded to him. He nodded back, deep brown eyes scanning my uniform. For the next twenty minutes I walked around the grounds. I ran into the other Secret Service man— Franklin—who was doing the same. We didn't speak. I was trying to walk off twenty-four hours without sleep and a stiff bourbon. It wasn't working.

Just before eleven a young man came running out of the Library toward where I was standing against an oak tree trying to look alert.

"Lieutenant Pevsner?" he said.

"That's right."

"Phone call for you. Follow me."

I followed him back into the building and into a small office not far from the Oval Office. A woman sat typing in the office and a phone rested on a desk off of the receiver. I picked it up.

"Lieutenant Pevsner," I said.

"Colonel Saint," he answered.

"Nothing here that I can see yet, sir," I said.

"Look again, Lieutenant," he said. "We have definite information that Gades flew to Kansas City one week and one day ago. He's been eating steaks and waiting for a chance to get Truman."

"He's not around here," I said, looking around the office

at the woman typist, who reminded me of Bulldog Turner of the Chicago Bears, and at the secretary, who looked a little like Clifton Webb.

"Some FBI crackpot has an idea. Thinks Gades will make his move today, one month to the day Gades's brother died," Saint said. "Something about the date circled in an appointment book in a hotel room Gades might have been in."

"He might be right," I said.

"The time was noted," said Saint. "Three P.M. What do you think?"

"I don't," I said.

"Find him," said Saint.

"Will do, sir," I said.

Saint hung up, and I went outside to hang around. I didn't know how to find Gades. I watched people come and go—delivery vans, a mailman. None was Gades. I was sure of that.

Noon turned the corner and Truman came sauntering out of the building with Koster and Franklin close behind, looking everywhere. Truman tilted his head back so he could see me from under his hat and motioned at me with his cane. I followed him.

"Called Bess," he said. "Told her we'd be having company. You like fried chicken?"

"Like it fine," I said, walking at his side.

We didn't take the car, which made it more difficult for the Secret Service men and me, but it was a clear, not-too-hot day and the walk helped wake me up. The walk to the gabled Victorian house on Delaware Street was probably longer than most seventy-year-olds would like to make, but Truman did it talking all the way, mostly about Andrew Jackson.

"No sign of him?" Truman asked as we went up the wooden steps. He wasn't talking about Andrew Jackson this time.

"Not yet," I said.

"Wouldn't want him to try anything around the house," he said.

"I'm watching, sir," I said with what I hoped was a reassuring smile.

"There's watching and there's watching," Truman said,

pausing on the porch and looking at the two Secret Service men, who had stopped at the bottom of the steps and were casually scanning the quiet street. "Sometimes you miss what's important because it's so damned obvious that you never consider it."

"I'll keep that in mind, sir," I said.

Lunch was hot and not too spicy. Mrs. Truman served the lunch herself, but the cleaning up was done by a young woman wearing an apron and not meeting my eyes when I looked at her. The Secret Service men ate in the kitchen, though I found that Truman had invited them to join us.

"Last Secret Service fellows insisted on working shifts and getting their own food," Truman said. "These boys are less formal. Better that way. How's the chicken?"

It was fine, and I said so.

"Bess likes cooking, or so she says. Hated the White House sometimes. Plenty for her to do, but not the things she liked doing. It all happened too fast for her. One minute I was a failed Kansas farmer who couldn't keep a hat business open and in ten years I was a judge, a senator, vice-president, and president of the United States. Hard to believe. More peas?"

I said no thanks and checked my watch. It was almost one. If Gades was going to make his move at three, he'd have to show up soon. I was considering suggesting to Truman that we stay around the house till after three, but he rose, pushed away from the table, and announced that we'd better be getting back to the Library.

Mrs. Truman, who had joined us silently for the lunch, accepted my thanks and asked her husband to come home early.

"Margaret promised to call," she said.

"Then by all means I'll be back early," he said with a smile.

The meal hadn't made me more alert. I'd eaten lightly, but it was getting late in the afternoon and the walk wasn't having the effect I'd like. The Secret Service men, as always, were silent, and Truman talked animatedly about Hubert Humphrey and the Pope's promise to send the Vatican documents on microfilm as soon as they were ready.

"Don't know what I'll do with them," Truman said, the

late-afternoon sun glinting off his glasses, "but you don't turn down an offer like that."

Nothing had changed at the Library. The same workmen were there. The secretary who looked like Clifton Webb was standing at the door to the replica of the Oval Office with a sheaf of papers in his hand. Truman took his left hand out of his pocket and took the papers and hurried into his office.

Koster ran a hand through his brown hair to make sure no loose strands marred the image. He took his place in front of the door and looked stonily at me to let me know that he wasn't up for idle conversation. Franklin scanned the narrow corridor and checked the doors. He turned to us, blinked his cold blue eyes, and nodded to indicate the place was clear. Then he wandered off to watch the rear of the building. My Timex told me 1400 hours was approaching. Saint's information seemed flimsy with Bess Truman's chicken, peas, and lemonade resting heavily in my stomach and a warm Missouri sun sparkling on the grass as I stepped in front of the building.

The whole Gades business seemed dreamlike, Colonel Saint's dream. I found an oak tree in front of the Library, loosened my tie, and sat in the shade where I could get a good look at anyone approaching the building on foot or in a vehicle. Birds above me chirped away, and once in the next hour I saw a cardinal and the second mailman of the day. I checked the mailman carefully. I'd once read a story by Chesterton about a criminal who disguised himself as a mailman because mailmen seem so much a part of the landscape. But this mailman was short and pudgy and definitely not Carl Gades.

I closed my eyes and began to go over the images of the day since I had arrived. I selected, checked faces and hands, and pulled myself up and awake when the image of Truman's dining room began to fade. My eyes scanned the Library, and I listened. Only the echo of a carpenter hammering away inside.

I had a sudden feeling of nausea. I wasn't sure what caused it, but I had to stand up. My legs were trembling. Maybe it was the lack of sleep, an allergy, or too much food for lunch; but something wasn't right.

"Sometimes you miss what's important because it's so damned obvious you don't see it," Truman had said.

Chesterton's invisible mailman. He'd been standing next to me, walking at Truman's right hand, looking at the former president's back through the window of the Library in front of me. The Secret Service man, Franklin. In the morning his eyes had been brown. Less than an hour ago they had turned blue. I was sure of it. I checked the images in my memory. Confirmed. I moved down the hill, straightening my tie, and went over other images. Franklin's nose, profile. Altered. Not quite Gades, but not unlike him. Little things could take care of that. And then I checked the hands. I stopped, closed my eyes, and compared Gades's left hand with Franklin's. A tiny white scar, a blemish the size of a tack head, the pattern of the veins. I started to run and checked my Timex. It was a few minutes before three.

I could have called for Koster, but I wasn't sure if Koster was Secret Service or Gades's helpmate of the month. So I ran behind the Library where Franklin was supposed to be stationed. He wasn't there. I considered running to the window of Truman's office and telling him to get the hell out of there, but I fought down the panic and the memory of lunch. I had no weapon. I hadn't expected to need one. The damned Secret Service was supposed to supply the firepower. I ran to the wall and crept along until I got to the window. When I looked inside, my head went light and I considered diving into a migraine.

Franklin was standing in front of Truman's desk and the ex-president was looking up at him. Franklin was doing all the talking, but I couldn't hear a word. Franklin, hell, it was Gades! And he was looking at his watch. I leaned back against the wall and checked mine. If mine was accurate and his was, too, it was about three minutes to three. I hoped Gades's sense of poetic justice was operating.

I considered a leap at the window, but there were too many things that could go wrong. The window might not break or, if it did, I might be so cut up that I couldn't do anything except get myself killed along with Harry Truman. Even if I did get through the window and on my feet, I didn't think I was a hand-to-hand match for Gades. Gades liked to kill with a knife, but he was known to carry a gun. He might be impetuous, but he was no fool.

So, I hurried for the front of the Library, managing to trip once and rip the knees of my dress greens. There was no time for checking credentials. I went right for the Oval Office where Koster was standing. He looked at me, saw a panting madman with a torn uniform, knew something was up, and took a defensive position in front of the door. It was a good sign. A Gades man, knowing his boss was inside and about to commit murder, would have had his weapon out and would have put two holes in me by now.

"Hold it Lieutenant," Koster said calmly.

I stopped, looked at the door to Truman's office, and hoped that it was reasonably soundproof. What was I doing? As I stood at an impasse in front of Koster, I pulled up the image of the original White House Oval Office I'd once visited. I found the door and fixed on it as I had left the room. The door was thick and solid. I did the same for the replica Oval Office behind Koster, recalling it from the second I'd looked at the door when I'd entered the room with Truman. It was equally thick. Knowing Truman's desire for detailed authenticity, I was confident that Gades and Truman wouldn't hear us in the hall unless we shouted.

"Koster," I said, trying to control my panting. "How well do you know Franklin?"

Koster tilted his head like a curious bird.

"Come again, Lieutenant?"

"When did you meet Franklin?"

I looked at the door and considered trying to rush past him, but I didn't see how I could make it even if I were lucky enough to catch him with a knee to the groin or an elbow to the stomach.

"Three days ago," he said. "He was assigned to bolster protection for the president when word came through that there might be an attempt on his life. What's your point?"

"Did you get a call? Did he have papers?" I asked, glancing at my watch. We had less than two minutes.

"Papers, a call came through," Koster said. "We talked. He . . ."

"His eyes change color," I said.

"His eyes?"

"They were brown this morning. They're blue now. You think of any reason?"

Koster tried to remember his partner's eyes.

"Why?" he asked.

"Maybe the brown contacts bothered him. He had to take them out so he could see clearly when he killed Mr. Truman."

"Killed . . . Are you saying that Franklin is . . ."

". . . Carl Gades," I finished. "And I just saw him in there," I nodded toward the door, "with Truman."

"Let's find out," Koster said, reaching for the doorknob but keeping an eye on me. I didn't move forward. The door was locked. Koster considered knocking, thought better of it, and looked at me.

"The door's solid," I said, "but the frame is new. If we both go at it, we might be able to get it down."

"Might," he said. "Let's do it."

There wasn't much room to move. We got against the far wall and together went for the Oval Office door. Our shoulders hit together and mine went numb, but the frame splintered and we tumbled in. I went down on the floor. Koster kept his feet and took in the room.

Gades was standing next to the desk, a good fifteen feet or more from Koster. In his hand Gades held a small revolver. Truman sat behind the desk, his mouth a thin pink line.

"About thirty seconds," Gades said, aiming the weapon at us. "Then our little Mr. Truman will feel steel entering his bowels and he'll know a little of what it is like to die as my brother died."

I got to my feet shakily and stood next to Koster.

"Your brother died," Truman said, "because he was a murderer and he paid the penalty for that crime by living out what remained of his life behind bars where he belonged."

"You could have saved him," Gades spat, not taking his eyes from me and Koster.

"I made some tough decisions when I was in office," Truman said evenly. "That was not one of them."

"Shut up old man," Gades said. "Shut up and watch the clock."

I wondered how much of a chance I'd have at surviving if I made a run at Gades. Not much. I might divert him enough for Koster to get his hands on him, but Gades had killed before. He could probably take both of us out in less than a second.

"Have you every played stud poker?" Truman asked.

"Stud poker?" Gades asked, and then laughed.

"One card in the hole, four up," Truman explained. "Everything in sight but the hole card."

"You can talk till I put the steel in your belly, old man," Gades said. "What did you have for lunch? Ah, yes. Chicken. Let's see what it looks like when it comes running out on the floor."

Gades kept his eyes on us.

"The trick," Truman said, "is to get the other fellow looking at the wrong cards. It worked with Churchill. It worked with Dewey. It worked with Stalin, and by God it'll work with you."

The next few seconds were a series of perfect images. I held them and savored them. I still have them in detail. Truman's hand had inched to the handle of the cane on his desk. He had been sitting absolutely immobile as he had talked. He had looked the old man, but in those few seconds, Harry Truman's cane swished upward under Gades's hand and Gades tried to turn the weapon in it away from us and toward Truman, who was on the rise. The gun hand went up in the air and the bullet cracked through the ceiling. Truman, now on his feet, brought the cane down with two hands on Gades's wrist. A bone broke with a sharp crack and the gun fell to the floor. Koster moved forward as Gades reacted by reaching into his jacket. The knife came out in the unbroken hand. Gades's teeth were clenched in hatred as he lunged forward over the desk. Koster was within a foot of the would-be assassin when Truman's cane cracked down on Gades's head.

Gades stagged backward, dropping the knife, and Koster hit him with a right that would have pleased Rocky Marciano.

"Little," grunted Truman, looking over the top of his glasses at the unconscious Gades on the floor. "Man doesn't know the game, he shouldn't take a drink in the dealer's parlor."

The hall was alive with people who had heard the door breaking and the gunshot. The secretary and typist and a few white-clad painters stood at the broken door trying to see what had happened.

"Show's over," said Truman. "Permanter, get that door fixed and call an ambulance. Everybody back to work."

They left reluctantly, missing Koster and me picking up the limp Gades.

"You did a fine job, Mr. President," Koster said, straightening his hair after he had secured Gades in a chair.

"Just be sure he's not playing possum," Truman said, looking up at the hole in the ceiling.

"He's not, sir," Koster said.

"Faced worse than that," Truman said looking at the unconscious Gades, "back in World War One. Hell, faced worse than that across the conference table."

"Still," I said, wearily wondering if Colonel Saint would be happy enough to pay for the new dress uniform I needed. "You took a big chance."

Truman grinned a broad campaign grin, leaned forward, and pointed to the famous sign on his desk that read:

THE BUCK STOPS HERE.

A FATAL TRIP

★ ★ ★

K. T. Anders

Ivan Popov had drunk too much vodka the night before. His head felt as big as an onion dome on top of St. Basil's as he showed his pass to the security guard, then waited for the elevator in the big gray-and-sand-colored KGB building in Dzerzhinsky Square in the middle of Moscow. Perhaps, he thought, walking as gently as possible down the hall to his office in the Operations Department, First Chief Directorate, just perhaps no one would notice that he was an hour late.

But Valentin, the burly man who shared his cubicle on the fifth floor, was waiting for him. He raised bushy black eyebrows and wagged a finger as Popov walked through the doorway.

"Shame, Comrade. The State cannot prosper if its servants do not arrive promptly to fulfill their duties."

Popov made an obscene gesture and sat down gingerly at his desk.

"Toilet paper," he whispered.

Valentin rose from his chair like a great goose, all flapping arms and legs. "Where?" he cried, already halfway to the door.

"No, no. Last night." Popov grabbed his aching head. "And for goodness sake, speak quietly."

Valentin landed back in his seat with a thud. "How many rolls did you get?"

"Six. I invited Misha over and we celebrated until two A.M."

Valentin's eyes misted over. "I haven't had toilet paper for six months," he said.

"I hear there may be another truck on Gorky Street around five tonight."

"No, rumor has it they're selling chickens on the Sadovaya then." Valentin shook his head. "My wife wants to make Chicken Kiev for my son's birthday."

Popov shrugged. "Life is full of choices, Comrade."

Valentin shot him a dirty look, then turned back to his own desk. "I nearly forgot," he said over his shoulder. "Grusha wants to see you."

"Grusha?" Popov's face went pale.

He tried to keep a low profile around his boss, Arkady Pyotr Grusha. Unofficially, Grusha was known throughout the Operations Department as Old Wall Head, because his subordinates had learned that once he'd made up his mind, it was like talking to a wall to get him to listen to anything else. Popov knew from firsthand experience.

For five years, Ivan Popov had been perfectly content with his job as an Intelligence Analyst in the cryptology section of the KGB. A timid, bookish man, he was overwhelmed when, six months ago, his name came up for promotion to Senior Analyst in Charge of Intercepted United States Naval Coded Intelligence. But somehow a clerk in personnel had confused his name with a Clandestine Operations Agent named Igor Popov. Igor had also been up for promotion in his own department, but unfortunately, had been killed on his last assignment. In a bureaucratic mix-up, Ivan's records, instead of Igor's, were placed in the Deceased file, and Ivan was given Igor's promotion into the Clandestine Operations Department. According to the official record, Ivan Popov was dead. Which made things a little sticky for him.

Since the State never admitted to making a mistake, it was difficult to get the error remedied. Ivan Popov had gone to Grusha right away with his problem. Grusha listened impassively as Ivan insisted he was not Igor. Then Grusha reread the file before him, which noted that agent Igor was a master at assuming a false identity to attain his objective.

"Communism is the best of all possible worlds," Grusha had said after thinking for several minutes in silence. "The State always acts in the best interest of the people. Therefore, this has happened for the best." He told Popov that he was lucky to have such a high-paying job, that one seldom got a second chance in life, and that he should go back to work and stop complaining.

So for six months, Popov had been struggling to become invisible in the nest of spies that was the Clandestine Operations Department. His nervous system was a wreck. He had succeeded in creating a niche for himself as a backup agent and was known to give excellent desk support to his fellow operatives, but he lived in dread of the day he would be called upon for an actual mission.

And now Grusha wanted to see him.

"Did he say what he wanted?" whispered Popov to Valentin, running a nervous hand through his unkempt brown hair. As usual, he'd forgotten to comb it this morning.

"No, just that it was priority. You better get in there."

Popov grabbed a fistful of papers relating to his current case—the entrapment of an innocent American businessman who was selling computers to several farm collectives around Moscow. Or rather, the field operative was entrapping; Popov was providing his usual backup at the office. He could feel the vein in his neck throbbing as he shuffled down the hall to Grusha's office. He hoped the director was only looking for an update on the entrapment case.

Grusha's secretary, Sonia, flashed her steel tooth and swung her hips as she showed him into Grusha's sparsely furnished office. Grusha was on the floor doing push-ups, his graying hair matted with sweat against his skull.

"Ah, Popov," said Grusha, puffing to get his ungainly frame upright. "A healthy body complements a healthy mind. Directive 536802B." He slapped his subordinate on the back, sending a bolt of pain through Popov's head, then sat behind his battered wooden desk. He frowned at the clock on the wall. "You're late, Popov."

"My apologies, Comrade Director," said Popov. "I . . . I was in the field this morning checking on the camera equipment for that entrapment case we're working on."

"Fish eggs," boomed Grusha with a wave of his hand. "I'll get someone else for that."

Popov could hear the time bomb begin to tick. He wondered how many hours of safety-behind-the-desk remained to him.

"We've almost got him, Comrade Director," he said, shuffling the sheaf of papers. "He's on film doing rather private things with a young boy we hired, and. . ."

"I've been looking through your file," said Grusha, ignoring him. He ran his eye over Popov's angular features and skinny frame. "To look at you, I'd never have guessed your background. We're underutilizing a man of your talents."

"My talents?" said Popov faintly. His knees began to quiver and he groped for the steel-frame chair opposite his boss.

"Remarkable. Not many men have the backbone for wet operations."

The vein in Popov's neck beat wildly. "Ah, *wet*," he said. He hadn't realized that Igor Popov had been in the KGB Wet Department, the department responsible for murders and assassinations. When he could control his voice, he pleaded with the man across the desk. "I'm not the man I used to be, Comrade Director. I've dried out."

"I understand." Grusha's eyes looked sympathetic. "Six months at a desk job can sap your nerve. But we'll remedy that. Time to get back into action."

"Action? No . . . no, I'm too old for action." Popov shook his head vigorously, causing the room to spin dizzily around him. He wished he didn't have this numbing hangover. He couldn't think fast enough.

Grusha laughed. "You're only twenty-nine, Comrade. And you did an excellent job eight months ago with that spy we caught in our missile factory."

Popov swallowed hard, tried to still his shaking hands. "You don't understand, Comrade Director. I'm not the right man. There's been a mistake. . ."

Grusha laughed again, his heavy jowls shaking like an English bulldog's. "You're too modest, Comrade Popov. But that's an admirable trait in a man of your experience. Now let me tell you what we have in mind for you."

The Director reached for the wooden box on his desk, extracted a Cuban cigar, and rolled it between his lips.

"The American government is in chaos," began Grusha, leaning back in his chair. "The vice-president got into some trouble and resigned. One of their senators was made vice-president. Then the *president* got into some trouble, and *he* resigned. Suddenly this senator has become the president of the United States. The American public is confused, hasn't the faintest notion what's going on or who's in charge. And it certainly doesn't trust its own government."

He smiled and lit the cigar. "Sounds like a perfect scenario, doesn't it? Just the right moment for the KGB to capitalize on the situation. Our own secretary general, Comrade Brezhnev, has decided that it is impossible to negotiate world power with a man the world not only doesn't know, but has never heard of, so he has offered to meet with this new president."

Grusha paused and looked at Popov, who was huddled in his chair. "Are you following me?" he asked. Popov nodded miserably.

Grusha took another puff on his cigar and watched a circle of blue smoke rise above his head like a halo. Popov touched the jumping vein in his neck and stared at the floor.

"It is well known," continued Grusha, "that the American press distorts all friendly overtures by the Soviet Union. So although this new president has sent a message to Brezhnev vowing to continue the détente begun by Nixon, he has also agreed to meet the premier privately, man to man, so that they may assess one another without the press jumping to conclusions. This meeting will take place at sea, in complete secrecy. Well, what do you think, Comrade?''

Popov said nothing, but stared at Grusha with bleak eyes.

"It's the perfect opportunity, Popov. While the American people are confused and distrustful, we can further augment the chaos. We can throw the country into such turmoil that it will be ripe for a left-wing takeover.''

Grusha paused. Popov knew he was expected to ask what course of action Grusha was proposing, but his head was thumping like the Moiseyev Dance Troupe and he couldn't bring himself to speak.

Grusha narrowed his eyes. "You are probably asking yourself what it is that we can do to capitalize on this turmoil.''

Popov nodded carefully.

"We will assassinate the new American president,'' said Grusha.

Popov's eyes bulged. "Assassinate the president of the United States?''

Grusha smiled widely. "I thought that would excite you.'' He leaned forward and lowered his voice. "If we succeed, I will probably become head of the KGB. You will take over as Director of Operations.''

The ache in Popov's head had assumed cosmic proportions. "Comrade Brezhnev has approved this?'' he asked incredulously.

Grusha snorted. "This is not a matter for the premier to know. This is a KGB matter. If the premier knows, he will be implicated, and he must remain innocent. But we can accomplish this on our own, especially with a man like you.''

Popov was sweating visibly. "Believe me, Comrade Director, I'm not your man. You don't understand. . .''

"This will be a mortal blow to American morale,'' continued Grusha. "We must act quickly. At the moment the country doesn't even have a vice-president. The people will be left leaderless. It is a brilliant plan.'' He sucked on his cigar with satisfaction.

"Comrade Director, please listen to me. I've never even seen a real gun, let alone used one. I. . .''

"Yes, I know all about it, Popov. Your methods are more

subtle. I've taken that into account. Wait till you hear the plan.''

For the next twenty minutes Grusha spelled out the details as Popov's insides shriveled to sawdust. Then Grusha dismissed him. Dazed, his legs like rubber, Popov barely made it back to his office. Valentin helped him to a chair.

"What happened?"

Popov blinked rapidly to keep the tears from spilling out of his eyes.

"You'll never believe it."

His office-mate leaned against the desk and folded his arms.

"Come on, Popov. It can't be as bad as all that. Did he fire you?"

Popov looked up miserably. "Can I trust you?"

Valentin hooted, his bushy eyebrows wiggling. "Do you want to see my security clearance?"

Shivering, Popov motioned to Valentin to open the bottom drawer of the file cabinet. He grabbed the bottle before Valentin had even straightened up, and he took a deep swig, letting the vodka roll down his throat. It steadied his hands, but didn't quell the fear that hammered in his chest and echoed agonizingly in his aching head.

"I've been given an assignment," whispered Popov.

Valentin nodded. "An assignment meant for Igor?"

Popov mopped his sweating brow and looked at him in mute terror. Valentin pulled up his chair.

"Want to tell me about it?"

Popov started slowly, speaking in a whisper so that Valentin had to hunch forward to hear him. As he talked, Valentin's eyes widened.

"And they want me to use a poison capsule with a dart needle," finished Popov. "They'll give me a special shoe with the capsule in the toe. When the tip of the shoe hits against something, the needle pops out automatically. The capsule's very small. I guess the poison is so strong it has to be sealed."

"Ricin." Valentin nodded. "A little drop'll do you."

Popov looked puzzled. "A little drop? . . ."

Valentin shrugged. "I read that somewhere."

Popov took another swig from the bottle. "I'll be part of

Brezhnev's entourage. I'm to get next to the president, or be near where he passes. Then at some point I'm to step forward and accidentally touch his leg with the toe of my shoe. The president won't even realize he's been hit. It'll be three days until he dies, and no one will be able to trace it back to that innocent touch.'' Popov ran his handkerchief around the back of his neck and stared at his friend.

''Just like when they hit Georgi Markov in London with the poison umbrella tip,'' agreed Valentin. He shook his head. ''Pretty good plan. You'll be a hero. Probably get the Order of Lenin.''

''I don't want the Order of Lenin,'' wailed Popov, but Valentin had already gone back to his own desk.

''I'm going to lunch,'' he said. ''Good luck.''

A stiff wind had come up, buffeting the helicopter as it took off from the deck of the Russian aircraft carrier, crossed two miles of choppy water in the Atlantic Ocean off the coast of Bermuda, and approached the United States vessel. Popov looked down to see the postage-size American aircraft carrier rocking violently in the sea below, its deck listing right, then left. We'll never be able to land, he thought. And even if we do, we'll slide right off. He closed his eyes. Icy water closed over his head as he fought for survival in the churning sea. A shark grabbed his leg with a sudden jerk, dragging him under. He opened his eyes in terror, but the jerk had only been the helicopter settling on the deck of the USS Courage. By some miracle they had made it safely.

From the window Popov could see the American crew lined up smartly at the edge of the runway. He fought tears of relief as he scrambled down the steps and took his place in the retinue of five men around the chunky figure of Premier Brezhnev.

The party cleared the helicopter blades. Popov was nearly rigid with fright as the American Secret Service came forward to perform a security check on the Russian delegation, but the tiny capsule in his shoe went undetected. Standing at attention, eyes on the tall, smiling American, Popov watched President Ford come forward to meet Secretary General

Brezhnev. The two world leaders shook hands on the windy deck.

An unusual moment in history, thought Popov, a private moment that no one present could ever admit had taken place. He shivered in the wind, feeling a clammy sweat crawl down his back. No one but he knew quite how unusual it was going to be.

To give him maximum opportunity for contact with the American president, Popov was detailed as Brezhnev's personal aide. As the premier and the president walked across the heaving deck to the center structure, he fell into step behind Brezhnev and slightly to the right. For a moment he was directly behind President Ford. Fascinated, he stared at the trousered leg only a step ahead of him. Four inches of empty space separated him from his target and the opportunity to change the history of the world.

Popov whimpered like a baby.

Heavy with its armament, his right foot felt like a tank. He tried to bring it forward into position, but it dragged behind him like a reluctant soldier, causing him to walk with a pronounced limp. The Russian Security Agent beside him glanced at him sharply.

"Hit my foot as we got out of the helicopter," said Popov.

The American Secret Service moved into position, forming a phalanx around their leader, squeezing Popov further to the rear. He almost breathed a sigh of relief as the president's leg disappeared into a forest of knife-pleated trousers. Would he be able to get close enough again? And would he be able to go through with it even if he did? Popov shuddered, grateful for the excuse of a brisk wind.

Ford and Brezhnev, two interpreters, and ten Russian security and Secret Service agents stepped into the huge elevator that would take them below to the captain's quarters. Popov tried to maneuver himself to the president's left, but Brezhnev stepped in front of him and Popov was left facing the premier's back. As the party walked down the narrow corridor, the American president went first, followed by the Russians. Popov found himself bringing up the rear. He concentrated on putting one foot in front of the other in a normal fashion.

The vein in his neck was throbbing as they reached the captain's quarters. The two leaders disappeared inside, accompanied only by two interpreters. Popov took a deep breath. His already queasy stomach rolled sickeningly with the rocking ship. The opportunity for contact with the president was half gone; would he have a better chance on the way out?

The Russian and American security agents took up positions just outside the door, eyeing one another suspiciously. A half hour passed in silence. Popov shifted restlessly, rubbed his sweating palms on his pants. He tried to ignore his shoe, but his eyes, fascinated by his lethal toe, would slide down uncontrollably, only to bounce back up under the scrutiny of the Secret Service.

At last the door opened. The agents fanned down the corridor, clearing the way for the two leaders to pass. Popov took his place next to Brezhnev, trying to wedge himself between his leader and the president. But it was to no avail. The two men stood close together, still in conversation as they walked down the corridor. The two interpreters followed closely behind.

The party again entered the massive elevator that would take them back to the flight deck. Little rivulets of sweat trickled down from under Popov's hat, tickling the hairs on the back of his neck, making him grin foolishly, despite his anguish. He only had a few moments left. What would the KGB do to him if he failed?

The elevator doors opened to the flight deck. Again the American navy in dress blues stood smartly saluting in the cold wind. Popov wished he were back at his old desk in cryptology happily decoding their secrets instead of walking the decks of their ship. In a panic, he rushed forward and stood to the side of the elevator opening. The president would have to pass him now. It was his last chance.

He stood stiffly, heart hammering like a jack drill, weight on his left foot, leaving his right free to swing forward with a little kick the moment the president walked in front of him.

President Ford stepped out of the elevator, barely a foot

from Popov. The Russian felt light-headed. This was the moment. He was going to do it. He clenched his teeth. Forward! his brain screamed. His foot hung like a deadweight at the end of his leg.

Suddenly, Ford lurched sideways. From what seemed another galaxy, Popov heard a muffled cry. He felt a hand on his shoulder, and found himself staring directly into the president's eyes, not four inches from his own. The Secret Service men jumped forward. The crew of the *USS Courage* looked nervous, but Ford was smiling.

"Just tripped," he said, pointing to the elevator floor that didn't quite match up with the deck.

He smiled reassuringly at the officers around him. Everyone smiled and nodded in return.

Everyone except Popov. He stood, frozen, his eyes glazed.

"Sorry, son," said President Ford. "Did I step on your toe?"

Popov nodded mutely, unable to speak. A creeping wetness penetrated his right sock. Gently he wiggled his toe. It squished. The capsule had been rigged to snap the needle out of the front of his shoe on impact. But the moment President Ford stepped on the top of his shoe, the capsule ruptured, spreading the deadly Ricin onto Popov's own foot.

After the Russian helicopter was out of sight, the president's helicopter took off from the rolling deck of the *USS Courage*. Winthrop McCall, deputy director of the CIA, sat next to the president.

"Well done, sir."

"I'll admit I was nervous, Win," said Ford. "I wasn't certain I'd be able to identify the officer in time. But your description was quite exact."

"We have an excellent source inside the KGB," said McCall, his thin lips curving slightly. "Code name Cupid. He gave us all the details. It was an ingenious plan."

"Please express my appreciation to Cupid."

"We've averted a major incident. Not to mention having saved your life."

"I hope I didn't hurt that poor boy's foot. Did you see the look on his face?"

"I'd hardly call him a poor boy, sir," McCall answered grimly. "According to our information, his name is Igor Popov and he's a highly trained assassin from the KGB Wet Department."

McCall looked out the window. He hadn't told Ford that stepping on the Russian's foot would break open the poison capsule, killing the man who planned to kill him. There were some things it was better for a president not to know.

"Will the KGB punish him for failing?" asked Ford.

"Sometimes failure is its own punishment," mumbled McCall, clearing his throat.

"I felt like a fool stumbling like that. And in front of the Navy, too. I was a football player, you know." Ford chuckled. "How soon do we tell the crew of the *Courage* what really happened?"

"I don't think we should mention it, sir. If the Russians discovered we knew of their plan, Cupid would be compromised."

"Uhmm." Ford frowned. "Boy, I hate having the military thinking they have a clumsy commander in chief! But I suppose you're right." He sighed and shook his head. "All those sailors will just have to think I'm a little unsteady on my feet."

An hour later, the helicopter curved in a wide arc and prepared to settle on the South Lawn of the White House. A cluster of reporters had gathered to greet the president, whom they thought was arriving from Camp David after deciding on his choice for vice-president.

President Ford stepped from the helicopter to the top of the stair ramp and waved to the reporters as the flashbulbs clicked. McCall stood behind him.

"Actually, sir," said McCall as the president prepared to descend the stairs, "in the interest of the national security, I think you should keep up the image."

Ford paused. "What do you mean?" he said over his shoulder.

"We don't want the Russkies to think anything funny went on here today. If you tripped a few more times, it would give us great credibility. Today wouldn't look out of the ordinary."

Ford blinked and turned to face the CIA man.

"You mean you want me to go around stumbling all the time?"

"It would safeguard our position."

"That's going a bit too far, McCall," snorted Ford. He started down the steps, smiling and waving at the reporters.

Behind him, McCall cleared his throat loudly. Ford paused on the last step and glared up at him.

"There is no higher priority than national security, Mr. President," said McCall.

The president and the deputy director of the CIA stared at one another briefly, then Ford turned to look at the eager reporters before him, cameras whirring, pens poised above their notebooks.

His smile was strained. "Hello, everyone," he said.

Then he tripped off the bottom step and stumbled into the crowd.

ABOUT THE EDITORS

A master of mystery anthologies, MARTIN H. GREEN-
BERG has compiled over two hundred short story collec-
tions, including several with Francis M. Nevins, Jr. A noted
scholar, Mr. Greenberg resides with his wife and daughter in
Green Bay, Wisconsin, where he teaches at the University of
Wisconsin.

FRANCIS M. NEVINS, JR., is a professor of law at St.
Louis University. He is, additionally, a novelist and an Edgar
Award Winner for his biography, *Royal Bloodline: Ellery
Queen, Author and Detective*. Mr. Nevins was the sponsor
for Ballantine's successful series of Cornell Woolrich novels.
He also wrote the definitive biography of Woolrich—*Cornell
Woolrich: First You Dream, Then You Die*.